T0354804

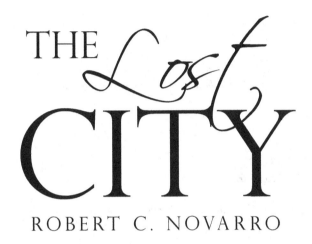

THE Lost CITY

ROBERT C. NOVARRO

authorHOUSE®

AuthorHouse™
1663 Liberty Drive
Bloomington, IN 47403
www.authorhouse.com
Phone: 1 (800) 839-8640

Published by AuthorHouse 02/24/2017

ISBN: 978-1-5246-7356-7 (sc)
ISBN: 978-1-5246-7354-3 (hc)
ISBN: 978-1-5246-7355-0 (e)

Library of Congress Control Number: 2017902806

Print information available on the last page.

This book is printed on acid-free paper.

Also by Robert C. Novarro:

Scarred
Bound by Bloodf
Il Castrato
My Love Possessed
The Eye of the Beholder
Devine Retribution

DEDICATION

To the two women in my life that are so important in my career. My wife, Angela who is always supportive of my endeavors and my cousin, Joan whose critical eye and editing pencil are invaluable to me.

PROLOGUE

Throughout mankind's history, centuries old legends and myths have come down to us, sometimes through tantalizing clues, and other times from the spoken word, to spark the imagination as well as to evoke the dreams of hidden, buried treasures. Names of fabled or lost cities such as Atlantis beyond the Gates of Hercules, Aztlan in Mexico, Helike in Greece, El Dorado in South America, La Ciudad Blanca in Honduras and Shangri la in Asia as well as Paititi in Peru are just a few of the many names of lost cities that been whispered from generation to generation.

Add to that list, one other, the lost city of Nakanjo that had vanished somewhere in the thick, lush rainforest in Guatemala. The **Saga** that was told describes how the Mayan rulers of this city built splendid temples, decorated their bodies with gold, jade and semi-precious stones. Led by such famous rulers as Smoke Serpent, Jade Ocelot and Jaguar Claw, Nakanjo grew into a large urban center, famous for its culture and fabulous wealth. And then, for no apparent reason, the city seemingly disappeared from the face of the earth. For centuries, the legend of Nakanjo grew ever dimmer, buried amid the seemingly impenetrable rainforest of Meso-America.

Then, in the 16th century, the tale was once more brought to life when an invading force of Spaniards, led by Cesar de Leon, and later his son Juan, learned of the legend of Nakanjo from the natives and they were determined that the riches of the city would belong to them. And so, they marched out, resolute in the belief that though the jungle had grown over it so thoroughly that it could not be detected, they were destined to uncover the city's mysterious location and gain its fortune.

But it was not until the late 20th century that a modern-day archeologist named Martin Cummings and his wife Esmie came upon an archaic map drawn by a **Scribe** who was a Dominican Brother who had marched with the conquistadors. The map had been in the possession of an old Indian and appeared to show the way to the ancient city of Nakanjo. With this discovery, the **Search** was once again reborn. Along with these scientists, there suddenly appears a man named Armand Thierry who uses his wealth and influence as an illegal arms dealer to illicitly steal valuable art objects from sites of ancient civilizations and display them in his many homes around the world.

This fictitious story is based somewhat on the real events of how man's greed for wealth and riches can completely destroy those who lust after it.

"Lust for possession and greed has ravaged the soul of humanity, metastasizing throughout society..."
Bryant McGill, Voice of Reason

THE SAGA

CHAPTER 1

NAKANJO, MAY, 451 A.D.

The ceremonial ritual for the dead played out before the assembled populace who watched silently in the Mayan city- state of Nakanjo in the spring of the year of the Christian calendar 451. Family members and priests wore high headdresses made of the plumes of exotic birds, and capes of animal skins. They swayed to the beating of drums as the litter of the deceased King Smoke Serpent was borne by four warriors on the way to the central pyramid. Behind them marched his wife Queen Sparkling River, his oldest son, Moon Jaguar, and his youngest son, Jade Ocelot. The body of the king was adorned in all his finest clothes and a carved jade mask which covered his face. The litter bearers carried him carefully to the top of the pyramid as the eyes of the inhabitants followed them up the stairs. The great king, conqueror of many Mayan cities around Nakanjo, was then taken down a central staircase by torchlight where his body would lie for eternity.

Taking an obsidian blade out of his sheath, the priest approached the royal trio. The queen stuck out her tongue in preparation. Her tongue was split and the blood drops collected on bark paper along with copal incense and it was burned to appease the malevolent Ah Puch, the god of death, so the king might enter freely into the next world. The priest went to each of the sons, 18-year-old Moon Jaguar and 13- year-old Jade Ocelot, to repeat the same bloodletting ritual to ensure their father's safe passage. The two boys didn't utter a sound as their tongues were split.

With a few utterances made by the elderly priest, the body was placed in a cavity in the stone chamber and then roofed with a glyph-covered flat stone. The priest led the others out to the top of the pyramid. As soon as the common people saw them, a great wailing rose to the skies above. The

1

funeral procession came down the stairs as the queen and her sons, guarded by soldiers, made their way back to the palace. Once the ceremony for the dead king was completed, the pyramid was to be readied for the ceremony that would install Moon Jaguar as the next king of Nakanjo.

By the next day, the sorrow for the death of the old king would be completely erased by the jubilance of the citizens for the installation of Moon Jaguar as their new king. The soon- to- be king called the chief priest into his chamber. Bowing, he said, "You called for me, Lord?" Moon Jaguar surreptitiously waved him closer.

"Is everything in place?" he asked.

"Lord, your plan is already in motion."

"Good! I will soon be rid of my younger brother."

"Yes, my Lord."

"He will always be a threat to overthrow me. He must be eliminated today before my ceremony." The timbre of his voice was arrogant and haughty. "Do you understand?"

"I do my Lord but what about the Queen Mother?"

"Do not harm her. In time, she will forget about Jade Ocelot."

"Yes, my Lord."

"Go now and see to it that everything is in place." As the priest bowed and left the room, a crooked smile appeared on the prince's face. He thought back to his years under his father's tutelage to become a great warrior and ruler. Even though there were five years between the brothers, their father would often pit the two against each other in physical trials of strength. Although the older brother would come out victorious, Jade Ocelot would sometimes be able to turn the tables by outwitting Moon Jaguar. His father would laugh when this would happen and the older brother swore that when he was made king, he would eliminate this supposed threat to his authority.

Queen Sparkling River could say nothing about how her youngest son was being treated. Her duty was to give birth to sons for her husband and she had fulfilled her obligation. The raising of her sons was exclusively in the hands of their father, Smoke Serpent. Daily she observed Moon Jaguar become more and more of a bully to his younger brother at the insistence of their father. It was only in their private moments between mother and youngest son that she could lift her son's confidence by advising him to

2

"stay strong and someday your turn will come." That was the only thing she could secretly do for him so that her husband did not find out that she was disobeying his direct order to her.

Behind the wall of the prince's chamber, the queen's handmaiden listened at the door. When the plot was revealed, she hurried to the queen's quarters. She found Prince Jade Ocelot by her side. The maiden, who was out of breath and bowing, was beckoned by the Queen to enter.

"What have you learned?" The servant looked at the young prince with a worried look that did not escape the Queen's attention. "Come closer."

"The young prince will lose his life before the coronation ceremony of your older son, but your life is to be spared." Sparkling River did not hesitate. "Tell my brother Jaguar Claw to gather those who are loyal to us for we must leave immediately!" As she rushed from the room, Jade Ocelot commented,

"What is wrong, mother?"

"We must go away from here right now!"

"But what about my brother's installation as king?"

"Certain events make it impossible and unwise for us to stay. Come with me!" When she walked to the door, the prince followed in her footsteps.

The sun had reached the apex of its climb and a feather- caped and crowned Moon Jaguar was ready to be escorted to the top of his temple. Before he could set foot outside, the chief priest entered the room, bowing. Moon Jaguar smiled in delightful anticipation of the expected good news. "Lord," the chief priest began. From the expression on his face, Moon Jaguar suddenly realized that something had gone awry. "Your brother is gone."

"Gone where?" the prince demanded loudly.

"I do not know Lord, but your mother is also missing."

"Somehow they learned of my plan. Find them and kill them both!" ordered Moon Jaguar. The chief priest bowed and scurried away. Pulling his emotions together, the soon- to- be king began the march to his temple escorted by warriors dressed in jaguar skins. They all climbed to the top as Moon Jaguar ensconced himself on his throne. Ceremonial dancers squirmed in wild abandonment and lurched themselves about to the rhythm of drums. The dancing stopped and the temple chief, with raised hands, called upon the people to acknowledge their new ruler. A great roar rose from the populace below. Next the chief priest called upon the multitude of gods and goddesses to bless the new king.

With a wave of his hand, King Moon Jaguar called upon the sacrificial victims to be brought up. With their hands tied behind their backs, over 200 Indian warriors from the city-states of Tikyu and Ixakbe were marched up the steps, and one by one their hands were untied and they were placed on their backs upon a raised circular stone. Warriors from Nankanjo took the appendages of the first prisoner and pressed down, forcing his chest to rise up. The priest came forward and prayed to the gods above to accept this sacrifice, and when he was done with his incantation, drove the sharp knife into the chest cavity to remove the victim's still beating heart. It was thrown into a fire brazen where it was consumed by the flames which gave off black smoke. The warriors lifted the dead body and tossed it down the temple steps. The next victim was brought forward and the ritual repeated. As he watched, the new king could not help but wish that the next victim was Jade Ocelot. *They must be found immediately and disposed of before he is able to seek his vengeance!*

The flight into the jungle by the queen and her son was led by a warrior and the queen's half-brother Jaguar Claw. Queen Sparkling River had devised a plan in the event that her younger son was threatened. Now they tore through the dense foliage. With them traveled her brother's loyal followers of the royal guard as well as servants in her retinue. She knew that once Moon Jaguar discovered their escape, he would send warriors to destroy all of them. She had never trusted her son's advisor, the chief priest who fawned and bowed in front of her and then went back to her husband to reveal anything he had found out about the queen. *He is a backstabbing snake!*

Jaguar Claw led the group to the nearest city-state in which they hoped to find refuge from Moon Jaguar's persecution. This was the city of Tikyu in which Sparkling River's sister, White Orchid was queen. She had been given by their father to the Tikyun king, Tall Tree, as part of a treaty of peace, but to Smoke Serpent it was a ploy to pacify Tikyu so he could conquer Ixakbe, another city-state. Once that was accomplished, he turned on Tikyu and absorbed them into his empire. The treasure he extracted from both cities made Nakanjo a powerful city-state. Each year both cities were required to send a large number of their warriors to be sacrificial victims on the altar to appease Nakanjo's gods. This betrayal by Smoke Serpent to the Tikyun king eventually led to the elderly king's demise, leaving his queen to rule the city. Sparkling River wasn't sure what kind of reception she would receive from her sister, but there was no other place to go.

After many long days of exhausting travel, they were met by a patrol of Tikyun warriors dressed in the skins of jaguars, the skull of the animal used as a head adornment. Immediately the Tikyun warriors lifted their spears and war clubs in the air and waved them threateningly about as insults were exchanged by both sides. The Nakanjon queen held her hands up and demanded silence. The warriors of Tikyun began to calm down. "Take me to your queen," she ordered. The leader of the Tikyun group demanded, "Who are you to order us about Nakanjon woman? You are all our prisoners!" Immediately, the warriors of her retinue took a defensive stance.

"I am Sparkling River, Nakanjo's queen. I demand to be brought before your queen, White Orchid, who is my sister!" The Tikyun party stood mute for a moment. Then the Tikyun leader shouted,

"You lie! All Nakanjons are liars!" At this insult, her half-brother Jaguar Claw raised his war club over his head to strike down the man who had insulted his sister.

"Hold, brother!" she told him and her brother backed away. "Take me to your queen now! If she finds out that you harmed me, you and the others here will be the next to be sent to Nakanjo as sacrifices to have your hearts ripped from your chests!" The Tikyun warriors looked at each other until the leader announced, "Come!" Some of the Tikyun warriors led the way while the others took positions behind the uninvited intruders.

After some time, the jungle opened to cultivated land where rows of corn, squash, beans, and chili peppers were being grown, and the hot burning sun blazed down upon them. Those working in the fields stood up to watch the queer procession pass before them. From the fields, they were led to the outskirts of Tikyu where the indigent people lived in their ramshackle huts. Once they realized who was parading before them, hateful stares followed them. Jade Ocelot and the others were led into the broad avenues and the central plaza of the city that faced the largest palace. In comparison to Nakanjo, this city was much smaller. The plaza was filled with farmers selling their produce, and buyers looking from stall to stall. As the group approached, the busy activity stopped and more detestable stares were fixed upon them. Some of them even hurled verbal insults at the trespassers.

Coming to the bottom of the stairs of the palace, they were waved on to the top. They passed the flat circular stone, splattered with dried blood left from the victims who had been sacrificed to Tikyun gods. At the top, they were taken into the coolness of the roofed anteroom before two armed guards opened the door to the throne room. Inside, Queen White Orchid regally sat on her throne conferring with the chief priest. She did not turn to see who had entered the room. Finally, when she had finished with the priest, she turned to look at the group. At first, she had no reaction as she gazed them up and down and then the realization that her brother and sister stood before sunk in. She rose from her throne and ran down the stairs as she used to do when she was a young child. "Brother, sister," she said gleefully. "It has been such a long time since I've seen you!"

"Sister," Sparkling River responded as they embraced. "It has been a long time. After sister and brother embraced and she was introduced to Jade Ocelot, White Orchid inquired, "What are you doing here and how did you get permission from your husband?"

"Smoke Serpent is dead."

"I cannot say that I'm sorry to hear this news. He has been a bane to my people."

"I understand how you and your people feel."

"Who sits on the throne of Nakanjo now?"

"My eldest son Moon Jaguar, and that's why we have come to you." The Tikyu queen led her sister to her private room. "Moon Jaguar intended to have my younger son Jade Ocelot killed. We escaped from the city before it happened." Upon hearing the news her younger sister's eyes, widened in horror. "How can I help you?"

"We need to take refuge here under your protection. We need to be hidden in the city when our pursuers come for us."

"It will be done, sister.

"Where are your sons?"

The question brought tears to the eyes of White Orchid. "Both are dead," she sobbed but this is my daughter, Cooing Dove. A young girl of

6

about 12 stood next to her mother. She possessed great beauty with long black hair that reached mid-way down her back, but she was extremely shy. She bowed her head to the family she had never met.

"Do not worry, I will make sure you and your son will never be found." The two sisters embraced once more.

It was inevitable, and by the next day an envoy from Nakanjo, carried on a litter backed by the city's warriors, showed up in Tikyu. Immediately, Jaguar Claw, perched high in the queen's palace, recognized the chief priest and king's advisor Screeching Owl, dressed in all his finery, backed by at least 100 warriors armed to the teeth. The population of the city scattered in all directions. "Bring me your queen!" he shouted authoritatively. Jaguar Claw arrived in the throne room and imparted the unpleasant news. "Go to my room," White Orchid advised her sister and other guests. On the left wall is a panel that opens to a secret room. Stay there and you will be safe." She sent her handmaiden to show them the way.

After they were gone, the palace guard came running in. "The chief priest of Nakanjo demands that you meet him outside!" Bristling at the insult, but knowing full well what would happen to her city if she refused his order, she left, accompanied by her entourage of advisors. She walked majestically down the building steps to the Plaza of the Sun and stopped before the older man in his litter.

"Lord, to what do I owe your visit?"

"Where are they?"

"Where are who, my Lord?" Screech Owl's eyes became like slits as he stared at her.

"Where are your sister, brother, and her son?"

"Have they left Nakanjo?" she asked innocently.

"Have you given sanctuary to them in your city?"

"No Lord, I haven't even seen them. This is all a surprise to me."

"And what would happen if I sent Najanko warriors to search the city. Would they be found here?"

"No, my Lord. But if it is your pleasure, then give the command." With a wave of his hand, Screeching Owl sent the warriors to search the city.

When he climbed out of his litter, his personal body guards followed him up to the top of the queen's palace. He shouted, "Search this place!" Immediately his guards rushed around tossing things aside and breaking them. White Orchid held her silence while her room was turned upside down. Screeching Owl watched her face carefully to detect any nervousness in her demeanor. The queen stayed steadfastly calm in the whirlwind of destruction around her. Finally, the guards returned.

"My Lord, there is no one hiding in here."

The old priest gave her a withering stare. "If they are found anywhere in this city, it will be your people who will suffer for it!"

"I tell you they are not here!"

"Come with me," he ordered her. They returned to the Plaza of the Sun to wait for the other warriors. One by one they returned with the same answer.

"They are not here, Lord." Climbing back into his litter, he was raised off the ground. But before he left, he warned White Orchid, "If they arrive here, take them prisoner and send me word. My Lord Jaguar Moon's wrath would burn this city to the ground and your people will be scattered to the four winds. I warn you!" The litter was turned around and the entourage left the city.

The old fool!

For most of his young life, Jade Ocelot had watched his older brother take lessons from his uncle in the art of warfare. Smoke Serpent wanted his eldest son Moon Jaguar to be fully prepared to rule and govern his city. One of his responsibilities would be to lead his army into war with surrounding city-states. Smoke Serpent, during his rule, had taken Ixakbe and Tikyu and made them subservient to Nakanjo. He instructed Jaguar Claw to prepare Moon Jaguar for other conquests.

Jade Ocelot was reduced to watching his brother in training while he stood looking from afar. Occasionally, his uncle would give him some lessons when his older brother was gone, but this was in secret. "After all," his illustrious father would say, "Your brother is the one who will inherit the throne."

Now with Moon Jaguar as his enemy, Jaguar Claw was making up time trying to instruct the young prince. He was instructed in the use of long distance weapons such as the blow gun, atlatl, and the spear, but most of the time was taken in the face-to-face combat that kings were used to. First was the 42-inch war club which could stun, cut, or break bones.

"Hold your club higher to defend yourself!" his uncle yelled as he came forward with his own club. Swinging down on his nephew's weapon, he knocked it out of Jade Ocelot's hand. The prince watched it fall to the ground while his hand stung from the blow.

"What did I do wrong?" the boy asked petulantly. His uncle could sense the frustration in his voice.

"Keep a tighter grip on the handle. Pick it up and we'll try again." Over and over, they practiced until Jade Ocelot was finally able to ward off his blows. "Now you attack me!" The prince came at him at full tilt but Jaguar Claw easily side-stepped him and pretended to strike him in the back with his club. "My club would have stopped you in your tracks and you would now be tied up and ready for human sacrifice to the gods."

"What should I have done?"

"Never run at full speed. You can easily be out maneuvered by your opponent."

"There is a lot to remember."

"Remembering will keep you alive. Forget and you are dead! Do not get frustrated because that will lead to mistakes. Focus on my words and actions. It is inevitable that you will someday meet Moon Jaguar in hand-to-hand combat. He is a superior warrior but with my instructions and your daily practice you will be his equal. Now, pick up your bronze hand axe."

"Yes, Uncle." Jade Ocelot's confidence had gotten a much-needed boost and he threw himself into his lessons. Jaguar Claw instructed his nephew repeatedly with defensive and offensive drills.

The sun rose to mid-morning as both of their bodies glistened with their sweat as they took time to rest. Jade Ocelot stood breathing heavily while his uncle did not seem exhausted at all. "How is it Uncle, that you don't seem tired?"

"I have stamina, something you will need to acquire with the skill of using your weapons. You will need to work even harder than your brother who has had years more experience than you. You will need to work even harder to catch up to him. Do you understand?"

"Yes, Uncle."

"Now come at me and attack!" His nephew remembered not to throw himself at Jaguar Claw but instead remained in control. "Look and see how

I have placed my feet." His uncle easily blocked the blow of Jade Ocelot. "Did you see how I did that?"

"I did, Uncle."

"Now block my attack!" Jade Ocelot took a similar stance and he easily thwarted his uncle's axe. Practice continued over and over. "That's better, but meet my attack by extending your axe toward mine.

Jade Ocelot did as his uncle instructed. "Like that?"

"Yes, that's it!" Once again, he charged toward his nephew who successfully blocked the thrust of his weapon.

"I understand now."

"Good, tomorrow we start with hand-to-hand combat with knives. When Kinich Ahau arises in the sky, we will get up early and start again." Jaguar Claw took the weapons and walked into the coolness of the temple entrance. Jade Ocelot was walking behind when he caught some movement in the peripheral vision of his left eye. He saw a young girl with long ebony hair quickly turn the corner. Even in the few seconds that he had caught sight of her, he could tell she had a rare beauty.

"Wait!" he called after her but she was already gone. Running to the spot where he had seen her turn the corner of the pyramid, he looked around but she was nowhere to be seen. Shrugging, he made his way back to the temple door. *Was that my cousin, Cooing Dove?*

CHAPTER 2

NAKANJO, MARCH, 452

Moon Jaguar sat on his throne as his chief advisor Screeching Owl approached him, bowing. Next to the king sat his queen, Silver Moon, the king's first cousin. She was a beautiful creature with a round face and sparkling eyes. Moon Jaguar had been in love with her for a long time and once he became king there was no doubt in anyone's mind which female he would choose as his new royal mate. Her abdomen was slightly swollen by the 4-month fetus she was carrying. "My Lord, we have searched thoroughly for months but your mother, uncle, and brother cannot be found." The king turned his head to his advisor.

"It's fine. The little worm of a brother of mine does not have the heart to return here. Only I have the true heart of a king."

"My Lord, there is even more serious news of a disturbing nature to tell you."

"What is it?" the king sighed impatiently hoping that his advisor would leave his presence soon.

"The land is not producing crops as it once did. If this trend continues, we will soon be looking at widespread hunger in the city. Even now, there are some shortages. Already, there is grumbling among the populace because of the lack of staples like maize, squash, beans, and chili peppers in the marketplaces. It is also reported that secondary foods such as cassava, avocado, and pumpkin are becoming scarce."

"Has the god Yum-Kaax turned his head away from his people? What are we to do? Can we continue to slash and burn the jungle for planting along the outer reaches of Nakanjo?" the king questioned.

"Farming further away from the city may work but it will mean longer trips from the fields, and the allocation of more warriors to guard these new fields."

"This will need to be done."

"Do I have your order to do this?"

"Tell the farmers I command them to slash and burn, then plant and farm beyond the lands already designated. This plan must assure us of continued good harvests. How can we curry Yum-Kaax's favor back on the city?"

"Only through a public blood-letting ceremony to the agricultural god to beg him to look on this city with beneficence once more."

"Tell my army to go out and find more sacrificial offerings to our god." Moon Jaguar waved his hand in dismissal. Screeching Owl stood without moving. "Did you not hear me? Go and let my commands be obeyed!"

"I'm sorry My Lord, but the god requires royal blood if he is to be persuaded back to our side."

"Then prepare for it tomorrow. Make an announcement to the populace that it will be done in the Plaza of the Sun before the temple when the sun reaches its highest point in the sky." Bowing, his advisor left to make the arrangements for the next day.

The sun had reached its apex by the next day and a group of warriors led the king, dressed in his finest robes, up the stairs to the temple's highest platform to the silence of the people. The temple priests approached the king. The chief priest carried a sharpened knife. He neared the king who stuck out his tongue. In a quick cutting motion, the king's tongue was pierced. A knotted rope was passed to the king who threaded it through the top of his tongue and out through the bottom. Each drop of the royal blood was allowed to drip onto a piece of cloth.

When the ritual was finished, the blood-soaked cloth was held up and presented to the people. A great roar arose from below. The chief priest quieted them by holding his hands in the air. Immediately, the crowd quieted and he spoke. "May this blood sacrifice by our king, Moon Jaguar, bring the god Yum-Kaax's favor back on his people!" This time the populace moaned their response so the god could hear them.

Turning, the chief priest dropped the bloody cloth in a flaming brazier as they all watched the smoke rise to the god above. The moaning below grew steadily stronger.

The warriors escorted their king down the temple stairs and through the crowd before they reached the palace. Moon Jaguar entered his residence and silently prayed for the god to answer the sacrifice he had made for his people. Silver Moon waited inside the tunnel avoiding the day's heat and humidity to welcome her husband back from his ordeal.

Two years of training had changed the unproven Jade Ocelot and turned him into a skilled warrior and leader. Jaguar Claw was soon training the warriors of Tikyu in the way of Nakanjo war making.

Each time Jade Ocelot was in training, his cousin, Cooing Dove would wander closer and closer to where the 15-year-old was working, but continually hid herself from the two men. But one day she threw caution to the wind and stepped out from the shadows and into the sunlight. Jaguar Claw, caught by surprise, yelled out, "What are you doing here, girl?"

Cooing Dove stopped in her tracks "I just wanted to watch…"

"Go away, girl! This is no place for females!" exclaimed Jaguar Claw. Cooing Dove was about to turn around when Jade Ocelot spoke out. "Let her stay, Uncle!" The young warrior had noticed his cousin's trepidations as she shyly drew closer to see him work out each day. He liked her attention.

"She has already distracted you from your training once today and once is too many times!"

"But Uncle…"

"I only give a command once, girl. Now go!" Cooing Dove did not hesitate this time and ran as fast as her feet could carry her. Jade Ocelot watched her as she retreated into the temple. Jaguar Claw lunged at his nephew sticking the unsharpened end of the knife into the young man's stomach.

"Ah!" he screamed out as the practice weapon left a bruise on his flesh. "I was not ready, Uncle!"

"That is the point," he replied to his nephew sternly. "Your lack of focus could make you a fatality. By looking away in a battle, even for just a few seconds, you could be killed!"

"I understand, but I feel as if I could now take on and win against any opponent."

"I am the one who will let you know if you're ready, and right now, you are not. Do you have any other questions?"

"No, Uncle."

"Good, now attack me!"

It was after his training and the subsequent washing of the grime and sweat from his flesh that Jade Ocelot went searching for his young cousin. In time, he found her with other girls, gathering flowers from the fields.

As he walked toward the chattering females, one of them caught sight of him approaching. They giggled and fled, leaving Cooing Dove behind. "I did not see you coming," she revealed to him as he drew near.

"I wanted to surprise you."

"You have." Once more she bent over to avert his eyes and began to pick wild flowers again.

"Cooing Dove, I am trying to explain about what happened earlier in the day." His cousin stood up with a bouquet of yellow and purple orchids.

"What are you talking about?" his cousin asked nonchalantly.

"Surely you couldn't have forgotten the tongue lashing my uncle gave you this afternoon."

"Oh, that. I have not given a second thought to it, cousin." He knew she was lying. Taking her by the arm, he gently pulled the dark beauty toward him. "I like it when you come to watch me."

"I had no idea that you had noticed me."

"Any man with eyes would notice you because you are as beautiful as the orchids you carry in your hand," he retorted unable to stop himself from blushing at his own words. The young girl smiled, diverting her eyes from his glance.

"You mustn't say such words to me."

"And may I ask, why not?" His chest puffed up with indignation.

"I am a princess of the royal blood."

"I too am of royal blood. Who better to compliment you?"

"But these are the words of someone who is in love. We've rarely been with each other alone over the past two years."

"I knew from the first time I met you that I wanted you as my wife, and I felt that you had the same feelings for me. Am I wrong?" Cooing Dove shook her head back and forth as whispered, "No."

"Good. Then let me escort you back to the palace."

Cooing Dove had just experienced the "Descent of the Gods". She had just turned 14 and as all female virgins upon reaching puberty, she wore the traditional red shell on her belt. Jade Ocelot already wore the white beads in his hair to indicate his passage from boy to manhood. Usually an tanezumab or matchmaker was sought by parents to find the perfect match for their children.

Both queens had noticed the attraction between their son and daughter, but it was White Orchid who approached Sparkling River. "Sister, have you discerned how close our children are becoming toward each other?"

"Yes, I have to admit that there seems to be a genuine affection between our two children."

"I've been thinking that perhaps a marriage could be arranged between them. What do you think?"

"I have been having the same thought as you, sister."

"Do you think that Jade Ocelot would be agreeable to such an arrangement?"

"I am sure he would be."

"It would be an arrangement with multiple advantages."

"In what ways?"

"First of course, we would bring together two people who are in love with each other."

"This is true."

"Secondly, Tikyu has been without a king far too long. Jade Ocelot would make a fitting king for this city."

"But would your people accept him as their king? After all, he is from Nakanjo, a city that dominates your own city."

"I'll admit that there was uneasiness among them when you arrived here seeking sanctuary. But as time has gone on, they've become more accepting of you and your family."

"I agree."

"Thirdly, with Jaguar Claw training our troops, they have a good chance of overcoming Moon Jaguar and unseating him. By the gods, your son should take his rightful place on both thrones."

"We are in complete agreement."

Both young people were approached about the possible coupling of the two families and they enthusiastically agreed to the marriage. Within a few weeks, the ceremony was scheduled. Jade Ocelot in his best finery, accompanied by his uncle and mother, walked to the home of White Orchid. Along the way, the people of the city wished him well. The priest blessed the two of them and prayed to the gods that their union would be fruitful. After the ceremony, gifts were given and a feast of turkey tamales, potatoes, beans, and tortillas were served to the wedding party and their guests.

CHAPTER 3

Marriage and married life proved to be satisfying for the happy couple. But Jade Ocelot's mind always returned to the same issue. *When will I be told that I am ready to overthrow my brother?*

For years, he kept asking this question of his uncle and for years the answer was always the same. "You are not ready yet!" He was not eager to inquire of his uncle the same query but now that he was married, he had hopes that the response would be different. "Am I now ready to take Nakanjo?"

"You are!"

Jade Ocelot was completely taken aback by his answer.

"When do we attack?"

"You misunderstand," Jaguar Claw shot back. Now his nephew was completely confused about what he heard. At last, he found his voice. "In what way?"

"We cannot attack the city yet. Instead, we must make an assault on their weakest point. If we succeed we will go ahead and plan our invasion."

"And what is their weakest point, Uncle?"

"Our scouts have witnessed the Nakanjo farmers cultivating ground even further away from the city with a few warriors on guard for protection."

"To take this extreme measure, the city must be experiencing food shortages."

"Exactly."

"If we can destroy the crops, we will strike a blow against my brother."

"It will also create discontent with his rule. What better way to defeat Moon Jaguar then to stir up his people against him?" Jade Ocelot's mouth turned upward in the corners into a smile.

"And when will this happen?"

"We must first pray and provide human sacrifice to Voting that we will be successful in this first part of the plan."

Sacrifices and prayers were offered at the great sun temple to the satisfaction of all who witnessed it. Two days later, a small party consisting of the warriors who had accompanied Jade Ocelot's family and a few of the more promising of the soldiers of Tikyu, made a foray into the jungle.

In three days, the war party came upon the fields for which they had been searching. In the heat of the day, about 30 men worked on the fields while the others hauled water from the Rio Los Esclavos. About 14 warriors stood idly, watching the work being done, and appeared to be bored with the process. With hand signals, Jade Ocelot indicated that his party should surround them. When everyone was in place, uncle and nephew emerged from the foliage with war whoops. Immediately, the others made an appearance running toward the workers. A volley of arrows flew into the air striking some of the farmers and soldiers. The other soldiers rushed to meet the attack while the farmers took off in the other direction.

One warrior met Jade Ocelot and struck his club straight toward the young man's head. Deftly Jade Ocelot slipped to the side, making the warrior miss his target. With a quick swipe, the prince's blow hit his enemy in the small of his back. The sound of bones cracking could be heard as the warrior collapsed to the ground and lay helpless. Standing over his enemy, Jade Ocelot swung a well-placed strike to his head. He turned around to see that the battle was already over. Their surprise attack proved to be victorious.

The field was littered with the dead, but none were from their party. Three of Nakanjo's soldiers were tied and subdued. On the king's order, the field was set ablaze and they began their trek back. As they walked, Jaguar Claw spoke up. "You fought well, Lord! You have even surpassed your brother." It was the first time his uncle ever addressed him with deference. With his chest filling up with pride he answered, "Thank you, Uncle."

Moon Jaguar stood outside his bedroom chamber, the sound of his wife's shrieking reverberating down the hallway. One last horrific scream and the noise suddenly ceased. Silver Moon stopped the screeching that had lasted into the afternoon. One of the queen's retinue came walking out. "Well, is my son born yet?" asked the king.

"Lord," she addressed him fearfully not knowing how he was going to react. "Your son did not live." His eyes became malicious and his expression was one that could have killed someone. With a giant swing, he cuffed her across the face so that she landed on the floor. Screeching Owl, his advisor, emerged from the room. "Go!" he ordered harshly as the maiden got to her feet and ran away.

"The girl lied! She said my son was dead!"

"It is true, Lord. He has died." He stared into his advisor's unemotional eyes and queried, "How could this have happened?"

"The child was breached. The women tried everything to turn him but it was impossible."

"This was Silver Moon's doing!" his voice raged.

"No, my Lord, your wife had nothing to do with it."

"Then one of her attendants is at fault! Point them out to me and they will be executed!"

"It was no one's fault, Lord."

"Someone is to blame and I will have my vengeance!"

"It's the gods, my Lord. The priests have said that the omens were not good if the child were to be born on this day." Crestfallen, Moon Jaguar inquired,

"And what of my wife? Is she dead too?"

"No, Lord. She has lost a lot of blood but is resting after this ordeal."

"Go back inside with a cloth and tell one of her attendants to dip it into her blood until it is soaked and bring it out to me."

A young girl carried the bloody cloth out to Moon Jaguar. Taking it, he marched outdoors and delivered it to the temple priests. "We are remorseful to hear the news of your son's death, Lord." Waving his hand as if to brush away the bad news, he replied,

"Enough of that! I have brought you a bloody cloth of my wife's blood. See to it that it is burned in the brazier and pray to the gods that my next son will be born alive." The priest took the cloth and he incanted a prayer

19

before he dropped it into the fire. It burst into flames quickly sending up a brilliant light. After a few minutes, the flames died and only the black curls of smoke remained.

"It is finished, my Lord." Dismissing the priests, he retraced his footsteps down the temple stairs back into his palace. Taken by surprise, the king found a gathering of dirty and exhausted farmers, escorted into the throne room by his warriors. His chief advisor stood apart from the others to observe the encounter.

"What are they doing here?" he said with great repugnance.

"My Lord," one of his warriors began. "These men have come with disturbing news." *What else could go wrong today?* Bowing his head reverently, one of the farmers began to speak.

"We were attacked, my Lord."

"What are you talking about?" he demanded in a threatening voice.

"We were working in the new fields when we are attacked."

"Why aren't the guards here?" exacted the king, rapidly losing his patience.

"As far as we know, they have all been killed as were some of the other farmers."

"And the cultivated food, what became of that!"

"I'm not sure, my Lord but we smelled smoke as we ran. I can only assume the fields were put to the torch."

The king's eyes narrowed with fury. "Who dared to attack me?"

The farmer cast his eyes down on the floor and mumbled, "I'm not... not sure, Lord."

"Liar!" he screamed at them. "Tell me the truth before you all find yourselves lying on the sacrificial stone with your hearts beating in the priest's hands!" he pointed an accusing finger at them.

Involuntarily, the farmers collectively shivered with terror. "I glanced over my shoulder and thought I saw your brother lead the attack." Moon Jaguar bristled at this unwelcome news.

"You are sure?" demanded the king.

"As far as I could tell, my Lord, yes it was Jade Ocelot. He was older and taller but it was your brother."

The king was caught by surprise by the answer but his temper quickly was refueled. "Get them out of here!" he commanded his soldiers. The farmers were shuffled out of the door. Turning to his advisor, he stated, "After all these years, he is still alive?"

"It would seem so, my Lord." Moon Jaguar's hands balled up tightly into fists as his body trembled with antagonism.

"Search the jungle and find him! Bring him back to me alive so that I can have the pleasure of separating his head from his body after his heart is torn from his chest!"

CHAPTER 4

The army of Tikyu was on the move. Jade Ocelot was dressed in regal finery as four warriors carried him aloft on a litter. By his side walked his constant advisor and uncle, Jaguar Claw.

The day was hot and steamy but the warriors marched forward in uniform step, dressed in colorful feathers and grotesque helmets made from fierce animal heads. In their hands, they carried war clubs and spears for battle. Their eyes stared straight ahead, focused on their destination of the city-state of Ixakbe.

As the party approached the outer crop fields of the city, the farmers who were toiling at their work stood in stunned soundlessness, but this emotion was speedily replaced by utter panic. They ran screaming from the fields and toward Ixakbe for protection.

Jade Ocelot's soldiers howled with a warrior's cry for blood but their king held up his hand. The men immediately fell silent. "We will only fight if we are attacked!" he bellowed out his reminder to them. Jaguar Claw had not agreed with his nephew about this mission to establish a peace between the two cities, but Jade Ocelot was now a man and a king. His orders must be obeyed. Another signal from the king's hand and the army continued its march. Sandaled feet tromped ahead circumnavigating the cultivated fields of crops and growing ever closer to the city of Ixakbe.

As they approached, the sound of screams could be heard as they rose in the sky and echoed between the temples that surrounded the plazas. At last, the army stepped foot into the city to see the women carrying babies in their arms and holding the hands of their children as they ran to the main plaza for protection. Their husbands, brothers, and sons quickly took up their weaponry and gathered to meet the oncoming threat. A litter bearing the Ixakben king, Scorched Mountain, was carried to meet the oncoming threat, his warriors quickly followed. Scorched Mountain was an elderly man in his 60s, with white hair, whose teeth were few and far between. His face was sagging and looking like distressed leather. Jade Ocelot held up his hand and the army came to a halt. Scorched Mountain's litter stopped a few feet from the King of Tikyu. "You have come here to make war on my people?" the old king demanded.

"I am here seeking peace between our two great city-states."

"And yet you come with your warriors carrying battle weapons. How do you explain that?"

"My warriors will not use them if your soldiers refrain from attacking us." Scorched Mountain stared intently on the Tikyun king.

"I do not recognize who you are. Identify yourself!"

"I am Jade Ocelot!" The old king's eyes widened as he suddenly recognized the man threatening his city. Pointing his shaking arthritic index finger at his antagonist, he yelled,

"You are no Tikyun! You are the son of our mortal enemy, Smoke Serpent and the brother of our current tyrant, Moon Jaguar of Nakanjo!" He spits the words from between his lips. "Moon Jaguar takes away our strongest, youngest men to be sacrificed on the altar of your gods. Tell me why I should believe anything you have to tell me." The king of Tikyu gazed on the faces of the untrained old men and young teenage boys who made up the opposing army.

"I come seeking an alliance between our two great cities."

Scorched Mountain sneered at Jade Ocelot's offer. "You could easily defeat my men and overrun the city. Your offer of peace is some kind of trickery!"

"It is no trick! I seek to overthrow my brother, Moon Jaguar, who has tried to kill me for many years."

"This is a fight between two brothers! What does this have to do with Ixakbe?"

"When my brother is overthrown with your city's help, as king of Nakanjo, I will ask you to keep our alliance so that the three cities would become the most powerful force in this land. What do you have to say to that?"

"And what about the sacrificing of my warriors?"

"That will come to an end." Scorched Mountain looked suspiciously on this proposal but knew if he refused the offer of peace, Jade Ocelot's army could efficiently wipe out his warriors and take the city as his own. He sat back in capitulation.

"Let it be done!"

"This is my uncle, Jaguar Claw, whom I will leave here to train your troops. When that is done, our two armies will march against my brother, our mutual enemy."

"Come into the city and feast with us as new allies," the old king declared. After Jade Ocelot agreed, Scorched Mountain led the Tikyun king and his warriors to the plaza of the palace. The people of Ixakbe, once they understood they were not under attack, came out of their hiding places and rejoiced in the street hailing the new alliance of the two city-states.

They all ate and drank until sunset was drawing to a close. Saying goodbye, Jade Ocelot led his men back to their own city.

Moon Jaguar should have been content with himself, but he just could not convince his troubled mind after his first wife died during childbirth. Each day he watched his new wife as Ruby Hummingbird's womb swelled with their child, but his pleasure was only momentary. With the command of more soldiers to watch the agricultural fields, he had stopped other raids, but his mind continued to be ill at ease. The use of newly seeded fields yielded a better crop for his people, but its distance left its transport vulnerable to further raids by Jade Ocelot.

The image of his brother and uncle clouded his thoughts and there was no escaping them. Scouting parties went out in different directions each day and Screeching Owl recounted to the king that there was nothing to report. Each time, Moon Jaguar went into an uncontrollable rage. "Find him, I tell you and that traitorous uncle of mine! Someone is surely hiding them away!"

"Lord, they will be found," His advisor prayed his words would come true. "But it takes time to look in every corner of the jungle."

"Must I do everything myself? Give me no excuses or you will find yourself on the sacrificial altar"

A trace of sweat appeared on the advisor's forehead as he bowed and backed out of the room, repeating, "Yes, Lord…yes, Lord."

Moon Jaguar stormed out of the throne room, his two body guards trying to keep pace with him. "Wait here!" he yelled at the men as he entered his wife's chamber. He saw Ruby Hummingbird being fanned by her ladies of the court. "Go!" he commanded and the young women fled from the room. His wife gazed at him and held out her hand. Moon Jaguar always found solace in the arms of his wife. "What troubles you so?" his concerned mate inquired. The king had promised himself that he would not burden his pregnant wife with state problems but now he felt as if he had nobody else to turn to.

"I have not wanted to encumber you with my problems."

"I am asking you what has you so upset." He laid his head on her shoulders and she stroked his hair.

"It's my brother."

"What about him? I thought he was dead."

"I assumed he was after all this time but something has made me doubt my assumption."

"Tell me, my love," she cooed in his ear.

"Moons ago, our new fields were attacked but I was reticent to tell you about it." He laid his hand on her swollenness as an indication why he had kept the news from her.

"You must divulge to me what you have kept hidden."

"When the farmers returned from the field, they related to me that one of the attackers looked like my brother."

"This is foolishness. Jade Ocelot could never have survived in the jungle for that length of time. Don't you see? This was a mistaken image of a frightened man running for his life. Is this what has been troubling you for all this time, my love?" Her soothing voice had the power to slow down his heart rate and he breathed easier.

"Yes! I've sent out search parties to find him but all have been unsuccessful!"

"They are probably unsuccessful because your brother is nothing but a pile of bones lying in the jungle." Soon the king was second guessing himself about the search parties. He stood up and walked to the door. He addressed one of his guards and commanded,

"Tell Screeching Owl to call off all the search parties."

With a bow, he responded, "Yes, my Lord," and took off down the hallway. Moon Jaguar walked back to his wife and sat down beside her.

"You have done a wise thing," she told him taking his hand. "The raiders were probably just jungle tribes. Your added troops to the fields will most likely end their raids."

"Yes, you are most prospectively correct." Moon Jaguar breathed a sigh of relief as the lines of worry on his forehead slowly dissipated.

With a clap of her hands, her ladies returned and began to fan the royal couple. He rested his head on Ruby Hummingbird's shoulder and was now totally at ease as his eyelids began to flutter into slumber. She laid her hand on the side of his cheek and gently caressed the green jade earring hanging from his lobe. *His brother must be deceased after this much time,* she told herself. *The farmer had to be mistaken about what he claims he saw. Still what if it is true? The only reason he would have returned would be to usurp the throne from my husband.*

As a young girl, Ruby Hummingbird had seen in her own city of Ixakbe, the bloody aftermath of a contentious civil war between her father and her uncle. The whole city had suffered as a result with starvation and pestilence in every household. It was at this point that Smoke Serpent, the father of her husband and the king of Nakanjo, had invaded her city and took her father and uncle to the sacrificial altar and dispatched them with the quick slashing of the flesh on their chests. She was taken prisoner and married to Moon Jaguar. It had been difficult at first with her new spouse because of his inflammatory temper, he was more easily comforted with soothing glances, lulling touches, and gentle words. *No, a civil war would do much harm to my husband, to Nakanjo, and to my baby.* She felt the child she was carrying suddenly kick. *The child is in agreement with me.*

A runner rushed into the palace and dropped to his knees once he reached Moon Jaguar and Ruby Hummingbird. She was days away from delivering their baby. The king's retinue had gathered in the throne room. Everyone was shocked by this sudden interruption by a common soldier. "What do you want?" the king inquired in a condescending tone of voice.

"Lord…" the soldier gasped trying to regain his breath.

"Speak up, speak up!" he barked losing his patience.

"Husband, calm yourself," advised his wife as her hands lay on top of her swollen womb.

"What is it?" Moon Jaguar inquired in a more serene timbre.

Pointing west with his hand, he replied, "An army approaches the city!" The king sniffled sardonically. Moon Jaguar rose from his seat and postured with a resounding voice,

"Nobody would dare try to overthrow me!"

Turning toward his advisor, Screeching Owl, he instructed him. "Have my soldiers gather in this courtyard ready for battle while I get ready. As the king walked to his room to be changed, his wife tottered after him saying,

"Be careful my husband!"

The king was dressed for war by his servants in plumes of exotic birds. They also placed jade jewelry with plugs on his ears and nose, and bracelets on his wrists. He rushed down the stairs where his litter was waiting for him. He waved to his soldiers as the army marched forward. He was met by his runners who brought him the latest news. "Lord," the first one greeted him. "It seems that the armies of Ixakbe and Tikyu have joined forces to march on us!"

"There is nothing to worry about. The warriors of Nakanjo are better trained and equipped than the invaders." Before nightfall, I will have the hearts of those in rebellion torn out of their chests." Once again, the army of Nakanjo moved forward. After a while, another runner approached. His news was alarming.

"Lord, the leaders of the rebellion have been identified as your uncle, Jaguar Claw and your brother, Jade Ocelot." The king bristled with the news.

"At last, the traitors have shown their faces! They will all be left slain on the battlefield except for my uncle and brother. They will learn what it means to go against my will!"

The two opposing armies met in an open plain facing each other. Moon Jaguar had his litter carried forward to within a few yards of the enemy. In a loud voice, he commanded, "Warriors of Tikyu and Ixakbe disband immediately and go back to your respective cities. But first bring me my brother and uncle!" The enemy did not move. Two men stepped out in front. Moon Jaguar recognized them instantaneously. Jade Ocelot shouted, "It is I brother, Jade Ocelot!

"I should have killed you when I first had the chance!"

"I suppose you should have, but today only one of us will be alive to walk away from the battle in victory while the other's blood will be spilled on the battlefield."

"Uncle, it is good to see you again. Before the daylight has faded, your head on a spike will decorate the palace courtyard!"

Jaguar Claw lifted his arm and pointed toward him. "Your days as ruler of Nakanjo are numbered and your name and memory will pass into ignominy!"

Moon Jaguar slipped from his litter, his right hand grasping a war club with five sharpened blades glistening in the sun. Raising it over his head, he let out a shrill whoop and the Nakanjan warriors yelled back as they raced forward. The two armies clashed with heads crushed, limbs broken, and faces smashed.

Jade Ocelot had wanted to battle in single combat with his brother, but first had to fight off his army. Warriors who rushed toward him were sliced down until the soil around his feet was saturated with his enemy's blood. Blood spatters decorated his exposed skin as he moved headlong into the next group of Nakanjans. Once more, he swung his war club and heard the grunts and screams as his enemies fell before him. Jade Ocelot's army steadily pushed the warriors of Nakanjo back, their number advantage was taking its toll. He took a quick look to the right to see his uncle decapitate his opponent with one strong swoop of his club. Two more of the Niranjan warriors approached them but they were speedily dispatched - one with a blow to the head and the other with a blow to the spine after he had deftly avoided the warriors spear.

It was out of the corner of his eye that he saw Moon Jaguar enter his litter as the bearers ran back in the direction of Nakanjo. He was not the only one to take notice. Word spread that their King Moon Jaguar had left the field of battle. Immediately, his army broke ranks to follow him. With a war whoop from Jaguar Claw, the two leaders followed the retreat, killing all the stragglers they came upon.

The people of Nakanjo stared frightfully as the king's litter raced past them. Not since the reign of Smoke Serpent, Moon Jaguar's father, had the city been in such jeopardy. Panicking people either sought shelter in their homes or in the jungle beyond the city. The king's army stood before Moon Jaguar listening for his order. "Defend the palace!" their lord commanded them as he retreated inside. The defenders turned to meet their approaching enemy, the first of whom entered the far side of the city. The sound of their sandals pounding on the pavement as they grew near sent up a terrifying racket, but before they attacked, Jade Ocelot let out a whoop. The army came to a halt. The warriors of Tikyu and Ixakbe sought revenge for the decades of repressive rule and the sacrificing of their young men. Their emotions filled them with blood thirsty rage that had been far from sated.

Jade Ocelot and Jaguar Claw stepped forward with the nephew speaking out. "Warriors of Nakanjo," he began. "You know who I am. I'm Jade Ocelot, the second son of Smoke Serpent. I do not want the blood of any more of my people to be spilled! Moon Jaguar has proven himself to be a weak king and not a true leader of a great people! Follow me and help me remove him from the throne where he is not fit to sit!"

His uncle now began to speak. "Bow to the true lord of Nakanjo, a king who will bring back the greatness of the people!" Moon Jaguar's soldiers looked at each other but said nothing. Jade Ocelot decided to take a risk. He moved towards them bearing his naked chest. *They will either stab me in the chest or let me pass and follow me.* As he got closer, the warriors of Nakanjo looked once more at each other. At last, the soldiers parted to let Jade Ocelot enter. They joined their former enemies and followed in the path of their new king and marched up the steps to the palace.

CHAPTER 5

NAKANJO, FEBRUARY, 461

The lake appeared to be a floating garden. Flat boats were festooned with garlands of vibrantly hued white and yellow orchids, violet coqueta, and red and pink poinsettias. The people of Nakanjo boisterously enjoyed the installation of their new king, Jade Ocelot. Right beside him stood his very pregnant wife, Queen Cooing Dove. Next to the queen were the two people who enabled him to reach this point, his mother Sparkling River, and his uncle, Jaguar Claw. The jade ornaments of authority were placed on his ears and nostrils by the chief priest and the plumed cape made of green and red quetzal feathers was placed over his shoulders. There was a great roar from the crowd when their new king raised his arms into the air, his war club in his fist

A day of festivities had been planned for the people. There was plenty to eat and drink for all. "The people are in total agreement with your installation." Jaguar Claw proclaimed.

"As my first act as king, I appoint you my Uncle, as my Chief Advisor."

"Thank you, Lord. I am honored." The new king and his family climbed the temple steps to the palace. "There will be a new prosperity for our people since Tikyu and Ixakbe are now allies rather than enemies."

"This is true."

"For my second command, a new temple will be built and dedicated to the war god, Votan, in appreciation for my victory over my brother."

As they made their way up, Jade Ocelot looked at the severed head that was placed on a spear atop the temple for everyone to see. It was the head of his brother's advisor, Screeching Owl. The king remembered how his warriors had found him cowering in his room and how he was dragged screaming and thrown down before Jade Ocelot's feet. Blubbering with tears streaming down his cheeks, he proclaimed, "It was entirely your brother's doing! I swear that I took no part in his murderous plot against you!" Moon Jaguar had already been found, captured, and imprisoned. Jade Ocelot would deal with him later.

"There was a reason that you were named Screeching Owl. You stay out of sight until it's time for the kill. I will not give you another chance to assassinate me. I've already ordered that you be sacrificed to the gods. Take him and keep watch over him and prepare him for the ceremony." Two guards came and dragged the prisoner away.

"No, Lord! Please, I am loyal only to you!" His screams echoed down the hallway. The king turned to Jaguar Claw instructing, "Bring my brother's wife to me. Treat her respectfully."

"Yes, Lord." Jade Ocelot handed his weapon to the nearest warrior and waited for his sister-in-law to be brought before him. Ruby Hummingbird was carried in on a litter, bringing her newborn daughter to whom she had given birth during the battle. Jade Ocelot walked over to her.

"Sister," he called to the proud woman. "You need not fear for yourself or your child since you will be honorably treated as a noblewoman in my court."

"What of my husband?"

"I am sorry to tell you that he must pay with his life." Moon Jaguar's soon-to-be widow did not say a word. "Bring her back to her room," he commanded.

A warrior entered the room and got on one knee. "All is ready for the sacrifice."

"Come with me," Jade Ocelot instructed his family. They walked into the bright sunlight where the chief priest was waiting. "Bring him forward!" The former chief advisor had been stripped of his clothing and his entire body painted with blue indigo mixed with clay mineral. He was brought to the sacrificial stone, his demeanor silent and more accepting now of his inescapable fate.

Laying him on his back, his feet and arms held down allowing his chest to rise, the chief priest held his knife in the air just above the victim's chest. After an incantation, the priest plunged it, piercing the flesh. The still beating heart was thrown into the burning brazier and sizzled as it was engulfed and consumed by the flaming fingers of the inferno.

Jade Ocelot stepped forward, the warrior handed him back his weapon and with his war club, with one powerful swing, the king lopped the head off the body. It was then that the head was displayed to the public. The body of the traitorous advisor was thrown down the stairs, while the head was staked on a spear and displayed to those below.

Now when he walked back from his installation, he knew he had to deal with his brother. "Give me your knife," he ordered his new advisor. His uncle did as he was ordered.

"What do you have planned?" Jaguar Claw inquired.

"I must go to my brother." His mother Sparkling River drew back. She had no interest in seeing her eldest son.

"I will come with you," offered Jaguar Claw.

"No! I must do this alone."

"As you wish, Lord."

The king walked down the cool passages of the temple until he came to a room where two guards were stationed. "Open the door and close it once I'm inside. But remain outside". The guards obeyed their new king. The doors closed once he had entered. Sitting on the floor, was the defeated, once powerful ex-king of Nakanjo. He looked up and stared at his younger brother in his finery, the clothing he had once worn as king. "How long do you intend to keep me here in my humiliation?" the former king demanded.

"It will be over soon," he answered back in a calm voice.

"Good!"

"I have a proposition that I would like you to consider."

"I am your prisoner. Do with me as you will." Jade Ocelot took the knife he had been carrying and slid it on the floor to his older brother.

"Do you want me to do your job?" he laughed maniacally.

"If you take your own life, I will see to it that you are buried as a king and given all the honors as such. Besides, it will spare you the shame of being a human sacrifice."

"What of my wife and child?"

"They will remain as part of my court. All this I promise you if you will just take the knife, cut your wrists and let your life blood drip into these two bowls." Next to where his brother sat, the two bowls had been placed for just this purpose. The room grew deadly hushed until Jade Ocelot spoke up. "What is your answer?"

"If you do what you have promised, I will do as you ask."

Before he turned to leave, he uttered, "Goodbye, brother."

Moon Jaguar did not answer and waited for his younger brother to depart. Once the door was reclosed, he lifted the knife and held it to the flesh of his left wrist. With a quick motion, he sliced through as the blood began to drip out. Swiftly, he took the weapon and cut his left wrist. Dropping the bloody knife to the floor, he held both his wrists over the bowls as his life poured out. Placidly, he thought about his days as king and how it all had come crashing down around him. He thought about this until a light-headedness began to overtake his consciousness. He tried to stay aware of his surroundings, but as the minutes passed, so did his life. At last, his body fell back on the floor and he passed through this life quietly.

The mood of the people of Nakanjo had become visibly upbeat when the civil war ended between the two brothers and Jade Ocelot had been established as king. Without worry of attack from its two sister cities, Ixakbe and Tikyu, warriors were no longer needed to guard the agricultural fields and the city could devote more time in enhancing Nakanjo.

Immediately after receiving the symbols of his new status, jade and gold ornamentation worn on his body, Jade Ocelot ordered the building of a temple dedicated to the god of war, Votan. Workers began to cut blocks of stone from the limestone bedrock quarries. From there, the blocks were pulled and pushed until they were put in place on the left side of the Temple of the Sun. The blocks were sealed together with mortar called quicklime, made from limestone that was burned down and then mixed with water and sand. The final step was the pulverization of limestone which was mixed with water to make stucco and used to smooth over and mold onto the façade.

Each day Jade Ocelot took pride as the temple rose into the air. It was the topic of conversation for all the people in the city and became a source of pride and bonding for the citizens. Steles were written telling of the great victory of the king over his brother.

When the dedication day arrived, the king, with Jaguar Claw and the chief priests, stood at the top of the temple, the populace staring up from below. Braziers were lit on either side of the stone altar and the curling black smoke rose into the air like a serpent. His wife Cooing Dove and his baby, a son named Bird Jaguar swaddled in cloth, stood in the background. Only one person was missing in this celebration. Unfortunately, his mother, Sparkling River, had died before the temple had been completed. She had been buried with her husband, her body adorned in gold and jade ornamentation as befitted a queen.

Jade Ocelot had already had his tongue split and a rope passed through it so that droplets of his blood could be collected on leaves and thrown into the fire as a sacrifice. The blood collected from his brother's suicide was also dropped into the fire in devotion to Votan for the king's triumph.

Once the temple had been completed, another one was begun on the right side of the Temple of the Sun. This was to be dedicated to the god of rain, Chaac.

It was during this time, with everything running smoothly, that the first problem arose. A message from the Ixakben king, War Club, arrived announcing that they would no longer be a part of the alliance. When the messenger was dismissed, the king turned to his uncle for a private audience. "Why do you think he is pulling back from his agreement?"

"Lord, it could be any number of reasons. First, he might have used the agreement to be rid of your brother's domination. Once that was achieved, he saw no reason to continue his loyalty to you. Or perhaps he does not want his city to be involved in any further wars. But more likely, it has to do with the influence his wife, Lady Sun, has over the old king."

"You must go to War Club as my emissary and convince him that for the sake of his city's safety and independence, he must renew his alliance with Nakanjo."

"Yes, Lord."

Transported on a litter and bedecked with gold and jade which reflected his importance in the court, Jaguar Claw arrived in Ixakbe. His reception by the people of the city reflected a change of attitude toward Jade Ocelot. His reception was cold and distant. The emissary was brought before War Club. Sitting to the right of him was the queen and on the left sat their 12-year old son, Sharpened Spear.

The Ixakben king sat without moving, his look just a blank stare into space. "Lord", Jaguar Claw began. "I have come here at my Lord Jade Ocelot's request to have our alliance between us reestablished." It was not War Club who answered.

"The King, my husband, does not believe that keeping an alliance with you will benefit Ixakbe in any way." Lady Moon was a beautiful female, much younger than her husband, but as deadly as the venomous scorpion.

Jaguar Claw ignored the queen and continued to address War Club. "Lord, the alliance is a mutual protection for all three cities. If Ixakbe strikes out on its own, you can expect no help from Nakanjo or Tikyu."

"And there is the problem," Lady Moon interjected. "The two cities share a familial connection that we Ixakbens don't share. We are treated as outsiders by the two cities."

"Nothing could be further from the truth. We honor Ixakbe for its contributions during our civil war and respect you as a great society!"

"Words, just words that now fall on deaf ears! Your king's actions speak much louder!"

This time, the emissary addressed the queen. "And what actions would that be, my Lady?"

"You have the audacity to interrogate me? It is just one example of Nakanjon arrogance!"

"This is not true, great king," proclaimed Jaguar Claw once more speaking to the king. War Club continued his unfocused gaze, a drop of spittle running down the corner of his mouth.

Lady Moon rose from her seat with great majesty. "Be gone!" she sneered and waved her hand as if she were swatting a lowly mosquito. "The alliance is broken and can never be repaired!"

Bowing, Jaguar Claw retreated from the room, walked down where his litter was awaiting and got in. "Back to Nakanjo," he instructed and he watched the hostile stares of the people as he passed. *Now I must break the bad news to my nephew.*

Lady Moon was nobody's fool. After her husband's death and internment, and the ceremony of her son, Sharpened Spear, making him king, his mother Lady Moon as Queen Regent looked for another alliance of protection. Even though Jade Ocelot had offered such an arrangement, he was still Smoke Jaguar's son and Moon Jaguar's younger brother, both of whom had used her people for sacrificial purposes. Therefore, she sent her emissary to the nearby city-state of Quiribal to propose a coalition.

There was a divisive rift amongst the nobility brewing against Lady Moon's attempt to align with Quiribal, their traditional enemy. They saw the breaking of the treaty with Nakanjo as a grave error since Jade Ocelot was nothing like his other male relatives. The leader of the opposition was the previous Ixakben King War Club's half-brother, Swift Arrow.

"What if the queen's emissary comes back from Quiribal with the city's agreement for an alliance?" one of the royal dissenters inquired.

"We must send our own emissary to Nakanjo saying that we are ready to overthrow the queen to reestablish our agreement."

"Even if the Quiribal king refuses, the queen can go to the king of Kaminche an even larger and more war-like city state."

"And there lies the problem. No matter who she seeks to join us to protect her son as king, these city-states will look only to swallow us. She barters for peace from a weak position. Any city-state that agrees will only be looking for the opportunity to invade us and take us over."

"This is a dangerous plan that she pursues."

"Lady Moon must be stopped at any cost!"

Unknown by most the citizens of Ixakbe, Lord Swift Arrow, with a small contingent of nobleman, made their way to Nakanjo. Once he was announced, he was granted an audience with Jade Ocelot. As always, Jaguar Claw, his uncle, stood by the king's side. Bowing, Swift Arrow began. "Lord Jade Ocelot, we come here to implore you to reestablish the alliance that once existed between our two great cities."

The king looked down silently at the Ixakben lords before him. At last, he responded. "Your queen does not seem to share your opinion. Lady Moon has already turned down such an offer of alliance from me."

"Mighty Lord, there is great disagreement amongst the nobility to the queen's decision to break with Nakanjo."

"What would you have me do?"

"Send some of your warriors to help us overthrow this foolish queen."

"I do not seek to depose the rightful ruler of Ixakbe."

"Lord, she has already sent emissaries to Quiribal for a joining of forces. If this doesn't happen, it is rumored that Lady Moon will seek a treaty with Kaminche to the east. Once this is done, it will be only a matter of time until we are subjected and invaded. Then this menace will be right next door to you. We beseech you to rejoin our cities to make Ixakbe a buffer between our mutual enemies."

While the king was deep in thought, Jaguar Claw bent over to whisper something in Jade Ocelot's ear. Listening intently, his advisor pulled away. "You will be shown into the anteroom to await my decision."

"As you wish, Lord."

As the group was led away, Jaguar Claw spoke up. "It would seem to me, Lord that we must back this faction against their queen."

"This is an Ixakben internal affair that has nothing to do with Nakanjo."

"Lord, Swift Arrow sees things clearly. Once an alliance is established with our enemies, it would not be long before Ixakbe is subjugated. The Kings of Kaminche or Quiribal will then turn their attention on us. It will not be long before we are staring at another war. Even with Tikyu's warriors beside ours, we would be hard pressed to hold them back!"

"Still, Lady Moon has refused our offer of alliance between our cities. Unless she changes her mind, I believe we must stay out of it." Suddenly, they were interrupted by the crying of a baby. "Is that my child crying?" The king's attention had been diverted. He rose to find out if his son was alright.

"Lord," Jaguar Claw called out to the king as he walked away. "What about the Ixakben delegation? They are seeking an answer from you."

"Tell them that I'm not willing to interfere in Ixakben affairs." Jade Ocelot left the room. His uncle watched as he walked away. *My nephew is too much involved in family matters and not enough involved in the affairs of Nakanjo. The decision not to support Ixakben nobles against Lady Moon will only postpone the inevitable. We will soon find ourselves in a war of survival against our common enemies. I must somehow influence Jade Ocelot so that he understands the dire consequences of his decision and it must be done sooner rather than later.* Jaguar Claw called out to one of the guards, "Show the Ixakben delegation back in!"

Chapter 6

It didn't take long for the King of Quiribal to respond to Lady Moon's proposal for a treaty between the two city-states. A procession of warriors from the city suddenly showed up, led by a Quiribaln prince, Holy Snake Lord, the youngest son of the King of Quiribal. Dressed in the finest of textiles, with his ears and throat adorned with the most luxurious jade earrings and nose pins, arms and neck dripping with gold jewelry, he was carried by litter into Ixakbe.

Lady Moon caught by surprise by this visit, hurried down to meet and welcome him to the city. Holy Snake Lord looked down arrogantly at the queen without getting out of his litter. "Lord" the queen began, "I greet you in friendship from the people of my city." Holy Snake Lord cast his gaze slowly around before he answered,

"Not much of a city is it." Instantly, the queen began to have grave regrets about her idea of linking the two cities.

"My Lord…"

"My name is Holy Snake Lord, Lady Moon."

"Please come into the palace where I can offer you food and drink after your long and dusty journey." Not saying a word in response, he disembarked from the litter, following the queen inside, a group of Quiribaln warriors armed with war clubs and spears behind him. Before they arrived in the throne room, Lady Moon told a servant, "Get my son and send him here right away." The servant ran to complete her task. With a clap of her hands, servants entered carrying trays. Bowls of guacamole served with masa (corn tortillas) and Poc Chuc (marinated pork) were brought in. Cocoa served hot was also offered.

While the Quiribaln prince dined, the queen's son, Sharpened Spear, appeared from the doorway. "Mother, what is happening?" he inquired as he watched Holy Snake Lord eat.

"My request for an alliance between Ixakbe and Quiribaln, I believe, is about to come to fruition. Come and I will introduce you to the prince." Mother and son drew closer to their guest.

"Welcome, great Lord to our city. Your visit brings us great honor," Sharpened Spear greeted him. By this time the rest of the court, including Swift Arrow, had come into the throne room.

Holy Snake Lord looked up momentarily from the meal to gruffly ask, "Who are you?"

"I am Prince Sharpened Spear, Lord." Holy Snake Lord gave him a casual look and went back to his meal. As the entire court watched, the prince took his time eating. Finally, a belch announced the end of the meal.

"Prince Holy Snake Lord, are you here with an answer from your father to my request?"

"I am." Lady Moon and her court nervously anticipated his answer, but he did not say another word. Finally, the queen spoke up.

"And what is his decision about forming an alliance with my city?" Once again, the prince belched before responding.

"My father will honor your request." Lady Moon was greatly pleased by this answer, while Swift Arrow and some of the other noblemen became despondent.

"Thank you, Lord," the queen answered exuberantly.

"But my lord father has two conditions before he will come to an agreement with you."

"And what are his demands?"

"First, since you are a widow, he requires that we be married."

The queen would never have wed such a lout but she was willing to do anything that would ensure that her son remained king of Ixakbe. "I agree. And the last request?"

"That any son that we may have become the legitimate heir to the throne."

An audible gasp rose from the queen and her court. "But my son is already king here."

"During our marriage ceremony, I will be made King of Ixakbe!"

"And what is to become of my son, Sharpened Spear?"

With a quick wave of his hand, Holy Snake Lord summoned a pair of his soldiers who ran to the young boy.

"Nooo!" his mother screamed as she ran defensively toward her flesh and blood. Before the Ixakben guards could respond to this threat, Quiribaln warriors cut them down.

Lady Moon stood before her son, blocking him with her body but the foreign combatants showed not a shred of mercy. While one of them grabbed her by the hair and dragged her away, the other took hold of the prince. "Mother, help me!" were the only words he could shriek out before his throat was slit. The noblemen of Ixakbe watched in terror as their prince crumpled to the ground, his blood pooling near his head.

Horror was etched on every Ixakben face as they had watched the tragedy unfold before them. The bloody body of the boy was dragged out as his overwrought mother cried out his name over and over.

"The ceremonies will take place in two days! Leave me now everyone, I am tired!" announced Holy Snake Lord.

NAKANJO, APRIL, 461

Rumors had spread around Nakanjo but were not confirmed until the first refugees arrived from Ixakbe. Among them were the noble Swift Arrow and a few members of Lady Moon's court. Swift Arrow approached Jaguar Claw to ask for an audience with the king. "Please implore your lord to see me right away!" From the tone of his voice, Jaguar Claw realized that the awful rumors about what happened in Ixakbe must be true.

"Wait here and I will speak with him immediately!" The king's advisor went to the throne room to find Jade Ocelot, a pregnant Cooing Dove, and Moon Jaguar's widowed wife, Ruby Hummingbird, eating together. Getting Jade Ocelot's attention, his advisor whispered, "A group of Ixakben nobles are here to speak to you, Lord."

"Now?" Jaguar Claw was shocked by the King's annoyed response.

"Yes, Lord. They bring news from Ixakbe." Getting up from his chair, he moaned,

"If I must." Jaguar Claw led his king to where the Ixakben nobles patiently lingered. As they walked, his advisor thought, *those are small things, weaknesses, that I have seen in Jade Ocelot character that do not bode well for a king.* He shelved these ideas as they approached the nobles. The Ixakbens bowed in deference to the Nakanjo king's status. "Swift Arrow, it is good to see you again."

"It is good to see you too but the circumstances by which I come to you have gone from bad to worse!"

"What do you mean?"

"You already know that Lady Moon was looking to ally Ixakbe with another city-state after our break with the alliance with Nakanjo."

"Yes, I know this."

"The Quiribal king sent his youngest son, Holy Snake Lord, for what we all thought were negotiations."

"That didn't happen?"

"No, Lord. Instead of parleying, he demanded that Lady Moon marry him and that he become king."

"That would be unfeasible since Lady Moon's son Sharpened Spear is the prince and our soon-to-be king."

"Not anymore."

"What are you saying?"

"Before our eyes, Holy Snake Lord ordered Sharpened Spear murdered."

Jade Ocelot's eyes opened wide with disbelief. "Why have you come to tell me this?"

"Lord Jade Ocelot, our city needs your help!"

"I am sorry for your loss but the alliance between our two cities no longer exits. My hands are tied in this matter."

"Lord," Jaguar Claw whispered in his sovereign's ear, "Quiribal now becomes a direct threat to Tikyu and our city." Jade Ocelot listened but did not answer. Instead, he addressed Swift Arrow and the other Ixakbens.

"I am sorry to hear about the death of your king and your queen's problem. You and the other refugees are welcome in my city but I can no longer offer you any assistance." With that the Nakajoan king made his way back to the throne room. In a placating tone, the king's advisor told the nobles, "I will try to speak to him." Crushed by what they had heard, the Ixakbens left the palace.

Running to catch up to the king, Jaguar Claw said, "Lord, I believe not helping Ixakbe may lead to our city's demise!"

"You are wrong, Uncle. Along with the Tikyuns we can stand up to any invader and turn them back."

"If we don't address this problem, we will be overrun with other Ixakben refugees. Our food supply could never stand the strain. Besides, the altars of the gods have not had blood sacrifices for almost a year. The people grow uneasy about the lack of victims to be laid out on the altar. War with Quiribal will provide us with captured warriors for sacrifice that we need to offer up to our gods.

"It was my decision to end blood sacrifices in this city. They will be replaced by royal blood instead."

"Lord, this is a dangerous move!"

"Uncle, you forget your place! You may advise me, but I make the final decisions for the good of my people!" As Jade Ocelot walked away, all that Jaguar Claw could do was stand flabbergasted. *Did I support the wrong brother? Only time will tell.*

The mood in the city of Ixakbe was quiet desperation and fear. After Swift Arrow and others had taken flight from the city, King Holy Snake Lord decreed that warriors would be guarding the main thoroughfares in and out of the city. They were not placed there for the defense of the city, but to prevent its citizens from fleeing Ixakbe. Their orders were to catch anyone trying to leave the city unlawfully. The captives were taken to the sacrificial stone to have their bloody hearts torn from their chests; this included men, women and children. Soon the stone dripped with the red blood of its people futilely trying to escape.

The installation of the Quiribalan prince as king was followed the next day by his marriage to Lady Moon. The day before, she had witnessed the burial of her son, Sharpened Spear, in the main temple. Tearfully, she had to be pulled away to ready herself for the wedding. With her eyes red from crying, she went through the ceremony as if she were dreaming, but the dream turned into a nightmare.

The nobility who were left were commanded to join the celebration. All those who attended were eyewitnesses to the king's gluttony and drunkenness. Platters of deer, fowl, and fish were served, with jugs of balache made from the bark of the leguminous trees which are soaked in honey and water until it fermented. "Drink, Eat!" he dictated slurring his words. Very few partook of the meal, including the queen.

Finally, Holy Snake Lord stood unsteadily on his feet and yelled, "Go away all of you! This is my wedding night!" The Ixakben lords could not wait to be dismissed and readily left the whole scene behind, except for a mixture of Quiribaln and Ixakben warriors deemed loyal to the new king.

Grabbing his new wife roughly by the arm, he pulled her up from the chair. "It's time to make a future king!" Filled with revulsion and disgust for her new husband, she was pulled sobbing to the bed chamber. He exposed himself to her and staggered in Lady Moon's direction. He tried to mount her on the platform bed, but she pushed him off so that he landed on the floor and there he lay for the rest of the night.

She stared at him for a while, grateful that he wouldn't bother her that night. *Still, there will be other nights that I will be forced to give in to his sexual advances. How I regret going to Quiribaln for an alliance. My son is dead, my life turned upside down, and my city in captivity. I pray to the gods for our redemption!* Quietly leaving the bedroom, she stayed in the ante-chamber in case he would awake. The night was spent crying and worrying.

By the next morning, Lady Moon went back to the room to find her husband in the same spot as he was the night before. She climbed over him to lay down and tried to get some much-needed sleep.

Later in the morning, the king awoke groaning, his head feeling like it was on fire. He slowly rose to his feet to find his bride still in bed. Despite his pain, he smiled triumphantly. *I wore her out last night.* Yelling at the warriors outside his door, he said, "Find my chief advisor!" In time, his advisor, Snake Jaguar appeared.

"My Lord, you sent for me?" Holy Snake Lord pointed to his queen. His advisor smiled. "Congratulations, my Lord. Before too long, you will have a son to follow you."

"I have another command to my warriors!"

"I am listening, my Lord."

"I want them to scour the jungle to find more sacrificial victims."

"Lord, what if they were to meet anyone from Nakanjon or Tikyun denizens?"

"Defeat them and take them prisoner like any other barbarians that they find! The gods require more blood."

"I hear and obey, Lord." As Snake Jaguar left the room, Lady Moon began to stir. Her husband moved to the side of the bed. "Wake up!" he ordered his wife, shaking her. The queen awoke realizing that her serious situation was still real.

"What do you want from me…Lord?"

"I want what I had from you last night!" There was no escaping him this time as he gruffly took her. She kept repeating, *I will kill him some day! I will kill him some day!*

CHAPTER 7

NAKANJO, JULY, 461

"Lord, two messengers have arrived at the palace."

Jade Ocelot looked away from his romping children and towards his uncle. "Bring the first one to the throne room. I will join you in a little while."

Jaguar Claw moved to the anteroom where a messenger from Tikyu waited. "Come with me." The two made their way to the throne room where they waited and waited. At last, the king made an appearance. The messenger bowed in deference to the King of Nakanjo.

"Why have you come to me from Tikyu?"

"Lord, I bring sad and happy news."

"What is the sad news?"

"Your aunt, Lady White Orchid has died."

"This is indeed sad news," Jaguar Claw said reacting to the news of the passing of his half-sister. Jade Ocelot nodded in agreement.

"And the good news?"

"Your cousin, Lord Shield is now king."

"Send my cousin salutations and congratulations upon his ascent to the throne and my grief at the passing of the queen, his mother."

"I will, Lord."

"Tell him that the bond and unity between us remains as strong as ever."

"Yes, Lord." The messenger was about to turn and leave until Jaguar Claw said, "Wait! Let me have a moment of your time, Lord." The two men stepped away beyond earshot.

"What is it, Uncle?"

"Lord Shield is a mere 15 years of age and has not had the experiences that you had at the same age."

"What do you suggest?"

"Send back with this messenger a contingent of our warriors to protect Tikyu from any incursion from Holy Snake Lord." The king thought for a while and nodded.

"Give word to the general about my order to march to Tikyu."

"Yes, Lord." As Jaguar Claw sent word, the king spoke to the messenger. A second messenger entered and bowed. Jaguar Claw recognized him as a farmer of their city. The man was sweating and breathing heavily as if he had run all the way there.

"Why have you come to me?" inquired Jade Ocelot.

"Lord, our farmers were attacked while working in the fields."

"Attacked? Attacked by whom?"

"By warriors from Quiribal and Ixakbe."

Jaguar Claw couldn't help but rejoin upon hearing the report. "And so it begins!"

"How many were slain? The king queried in a concerned voice.

"Very few. It was clear that they were there to take captives with whom they marched off."

"Are you the only one to have escaped?" the counselor wanted to know.

"I was, Lord. I pretended that I was dead and waited until they evacuated the fields before I ran here." At this point the farmer was dismissed from the room.

"Holy Snake Lord is testing us," Jaguar Claw concluded. "With a weak Tikyu to the north of us, he is hoping to isolate Nakanjo and invade!" Jade Ocelot was deep in thought.

"I will send another contingent of warriors into the fields to protect our farmers and crops.

"With two contingents gone, this will leave our city open to attack!"

"I will send an emissary to Holy Snake Lord in Ixakbe to try and establish peace between our two cities."

"Lord, he is not looking to find peace with our people. He wants to take this city for his own!"

"The King of Ixakbe can be reasoned with if he is approached in the right manner."

"And what manner is that, Lord?"

"Unthreatening, of course."

"Holy Snake Lord will only see this as a sign of weakness. We must strike back at Ixakbe with swiftness and ferocity. It is the only language he will understand!"

"That will only antagonize him!"

"That is what should be done. We must take captives from their city to sacrifice to our gods for victory!"

"I have told you many that there will no longer be any human sacrifices in Nakanjo. Not as long as I am king!" Jaguar Claw wished he could turn his nephew's mind around.

Jade Ocelot thought, *There is only one way I can get my uncle to see things my way.* "I appoint you as my emissary to the King of Ixakbe."

"Me? I have no experience in peacemaking, but only in war!"

"That is why you will be the perfect choice."

"I don't understand, Lord."

"As a war general, you will be able to negotiate from a strong position."

"I don't think…"

"This is my decision! Carry out my orders!" With that, Jade Ocelot left his counselor alone with his thoughts. *This will inevitably lead to the fall of this city and our people scattering in every direction. Nakanjo will be no more!*

It took days before the litter carrying Jaguar Claw to Ixakbe arrived at its destination. The litter, carried by four bearers, was followed by a party of 20 heavily-armed warriors. The advisor might be there for peaceful negotiations, but he was going to be prepared if they were ambushed.

Passing Nakanjo's agricultural fields, he noticed the water in the lake had receded because of a prolonged drought. The farmers had to work much harder to water the crops. He had been told there was grumbling in the city because the people blamed this on the lack of human sacrifices to the rain god, Chaac. He had spoken to his nephew several times about this topic, but Jade Ocelot stubbornly refused to change his mind. *I will need to press him harder.*

Moving on for the next few days, the emissary's party eventually spotted the tops of pyramids of Ixakbe rising above the rain forest canopy. "Be on alert in case we are ambushed!" he warned his guards. The warriors fingered their weapons nervously.

Before they could reach Ixakbe, they were confronted by a scouting party of Quiribal soldiers. The Nakojon soldiers from the city took a defensive stand. The leader of the group called out, "Identify yourself!"

"I am Jaguar Claw, emissary of Jade Ocelot, King of Nakanjo. I've come to speak to your king on an urgent matter!" The Quiribalan looked suspiciously at the foreign warriors. "If you disarm your men, I will take you to the palace!"

"My men will keep their arms but they will not be the ones who will strike the first blow! Take us there now!" As soon as Jaguar Claw identified himself, his reputation as a great warrior was recognized. Although he wasn't sure about the Nokajon, the Quiribalan leader felt that caution was the better part of valor and waved them forward.

It wasn't long before they entered a large stone-laid avenue. All around them, new pyramids were rising. Workers covered in limestone dust labored to move cut blocks of stone. The pyramids already erected were being whitewashed by laborers. Quiribalan warriors stood guard and "encouraged" the workers to work harder.

As they got further into the city, the populace turned to witness the scene. Their faces seemed drawn with anxiety and their bodies somewhat feeble. *The citizens of this city have paid an awful price for their queen's decision.* They approached the bottom step of the main temple where guards were stationed. The two Quiribalan soldiers conversed with each other. The guard at the temple approached the litter. A look of disgust crossed his face. "What do you want here?"

"I wish to speak to your king, Holy Snake Lord."

"For what reason?"

"That is something I will only discuss with your king." The guard was immediately put off by the rebuff.

"Stinking Nokanjon! Watch your tongue!"

Jaguar Claw got out of the litter, his obsidian war club by his side. "It would be smarter of you to watch your own tongue before I cut it out of your mouth!"

The guard frowned and then answered, "Wait here!" Sending another soldier up the stairs, he returned in a few minutes and spoke to the guard. "You may go up by yourself and you must leave your weapon with me."

"I will go on my own because one Nokanjon warrior is worth 20 of yours!" The guard seethed at the words. "I'm not leaving my weapon with you!"

"You must give it to me! It is my king's demand!"

"Then let him or you come and take it from my hand!" Jaguar Claw moved into an attack stance.

"Keep your damn club! Follow me!"

Jaguar Claw followed the guard up the steps to the top. He was then escorted into the throne room where Holy Snake Lord was seated, a bowl of mangos on a table by his side. The king ate the yellow pulp and slurped the juice of the fruit that ran down his chin onto his clothing. Jaguar Claw noticed his queen, Lady Moon sat below him. Her eyes were vacant. She remained expressionless.

The king noticed that the interloper was armed. He turned toward his guard and screamed, "I told you to disarm him!"

"Do not blame him, Lord," Jaguar Claw advised. "He was not man enough to take it from me!"

"Get out!" the king yelled at the guard who scurried out of his presence.

"Lord, my name is Jaguar Claw..."

"I know who you are!" he replied going back to continue eating the fruit.

"I am here by order of my king, Jade Ocelot to negotiate a peace between us."

"You entreat me for peace between our two cities and yet you carry a war club in my presence! That's not a very peaceful gesture on your part!"

"I carry it for my own protection and not to be a threat to you." The king laughed hysterically and turned toward his wife.

"He is very funny, isn't he my queen?" Lady Moon remained impassive.

"Before we begin our discussion, I must ask where our people are who you have violently taken by your warriors?"

"Your people? What could I possibly want with your people?"

"Some farmers were killed and the rest were herded away as captives, but your warriors were not completely thorough."

"I don't know what you're talking about," he shrugged indifferently.

"One of the farmers played dead until your warriors left, and he ran back to Jade Ocelot and myself to relate the entire incident."

"You must be a madman because you are talking out of your head!"

"I have come to ask for peace between our two cities."

"Peace, you want peace?"

"That is my king's request."

"And yet I am told you have sent a contingent of your warriors to Tikyu! That is not a peaceful move. It is a direct threat to my city!"

"Our warriors are not a threat to Ixakbe."

"Tell it to the wind for your words have no substance!"

"I give you my word!"

"A Nokonjan's word is worthless!"

"Then you're saying that there is no chance for peace between us?"

"Precisely! Now go back to your king! You bore me!" Using his hand as if he were shooing a fly, Holy Smoke Lord dismissed him and returned to his mangos.

Jaguar Claw left the interior of the building and came down the stairs of the temple. Climbing into his litter, he thought, *My nephew will not be happy about this bad news.*

Walking up the steps to the palace, the king's advisor brushed off the dust of the road from his clothing and entered the king's chamber. "I must talk to you privately," Jaguar Claw indicated to his king. Jade Ocelot looked at him with a frown. *He's more interested in being with his family than dealing with issues that affect our city.*

Reluctantly, the king led the way to the anteroom. "I can tell by the concerned look on your face, your news is not good."

"My overtures for peace were soundly rejected by Holy Snake Lord. He would not listen to anything I had to say."

"Why is that? Did he give you a reason?"

"He gave me several reasons. First, he has interpreted our move to send warriors to Tikyu as a threat against his city."

"Did you not explain to him that we have no intent on marching on Ixakbe?"

"I did, my Lord but he would have none of it."

"This is very distressful and disturbing news."

"I know, my Lord."

"You indicated to me that there was another reason for his refusal for peace. What is that?"

"He objected to the fact that the warriors had carried weapons into his presence."

"Did he ask you for them?"

"He did, my Lord but I refused his request." Jade Ocelot gave him a condescending look.

"And why is that, Uncle?"

"After all, our people were killed and taken captive by their warriors. Why would I jeopardize my life or that of my men? They cannot be trusted!"

"This was a foolish decision on your part!" His voice remained calm but was strained by what he had just been told.

"Finally, I made the point of asking about their attack on our fields."

"It is no wonder he spurned your proposals for peace between our cities!" This time, he did not hold back his antagonism towards Jaguar Claw. "I never told you to bring that up to him."

"He lied! He denied even knowing about the attack!"

"Did you really think he would admit to it? We have no proof of his culpability!"

"What about the farmer who escaped the raid?"

"It is simply the word of an ordinary citizen and not a soldier. I'm extremely dissatisfied by your failure to get the job done! Now, I suppose we need to prepare for war. *The man is delusional.*

Jade Ocelot was about to leave when Jaguar Claw called to him, "My Lord, there is another matter that must be addressed. The king stopped and turned back.

"And what is that?" he remarked, his impatience sounded in his voice.

"As you know, Chaac has not seen fit to provide us with rain for over a month. Things will soon become serious for our people if it goes on much longer!"

"I have cut my tongue until it has become soar. The priests use my blood on the altar of the rain god but it is no use. The god turns away from our imploring prayers for rain."

"It is not enough of a sacrifice, Lord!"

"I refuse to have this discussion with you again. You already know my feelings about human sacrifice."

"I do, my Lord but it is not helping our situation. Must we wait until the crops all shrivel in the heat and our people are starving before we try another way?"

"You are exaggerating the situation to make your point. We have not reached that disastrous situation!"

"I realize that, but the water from the lake shrinks daily. Even the melting mountain snow flowing into the river is beginning to dry up."

"Again, this is a hyperbole on your part. I have faith that Chaac will look favorably on us again and provide us with life-giving rain."

"The people of Nakanjo are not so convinced. Every day I hear complaints about the lack of rain and the beginning of some shortages of food in the marketplace."

Jade Ocelot lost his temper and petulantly replied, "I forbid you to ever bring this subject up to me again, do you understand?"

"What if word of this reaches Holy Snake Lord's ear? Perhaps he will think that in our weakened condition the city could be easily overrun by his warriors."

"I warn you for the last time! Do not speak to me of this again!"

This situation cannot go on this way indefinitely. Although Jade Ocelot was his king and nephew, Jaguar Claw began to think the unthinkable- treason!

CHAPTER 8

IXAKBE, JULY, 461

Lady Moon sat sobbing at her fate and that of her son. None of her ladies could find anything to say that would comfort her. She was surrounded by people yet she was all alone. The queen spent days in mourning, staying out of her husband's way. At night when her royal husband had used her, Lady Moon got up, not being able to sleep and wandered around the building. Her face became increasingly haggard looking, and she took little sustenance, just enough to keep her alive, although very often she wished for her own death. Lady Moon was becoming ever more desperate.

In another part of the temple, the king, Holy Snake Lord, sat with his counselor, Snake Jaguar in the throne room. The leader of Ixakbe sat, his forehead wrinkled in thought. His advice-giver finally inquired,

"Lord, what are you thinking?" Holy Snake Lord called one of his loyal Quiribal guards to him.

"Bring this message to my royal father. Tell him to send over all the warriors he can spare. I am about to extend his empire again. Go now!" The warrior took off out the door.

"You are going to attack Nakanjo, aren't you?" The king nodded.

"Before I attack the heart of Nakanjo, I must cut off their extremities." Snake Jaguar looked puzzled.

"What do you mean, Lord?"

"Jade Ocelot sent Jaguar Claw to seek a peace treaty with us. This is extremely telling as to the mind of the Nokajon king."

"He deals with us from a position of weakness!"

"Exactly, even if he believes he is in a strong position, he does not want to risk war with us." The king smirked with confidence.

"But what do you mean about cutting off the extremities?"

"Jade Ocelot and his uncle expect me to attack Nakanjo, but that's not what we'll do."

"What do you have in mind?"

"When my father's warriors arrive here, we will march on their only remaining ally, Tikyu."

"You mean…"

"Yes, Nakanjo at that point will be virtually surrounded. Jade Ocelot will need to yield the city to me!"

"Brilliant, my Lord!"

"I want to personally witness the moment when the hearts of the king and his uncle are ripped from their flesh and thrown into the fire of Votan. As for those Ixakbens who abandoned me to join Jade Ocelot, once their hearts are taken, their heads will be cut off and put on spears that will decorate the outside of the god's temple. With this, all of my enemies will then learn what it means to oppose me!"

"A most deserving fate for the traitors who betrayed you, my Lord," the king's advisor sniveled in enthusiastic anticipation. "I've heard rumors from Nakanjo that their king is rapidly losing his popularity. There is grumbling among the people, they say."

"Tell me more about this grumbling in Nakanjo."

"I have been told that Jade Ocelot has banned human sacrifice and that only royal blood be used as offerings to the gods."

"Now I know he is a fool! What else do you hear?"

"They say their gods have turned away from Nakanjo. This has resulted in some drought in the fields. I hear that it will not be too long before the people will start facing starvation."

"Nakanjo will soon be ripe for plucking!" The two men laughed heartily.

Just outside the throne room, ensconced in the hallway, Lady Moon walked the length and breadth of the temple when she found herself eavesdropping on her husband and his advisor. Her heart pounded so loudly in her chest, she was afraid the two men inside would hear it. She hurried away before she could be caught. *I should never have broken my alliance with Jade Ocelot. All the tragedy that followed was due to my ignorance. If I could only go back in time, I would change my fateful decision. But I could do something now about disrupting my husband's plan, but how shall I do it?*

She went to one of her ladies she thought she could trust. "Evening Star, I must talk to you!"

"Yes, my Queen?"

"Do I still have your loyalty?"

"You do, my Queen."

"And your husband's allegiance. Does he hate Holy Snake Lord as much as we do?"

"He does."

"Then tell him to bring a message to the King of Nakanjo from me."

"What is the message?"

"Tell him that my husband has sent for a force of Quiribalan warriors from his father to lead an attack and capture of Tikyu. Once he has taken the city, my husband will have Jade Ocelot surrounded. Tell your husband to leave immediately, but be careful. My husband has ordered that all caught leaving the city without permission will be put to death. Tell him to be very careful. Now go to him!" Lady Moon watched as she left. For once, after so many months of grief, a small smile appeared on her face. *Now it is time to take back the power that has been stolen from me.*

NAKANJO, JULY, 461

An exhausted and wounded Ixakben warrior appeared at the edge of the Mayan city of Nakanjo asking to speak with the king. One of the city's warriors took the runner up to the temple palace. The warrior from Ixakbe had a nasty gash between his shoulder blades which was covered with coagulated blood and was attracting flies. "Wait here," the Nakojon warrior instructed him. In a few minutes, the warrior came out with Jaguar Claw. The consultant looked at the wounded warrior.

"Why do you request to see our king?"

"I have a message from my queen, Lady Moon."

"Tell me the message."

"I was instructed to tell the king directly. I fought my way out of Ixakbe to bring this message to only the king!" Dismissing the guard, the king's consultor led him to the throne room where Jade Ocelot was holding court. Jaguar Claw went up to the king and whispered in his ear. Once he had finished, Jade Ocelot announced,

"You are all dismissed!" All the court left by the nearest exits. Jaguar Claw went out to guide the messenger in. The wounded man tried to bow but the pain was becoming increasingly more intense. "What is it that you've come to tell me?"

"Lord," he began. "My wife, an attendant to Lady Moon, came to me with a message from the queen."

"Go on."

"Lady Moon bids me to tell you that she overheard her husband and his advisor speaking together. Holy Snake Lord is waiting for more warriors from his father before he attacks Tikyu. His intention is to surround you, forcing your hand to give up your city to him."

"Lord, this is important news…" The king prevented Jaguar Claw from speaking further.

"Guards!" King Jade Ocelot called out. Two guards came in. "Take this Ixakben and bind up his wounds. Then allow him to rest and take some food and water."

"Thank you, Lord," expressed the messenger. As soon as he was escorted from the throne room, Jaguar Claw advised,

"We must act on this information and go to our ally's defense!"

"I agree," the king made note. "A peace treaty with Ixakbe is no longer viable."

"This is true, my Lord. Allow me to lead our warriors to Tikyu for its defense."

I'm in accord with your thinking, however one thing needs to be changed."

"My Lord, what is that?

"Instead of you, I will lead my warriors to defeat Holy Snake Lord and his army."

"It is not safe, my Lord. You are needed here to boost the people's morale. I would be a poor substitute to do that job."

"Enough, Uncle. You must defend this city in case this plan is a ploy. If you sight the army approaching, send me word and we will return. Holy Snake Lord and his army will be caught between us. He'll have no chance to take this city." Although Jaguar Claw didn't like the idea of putting his king in danger, he reluctantly submitted to his nephew's request.

The next morning saying goodbye to his queen, Cooing Dove and his son, Bird Jaguar, the king, came down the steps dressed in full war regalia and climbed into the waiting litter. They led the way with 500 warriors following.

He could not help but think back to the time the king was just a boy and how he led him and his half-sister out of Nakanjo and into Tikyu. *Circumstances have certainly changed. Now, Jade Ocelot is not only a man, but a king who is the head of his army.*

At that moment, the king's uncle began to beef up Nakanjo's defenses in anticipation of an attack. Days went by while Jaguar Claw kept the populace's minds busy with defense activities and not on the fact that their king was missing from the city.

Each day, Jaguar Claw sent out scouting parties to bring any evidence of an army marching on them, and each day they came back with nothing new to report.

Day after day, Jaguar Claw waited impatiently for some sort of news from Tikyu. The roads remained clear, no messenger came to bring news of a great victory, but also there were no runners bringing news of disaster. *I thank the gods for that!"*

He would have made blood sacrifices if a triumph were to occur, but his king had strictly forbidden it. Instead, he went to the priests to have his tongue pierced and the blood burned at the altars. The king's dutiful wife would join him, having her blood taken too. Never once did she complain or show any fear for her husband's wellbeing. She remained composed to all the court. Cooing Dove would even be carried around in a litter with her son so the people could see who they were fighting for. She gave the people courage when their confidence appeared to be waning.

On the morning of the eighth day, Jaguar Claw took his usual spot at the top of the palace and watched for any messenger on his way to Nakanjo. The sunbaked land was already sending up waves of heat into the dry air. He searched in vain for any movement in the distance. Jaguar Claw was about to give up and go into the cooler interior when he thought he saw some slight motion in the far distance. Raising his hand to his eyes, he tried to shade them to get a better look. *Yes, someone is coming! someone is coming.*

As he waited, his heart nearly jumping out of his chest, a man wearing a Nakanjoan warrior's gear became very clear. *Thank the gods!*

Jaguar Claw stood on top of the palace pyramid and shaded his eyes from the harsh light of the sun. *Yes, I can distinctly observe a runner coming toward the city. It must be a message of victory!*

Before he could enjoy the feeling of elation, he looked at the runner again as he drew closer. *He is not a Nakanjoan but a Ixakben! Are we under attack?"* Behind the Ixakben warrior ran a mixture of Tikyun and Nakanjoan warriors. *It is defeat!* Running inside, Jaguar Claw gathered as many warriors on guard in the building to meet those who were coming from the battlefield. Walking into the Plaza of the Sun with his armed entourage, the first runner came to a halt and dropped to the ground before Jaguar Claw. "I should kill you Ixakben!"

"Lord, I am here with a party of warriors from Ixakbe who turned against Holy Snake Lord during the battle.

"Then it was a triumph?" The other warriors who followed also quickly dropped to their knees in front of him. A Nakanjoan warrior answered, "No, Lord, they came at us from all sides of the city!"

"What happened to the king?"

"He fought bravely for some time, Lord. Jade Ocelot drove the enemy back time and time again but eventually it was of no use!"

"Why is that?" he asked, his voice filled with concern for his nephew.

"Although my lord held his ground on top of the main pyramid of the city with some warriors, the rest of the city of Tikyu was soon inundated by Quiribalan warriors and some of their Ixakben allies. Jade Ocelot and his men were soon isolated from the rest of the army and then surrounded!"

"Then my nephew is dead?"

"No, Lord. He and the warriors who fought with him were tied by rope and he was marched away as a prisoner!"

"Then he has been taken for sacrifice?"

"I'm sure of it, my Lord."

"Are we in imminent danger of attack?"

"Holy Snake Lord has started back to Ixakbe with his army and prisoners."

Turning to one of the guards, Jaguar Claw ordered, "See to it that these men's wounds are bandaged and that they are fed."

"Yes, Lord."

The elder statesmen walked up the stairs and back into the temple. *Sadly, I can do nothing to save my nephew from his fate. This procrastination about dealing with the Quiribalan prince earlier has led us down this inevitable end of the road. If my nephew, Moon Jaguar had remained as king, this would never have resulted.* He shook his head back in disgust.

As he entered the palace, the elderly chief priest was waiting for him. "I can tell by your expression that the news wasn't good."

"You read my face accurately. The army was defeated and Jade Ocelot was taken prisoner with some of this city's warriors. I must take on the defense of the city before Holy Snake Lord's attention turns toward the attack of Nakanjo."

"But first you must be anointed as the new king."

"My nephew is still alive and king of this city."

"It is only a matter of time before Jade Ocelot meets his untimely end. If the city is to stand strong, they must see their king in control. There is no other choice we can make!" Jaguar Claw could not find words that would deny what he said. He knew the people would fight harder seeing their king out in front of them. "But I must begin planning for the city's defense!"

"Your installation cannot take too long. We must do it as quickly as possible!"

Jaguar Claw followed the priest into the temple of the war god, Votan where the chief priest was joined by two other priests. Braziers were lit as the priest began his incantation calling on Votan to witness and approve the new king. When the ceremony was over, the chief priest prayed for the salvation of the city. "But we have no blood sacrifice to offer to Votan."

"Yes, we do!" Without a moment's hesitation, the priest slipped out his knife and cut his own throat. The new king was aghast at this sudden self-sacrifice. As he had prearranged with the two other priests, his clothing was stripped away from his body and the knife plunged into his chest. His still beating heart was torn from his open chest, held aloft after a prayer, and dropped into the brazier. It sizzled and spurted as it hit the flames. *I cannot allow this brave sacrifice to Votan to be useless. As the new king, I must protect this city and its people at any cost!*

Putting on the royal robe of feathers made from the sacred Quetzal bird, King Jaguar Claw went to the top of the pyramid so everyone could see him clearly. "My people!" he shouted so that all could hear him. "Our king is lost! As the new King I have a plan for the resistance of our city against the approaching invaders!" The populace shouted their approval in unison and with intense enthusiasm. "My first command is to build up the walls around the city…" The inhabitants endorsed this decision with a mighty roar, "but leave the eastern wall unfinished!"

The city lay hushed in tense anticipation of the attack. Earlier, scouts had reported to Jaguar Claw of the sighting of the invasion force heading east toward Tikyu. Days before, the king of Tikyu, Lord Shield had ordered the female nobility and their children into the jungle for safety. The new king watched the line of weeping women and their offspring as they left the city and their husbands and fathers behind.

With the Nakanjoan king's aid, Lord Shield divided the forces of Tikyun and Nakanjoan warriors and dispersed them to certain key points in the city. Then they stood and listened for every sound that might be a clue to where the attack would come. "I will direct the western and southern walls of the city," Lord Shield stated.

"And I will be responsible for the other two," specified Jade Ocelot. Both men gripped each other's arms in fealty to each other.

"May the gods favor us with a victory today!" The two men parted, each going to their specific areas to direct their warriors.

The jungle was silent-too silent! It was an indication that since the fauna in the area was disturbed by the intrusion of such a large group of humans, the animals had dispersed into other areas. Nakanjoan and Tikyun troops armed with their weapons waited in excited exhilaration for the sounds of the attack. They did not have to wait long.

The chilling war cries of the Quiribalan warriors filled their ears and made their hair stand on end. Jade Ocelot bellowed out a roar that his warriors picked up and they bellowed with him.

The first wave of enemy warriors came to the wall at a dead run, but arrows cut many of them down. A lethal flood of arrows from the invaders dropped some of the defenders where they stood. Another wave of warriors followed the first. Nakanjoan warriors drove them back but at a terrible cost in their ranks.

Jade Ocelot's warriors took hit after hit but still they fought on. The king realized that they could no longer hold the wall and directed what was left of his army to fall back to the first temple in the city. Once the enemy realized that the position was no longer being defended, they poured over it and ran down the main road while King Holy Snake Lord screamed for them to kill. Jade Ocelot looked across the city to the other walls where Lord Shield and his Tikyun soldiers had been standing. He saw that their wall had already been taken by their overwhelming numbers. As he and his warriors occupied the temple he knew he was in for the fight of his life.

The Quiribalan warriors had tasted blood and they had a strong craving for more. They came crashing into the building like the pounding of waves on the sand during a hurricane. With a few of his best warriors, Jade Ocelot took the high ground at the top of the temple and waited for the assault to come to him, a war club in one hand and a knife in the other. The first of the enemy reached them and the king and his warriors split heads and snapped bones as they dispatched them easily. The main force of Quiribalans reached the upper floor and poured in on them. Swinging his war club with deadly accuracy as his uncle had taught him, the enemy dropped, screaming in the throes of agonizing death. Still they came, more and more, until Jade Ocelot's arms became weary with fatigue. "Stop!" the voice of Holy Snake Lord screamed. Take the rest as prisoners!" The few of the Nakanjoan warriors offered little resistance. They dropped their weapons to the floor.

As their hands were tied and their necks connected to each other by rope, Jade Ocelot called out, "Where is Lord Shield?" A warrior carrying a head drew near. Holy Snake Lord took the head by its hair and lifted it aloft. "Here is your friend!" Lord Shield's eyes were opened wide when the club had struck, his lips parted as if he were going to say something while blood dripped from the neck.

"Why do you not hand me the same fate?" asked Jade Ocelot.

"I have something special planned for you! Take them away!"

For days, they were marched through the jungle trails with bound hands. There was little food or rest for the prisoners as they were prodded on by spears and shoves. At last, they knew they were approaching the city when the tops of the Tikyun temples peeped over the top of the jungle canopy. They were marched through the city with the cheers of some and the stares of others. "Take them into the temple but do not untie them! Station two soldiers to guard them! Bind his wounds!" he commanded pointing to Jade Ocelot. "I want him in good health." Turning to the chief priest, he instructed, "Get ready for the sacrifices to our gods!"

The prisoners were marched into a room where they were pushed to the floor. The men did not speak to each other but contemplated their awaiting deaths. After some time, slave girls entered with bowls of blue dye made of indigo from the leaves of the anil plant and mixed it thoroughly with palygorskite clay until it formed a pigment that was ready to apply. They were accompanied by the guards. The last of the 11 warriors were roughly yanked to their feet as the women smoothed the blue dye over their entire body. When they were done, the first prisoner was marched out. The rest knew where he was headed and within a few minutes, screams of the sacrificed drifted into the room. The first Nakanoan warrior had met his fate. The process was repeated over and over, as their numbers dwindled. Jade Ocelot took the time to gather his thoughts. *I said goodbye to my wife Cooing Dove, promising her that I would return. For the first time since we were married, I will need to break my word to her.* He regretted dismissing his uncle's advice to him. *I should have listened to my uncle's counsel and dealt sternly with Holy Snake Lord before he became this powerful.* All the misgivings he had now could not turn back the time.

The last of his warriors was covered in blue and marched out of the room. Once more, the shrieks of the populace filtered into the room. He waited for the moment when the slave women would smear blue paint over his body. Instead, Holy Snake Lord appeared. "Are you ready? It's your turn now!" Holding his head high, Jade Ocelot said,

"I ask for the right to die as a king!"

"You have no rights here. Only the ones I say you have and I deny you the chance to slit your wrists and die slowly."

"Holy Snake Lord, you are a king as am I. If circumstances had been different and our places exchanged, I would not repudiate your wish."

"But I am not in your position, thank the gods!"

"Your gods will abandon you sooner or later especially if you're thinking of going against Jaguar Claw."

"Tell me, Jade Ocelot. I'm curious. The story is that your uncle taught you the art of war. Is that true?"

"That's right."

"Then I will have nothing to worry about. Since I overcame you so easily, I will have no problem defeating him."

"Where were you when the fighting between our two armies was at a fever pitch?"

"I was directing my warriors…"

"You were waiting safely from behind the lines of your army. Not once did you lead any of the charges! You stayed well behind the lines out of danger!" Holy Snake Lord glowered and scowled.

"After your heart is ripped from your flesh, your head will be decapitated and your body will be thrown down the temple steps. Then I will have your head mounted on a spear in front of the palace so I can look into your dead eyes every morning. When I invade Nakanjo and take your uncle prisoner, his head will keep yours company."

"You will never see my uncle's head on a spear!"

"He will fall to me as you did. Come in!" he yelled as the slave women who scurried in and cowered at the sound of his voice. "Prepare him!"

"You will not see the day that you will defeat my uncle!"

"You will not live to see another day, Jade Ocelot!"

"Your day of judgement is upon you, only you don't know it," the prisoner cautioned him. Holy Snake Lord left in a hurry as the guards jerked the Nakanjoan king to his feet. The women spread the blue pigment across his body. When they were done, the two guards grabbed him by the arms and brought him outside. A great roar arose from the crowd below as the searing rays of the sun beat down on him unmercifully.

Once his eyes adjusted to the light, Jade Ocelot peered down the stairs where the bodies of his warriors lay scattered about. The captured king looked up to see the chief priest standing over the bloody sacrificial stone intoning the prayers to the sun god. Looking beyond this scene, he spotted Lady Moon sitting apart, her eyes dull and lifeless. When the priest nodded, Jade Ocelot was brought over to the stone and the binds that held his hands were cut. Quickly, his arms and legs were grabbed and he was lifted on top of the stone. His extremities were pulled down so his chest rose in the air. The king stared at the blue sky and the white clouds that slowly moved by. The priest appeared over him blocking his view of the sky.

As if he were dreaming, he watched as the chief priest raised the knife and his mouth moved in prayer, but Jade Ocelot could not make out what he was saying. He watched the blade plunge down and begged the gods that he could join them in their kingdom. A searing flash of pain was felt before everything blacked out.

CHAPTER 9

The first thing King Holy Snake Lord did every morning after he awoke was to stroll outside his bedroom and look at the head of Jade Ocelot on a spear. Each day the head deteriorated from the heat and humidity as birds nibbled at the flesh. After a week, the stench became unbearable but not for Holy Snake Lord. To him it smelled like victory.

For Lady Moon, who was newly pregnant and experiencing morning sickness, she could not bear the sight or smell of the head of the man who had offered her friendship. When she asked her husband to remove this obscene decoration due to her pregnancy and vomiting, he had soundly refused her appeal. She slept in another room. Her husband did not object.

As time passed and she felt the baby stir in her womb, all she could think of was her dead son, Sharpened Spear. Her depression was so great at times that she mulled over the idea of getting a knife and killing the new life in her. The noble woman reviled her husband so much that she hated the idea of giving him a son that he could have the chance to corrupt.

In another part of the palace, the king and his advisor, Snake Jaguar, spoke about the plan for Nakanjo. "I'm going to crush the city and Jaguar Claw under my heel as I did with his nephew!"

"My Lord, the gods adjudge this with their approval."

"See to it that blood sacrifices are made to Votan to ensure my victory over Jaguar Claw!"

"The chief priest has requested that you make a blood offering for your conquest over your enemy."

"Wait for me here."

Holy Snake Lord called for his litter to take him to the temple of Votan. Climbing up the steps to the top platform, the chief priest and his assistants were waiting for their king's arrival. "Is everything ready?" the royal personage demanded.

"We are ready to proceed immediately." The king looked over and saw that the brazier was already smoking. The chief priest prayed, lifting his arms to the sky to Votan for the victory of Holy Snake Lord over his adversary, Jaguar Claw. Calling on one of his assistants, the chief priest received the knife from him. He lifted the knife to the sky and called on the god's support in this venture. The chief priest nodded at his other assistant who brought over a piece of sacred cloth and the cord. Holy Snake Lord stuck out his tongue which was cut with the sharpened blade. Taking the cord from the assistant, the king passed it through the wound to ensure that the wound would bleed well. He was then handed the cloth and collected his royal blood droplets onto it. Taking the cloth, the chief priest walked it to the smoke-filled brazier, mumbled another prayer and dropped it in. The saturated cloth flared in a flash of flames that consumed the entire bloody material. The chief priest stood still and seemed enchanted by the fiery show. Once the blaze had slowly died down, he turned to the king. "Votan looks favorably on your endeavor." Holy Smoke Lord contemplated this statement finally answering,

"Let the will of Votan be done!" Coming down the stairs, he was once more carried by litter to the palace where Snake Jaguar waited for him. "It is done," he told his advisor. "Votan gives me his approval to attack Nakanjo!"

"It is a good omen, Lord." As he finished speaking, a noisy ruckus was heard from outside. One of the guards walked in with the scouting party the king had sent out to observe Nakanjo, the next city he would conquer. Both warriors fell to their knees before him breathing heavily. "What have you come to report to me?" he commanded.

"The city is being prepared for war, Lord."

"Be specific!"

"The city walls are all being made higher."

"Is there more?"

"All of the food has been harvested and brought within the walls." Holy Snake Lord turned to his advisor.

"They are preparing for a long siege."

"Lord, it would seem so."

Turning toward the runners he ordered, "Go back and come to me each day to report what is happening."

"Yes, Lord," they stated as they got to their feet and left the room.

"So, they are preparing for a long siege, are they?"

"The evidence reported would seem to indicate that."

"Jaguar Claw probably thinks that I will be licking my wounds after I took Tikyu. He assumes that it will take a while before I attack."

"What are you thinking of doing, Lord?"

"I will catch them all by surprise. Bring this order to my generals. Tell them to prepare my warriors for battle. We march on Nakanjo tomorrow." Snake Jaguar left immediately to do what he was bid. *By this time in two days, my victory over this area will be complete.*

NAKANJO, AUGUST, 461

"Our scouts report that Holy Snake Lord and his warriors are on the move," the new advisor Quetzal Jaguar counseled the new king, Jaguar Claw.

"Good, that means that Holy Snake Lord has taken the bait! See to it that everyone is in place and is ready."

"Yes, Lord."

The trap has been set! All I need is for Holy Snake Lord to step in it!

"Help me put on my battle garments!" he told his aide. The servant brought over his helmet made from a jaguar head, its long canine teeth resting on his forehead, and a cape made from the skin of the same carnivore. Jade ornaments around his neck and in his nose and ears were the last finishing touches to be made. Placing his knife in his belt, he lifted his war club in his hand and proceeded outdoors. The king took a look at the three finished walls that surrounded the city which had been worked on night and day to be completed. Around the walls there was a small contingent of warriors who were on guard for the enemy's approach. A larger group of warriors was stationed at the unfinished wall. He looked around at the temples in which bowmen were hidden. *Everything seems in place. Now all we must do is wait!*

A lit torch blazed next to the white stucco wall of the temple, just within his reach. He would use it to signal his warriors at the right time. Suddenly two runners appeared from out of the jungle. Jaguar Claw hurried down the steps to meet them. They fell to their knees as they approached him. "What is it?" the king wanted to know.

"Lord," one of them addressed him. "A vast army is now in the area of Nakanjo!"

"Take your places at the wall," he commanded. They stood and bowed and joined their companions. "Look to the palace and when I wave the torch, that will be the signal to retreat behind the wall," he reminded his advisor and then returned to the top platform of the palace temple.

When he had reached the top, the first of the Quiribalan warriors dressed in battle garb attacked the wall yelling war whoops. *Holy Snake Lord is testing our strength at the unfinished wall.* The builders quickly retreated inside Nakanjo as the enemy neared them. Jaguar Claw's warriors quickly closed ranks. Hand to hand battle ensued with Nakanjoan warriors easily holding them back. Holy Snake Lord appeared from the jungle and with a loud yell signaled for the rest of his warriors to attack. They rushed to the city, screaming at the top of their lungs, bloodlust in their eyes.

For a time, the Nakanjoan warriors held their own but the constant arrival of fresh enemy warriors stepping over the bodies of the dead and dying began to push them back. Jaguar Claw took the torch and swung it back and forth. Nakanjoan warriors broke rank and fled into the city, the enemy on their heels as the squeezed through the narrow opening in the unfinished wall. The Nakanjoan warriors turned to face their enemy, joined by others hiding behind the temples. Jaguar Claw rushed down the steps, again waving his torch before he tossed it aside to join his men.

The bowmen fired arrows at the enemy getting through the wall. In a matter of minutes, dead bodies cut down by arrows clogged the opening until it was practically impassable. The bowmen rushed to the unfinished south wall and poured down arrows on the enemy trying to clear away the dead. Their bodies soon joined those of their dead companions. At last, the opponents broke rank and fled back into the rain forest.

Those enemy warriors who had made it inside the city, seeing that their retreat had been cut off, panicked and started moving back under a heavy frontal assault. With a war whoop, Jaguar Claw led the attack of those in the city. His warriors rushed forward with him.

Jaguar Claw blocked the swing of the enemy's club with his own and with his other hand stabbed the Quiribalan in the stomach. The warrior screamed in pain and as the king withdrew the bloody blade, he finished the enemy by striking down his club on the enemy's head. A large crack was heard as the warrior sank to the ground.

The next warrior came at the king charging with a spear. Jaguar Claw knocked the instrument aside with his club. The enemy was shocked with the ease by which the king had accomplished this and did not notice when Jaguar Claw's club slashed across his face breaking his nose and leaving a large gash across his face. He was dispatched with a hard blow to the top of his head. All around him, his warriors were also slaughtering the enemy. All at once, the Quiribalan warriors dropped their weapons knowing that it was hopeless to continue. "Bind the captured prisoner's hands and those that have been wounded and take them inside the temple. Make sure they are guarded so that they cannot escape!"

"Right away, Lord," the soldier closest to him answered.

"You," he pointed to another soldier. "Gather a few of our warriors and bring our wounded men to the priests for help."

"Yes, Lord!"

With the other nobles, Jaguar Claw moved about the dead and wounded. Many cried out in pain begging for help, but one enemy warrior caught his eye as he tried to crawl away, an arrow stuck deep in his thigh. Jaguar Claw and the others moved toward him. Immediately, the king recognized the wounded man. The Ixakben nobleman, Swift Arrow, who had fled to Nakanjo when his city had first been taken over, drew close to the captured king. The royal personage of Holy Snake Lord was found among the wounded. The Ixakben king caste his eyes up at his enemy. "Today you die!" the wounded king boasted.

"Hold!" Jaguar Claw shouted out before his warrior could club the fallen king over the head. "For him to die in battle would be too much of an honorable ending for such a man! Take him to where the other enemy warriors wait their fate."

Two soldiers lifted him to his feet as he grimaced in pain and dragged him away. "You cannot do this to me. I am a king!" he kept repeating.

The altar of Votan that day ran red with blood once more- Quiribalan blood! After years of a policy banning human sacrifice established by Jade Ocelot, prisoners of war were prepared for the death ceremony. After the first day's sacrifices, the rain god Chaahk once more looked favorably on Nakanjo and the rain fell once again. The people rejoiced for the water that saturated the soil and nourished the plants.

King Jaguar Claw officiated over the sacrifices as each enemy warrior took his turn on the stone altar. By the king's side sat Cooing Dove mourning for her dead husband, Jade Ocelot. Jaguar Claw ruled as a Regent until her boy would come of age to rule the city himself.

After 30 warriors had given up their lives the first day, the king and his advisor Quetzal Jaguar visited the place where the rest of the prisoners-of-war were being kept. The captives sat leaning against the walls, their hands and feet bound together, their heads bowed. In the corner sat Holy Snake Lord. The king and his advisor drew near. Infection had already set in from the arrow still in his thigh.

The imprisoned king raised his head to see who approached him. "It's about time that you arrived! I sent word yesterday that I wanted to speak to you!"

"I am here now," Jaguar Claw's voice was low and unemotional. "Why have you called for me?"

"Do the right thing! Turn me loose and I will sign a treaty of peace between us."

"It is too late for that. You have made war on Ixakbe, and Tikyu as well as my city."

"You are wrong! I came to Ixakbe at the invitation of Lady Moon."

"This is true but the others you made war with gave you no provocation to invade them." The captive king's eyes grew narrow with wrath.

"Untie me this minute or it will go badly for you!" The king turned to his advisor laughing.

"He is out of his mind!"

"My Lord, he talks as if his situation were in reverse and you were his prisoner."

"Let me go now or you'll have to deal with my father's fury once he discovers what you have done!"

"You father has other sons. He will forget you soon enough." Holy Snake Lord's voice suddenly changed.

"Please, do not sacrifice me!" he whined in terror. The other prisoners turned to look at him as disgust registered on their faces.

"You will be the last to be taken to the altar."

"Then give to me my right as king to die by my own hand!"

"Did you grant that right to my nephew? No, instead he was led to the altar and killed, his head decapitated and fixed upon a spear for the birds to peck on, and for all to see." Holy Snake Lord gave no response to the accusation. "As you showed no mercy to my nephew, no mercy will be shown to you."

"You can't do that to me!"

"On the day of your sacrifice, your head will be hacked off your body and displayed on a spear for all of Nakanjo to see."

"No…no…no!" he moaned in a wretched tone of voice.

"Do not worry. You will not have too long to wait. I will make sure of that." The king and his advisor turned and left.

After Holy Snake Lord's heart was snatched from his chest and dropped into a fiery brazier, his head was taken and displayed on a spear. Within a few days, the vultures began to land and peck on the putrid flesh.

Word came after Nakanjo's victory over Holy Snake Lord and the people of Tikyu revolted against their conquerors and tormentors. Those that had been unable to flee were slaughtered where they stood.

Once the sacrifices were concluded, the citizens of the city began to put Nakanjo back in order. The king left Quetzal Jaguar to see that the city was cleaned up while he started out with his army to drive the Quiribalan from Ixakbe. Jaguar Claw refused to be carried in a litter but instead walked in front of his men, his well-defined body muscles rippling in the glaring sun.

After days of marching in ranks, the walls of Ixakbe began to appear through the tropical jungle's plant life. As they drew closer, the Nakanjoan warriors withdrew their weapons for battle. As Jaguar Claw talked to his men, one of them observed a runner coming from the city. The warrior approached them with speed. Drawing closer, the king realized it was an Ixakben warrior. The king watched with a wary eye until he dropped before him. Trying to catch his breath, the man cried out, "Lord, the city is yours!" The king looked at him surreptitiously.

"Is this some kind of trick to draw my army into the city so that we can be ambushed?"

"No Lord, this is no ruse. Word came to us of your victory over Holy Snake Lord. The Quiribalan's were first in disbelief. Yesterday, one of their scouts reported that your army was drawing near to Ixakbe. Every one of them fled the city." In his heart, Jaguar Claw believed these words. Still, he and his warriors cautiously passed the walls of the city. It was soon evident that what he had been told was the truth. A pregnant Lady Moon arrived in a litter to greet him. "My Lord," she greeted him. "I am so pleased to see you here."

"I had intended to drive away our enemies from your city but I see that it's no longer necessary."

"I am delighted to tell you that once they heard of your coming, they could not wait to abandon my city."

"I have a request of you."

"Just speak and it will be granted."

"I wish to retrieve my nephew's head and return it to Nakanjo." The queen pointed to the palace platform on top of the temple.

"You will find it up there." She turned her head sympathetically towards him. "I am sorry that I was unable to prevent your nephew's death."

"By sending me a message about Holy Snake Lord's attention to attack Nakanjo, I had enough time to plan his defeat. I thank you for your warning."

Taking a cloth from one of his soldiers, he went alone to the top of the temple. His nephew's face was no longer recognizable. As he lifted it from the spear and carefully wrapped it he thought, *Come nephew. I am taking you home.*

CHAPTER 10

The head of the former King Jade Ocelot was brought home to Nakanjo in reverent silence. The population lined up along the avenues to acknowledge his return. Although, at the end of his reign, his decisions were controversial and not popular, he had still been their king and that was not forgotten.

As the triumphant warriors led by Jaguar Claw neared the palace, Cooing Dove and Bird Jaguar came down to meet them. They were accompanied by the king's advisor Quetzal Jaguar. The king stopped the procession in front of the queen and prince. "Lady," Jaguar Claw began. "I have brought back your husband." The queen became visibly emotional and broke down in tears.

"I thank you," the nine-year-old Bird Jaguar uttered trying to handle himself like a man, and future king.

"A jade death mask will be made at my order so that he can join his father and brother in the next world," the regent king exclaimed

"Thank you, my Lord," the red-eyed Cooing Dove replied.

"For now, he will be interred in the temple until the mask is completed. At that time the burial ceremony will take place."

Taking the head wrapped in cloth, the king walked to the nearby temple and climbed to the top. *Rest easy my nephew.*

As the king walked down, he stopped to look at Nakanjo's progress after the battle. The east wall now matched the height of the others. The bodies of the dead had been cleared away and the debris removed. *It's looking more and more like the city I knew.* He was exhausted by the battle and the march to and from Ixakbe. The king was aware that old age was taking its toll on his aging body. Climbing up to the palace, he allowed his servants to divest him of battle clothing. A bowl of water was presented to him so he could wash his face and arms. His servants washed his legs. "Bring me something to eat and drink."

"Yes, my Lord," a servant answered and he rushed to complete his task. A platter of corn tortillas, Poc Chuc and avocadoes was brought in. Cool water taken from the river was presented to him.

After he was sated, he laid himself down and slept for hours. Waking in the late afternoon, a servant entered to announce, "Lady Cooing Dove has asked to see you." Feeling more refreshed, he said, "Help me dress quickly. When he was dressed, he commanded, "Bring her in."

The servant left and returned with the queen. She carried herself with distinguished grace before him.

"My Lord, I have come to congratulate you on your great victory."

"I am pleased that Holy Snake Lord is no longer a threat to our people and our way of life."

"This is true. I've come to thank you for my husband's return. I was too emotionally distraught to thank you properly before."

"I understand that you were overwhelmed, and I thank you for coming to me now." Cooing Dove hesitated to continue to speak and Jaguar Claw noticed her vacillation. "Come, speak your mind. There are no secrets between us."

"My Lord, my reluctance is not because I do not trust you."

"Then what is it?"

"It is about my son, Bird Jaguar."

"Is his health alright?"

"It is my Lord. I want to ask you a delicate question."

"Then ask me."

"When my son is of age to take his father's place as leader, will you prevent him from doing so?" the king rose from his chair.

"I believe myself to be king until the boy comes of age, and when he has, I will gladly step aside so that he can inherit his father's legacy." Lady Cooing Dove bowed saying,

"Thank you, my Lord."

"Is there anything else I can do to reassure you?"

"I ask you Lord to train my son for battle as you once did for my husband."

I remember the time Jade Ocelot saw the fleeing image of his future wife Cooing Dove after one of his first training sessions I gave him as a boy. Now I will be teaching his son.

"It will be my honor, Lady."

The Mayan city of Nakanjo prospered after the defeat of the Quiribalans. The gods favored the city with plenty of rain and as a result, abundant food. Human sacrifices continued to keep the gods in a positive frame of mind towards the city.

Jaguar Claw took on the training of the future king, Bird Jaguar, as he had promised his mother Cooing Dove. As he went through the lessons on battling an enemy warrior, he could not help but think back to achieving the same thing with Jade Ocelot. *Time has passed so quickly.*

A burial ceremony had taken place once the mask had been completed. The artisans had created a thing of beauty, made of jade and decorated with emeralds traded by the Nakajoans with the Indian tribes from Colombia. The disfigured head was carried ritualistically down the avenue by the present king. Walking up the steps of the pyramid dedicated to the sun god, Kinich Ahau, Jaguar Claw reached the top platform where the dead king's wife and son waited. With them was the chief priest who recited the prayer of the dead. Down below, the city's populace watched in reverent silence.

The four walked into the interior where a burial place had been constructed underneath the tile floor. Climbing down the stairs, he laid down the masked head of Jade Ocelot and placed golden necklaces next to the disembodied head. *You're home now, nephew.* Coming back up, the floor was sealed shut.

Months later a new stele was installed in the city and joined the other steles of previous kings of Nakanjo. The artisans had carved a close replica of Jaguar Claw in his battle adornment. In one hand, he carried his war club, and in the other he held the decapitated head of a Quiribalan warrior by his hair. Underneath the frieze of the king, glyphs that were carved told of the king's victory over his enemies.

The building of the city continued with new temples joining the skyline. A ball court was devised to bring entertainment to the people and new broad avenues were constructed giving rise to a shiny new metropolis. Along with the growth of the city came a boom in population.

The alliance between the three cities of Nakanjo, Tikyu, and Ixakbe was re-established and peace reigned throughout the valley. Such a strong coalition kept the King of Quiribal in check. He never sought revenge for the death of his son or the defeat of his warriors.

Various noblewomen took up the idea that Jaguar Claw should be married and start a family, but the king gently rejected all offers of marriage. He had no wish for connubial bliss and having children. Jaguar Claw had no intention of later starting a civil war between Bird Claw and any son he might have. The city had been in enough strife and he was not going to be the blame of more wars after his death. His intentions were noble and altruistic.

It was with great sorrow and devastation that the news of Jaguar Claw death after a nine-year reign traveled to the cities of the alliance. He developed a high fever that finally resulted in his passing. The body was dressed in his royal robe over his battle clothing. The war club he had used to defeat Holy Snake Lord was in one hand and in his left hand, he held his shield. His jade mask was decorated with brilliant green emeralds and blue-green turquoise. Fire opals studded his garments and his arms were encircled in amber and gold bracelets.

His body was carried to the pyramid dedicated to Yum –Kaax the agricultural god. He was laid to rest in a secret burial chamber revered by the people. The next day, the inauguration of Bird Claw as king took place. His status among the pantheon of previous kings was now solidified. The people rejoiced and celebrated upon the new king as he showed himself to the city in royal regalia. A new age had begun.

In the first year of his reign, Bird Jaguar married a teenaged noblewoman named Lady Evening Star. Within months, she became pregnant, but Cooing Dove, the king's mother, did not live long enough to see her grandchild born. It was rumored that she had died of a broken heart once her husband had been murdered.

The funeral procession carried the body to the site of her dead husband. Son and daughter-in-law walked gravely behind. The whole city turned out for the funeral. The body was adorned with a jade mask studded with yellow opals. Necklaces of lapis-lazuli graced her neck and on her arms hung gold bracelets. The queen was buried in the same funerary vault as the head of her husband, Jade Ocelot.

The growth of the city continued as five new pyramid temples were erected, totaling eight. The population growth put people to work building new homes and new avenues that would take its citizens across the city of Nakanjo.

Bird Jaguar presided over a city that ran like clockwork due to meticulous managing by the appointments of very capable officials. The people were well fed and satisfied with their comfortable lives.

The king also managed to keep the peace with the other two Mayan city states. Gifts were exchanged once a year to reinforce the alliances between the three cities. During royal celebrations, the kings and queens of the other cities were invited to come and join the festivities. One such occasion was the birth of the royal couple's first child. It was a baby boy whom they named Smoke Serpent.

When the child grew, it was his father who taught him the warrior way of hand-to-hand combat just as Jaguar Claw had once taught him. "But my father," the prince would ask, "peace has reigned in this valley for many years. What is the point of learning this? "My son, the only way peace can endure is if we remain strong and prepared for war, so it has been, so it will always be!" With this clear explanation, Smoke Snake threw himself into his lessons with his father.

Before long, Lady Evening Star found herself with child once more. When the day arrived of her childbirth, a girl was born to the royal couple. She was named Lady Six Sky. The raising of their daughter was left to her mother. At her mother's knees, she learned about court manners and how to take the reeds gathered by the women of Nakanjo from the lake to make decorative woven bowls. They were used in gathering fruit and berries from the fields and tropical rain forest to be sold in the open marketplace.

After his father died, Bird Jaguar became a king his people admired. He was diplomatic and humanitarian when the situation called for it, but he could be cruel and unforgiving when the laws were broken. Criminals who were thieves or murderers were condemned and jailed to become human sacrifice to the gods. They were marched out and had the hearts wrenched from their chest cavities during certain celestial alignments designated by Mayan priestly astronomers.

For more than 16 years, peace under the sovereignty of Bird Jaguar continued, but things began to change. Smoke Serpent was married to a Nakanjoan noblewoman called Lady Half Moon. The kings and queens of Ixakbe and Tikyu were invited to celebrate.

For months, the king and queen waited for the happy news of pregnancy from their daughter-in-law, but nothing followed. They continued to wait patiently for the news they so much desired but Lady Half Moon remained barren.

After a year, the king approached his son. "It is time for you to think about taking another wife."

"My Lord, I am in love with my wife and would never consider leaving her."

"Love has nothing to do with this," he barked angrily. "Your wife must bear a son if our bloodline is to continue!"

"My Lord father, I don't know..." Bird Jaguar interrupted.

"I know you don't know whom to marry. I have discussed this with my advisor and we have found a very worthy noblewoman, Lady Morning Star."

"I do not love Lady Morning Star!"

"Enough about love!" he screamed at his son. "I am the king and you will obey me!" Smoke Serpent left the room without saying another word to his father. The rift was never healed even though he married Lady Morning Star. When the king sent Lady Half Moon back to her parents, his son was devastated. In protest, he refused to touch his new wife.

Hearing of this, his father stormed after his son. "You will have a child with your new wife!" he commanded in a loud voice.

"In this and this only, I will not obey you, my Lord father." Smoke Serpent glared at his father. In an instant, Bird Jaguar was on top of his son with his strong hands around his son's throat. Smoke Serpent tried to break his father's deadly grip but he was unsuccessful. The lack of air asphyxiated the young man. Bird Jaguar's anger passed and when he saw that his son lay dead in front of him, his anger turned into grief.

Chapter 11

The gods turned their eyes from the king who committed filicide. Soon a new drought began as the clouds withheld their rain. Water levels dropped as the snow on the mountains continually withheld the flow of liquid. The crops began to dry in the constant heat of the sun.

No matter how many blood sacrifices were performed, they would not dissuade the gods from their anger of Bird Jaguar's deed. Soon the citizens were staring starvation in the face and the grumbling grew against their king.

A few people packed their possessions and left Nakanjo, but most of the others prayed to their divine beings for relief. Instead, they awoke one morning to the ground shaking and the distant mountains grumbling and spewing black smoke and ash. What followed was a tremendous earthquake that shook the city, collapsing buildings and temples.

Those who were not crushed by the building blocks or not swallowed up by the earth were so terrified by what had happened that they abandoned Nakanjo to the tropical rain forest. There was no one left in the city.

After some time, the growth of the jungle that had been successfully controlled for centuries slowly began to encroach and re-claim the Mayans city-state. No hands remained to cut the foliage back, and without it, jungle flora once more covered everything until the eye could no longer detect what men had once built. Nature had obliterated everything that man had created.

Over the centuries, all that was left was the myth of what had happened to the lost city of Nakanjo.

THE SAGA

CHAPTER 12

CADIZ, SPAIN DECEMBER 1494

Cesar de Leon was born of a noble but impoverished family on his father's side in Cadiz, Spain in December of the year 1494. His mother Sarah's family was labeled "Conversos", a name given to Jews who had converted to Catholicism. However, the shadow of the Inquisition constantly threatened their lives. They had seen what happened to such families who were accused of still worshiping the Jewish faith. They were spirited away in the middle of the night, either burned at the stake as heretics or never seen again. For Cesar and his family, their lives were always precarious. And so, it was that Cesar grew up with a hatred of the church that he kept well hidden.

As a young boy, his father apprenticed him to a goldsmith to learn a trade, but Cesar couldn't be more disinterested. Instead, he spent his days at the city wharfs watching the boats sail in and out of the harbor, and dreaming of navigating to foreign lands, contacting strange people of different cultures.

Each day, Cesar came home to a beating from his father. "Why do you continually fight against my wishes for a prosperous future for you?" his frustrated father finally questioned him.

"Father, I have no desire to become a goldsmith," he answered with mild defiance, for he knew that if he disrespected his father, another beating would ensue.

"And what do you wish to do?"

"I want to become a soldier and sail to the New World to seek my fortune." Even though Cesar and his two brothers had been brought up learning to read and how to defend themselves with a sword, he knew at an early age that as the middle son, he had no hope of improving his situation in Cadiz. What little the de Leon family had would go to the eldest brother Carlos because of the practice of primogeniture, while his youngest brother, Juanito, "little Juan" was destined to enter the local Carthusian monastery for a life of prayer with no contact with the outside world.

Still, his father forced him back into his apprenticeship, and although Cesar was resentful, he obeyed his father until he was 16. The young man packed up his few belongings after he read that a flotilla of ships was ready to raise their sails and travel to the island of Hispaniola. While his mother cried, his father reluctantly gave him his blessing, handed him his sword which he buckled around his waist, and a few gold reals to help him on his journey.

Hurrying to the wharfs, he wanted to sign up as a soldier on one of the ships bound for the West. Using a few gold reals his father had given him, he bought his passage. By the time he reached the Caribbean island of Cuba after months of seasickness, his pockets were empty. A notice on a building told of an expedition being outfitted for foreign conquest. He hastily ran to the wharfs before all the places could be filled. He waited for his turn to become a part of the expedition. At last, his turn came. "Name?" the man sitting behind a table with the book in front of him asked the young man.

"Cesar de Leon," he answered proudly.

"In what capacity will you be able to work on this voyage?"

"As a soldier." The big man guffawed out loud, setting the rest of the men on line to laugh in derision.

"And how old are you, soldier?"

"Twenty!" he lied hoping his expression did not betray him.

"Twenty, hey!" he responded skeptically.

"Yes, twenty!" He pushed the book towards Cesar and pointing his finger said,

"Put your mark here."

"I can read and write!" he retorted insolently.

"Then sign your name!

"Vamos! Apurate!" voices behind him grumbled impatiently. Before he could sign his name on the manifest, a voice from above asked,

"Who is holding up this line?" a distinguished man with a beard and moustache demanded from the balcony above the piers.

"This boy, sir! He says he is a soldier."

"Come up here!"

"Who is he," the curious lad queried.

"He is General Hernan Cortez, one of the leaders of this expedition."

"Come up here boy and don't keep me waiting!" Cesar ran into the building and up the stairs and announced,

"I'm here, sir!" Hernan took a good look at him.

"So, you are a soldier, are you?"

"Yes, General." Cortez withdrew his sword from its scabbard and commanded,

"Then prove it!" The others below watched in morbid curiosity.

Cesar removed his sword and took his stance. There was no fear reflected in his eyes. Cortez lunged toward the boy who parried his blow aside. Hernan was surprised and moved in for another blow. Each one he deflected and then Cesar turned the tables and came after the general. After a few such blows, the general was able to knock the sword down as it clattered on the tiled floor. "Pick it up and put it away." Cesar did as he was told. "You have skill, my young friend and boldness."

"Thank you, sir." Cortez sheathed his weapon and shouted downstairs, "Register him as a soldier!"

MEXICO, 1513

After waiting nine years, Cortez was at last commissioned to head his own expedition. There was a certain quality about Cesar de Leon that Cortez admired. He just could not put his finger on it. Maybe it was the bravado of his attitude or maybe it was the hunger for wealth he could sense by looking at him. Whatever it was, Hernan Cortez recognized his younger self in the young man.

The general made sure that he was trained by the best swordsmen in Cadiz before he appointed Cesar as a lieutenant in his army. The young man beamed from ear to ear.

It was then that Cesar was introduced to an Arawak Indian woman who had, as a converted Catholic, been baptized as Ladamma Maria. She became Hernan's translator and joined the expedition. The young man was transfixed by her exotic beauty. She was slightly taller than most of her tribe, standing at 5'6", with long hair as dark as a raven's wing, which hung to her waist. Maria's eyes were like two black coals, intelligently piercing, while her bright white teeth were set off by her brown skin. He fell for her tremendously hard but he kept his feelings to himself.

The leader of the expedition to conquer the lands west of Cuba, Diego Velazques de Cuellar, was installed by Christopher Columbus, the Viceroy of the Indies. The flotilla of ships sailed from Cadiz, bound for the island of Cuba.

Cesar recalled the weeks of sailing which were uneventful but for the bouts of seasickness among the soldiers. He was among those who hung over the rail trying to empty his stomach contents. There were also the occasional fights between 300 men forced to live in very close quarters.

When land was sighted, rowboats brought horses, men, supplies, and arms to the southern coastline of the island where they were unopposed by the natives. Quickly raising the Spanish flag, Cortez claimed this land for the king and queen of Spain. Immediately, a settlement was founded and named Villa de Nuestra Senora de la Asuncion de Baracoa and a protective wall was erected. A church and town began to take shape, but in all that time, not one native of the island had approached the compound. On a sunny morning, Diego Valesquez ordered Cortez and the troops he led to leave the village and determine if the island was inhabited by Indians.

Cesar joined his leader who was already on horseback. The pace was easy, and believing that they would not run across anyone, the two began to talk. But they were being closely watched and followed. Just beyond the path that was being cleared, the Tiano tribe, led by their leader the cacique, Hatuey, waited for the time to strike the unsuspecting foreigners.

The intensity of hatred grew amongst the native Tiano against these invaders. At last, with a war whoop, the Indians burst out of their hiding place and fell upon the unsuspecting Spaniards. Arrows flew in the air but bounced off the soldiers' armor. Still, a few found their mark where flesh was unprotected. Guns were fired, but it did not stave off the Taino's charge. Hernan and Cesar withdrew their swords and cut a wide swath into them as if they were harvesting wheat.

Like agile monkeys, some tribesmen jumped up behind the foreign horse riders and stabbed them with their knives. Cesar de Leon had just dispatched a brown-skinned warrior with a single blow of his sword when he turned his horse to the left. A Tiano warrior had climbed behind Cortez as he fought off a frontal attack. Cesar charged as the knife sank into the seam between armor plates in Cortez's upper arm. Hernan screamed out in pain. With a wide swing of his sword, the lieutenant cut down the attacker perched behind the general. *"Retirada!"* Hernan ordered and his troops withdrew from the field while some helped wounded comrades. Rifles were discharged preventing the warriors from following them.

Cortez recovered from his wound, and a week later another troop of soldiers went out, tracked the Indians down and entered their village. The Tianos brought out food looking for an amicable resolution. Once the food was eaten, the order to kill was given and the villagers were massacred, but their chief was kept alive. Days later, Hatuey, the captured chief of the Tianos was burned at the stake. Newly commissioned Captain Cesar de Leon oversaw the execution.

Cesar de Leon honed his skills as a conquistador under the tutelage of Hernan Cortez in the defeat of the Aztecs of Mexico. Once they arrived back in Havana, on the recommendation of his friend and general, he was commissioned as a general to begin the conquest of Guatemala.

He went to Ladamma Maria expressing his love to her. To his utter joy, she shyly answered," I'm in love with you too." Everything seemed to be falling in place to begin another life in the New World. He married the young Indian mestizo maiden with the permission of his general and they made love as husband and wife that evening. Very soon, she was pregnant.

His expedition was outfitted by the governor of the island with three ships of soldiers, armaments, and horses. As de Leon read the commission, he smiled with satisfaction until he read that the name of one of the missionaries was Brother Manolo Gallego. The conquistador fumed with rage. Cesar had met Gallego on the voyage to Havana and took an instant disliking to him. He was suspicious of all churchmen, but he had found out that the Dominican Brother had served some time as a judge of the Inquisition in Toledo, Spain. The young general petitioned the governor for someone else to lead the religious brothers, but he was flatly refused. This put a damper on his otherwise exciting expedition.

The two had had many "discussions" as to the role of the Spanish in the New World. None of them had ended well. "The main purpose of our trip," Cesar had insisted, "is to bring back gold and any other riches we may find!"

Manolo replied in disagreement. "You are wrong," he answered, his emotions under complete control. "It is to bring the word of God to these people and to save their immortal souls from the fires of hell and eternal damnation."

"No matter how many you convert to Christianity, they will still be heathens! Cesar ridiculed with disgust in his voice. He heard himself saying this even though he was married to a woman who was part European and part Arawak. "It is a total waste of time! Besides, who are we to get to work the gold or silver mines there?"

"I will not stand by and watch you make slaves of these people. I will not abide it."

"You will not abide it?" he laughed in derision. "Do you think the governor would support your contention? I assure you, he might express the same words but he is more interested in the riches than the conversion of souls."

Brother Gallego broke off the conversation when he realized that no amount of convincing would turn this man's opinion around. *I will not allow this man to get away with any abuse toward these people.* With a dismissive sniff, de Leon knew that this delusional monk would never get his way as long as he was heading this expedition.

A little over a month later, the sails were lifted and immediately filled with a wind that powered them in a westerly direction. Along with the men was an Ixakben woman named Blue River who had been captured and Christianized years before she had become a translator. A week and a half later, they caught sight of an overwhelming land decorated completely in green vegetation. "Land ho!" the sailor in the crow's nest called out forcefully. De Leon, on a ship christened the Santo Rosario, was called up from his cabin to view their destination.

Anchors were dropped in crystal blue-green water as a row boat from each of the three ships moved toward land. Cesar jumped into the shallow water and was the first to reach dry land. Blue River and Brother Gallego accompanied him. Taking the Spanish flag, the conquistador planted it in the sand saying, "I claim this land for their majesties the King and Queen of Spain!" No one came out to greet them. "Go!" he ordered the soldiers that had accompanied him. "Go a few yards into the jungle and see who might be around. If you find anybody, bring them back to me!" As the men moved inland, the monk called out,

"Do not hurt them and if they resist, let them go!"

"Bring them here as I instructed you!" De Leon marched over to where the religious man was standing. "I warn you, do not flaunt my authority at any time, but even more, not in front of my men! I am the authority here and you will obey me!"

"I answer to one authority only and that is God," he announced using his index finger to point to the heavens above.

De Leon watched as the soldiers lost themselves in the local flora, but he told himself, *This holy man must go, one way or another!*

CHAPTER 13

SAN CRISTOBAL, GUATEMALA, JUNE 1524

Where once there had been nothing but palm trees and a virgin green shoreline, there now stood a clearing with the beginning of a small town. Roughly hewn timber was transformed into buildings with thatched roofs and protective walls. Three Spanish galleons were anchored offshore and row boats were beached on the white sand.

Some buildings were used as soldiers' quarters, another as an infirmary, while another, with a simple handmade cross, was the church. The most impressive building in size was the one in which Cesar de Leon lived and worked. Behind his chair stood a small Indian boy who made sure the fan at the back of the conquistador's head kept moving in the humid air. Beyond the town were the fields in which their food was cultivated by natives used as forced labor. Their conquerors doled out punishment for those who were thought to be slowing down. There were pens that housed the horses, cows, and pigs had been brought over with the Spaniards. In a religious ceremony, the tiny village had been named, *San Cristobel*. Just beyond the town, surrounded by a crude fence, stood a few wooden crosses that were a part of the cemetery.

In the infirmary, Brother Gallego and two other Dominican brothers dressed in black habits and cowls bent over trying to ease the suffering of the sick and physically abused. Blankets laid about practically filled the floor with the ailing. Cool rags were placed on the foreheads of the feverish and native ointments were applied to the scars left by the whiplash as the brothers who had learned the native tongue tried to soothe them with comforting words. The soldiers, bloated with pride, made no attempt to learn and communicate with them. Moans and shrieks from the patients filled the sticky, humid air.

All at once, a young Spanish officer appeared at the door. "Are you Brother Gallego?" he catechized. The monk left a bowl of water and a wet rag he was using next to one of his patients on the floor and stood up.

"I am Brother Gallego, my son."

"General de Leon commands that you should come to him now. I am to escort you there."

"But I am in the middle of caring for my parishioners."

"His orders were for you to come to him immediately!" Shrugging in frustration, he turned to his other Brothers and advised, "Continue to take care of the sick. I'll be returning soon." With the young officer leading the way, the two men walked in the hot mid-afternoon sun. The men entered the building and the young officer announced, "Brother Gallego is here."

"You are dismissed!" the general proclaimed. The obedient officer took his leave and waited outside. Before he looked up at the Brother, the general yelled, "I swear there are more flies in this land than people!" With that, he cuffed the Indian boy who was standing next to him across the face and screamed, "Move that fan faster and keep those damned flies off of me!" The boy immediately moved his arms in a quicker motion.

"General, watch your language. Was it necessary to slap the boy?"

"That's the only way they learn. They're like animals that have to be beaten to get work out of them."

"You are wrong. They are becoming Christian souls who are now members of our faith and belong to Holy Mother Church."

"You are only fooling yourself! If we were to suddenly leave here, they would go back to their heathen ways!"

"You do not give them enough credit. They are innocent souls."

"And you give them too much credit," de Leon sneered at him with disdain.

"What about all those slothful heathen Indians that you are keeping in the infirmary? Many of them should be outside working again."

"Some are ill with fever and chills. The others have been whipped to within an inch of their lives. None are fit to do any work."

"Malingerers, all of them! They should all be beaten and driven out to the fields!"

"General, I beg you, for the love of God, do not do such a thing!" de Leon sat back with a smug look on his mustachioed face.

"I want them ready for travel in a few days, understood?"

"But why travel? We still need time to establish the town on this site."

De Leon yelled out, "Lieutenant Martinez, bring him in!" The officer led an Indian who was chained at the wrists and the ankles. Brother Gallego recognized him right away. It was an Indian who had been christened Felipe.

Turning toward the general, Gallego inquired, "Why is this man in chains?"

"He was caught stealing food from the fields last night and when he was about to be whipped this morning in front of the others, he screamed, 'Oro, oro'! I want you to question him about what he knows about gold! Brother Gallego began to question him in the Mayan tongue. Felipe animatedly began to tell his story which went on for a few minutes. Finally, de Leon interrupted exclaiming, "What is he jabbering about?"

The monk nodded to the prisoner and turned to de Leon. "He told me he knows of a city filled with gold."

"Now we are getting somewhere. How does he know this?"

"He is of a tribe that lives near the city's ruins."

"What is the name of this city?" Once more, the man answered.

"He says it's called Nakanjo."

"Where is it?" The brother asked him the question and Felipe answered. Gallago turned toward the general once more.

"He states that only he knows and he will lead you there if you spare him the whip."

"They are all so clever and conniving! Do you still believe that they are all innocent souls? Tell him I agree to dismiss his punishment, but if he is lying, he will wish for the whip after my men get through with him." The brother translated.

"Oro!" he repeated.

"Now you understand the urgency of why we are going into the interior. I will leave a contingent of men here to keep the peace. Everyone else will march with me. Make sure those you are caring for are fit for labor!"

As he walked back, the Brother thought, *Greed is human folly!*

The trek into the interior of the land left the Spaniards frustrated and exhausted after five grueling days. Added to this was the misery of constantly biting flies and mosquitos that seemed to be everywhere. Their exasperation was heightened by the armor they wore as they traveled. It was heavy and made the heat even more unbearable.

The members of the expedition were on heightened alert for any sudden attacks by local tribesmen. The calls of Black Howler monkeys set their nerves on edge so much that one soldier shot into the trees. "Save your ammunition!" shouted de Leon to his anxious men.

Felipe led the group, using a machete to clear away the underbrush and hanging vines. "I do not trust him," the general's second-in-command voiced to his superior.

"Do not worry. If we are attacked, he will be the first to die!" Turning to his translator Blue River, he inquired, "Ask him how much further we have to go." She got Felipe's attention and asked him the question. He babbled the answer before he continued to chip away at the vegetation ahead of them. "What was his answer?"

"He tells me it is a few days away."

"It is the same answer I have been given since we first started out on this expedition! Remind him that if he is leading us into a trap, he will forfeit his life!" She translated this to him as Felipe turned around, his eyes wide with wonder and kept repeating, *"Oro! Oro!"*

"Yes, I know," the perturbed officer answered gruffly.

Felipe led them to a clearing through which dappled sunlight came through the green canopy. The calls of disturbed Scarlet Macaws greeted them. A small brook of swift moving water crossed in front of them. The soldiers immediately fell upon the water and drank deeply. "Get them back in formation!" de Leon barked but before his order could be followed, a single arrow thudded into a tree close to where the general was riding. The alarm was raised as the men pointed their guns but there was no one they could see. Felipe turned to de Leon chattering away. "What is he saying?"

The translator replied, "He said that they are his people and not to shoot them. They are peaceful." Suspicion dominated the general's expression.

"Tell him to order them out into the open so that I can see them!" Once his order was translated, Felipe faced the jungle and clicked his tongue three times. Like shadows once engulfed in the darkness of the jungle, five warriors appeared. Their short dark hair was colored red with river clay with which they also decorated their bodies. They wore little in the way of clothing except a strip of leather that covered their genitals. Some of them appeared with a drawn bow and an arrow ready to be released, while others held their spears aloft in a threatening manner. "I should have you killed you!" Cesar screamed at their guide.

Once it was translated, the Indian answered, "Come back to the village to eat, drink, and rest. These people will carry your supplies. The trail near this point is elevated. My people are used to hard climbs. They will be a big help to you." Cesar looked around at his exhausted men, and although he did not feel comfortable with the offer, decided to accept it. He nodded to Felipe, who told the warriors to lead the way.

After about 30 minutes, the party came upon a clearing in which 14 hovels were situated. The sounds of the large group approaching brought the people out with curiosity. The native women were covered below the waist but wore nothing above. The babies and children wore nothing at all. They all gathered around Felipe and greeted him like a long-lost brother. "Come," Felipe told the Spaniards and led them to a large hut set in the middle of the settlement. Brother Gallego and his companion Brother Hermoza followed the others.

The interior of the hut was a bit cooler and the Indian women passed around pots of water that were greedily drunk. Once their thirst was quenched, they noticed the delicious aroma of cooking meat. Before too long, some Indians came in carrying a spit on which a white-tailed deer had been roasted. The Spaniards ate hungrily, allowing the grease to flow down their cheeks, into their beards and down their fingers.

When they all had sated their hunger, de Leon turned to his guide. "How many days do we have until we reach our destination?"

Blue River interpreted, "Nakanjo is about a three-day climb from here."

"We will resupply here and be ready to march tomorrow."

"As you wish."

The general posted guards outside their hut. He wasn't totally convinced that these natives were trustworthy. They were replaced every so often with new guards. The other soldiers in the hut drifted off into peaceful sleep.

By the next morning, the force was reassembled, but this time native bearers gathered up the Spaniard's equipment while Felipe once again lead the party. Very soon, they were past the flat terrain and moving over an elevated area. The terrain got more challenging as the incline of the topography got slowly steeper. Horses and Spaniards sometimes lost their footing, letting stones and pebbles career down below them. However, the Indians were adept at this kind of land and took to it as easily as mountain goats.

After the first day, the group made camp. Their muscles were sore and aching but the idea of the acquisition of gold and jewels gave them the motivation to move on by the next day.

Everything to the eye seemed to move in slow motion. The steam generated by the evaporating rain water appeared to take the form of floating spirits rising above their heads. The greenness of the jungle gave them the impression that it would go on interminably. Felipe and his tribesmen looked as if they were the only men in the party who still had limitless energy. Behind him, the Spaniards had long ago taken off most of their armor because of heat and exhaustion, and like the pack animals, trod lethargically on.

Past streams where both man and animal stopped to drink, and through tangled vines and overgrown flora, they continued in the hope of finding gold. They only stopped when the call of some wild bird echoed in the rain forest or to pitch tents for the night. It was on one of those nights that Brother Gallego walked to the general's tent. He found him hunched over a table writing. "Excuse me, General. May I see you for a moment?"

De Leon looked up from his page and closed his journal. "Come and sit down. May I offer you some fine port?" he queried, putting his hand on the bottle that was near him on the table.

"Not for me but don't let me stop you from pouring a drink for yourself." The general did just that and took a few sips.

"Now, how can I assist you?"

"In the morning, I'd like to return to San Cristobel. I would need only one soldier to escort me back." De Leon sat back in his chair and let out a big guffaw.

"And what would be your reason for returning?"

"So I can minister to the people of the city."

"There are other Brothers who were left behind to do that job. Besides, you are needed to make converts of any indigenous people we may meet along the way."

"Then your answer is "No"?

"That's correct. Furthermore, not one soldier here would volunteer to take you back after we have come all this way."

"You could order one of them to do this."

"And have an act of recalcitrance on my hands? The answer is the same. Have you looked beyond the tired expressions of my men? If you do, you will detect the burning desire in their eyes to acquire gold and riches. If you are so eager to go, you'll have to go by yourself."

"I would never survive!"

"Yes, that's true. I guess you'll have to stay with the rest of us." Gallego rose from his chair silently and walked out of the tent. De Leon went back to writing in his journal.

Brother Manolo Gallego returned to his tent and took out the journal in which he had been writing since they had left Spain. He wrote of his disappointment in the general's attitude, then recited his prayers, blew out the flame on the candle and tried to fall asleep on his cot. The heat made it almost impossible.

Morning dawned just as sweltering and oppressive as the days before it. The men rose from their sleep, ate sparingly from the food they brought along, and began to take down their sleeping quarters.

With his translator at his side, de Leon got hold of Felipe and shaking him, demanded, "How many more days of traveling?" His translator asked this of him. With wild gesticulations of his arms while he was speaking, the translator answered, "A few more days."

"A few more days?" he yelled, his voice resounding around the clearing. "I should kill you right now for leading us on a fool's chase!" Once more, Blue River translated the guide's gibberish reply. "He has told me that we are within a two-day distance to his people where we can resupply with food and water."

The general looked deeply into the woman's eyes. "Do you believe him?"

"I believe he is speaking the truth."

"Move on!" he yelled at the troupe. The party moved out.

By mid-afternoon, something moved in the underbrush before them and the Spaniards raised their guns and pointed to where the disturbance was happening. Stepping out of the leaves, short brown men, dressed in just a loincloth, skin covered with clay as protection from the sun, had their weapons drawn before them. Their expressions were not friendly.

The head man yelled at the top of his voice at them. The woman by the general's side began to translate. "They are the Quiche people, just one of the descendants of the Maya. They demand that we turn and go back where we came from."

"He makes demands on me?" Before the translator could answer, Felipe addressed the warriors. "What is he saying?"

"He is telling the chief that he is one of them." The Quiche antagonists stared until the chief smiled and dropped his bow and arrow. The others quickly followed his lead.

"What's happening?"

"They are welcoming us." With hospitable pats on his back, Felipe turned and told the Spanish something.

"Now what?" Blue River replied,

"Felipe wants us to follow them to their village where we can eat and rest." The party moved forward. Cesar was wary of the invitation. *None of these people can be trusted.*

After a few days of rest and nutrition, de Leon went to Felipe with Blue River and proclaimed, "I will wait no more! Take me to where I can find the gold you promised! When she had translated the words of the Spaniard, Felipe nodded his head vigorously answering,

"Si, Senor!"

"Good! I want to head out as soon as possible."

The order was given and his second-in-command, Lieutenant Martinez, spread the word amongst the troops and preparations were started. The lust for gold blazed in their eyes. Along with his other companion, Brother Gallego, who was still exhausted, he put their few possessions together and loaded them onto a mule. Felipe was now joined by other male members of the tribe who led the way out.

Once again, they started out in tangled vegetation and the sounds of Howler Monkeys screaming that their environs were being disturbed. "What if Felipe and his people are misleading us?" Martinez inquired of his superior.

"Then they will all taste the cold edge of my blade!" he retorted touching the weapon that dangled at his hip, the only gift he had ever been given by his father.

"The men are beginning to complain about how long this is taking."

"As long as there is the promise of gold at the end of the journey, they will keep going." And so, they marched on, the unmerciful warmth of the sun beating down on their bodies. Cesar was soon lacking in patience. "How much longer?" he confronted Felipe.

The Indian babbled something that de Leon's translator explained, *"Pronro estaremos alli."*

"It's always the same answer, "Soon, soon!"

"I am running out of patience! Tell him if we don't reach our destination by tomorrow, I will kill all of them!" Blue River translated as Felipe continued to smile and repeat, "Soon, soon, there will be gold."

Once darkness fell and the party stopped for the evening, Brother Manolo Gallego complained of not feeling well. Before he dropped off to sleep, he transcribed the events of the day in his diary. By morning when the camp broke, the monk was worse. The other monk approached de Leon. "General, Brother Manolo is quite sick."

"Get him ready to move out! I will not leave any stragglers behind. Now go!" The monk did as he was told and helped Brother Gallego mount the mule. The party moved forward at a slow pace as the sun once more roasted the expedition members. By midday, a new sound could be heard very faintly in the distance.

"What is that sound?" he demanded of his guide.

"It is the sound of the river which means we will soon be there," Blue River translated.

They soon found a clearing where a wildly rushing river was flowing downstream.

"Is it here?" Cesar de Leon commanded. Felipe pointed upstream repeating,

"Oro, oro!"

The party stopped to drink from the cold water in the river. Brother Manolo was given a cold compress to put on his head after he had quenched his thirst. The horses and mules were urged on as the river cascaded passed them. The group soon saw the source of the water, the mountains whose melting snow flowed first into a lake that fed the river.

Felipe approached the Spaniards excitedly saying, *"Estamos aqui!"* The woman who was acting as the translator told Cesar, "He is saying that we are here." Leon looked around him. The scenery was quite breathtaking but he questioned angrily, "Where is the gold?"

"Ahi, ahi!" Cesar's eyes followed where the Indian was pointing. He seemed to indicate that it was the high ground covered by trees and vegetation a mile or so from the lake.

"This is preposterous," he shrieked as he withdrew his sword from his scabbard. Once more, Felipe babbled something, still pointing in the same direction.

"He says that where he is pointing are the ancient ruins of a city named Nakanjo. It is within the city where the gold can be found." Brother Manolo's companion once more approached the general.

"General, Brother Manolo must be taken back to the Indian settlement. His fever is rising!"

"Go," the impatient leader barked. "And take a few of the Indians to lead you back!" The monk hurried toward his companion as a few Indians followed.

"Brother, the general has given us his permission to go back to the native village so that you can recover."

"Please hand me my diary," he asked. "I must be allowed to record in it before we leave." Gallego's fever was high but his brain faculties had not failed. Taking the book, he dipped his pen in the bottle of ink that the other Brother held and wrote,

"Today we reached a great city off the shore of a large lake."

The party started back but before they could reach their destination, Brother Manolo Gallego died. His body was buried in the jungle and a prayer said over it. His companion carried his diary back to the Indian village and then returned to the place of the Spanish settlement that was lapped by the waters of the Atlantic Ocean.

Eventually, his diary was returned to the convent of San Cristobel where it eventually found its way to Salamanca and it was placed in the library and where it was forgotten for hundreds of years.

"Where?"

"There, there!" Felipe kept pointing to the same place. Cesar stared in that direction but could only see three vegetation-covered hills. The female translator turned to Cesar saying, "He insists that it's over there!" She pointed in the same direction.

The conquistador looked once more with confusion. "If he's lying to me..."

"He keeps repeating the same word," his translator persisted.

"Tell him to go on!" Cesar de Leon waved his soldiers forward. As they approached, everyone noticed what seemed to be a line rising from the ground up on the hill. Then the line became perfectly visible. A path had been created that revealed steps escalating to the top. *So, they are not hills after all, but buildings!*

Excitedly, Felipe said, "Follow me to the top."

"He wants us to climb to the top with him."

"You two," he ordered pointing to a couple of soldiers. "Stand guard here." The rest of the troop started the climb. The stairs were steep and it took even more energy to climb. The Indians however, bounded up the steps as if they were used to doing it. They soon outpaced the Spaniards and waited for them to catch up. At last, Cesar and the others stood at the top. The general stood up and was aghast at the view. No matter where he looked, there was green undergrowth as far as the eye could see. Turning, he noticed a flattened stone on a pedestal. On further examination, he discerned a dried red substance that had stained the stone.

"This way, Spaniard!" Felipe's voice was raised again.

"He wants us to go inside." Cesar assigned another two soldiers to stand guard with Blue River. The rest moved into the relative coolness of the interior. Felipe lit the torches that were hung on the walls. When the interior was lit up, the Spaniards were amazed at the colorful paintings that covered the walls. On closer inspection, Cesar found the images disturbing. The upper and lower borders were adorned with skulls while the center panels showed men having their hearts ripped out on a stone that was like the one just outside. But the general's lust for gold outweighed his apprehension at what he was seeing.

"Where's the treasure?" de Leon blurted out. Felipe waved a few of the Indians over and together they lifted the center panel in the floor, revealing a staircase. Taking one of the torches, Cesar led his men down into the temple pyramid. There were several sarcophagi resting at the bottom of the staircase. "Get these lids off," barked the general. Struggling, the soldiers at last removed the lid of the nearest sarcophagus. Gasping, they saw a body with a jade death mask that was adorned with intricately designed gold necklaces. Without hesitation, they started snatching at the priceless items. Juan grabbed a golden bracelet and put it into a pocket in his uniform.

They were so busy robbing the dead that they did not see the Indians, this time armed with weapons, approach them silently from behind. With a war whoop, they threw themselves on the unsuspecting tomb robbers. Clubs came crashing down from above, stunning some of the enemy. Cesar screamed "Follow me!"

Using his instinct and memory of the Aztec attack in Mexico, he used his body weight and sword. The general began to push the Indians to the side, killing those he could. Near the top of the stairs, he received a blow to the back of his head. Although it stunned him, he made it outside. What he saw made him feel ill. Both Spaniards and White Egret lay slain on the floor. He moved to the top step and yelled down for help to the soldiers below but they were missing. He felt another blow to the back of his head and blacked out. His body pitched forward and he fell down the stairs.

CHAPTER 14

RAINFOREST OF GUATEMALA, JULY, 1524

Cesar de Leon didn't know how long he had been unconscious but he woke with a splitting headache. He moaned and touched the back of his head. His hair was matted with coagulated blood. He lifted himself and looked up. The general realized he had landed a few steps from the top. When he turned to look down, his heart stopped at what he saw. He recognized five bodies of his men with gaping bloody holes in their chests where their hearts had been. Their eyes were opened wide with terror. *They must have thought they killed me or I would now be in the same condition as my men.* His lips said a silent prayer to the Madonna for his good fortune. Yelling for anyone, he knew from the silence that followed that he was alone.

Climbing to the top, he looked at the sacrificial stone, red from the new blood that had been spilled on it. Making the Sign of the Cross, he made his way down the stairs, though he stopped a few times from vertigo, until his feet were once more on the hard ground. Seeing the horses a short distance away, he whistled for his black stallion, Caballero. The horse lifted his head from grazing, recognizing his master's call and made his way to him. With some difficulty, Cesar de Leon mounted his steed. *I don't know if the Indians are still around but I need to make my way back to the settlement.*

Spurring his horse, he followed his way back by using the path the Indians had cleared earlier. The horse plodded on under the blistering heat of the sun. Cesar was soon soaked with sweat as he discarded his heavy armor, piece by piece. When night fell, he tied up the horse and dropped to the ground to sleep in sweet relief.

In the morning, his priority was to find water for the two of them. The horse had eaten well with all the vegetation around. Once more, he got on the horse's back and continued at a snail's pace towards the Spanish settlement along the Atlantic Ocean.

Coming across a narrow creek, he fell to his knees and drank deeply of the cool water. His horse bent its neck and drank near him. All the supplies were missing, even his water bottle so he could not collect water for the rest of the journey. The rains came once a day but even though they were intense, they didn't last long. Cesar sucked on the leaves where water accumulated but it was never enough. The rain dropped to the forest floor but the sun's evaporation and the quick saturation of the ground left little for drinking. *Those lousy savages probably took everything we had with them thinking that we were all dead. But not me, not me. I'll live to see Havana again!* Remounting, he started on his way back.

Days and nights seemed like one huge blur and he wondered if he was even going in the right direction. Once or twice a day he slipped from his steed and fell to the forest floor. Each time, his horse waited patiently for its master to awaken and get back in the saddle. Then one morning, his horse dropped to the ground before he could mount it and never got up. He kneeled beside him and stroked his nuzzle for the last time. *Old friend, we saw each other through The Night of Sorrows when Cortez and the rest of us fought our way out of Tenochtitian while the Aztecs savagely attacked us, but now you are gone from me. Rest in peace, Caballero!*

Leaving his horse behind, Cesar de Leon started out on his own with determination. His pace was slower than it was on the horse, and he didn't cover the same distance each day, but his will remained strong. Day after day, step after step, he forced himself to move on. Staggering forward, he was forced to catch small rodents for sustenance, their blood minutely quenching his thirst.

Before he slept each night, he prayed that he would make it back to the settlement, and not wind up dead along the way. In the morning, his feet were sometimes so sore that he was forced to crawl. His hands became raw, and he broke down into tears of frustration, but he still clung stubbornly to life.

Then finally after weeks of struggling, he found himself in a clearing. Not far away, a familiar wall stood in front of him just a few yards away.

Cesar tried to call out for help but his dried throat could not make a sound. He continued to crawl along before a sentry on the wall caught sight of something moving and called out to the others, "There's someone crawling to the gate!" A contingent of soldiers emerged and hurried toward the stranger. His gaunt features and scruffy appearance made it impossible to identify him. He was carried inside the fort.

No one seemed to recognize him until Lieutenant Sandoval, who had overseen the settlement in the general's absence, exclaimed, "It's General de Leon!" Sandoval tried to question him but Cesar was now in the middle of delirium with a high fever. Days went by with everyone wondering where the others were.

He was provided with cold compresses, clean water for drinking, and nourishing food, but his fever never broke. He lay in the bed and appeared to be a shadow of the person he used to be. "Where are the others? Sandoval inquired.

"They're all gone, all dead!"

"What happened to them?"

"We were attacked by Felipe's people. Some of the men were used as human sacrifice. It was horrible!" Greed now took over Sandoval's questioning.

"What about the lost city of Nakanjo and its treasure? Did you find it?" A flood of memories came to Cesar like a nightmare. He shut his eyes tight hoping they would evaporate. They didn't.

"Let me give you some advice. Nakanjo remains lost and its land is cursed!" He then slipped into a coma.

SAN CRISTOBAL, GUATEMALA, SEPTEMBER, 1524

An armada of five Spanish galleons had sailed from Havana and arrived at the settlement in Guatemala. After getting word that de Leon's sortie had resulted in a disaster, the governor of the island dispatched a new general, Miguel Escarra to take his place. He brought orders for Cesar to return to Cuba.

For weeks before the ships arrived, de Leon lay on the cot on the edge of death, in and out of consciousness. During that time when he was awake, he babbled incoherently. The only thing that was clear was when he stated the names of the soldier who had died under his command while his pregnant wife Ladamma Maria sat by his side. Brother Tomas tried to care for him the best that he could, but no one held out hope that the general would recover.

When he woke, Brother Tomas tried to get him to eat. Cesar ate very little even though his wife kept encouraging him. His men came in to visit him with the excuse to see how he was doing. Instead they questioned him about the location of the lost city. Cesar never gave a straight answer. After a while, all of them were convinced that the blow to his head had damaged his memory. They hoped that in time he would remember.

This hope was dashed when five wind-filled sails come closer and closer to the shore until the order to "Drop anchor" was given. General Escarra was taken by rowboat to the beach, the Spanish royal flag fluttering in the breeze above his head.

Brother Tomas met him and escorted the newly arrived personage to General Cesar de Leon's bedside. Escarra read from the document the governor of Cuba had given to him which commanded that Miguel take Cesar's place. After he was done, General Escarra looked down but de Leon's eyes were a complete blank and he remained speechless. "This is his condition?" the general wanted to know.

"Except for occasionally calling out the dead soldiers' names, there is nothing more," Tomas answered in a subdued tone of voice. Escarra turned the patient's head. The wound was red and very noticeable. He let Cesar's head roll back in place on his pillow. Shaking his head, he left the tent.

The soldiers had gathered on the beach when Escarra stopped. "My first order is that three ships should be outfitted and supplied for the trip back to Havana! They will be ready to sail back in three days!"

"May I look after him on the journey back?" the brother inquired.

"By all means!" his answer was sharp and terse. "I've brought Brothers of my own on this trip."

"Thank you, General."

In three days, supplies, soldiers, and General de Leon, accompanied by Brother Tomas were all on board and the ships raised anchors. Two days later, the ships were hit by a raging wind and a driving rain that tossed them about. It got so bad that the soldiers begged for the Brother to hear their confessions. Through all this, the general never moved and never said a word.

Two somewhat damaged ships limped into port, the third having been sunk in the storm. While the sailors unloaded the ships, a litter drawn by a horse was sent by the governor for Cesar. Brother joined him to the Governor's Palace.

Once Cesar's cot had been taken off the cart, they arrived in front of the royal official. Brother Tomas bowed and said, "Your Excellency."

"This is General de Leon?" he quizzed in shock. "The man looks nothing like the one I sent out to start a settlement.

"It is him! An exploration to find the Mayan city of Nakanjo left him in this state."

"It is a great shame! Perhaps his horrible experiences have opened his soul to be possessed by the devil. I will order that he be taken to the Monastery of *Los Santos Inocentes* to be taken care of by the brothers."

"But Your Excellency, this monastery is to house deranged people; it is no place for the general!"

"They are equipped to handle him. This is my order!"

Tied into his bed by the Brothers, General de Leon gradually declined. He peacefully passed away a week later. After a Requiem Mass was said, he was buried in a pauper's grave at the back of the monastery cemetery.

CHAPTER 15

SAN CRISTOBAL, GUATEMALA, OCTOBER, 1524

The day of the funeral mass for her husband, an extremely pregnant Ladamma Maria was escorted down the aisle of La Iglesia del Anuncio dressed in black, with a lacy, ebony mantilla covering her tear-swollen face. By her side, she was escorted by Captain Mariano Sandoval, the man Cesar had left in charge when he began his expedition. Outside the church, the rumor mill began turning. "Look at her," tongues wagged. "Who does she think she is fooling. She is no lady!" One aristocratic woman recently arrived from Spain declared. "I know, the planters' wife. There's even a rumor that de Leon's mother's side of the family was Jewish!"

"Why then he shouldn't even be buried in sacred ground," the other woman clacked arrogantly.

Behind them, six men from de Leon's army acted as pall bearers as they marched the closed casket to the altar. The air in the church was filled with the scent of incense and the melting tallow of the candles. The priest waited at the altar, holding the holy water he would sprinkle on the coffin. Except for the attendance of the soldiers, the small church was sparsely filled.

It had taken the help of Sandoval, whose uncle was the Roman Catholic Cardinal of the city of Valencia in Spain, to pave the way for the former general to be buried in the church cemetery beside the dead soldiers who had been under his command. It was well known of Cesar de Leon that his love for the church could best be described as barely tolerable, and there had been some question by the church pastor as to whether he could be buried in hallowed ground. But this was all pushed to the side upon receiving the communique from the Cardinal who dispelled all charges against him.

And so, the funeral began with a disgruntled pastor saying the mass accompanied by two Indian boys who were now altar boys as well as newly baptized Christians. The Latin Mass was conducted and Holy Communion given them, then the funeral procession proceeded behind the church where lines of white crosses filled the cemetery. Sprinkling holy water on the casket while he chanted prayers, the pastor signaled and the coffin was lowered into place and shovels of dirt were thrown in to fill the gaping hole.

Less than 24 hours later, in the small house Cesar had built for his wife, the widow Ladamma Maria de Leon went into labor. Indian midwives were called in to help the woman give birth. Three hours of excruciating pain and pushing resulted in the birth of a son whom she would name Juan Cesar de Leon.

The baby boy was cleaned, his umbilical cord severed, he was wrapped in a blanket and given to his waiting mother. Although he was fair of skin, there was no denying that is broad nose was a trait of the Indian population. He squealed incessantly as his little fists waved back and forth, giving his mother the chance to say to herself, *My son will be a fighter!*

His mother was correct in her belief because although the boy carried a Spanish moniker, his facial features were more Indian than Spanish. Her son would be fighting endlessly for what he wanted out of life. Captain Mariano Sandoval stood up at little Juan's christening to become his godfather while his Indian wife became his godmother.

The gossips of the town were quick to point out, "He's a Mestizo, a mixed blood! He'll never amount to anything!" For the transplanted aristocrats of Spain, these upstarts, who looked like the natives, were hated more than the Indians themselves, for they had the crust to demand that they be treated as any other Spaniard from the old world. *"Advenedizos vergonzosos!"* they spat out anytime they caught sight of one.

Juan was left very little by his father, but he did receive two things; his name and the sword of his grandfather, and nothing else. As an infant and toddler, mother and son lived just above the poverty level with the support of many of Cesar's former soldiers.

When Juan reached school age, it was the influence of Brother Tomas, the former friend of Brother Manolo Gallego, who came to his mother to say, "Let me enroll the boy into school." Distressfully, his mother replied,

"He will only be ridiculed and taunted by the other boys!"

"Unfortunately, Juan is already receiving their animosity, but now he'll also receive an education. Without it however, he has no hope to raise himself up in this world." Reluctantly, his mother had to agree and the very next day, he was escorted by Brother Tomas to the mission school.

After two months of instruction, Juan was already ahead of many of the other students. It was now Summer and growing hot and sultry. The humidity stuck to one's body like another layer of skin. Juan was placed on a bench where other Indian children were learning the basics of reading and mathematics. It didn't take long for Juan's teacher, Brother Vicente De Vargas, to go to Brother Tomas to say, "The boy is very bright and has quickly picked up the work faster than the other pupils."

"What are you trying to tell me?"

"He does not belong in this setting."

"So, he belongs in the school of aristocratic boys?"

"Most definitely. I know you will be harangued by the parents of the boys who attend there, but it really would be the best place for him."

"They will not intimidate me if the boy possesses the ability to keep up with the other boys."

"In my estimation, he should have no trouble with that." Brother Tomas listened to his Dominican Brother, rubbing his chin thoughtfully with his long fingers.

"Tomorrow I will escort Juan to the school so that everyone understands that he has my support in being there.

"I will pray for you, Brother."

Taking a new uniform from the supply closet, he arrived on the doorstep of the de Leon's with the news. "Lady," Brother Tomas started. "It has been determined that your son has far too much intelligence to continue to study at the mission school."

"What do you plan on doing with him?" she inquired with skepticism. Brother Tomas held out the school uniform. "No!" she announced emphatically. "They will never accept him there!"

"They will accept him if I say that they should!"

"And when you're not there, what will happen to him?"

"He will learn to defend himself and develop a thick skin, both of which will hold him in good stead in the adult world."

"I don't know," Ladamma Maria said.

"Juan," Brother Tomas said when the young boy entered the room. "Would you like to attend school with the other Spanish boys?"

"Oh yes, very much!" His mother said reproachfully

"He doesn't understand what he'll be up against."

"Juan will be fine. After all, he is the son of Cesar de Leon and by birthright should attend. His mother could not argue that point.

"Very well." Handing over the uniform to his mother, he departed, saying, "I will pick him up a few minutes to nine in the morning and take him to his new school."

The next morning was like the days and weeks before, muggy and humid, when Brother Tomas picked up the uniform-clad Juan for his first day in his new school.

The lesson in mathematics was suddenly halted as the Dominican brother and the boy walked into the classroom hand in hand. The students, divided by appropriate age categories, and the brothers who were instructing them, stopped to stare at the two as they moved through the classroom. They stopped in front of the boys aged 6 to 9. "I have a new student for your class," announced Brother Tomas. The teacher stared at him with nervous anxiety.

"But Brother..." was all the teacher had time to say before the boy's escort spoke out.

"I have a new student for your class," he repeated emphatically. "His name is Juan Cesar de Leon." Brother Carlos, the teacher, looked at the child in the slightly large uniform and said, "Take a seat at the back bench, Juan".

"Go now and be a good boy," Brother Tomas instructed his young charge. Juan happily took his place amongst the other boys. His young classmates stared at him as he took his seat and it was only after Brother Carlos clapped his hands that they all regained their focus. The instruction of adding and subtracting numbers continued, but Juan was soon bored with the topic in which he was already proficient. In time Juan's attention waned and his eyes drifted around the room to the other teachers and students.

"Master de Leon!" the teacher's harsh tone brought back his attention. "Pay attention to your lessons!" The rebuke caused the boy embarrassment while the other students smiled as if to say, "You see this Indian boy doesn't belong here with us!" The boy sitting to the left of him whispered derisively, *"El Burro!"*

But the real problem was to come that afternoon at recess. Brother Carlos watched from the classroom window as the bully and biggest boy of the group named Jorge de la Campo, two years older than his classmate, pummeled Juan with his hands as the other boys screamed their encouragement, until the young mestizo fell to the ground, his face bloody and bruised. *"Ir a sasa a su madre indio! No preteneces aqui con nosotros!"* When the boys came in for religious instruction in the afternoon, all their teacher would say about the incident was directed to Juan. "Go outside and clean yourself up at the trough." Sullenly, Juan did as he was commanded and afterwards rejoined the others.

By the time the school day was over, the restless students couldn't wait for their dismissal. Juan remained behind for a time until he saw Brother Tomas as the door. The brother took one look at the boy's battered face and confronted his teacher. "What happened to him?" Brother Carlos simply shrugged. Brother Tomas' eyes narrowed in rage. "I'll ask you one more time. What happened?"

"The boy had an altercation with one of the other students at recess," he explained with no emotion.

"Why did you not stop them?" demanded Brother Tomas.

"I am a teacher, not a referee!"

"You are anybody I tell you to be!" the older monk reprimanded. "I never want to see this boy in the same condition again when he leaves your classroom! Did I make myself clear?"

"Yes, Brother." Taking the boy's hand, the monk stormed out of the school. Turning toward Juan as they walked, he said, "Our Lord teaches us to turn the other cheek when we are confronted with violence, but Our Lord would not want to see His people treated the way you were. You must fight back the next time you are hit. Do you understand?"

"Yes, Brother Tomas."

When Ladamma Maria caught sight of her son, she stared angrily at the Brother. "Is this what I can expect every time my son comes home from school?"

"Of course not. Juan's first day with his new classmates was a test of your son's will to survive amongst the aristocracy here in San Cristobal. Tomorrow it will be a different story, won't it Juan?"

"Yes, Brother Tomas."

The next day in class, the boys looked at Juan de la Leon and waited for the chance to see Jorge beat the little whelp down to the ground once more. "So, you've come back again, have you?" Jorge taunted him. "You didn't learn your lesson yesterday? Then I'll have to teach you your place once more!"

"Do not lay your hands on me again. For even though Our Lord has told us to turn the other cheek, He does not want his people to lie down and take a beating." The other boys laughed derisively.

"The little Indian boy has attained some courage since yesterday. Let's see what you'll do. I say you will do nothing!" He hauled off and slapped Juan hard against his cheek. The other boys began to egg Jorge on. The smile on Jorge's face drove Juan into a rage, and he punched his tormentor in the nose and dropped the unsuspecting boy to the ground. The other boys who surrounded them fell silent in shock. Jorge touched his nose and discovered that it was bleeding. "You hit me and made my nose bleed," the boy exclaimed as he lay on the ground.

"And if you get up and try to hit me again, I'll do the same thing!" Rising from the ground, young Jorge de la Campo brushed the dust off his uniform and offered his hand, this time in friendship. The other boys stared in disbelief. Juan shook his hand. "He's one of us now!" Jorge announced to the others and from that day forward, the two boys were the best of friends.

CHAPTER 16

As Juan grew up, so did the little village of San Cristobal. When he had reached his 18th birthday, the town was hardly recognizable. The little church of La Iglesia del Anuncio had been torn down and a cathedral was going up in its place. Already finished were the town hall and the government buildings that surrounded *La Plaza de Santo Nino*. The white-washed walls and bright orange tiles of the buildings reflected the brilliance of the hot Guatemalan sun. A bank, hotel, a post office, a larger school, and a military training camp soon followed. Beyond the town a few miles inland, plantations were carved out by the aristocratic families. Within a few years, coffee and sugar cane were being sent back to Spain in exchange for luxury goods brought back to the Guatemalan rainforest. *My father would not recognize this place if he were to come back today.*

He visited the graves of his parents every day laying flowers on the mound of dirt in front of the gravestone. Juan had been taken in by his godparents. The house that Captain Sandoval, his wife and three sons lived in was a modest abode. Juan shared a room with the oldest son, Cesar, named after Juan's father.

By the time the young man had finished his academics, he wished to enter the military academy. The same prejudice Juan faced in previous schools raised its ugly head once more when Mariano Sandoval recommended him for the academy.

A newly arrived aristocrat and general, Vizconde Guillermo de Altamira and his family moved into a hacienda on a sugar plantation that the viscount had ordered built for him. It was after his arrival that the military academy was established for the training of the sons of Spanish nobility.

Juan's application to join the academy was presented to the Viscount de Altamira by his godfather. Reviewing the application himself, the general looked up at the captain who stood before him. "The application reveals that this candidate's father was a nobleman."

"This is true, my Lord."

"The name de Leon is not familiar to me. What can you tell me about the candidate's father?"

"He was born in Cadiz, my Lord, of a noble family whose descendants date back for centuries."

"Still it does not seem to be well known to me."

"It is said that one of his ancestors fought by the side of King Ferdinand when the Moors were ousted from Grenada." Sandoval hoped this fabrication of the truth had not gone too far.

"Send him to me tomorrow morning so that I can see and talk to your godson."

"As you wish, my Lord."

The next morning, Mariano Sandoval accompanied his godson to the general's office inside the academy. A lieutenant sat outside the lavishly decorated office to announce each visitor. The young officer looked up when the pair arrived. He was taken aback by what he saw. "I am Captain Mariano Sandoval. We have an appointment this morning with the Vizconde." The lieutenant got up from behind his desk and knocked on the general's door. "Entrar" the voice behind the door declared. Opening the door, the lieutenant announced,

"There is a Captain Sandoval here to see you."

"Show them in." Waving the visitors forward, the young officer closed the door behind them. The general looked up from his papers to see the two men, the younger one with a sword strapped to his hip. The nobleman was quickly stunned by what he saw. "Captain Sandoval, explain yourself! Who is this Indian to you?"

"This is my godson, Juan Cesar de Leon who is applying for entrance into the academy."

"There must be some mistake," the general stated, looking for some explanation to this matter.

"There is no mistake, my Lord. This is the young man I spoke with you about yesterday."

"But…but, he is a Mestizo."

"Yes, my Lord. That is true." Guillermo stood up forcefully and indignantly inquired,

"Is this some sort of sick joke?"

"No my Lord, he is truly my godson and he wishes to enter the academy as a newly appointed cadet."

"Impossible!" the Vizcconde raved loudly. "This sort of thing just cannot be done!"

"Why, my Lord? He is of noble origin and it is his birthright."

"This is an outrage," the nobleman fumed. "You know perfectly well why he would not make a suitable cadet!"

"Why is that, my Lord?" Sandoval played innocent.

"He is of mixed race, partly Indian! That is why!"

"I have trained him myself in the use of the sword and rapier, my Lord."

"That doesn't matter. Are you blind, man? Can you not see what is plainly in front of your face?"

"I see my godson, my Lord, a young man who is worthy of a spot in the academy." Taking the application that was before him, the nobleman tore it furiously into tiny pieces.

"Never!" he shouted. "Not as long as I head the academy!"

"But, my Lord…"

"Get out!" de Altamira exclaimed with extreme impatience and annoyance. "Go on, the two of you leave my office and never return!" The two men turned and walked away.

"Are my dreams of becoming a soldier over already?" Juan asked his godfather as they walked outside the academy where a few of the cadets were talking.

"I can't say for sure, but I believe so." Suddenly, Juan heard his name called out.

"Juan Cesar de Leon! How have you been?" It was his old classmate Jorge de la Campo, who had graduated school two years before, who greeted him.

"How are you, Jorge?" they greeted each other with hugs like long lost brothers.

"Are you thinking of joining the academy?" Juan looked at the handsome young man dressed splendidly in his cadet dress uniform.

"I was, but I was denied entrance."

"What? You have noble blood!"

"Yes, but I am of a mixed race."

"Was that the reason you were given for your denial to enter?"

"Yes," he answered dejectedly.

"Do not worry. I will speak of that matter with my father."

"But the Vizconde indicated that while he oversaw the academy, it would never happen."

"Don't worry. My father will write an appeal to the king to make it happen. Just have patience." Six months later, Vizconde Guillermo de Altamira was recalled to Spain and another nobleman replaced him. Not long after that, Juan received a letter saying that he would be welcomed into the academy as a new cadet.

CHAPTER 17

Attendance at the academy was six days a week, with Sundays off for worshipping. The instructors of the cadets were trained in the Royal Academy in Madrid for many years, giving them years of experience.

On Juan's first day, many of the cadets looked down their noses at what appeared to them to be a person undeserving of a position reserved for the upper class of Spanish society. But his friendship with Jorge smoothed his entrance into the academy.

The cadets, who numbered just over 120, were positioned in four lines, each line facing the other. The Mestizo lined up opposite what appeared to be a fop, an effeminate young man who was the nephew of the Marquis de Mancera. His name was Sebastian. The instructors began the lesson by calling out certain numbers; each number represented a particular move that had to be demonstrated by the student. "One!" the instructor shouted and immediately the students went into an advance movement. "Two! And the students moved to deflect a blow from another sword. "Three!" the lunge was demonstrated as the students leaped forward, and on and on the cadets practiced displaying their proficiency for each of the moves.

Hours passed before the instructor called for a break in the lessons. Some of the cadets went outside for fresh air, but Juan decided to introduce himself to Sebastian. The young man removed a linen and lace handkerchief from his shirt sleeve and delicately dabbed the perspiration from his forehead. "Hello, my name is Juan Cesar de Leon" and he extended his hand. De Mancera gave him a look of icy indifference.

"How did an Indian like you gain entrance into this academy?"

"I received a special dispensation from the king because of my father."

"They'll let anybody in today! By the way, who was your father?"

"Cesar de Leon," he answered proudly. Shrugging, Sebastian sharply retorted.

"I've never heard of him."

Standing tall and filled with pride, he replied, "He is the Conquistador who established this town!"

"Really?"

"And by the way, I'm not an Indian. I'm a Mestizo!"

"It's the same thing!" The arrogant fop waved the scented handkerchief under his nose as if he were trying to rid a malodorous odor from under his nostrils. "Go away!" he ordered. "Your stench is becoming overpowering!"

"You insult me?" barked Juan. "Defend yourself!"

"Fight you?"

"Yes, are you afraid that I'm a better swordsman?"

"Impossible!"

"Then defend yourself!" A smattering of cadets still in the building overheard the duo shouting and gathered around to see what would happen. Juan took his stance and waited for his opponent to do the same. With the others looking at him, Sebastian had no choice but to fight this lowly personage. Crossing swords, the duel began. Each of them parried and lunged back and forth, the clanging of steel against steel reverberating in the building. The others yelled their encouragement for the Marquis' nephew, but Juan met the challenge.

The commotion drew the attention of their instructor who rushed in to stop the fight. "Put up your swords!" he demanded of them as he pushed his way through his students. "Who began this!" he screamed, his face as red as a tomato. He looked at the two combatants and yelled, "It was you!" he accused his finger indicted the culprit as he chastised Juan. "I knew allowing you into the academy was a mistake!"

"You are wrong," Sebastian calmly corrected. "I challenged him!" The teacher stared at the young man of royal blood and asked,

"Are you sure?"

"I'm positive!"

"Then ten lashes for you both to be given immediately!" The two were taken outside by the other cadets and marched to a place behind the building where punishments were dispensed. They were stopped in front of a grove of trees. Each boy was stripped of his shirt and their hands tied around the tree exposing their bare backs.

As their instructor cracked the whip to loosen his wrist, Juan turned to Sebastian, asking, "Why did you take the blame for me?"

"You have proved yourself to be a worthy opponent after all and…" Before he could continue, the lash of the whip struck Juan in the back producing a red welt on his flesh. Gritting his teeth, Juan did not make a sound. The next lash struck Sebastian's back. He never uttered a sound.

When they each received their ten lashes, they were untied and brought into the dormitory to have their backs attended. Their wounds were soothed with a salve that eased the pain, and then were bandaged. They gingerly put on their shirts and smiled at each other. That day, through their mutual pain, a friendship was forged in blood.

The academy closed for the Christmas holiday and the cadets were released to join their families outside of town on their plantations. For Juan, it was a short trip by horse to his godfather's small and crowded house.

He hadn't seen Mariano Sandoval for months and now he had a burning desire to know about his father. He remembered how, as a small boy, once he had seen other boys with their fathers, he was curious to know why his father was never around. He remembered how his mother reacted to the question, "Where is my father?" She immediately broke down in tears and could hardly get the words out of her mouth "He…he…"

"Never mind, mother," her little son said placing his hand in hers and soothing her emotional breakdown. "It's not important." Juan learned to swallow his emotions to calm his mother's feelings. Still the curiosity never abandoned him.

After his ninth birthday, his mother suddenly passed away. The doctor said it was her age, but Juan knew better. He was convinced she had finally died of a broken heart because of his father. It was at the cemetery that Juan saw the gravestone with his father's name inscribed on it. His mother's casket was lowered into the ground as their son thought, *Now, they are together in heaven.*

When he returned to his godfather's house, he had convinced himself that he needed to have this question finally answered. Juan waited for the evening when his godmother and her sons were soundly sleeping in their bedrooms. Before his godfather could excuse himself for the evening, the young man pulled up a chair to the table by which Sandoval was sitting reading the newspaper by candlelight.

"Godfather," he got his attention.

"What is it, Juan?"

"Tell me about my father." Mariano stared at the young man for a moment.

"I'm sure your mother told you everything she knew."

"She could never answer my question since it would always upset her."

"You mean your sainted mother never told you anything about him?

"No, never."

"I met your father onboard a ship from Cadiz to Cuba. I lived in the town of Arcos de la Frontera, a small town just outside of Cadiz. We sailed west with Hernan Cortez. In time, we were both made captains."

"The Conquistador who defeated the Aztecs?"

"Yes, that's right. Your father and I fought by his side during that campaign." Juan's eyes widened with utter amazement.

"You did?"

"Yes, it was your father who was assigned to defend the Spanish forces from the rear so the others could escape over the causeway."

"He did?"

"Yes, but the Aztecs attacked from all sides and many of our brave men were either killed or drowned in the water, being weighed down with all the loot they had pillaged."

"How did my father escape?"

"He fought his way like a madman, using the sword you carry to strike down any Aztec warrior who challenged him.

"And where were you at this time, godfather?"

"I was fighting back the Aztecs who were trying to cut off our exit from the causeway."

"How did he come to be a general?"

"He was so liked by Cortez that he went to the governor of Cuba and insisted that your father was more than qualified to lead an expedition of his own. That is how your father came to lead a mission here to Guatemala."

"But besides being brave and a great swordsman, what else can you tell me about him?" Mariano debated as to whether he should tell him about his father's mistrust of the church. He decided to leave it buried with his friend.

"He was a good man who was much admired by his men, and after Cortez was finished using your mother as his translator, your father married her. They were very much in love."

"How did my father die?"

"One of the Indian slaves who was working here told your father about a Mayan city named Nakanjo and that gold could be found there. Cesar assigned some men to accompany him to this city. When I volunteered to go with him, he told me to remain behind."

"What happened?"

"Months later, he returned on his own, severely wounded by a blow to his head. As I was going through his things, I found something." Sandoval rose from the table and walked over to the wall where he slid out a loose brick. He pulled out a cloth and returned the brick to its place. Sitting down and unwrapping the cloth, he revealed a four-inch wide gold bracelet studded with emeralds and semi-precious stones and fashioned by a long-dead Mayan artisan. He passed it to Juan.

"My father had this in his possession?"

"He did. When he returned he was incoherent. He never really regained his mind."

"And this bracelet?"

"He never said if he reached Nakanjo, but this bracelet seems to tell me that he did and some great disaster happened there. Most likely, his party was attacked by Indians and they were massacred with only your father surviving."

"*Dios mio!*" he exclaimed passing the bracelet back.

"It is yours now," Mariano said. "I have been saving this to give to his adult son. The time is right!" Juan stared at the gold bracelet which stirred up other questions.

"Do you think this bracelet is from the lost city of Nakanjo?"

"I have to believe it is and that your father lived long enough to bring it back here and give it to you one day."

CHAPTER 18

Two long years of intensive training in horsemanship and with different weapons finally culminated with the cadets graduating the academy. His godfather, Mariano, could not have been any prouder of the young man then if he had been his actual son. The lieutenant's uniform that the cadets received was made of a dark blue cotton material trimmed with bright red cord on the jacket. Juan and Sebastian lined up to hear which battalions they would be assigned to join.

The straight line of the cadets stood at attention in the yard next to the academy as the blistering sun beat down on them mercilessly. In a loud voice the instructor called one name after another alphabetically. The announcer finally called Juan's name. "Juan Cesar de Leon, 8th Battalion!" Juan nearly jumped out of his skin with elation. Jorge la Campo, who had graduated 4 years before, was one of the captains of that battalion. He wanted to yell in delight but the soldiers remained silent and in formation. It wasn't long before he heard, "Sebastian, Marquis de Mancera, 8th Battalion! *This could not have worked out any better. Sebastian and I will be in the same battalion under Jorge. I can't believe my good luck!*

Once every cadet's name was called and assigned, the newly appointed lieutenants at the academy were dismissed for the last time. Sebastian came over to Juan so that they could congratulate each other. "I can't believe our good fortune to be allocated into the 8th Battalion!"

"Why is that good fortune?"

"We will report to Captain de la Campo!"

"And why is that wonderful, Juan?"

"We went to school together and he is a good friend of mine!"

"Then let's celebrate at the tavern!" The two soldiers entered *"El Gato Siesta"*, the local watering hole where most of the male population of the town gathered to drink wine, socialize, and gamble. For Juan, this was his first experience in drinking alcohol.

The bartender came over to the two young men, "What will you have?"

"A bottle of your best Garnacha!"

Juan protested, "I have no money to purchase a bottle."

"Don't worry. My uncle is a most generous man. He sends me a stipend every month. This bottle of wine is on me. Bring it over to the table," Sebastian ordered the bartender. The man behind the bar brought the corked bottle of red wine and two glasses. He stood unmoving for a moment. "Well, open it," commanded Sebastian.

"Put your money on the table first," the man in the wine-stained apron retorted. "I know how you soldiers are, always trying to drink without payment." Sebastian slammed two gold coins on the table.

"Will this cover it?" The proprietor looked at the coins with greedy eyes.

"*Si senor*, here is your wine." The bartender uncorked the bottle and poured the red wine into each glass. "If there is anything more I can do for you gentlemen...

"Go away," rudely responded Sebastian. "We'll call you if we need you!" The bartender moved away as the two soldiers lifted their glasses. "To our glorious futures and financial independence."

"I'll gladly drink to that."

Juan lifted the glass to his lips and sipped. It tasted wonderful. "This is delicious," he proclaimed after he swallowed. Sebastian laughed out loud.

"You've never had alcohol before, have you?"

"What are you talking about?"

"This is your first drink of the grape."

"Not the first," he defended himself.

"Fine," Sebastian replied sarcastically. "Then drink up! We have to finish this bottle." Putting the glass to his lips, he gulped down the contents. "How do you feel?"

"I feel fine."

"Another bottle!" Sebastian called out to the bartender and it arrived without haste when he put two more gold coins on the table. Refilling both glasses, the two soldiers began to drink. It wasn't long before they were slurring their speech and feeling slightly inebriated.

A guitar was heard and before long, a Mestizo woman with bare feet began to dance for the patrons, her multi-colored striped skirt flowing around her body. Juan watched as the Mestizo beauty with hair the color of coffee and cream, lips as red as ripe cherries, and dark eyes that twinkled like the stars in an evening sky, danced closer and closer to him. When the song was over, she made a beeline to Juan and sat on his lap. Juan was shocked at her forwardness. "What is your name, handsome soldier?"

"My…my name is Juan," he stuttered.

"Dios mio! You are a virgin also?" The question made Juan cringe as the other male patrons raucously laughed. Before his companion could respond, the girl on his lap said, "Juanito, my name is Inez. Would you like to come up stairs with me?" She got to her feet and pulled him out of his chair. As she led him to the staircase, a large behemoth of a man with a black moustache and rotted teeth approached and tore the two apart grabbing the girl's arm. "Inez is with me," he shouted with great bravado.

"Get your filthy hands off me, Reynaldo! I am not your woman!"

"Let go of her!" a drunken Juan threatened. Reynaldo looked around at the others laughing raucously.

"And what are you going to do if I don't let her go, Juanito?" he mocked.

"I'll have to thrash you," he warned him. Juan never saw the hairy knuckled fist that crashed into his face. Juan dropped heavily to the floor like a bag of cement.

Juan woke up with a splitting headache as he lifted himself slowly from the floor. Next to him lay the unconscious Sebastian. Juan tried to focus his eyes. Once he did, he realized that they were both in a jail cell. "Sebastian, wake up," he said prodding him with his foot.

The other man groaned as he started to come around. "Where are we?"

"It looks like we've been locked up. Do you remember what happened because my memory is a bit fuzzy at the moment?"

"Don't you recall Inez?"

"I remember her, but not much more after that."

"You had a run-in with a guy called Reynaldo."

"I did?"

124

"Yes, he objected to the two of you being together."

"He did."

"Yes, you threatened him when he wouldn't let the girl go."

"I can't recollect that at all. What happened then?"

"He flattened you."

"He did?"

"And I, as your friend, got up to defend you."

"Thank you."

"Before I knew it, I was laying on the floor next to you."

Before Juan could answer, a loud voice screamed, "Atencion!"

The two soldiers groaned and slowly got to their feet. "Not even in the battalion yet and you've made disgraces of yourselves!" "Unlock the door!" a voice ordered the jailor. "Move out!" The two men marched out as Juan realized it was Captain Jorge la Campo who had raised his voice.

"Jorge, my friend," Juan began. "What happened last night is still very fuzzy to me."

"You will address me as Captain la Campo, Lieutenant. And as far as last night is concerned, I read the report that said the two of you were drunk and got into a fight with another man over a woman. Now move to the stables." Once they had reached their destination, he told them. "Clean out the stables!"

"But there are over a hundred stalls," Sebastian protested.

"That's right, now get to it," Marching away, Jorge left them to their punishment.

CHAPTER 19

There had been restlessness near some of the plantations miles east of San Cristobal by the local Indians. In fact, two of these plantations and haciendas were burned to the ground. The men who had lost their homes, and their neighbor, who thought he would be the next to be attacked, came into the town to petition the Viceroy of New Spain for more protection against these Indian raids.

General Emilio de Bivona, the younger son of the Duke de Bivona was ordered to take his battalions west of the town and put an end to these terrorizations. Immediately, the general called a meeting of his senior officers. "In two days, I will lead two of my battalions east to drive back the Cholti people who had been revolting against local Spaniards. Battalions 7 and 8 will march with me. Gentlemen, get everything in readiness."

The officers of the two battalions came back to the soldiers with their orders. "Men of the 8th Battalion," Captain la Campo announced, "In two days we march east to stop a rebellion by the Cholti people." The men raised their voices enthusiastically in affirmation.

"At last we will be a part of a campaign," Juan whispered to Sebastian.

"Perhaps some gold will be found and confiscated," Sabastian remarked. "Once I get enough, I'll buy a stretch of land, build a home and start a coffee plantation. Then I won't have to beg from my uncle any longer."

"There will be extra training sessions before we leave," the captain instructed. The men gave a collective groan upon hearing that. Three training stints involving battle readiness were held and Captain la Campo oversaw all aspects of the training.

After the first day's morning exercise, Lieutenant de Mancera approached his comrade. "I thought you told me la Campo was a friend of yours?"

"He is. We've known each other since we were boys."

"Well, he doesn't seem friendly to you. In fact, he barely acknowledges you!"

"He is our superior officer and besides, we got off on the wrong foot with him when we wound up in jail!"

"If you go back as many years as you've said, you'd think he could make the effort to be friendlier."

"If we were in his position, we'd do the same thing. He is our superior officer. He can't show us any favoritism."

Two days of drilling and packing food and ammunition prepared them for the third morning's march. Unlike the regular soldiers, all officers, despite their ranks, rode their horses out of San Cristobal. In the back of the ranks marched Indian bearers with the food and equipment. After attending Mass and receiving Communion, the town's population came out to cheer them off.

After a few days marching on dusty roads, the traveling became more hazardous as thoroughfares ended and thick jungle growth appeared. A few of the bearers took out their machetes to cut a wide swath into the green foliage. This forced a slowdown of the movement of the army. The general sent out a reconnaissance party of 20 Indians to help detect where the Cholti villages were located.

A few hours before the sun was to set, the soldiers were halted for the evening to set up camp by a narrow river. Fires were started for warmth during the chilly jungle evenings and to heat their food for the meal. The Indian scouts returned to the encampment to tell the general that the Cholti villages had not been located yet. After the meal, sentries were posted around the camp. Jorge came around to announce the schedule. Two men's names were called along with Sebastian's.

"I'm a lieutenant," Sebastian protested. "I don't get assigned sentry duty!"

"You'll do whatever I tell you to do. De Mantera, you'll take the first shift." Sebastian bristled at the assignment, but didn't say another word about it. "Lieutenant de Leon, you will spell him three hours later." Juan held his tongue. "Now get to your posts!" Those who had been assigned arose from the ground with their firearms and made their way to spots surrounding the camp.

The night was passing in relative peace and quiet. Juan and the others settled down to sleep before they would be awakened for the next shift of sentries. He didn't know how long he was asleep when he was roughly awaked by someone shaking him. "What...what is it?" the slumbering lieutenant asked, half-asleep.

"It's your turn," a fatigued Sebastian announced as he lay down on his blanket. Slowly, Lieutenant de Leon woke the other soldiers who were assigned sentry duty with him. Groggily, they stood erect, their firearms on the ready. Juan listened for the smallest sounds to indicate that they were being approached in the darkness, but only the sounds of nocturnal animals on the prowl could be heard. He marched back and forth struggling to keep himself awake. There were moments when he nodded off, but he always snapped back to attention when he felt himself succumbing to the temptation.

He couldn't tell how long he was out there before the sunlight began to brush away the dark of night. Juan made his way back to the camp where the soldiers had already been roused from sleep and were heating up breakfast. Juan sat down near his friend for *Desayuno,* or the first meal of the day. A plate of Catalan *Pan con Tomate* (bread topped with chopped tomato and drizzled with olive oil) was passed to him. Juan was ravenous and ate heartily. The water from the river helped him to swallow his food.

A blast from a horn meant that camp was to be taken down and the soldiers were to line up and get prepared for that day's march. Once everyone was in place, the Indian scouts were sent out. Mounting his saddled bay-colored Galician-bred steed, Juan kicked it in the flanks to urge it forward. They were led once again by the Indians who used their machetes to clear a path.

The heat of the day was once again upon them and the men sweated uncomfortably in their helmets and chest armor. Swarms of mosquitos tormented both man and beast. The heat and humidity rose in waves from the plant life into the sticky air. The pace of the military advance became increasingly slower and frequent stops were made as the temperature climbed ever higher.

Juan couldn't remember exactly when the first arrow struck its mark, but before anyone knew it, one struck a soldier in the throat. Immediately, there followed a host of other arrows that also found their targets. Swiftly, Captain de la Campo ordered the troops into a protective circle and fired off shots from their harquebus to hold the Cholti warriors back. The officers on horseback with drawn swords charged through the underbrush, scattering the enemy in different directions while the loin clothed, clay-smudged Indians kept firing off barrages of arrows.

Swinging his sword, Juan cut a slash across the chest of an Indian who screamed in pain as he collapsed. Turning his horse around, he watched as an Indian came up behind Jorge's horse and mounted it from the back. With tremendous force, the enemy drove his knife to the side of his chest that was not protected by armor. Screaming at the top of his lungs, Juan spurred his horse, charging the attacker and driving him off into the jungle. "Are you badly hurt?" he yelled out to his captain as the screams of the wounded and dying mixed with the blasts of gunfire that surrounded them. Juan swung his sword mercilessly as each Cholti warrior was cut down or turned away.

"I think I'm alright," but Juan could see that he was faltering in his saddle. He grabbed Jorge's horse bridle and lead him out of the jungle and into the defense circle of the Spanish soldiers.

Then, as quickly as the battle started, it ended. The war whoops of the enemy faded away as the soldiers stopped to check on their comrades. The body count of the dead Cholti warriors numbered over 30. The combined death of soldiers from the 7th and 8th Brigade totaled eight with six wounded including Jorge. Taking the captain from his horse to the ground, Juan quickly began to wad up cloth to stem the flow of blood.

"You saved my life," Jorge gasped from the pain.

"Be quiet so I can finish what I'm doing."

Sebastian came up by horseback asking, "Is he alright?"

"He'll be fine once I'm finished dressing his wound."

The dead soldiers were buried and the wounded were mounted for the trip back to San Cristobal. General Emilio Bivona commanded Juan and a few foot soldiers to start back home while he continued to pursue the fleeing enemy. Sebastian came to his friend, his hand opened to shake his hand. "Be careful!" warned Juan.

"Don't worry about me," his comrade laughed. "I'm like a cat. No matter what the circumstances, I always land on my feet." Mounting their horses, the two groups parted ways.

On the journey back to San Cristobal, two of the wounded soldiers died. They were hurriedly buried and two wooden crosses fashioned from sticks were planted in the soft soil of the mounds. They traveled through the section of the tropical rainforest that had already been cleared away. They would have made better time except for the burials, and the wounded had to be moved slowly.

When they at last arrived in town, the citizens helped the wounded down to be cared for by the local doctors. Juan took his friend to the army surgeon who looked after the officers. Juan gingerly removed Jorge from his horse and he groaned as he was brought into the surgeon's office.

The surgeon helped Juan situate the captain on a table and began to examine the wound. He removed the blood-soaked cloth that had been pressed to the flesh to stop the flow of blood. As the doctor removed it, Jorge moaned. The wound began to bleed a little through the clotted red mass at his side. Jorge had passed out on the table. "You must leave, lieutenant so I can examine the patient."

"Will he be alright?"

"I won't know until I can take a good look at the wound, and I can't do that until you have gone."

"Please send me word about his condition. I will be in the officer's quarters."

"Go now!" was the only reply he received.

Except for a few minor flesh wounds, Juan Cesar de Leon came out of the battle practically unscathed. Calling on his orderly to draw him a bath, he began to strip away his armor and perspiration- soaked clothing. Moaning, he lowered himself into the warm, soothing bath water. Juan closed his eyes and let the sensation carry him away from the last exhausting days. Without realizing it, Juan fell asleep in the comfort of the soothing water. He did not know how long he had slept, but when he awoke, the bath water had become cool.

Washing himself thoroughly, he rose from the water, stepped out of the tub and vigorously dried himself. Dressing in the clean uniform that his orderly had laid out, he waited nervously to hear from the doctor. He did not have too much longer. An Indian messenger came running to look for the lieutenant. "The doctor will see you now." His heart was in his mouth, the temples of his head pounded with pressure as he made his way to the surgeon's office. He found the physician sitting behind his desk. "Doctor, how is Captain de la Campo?" he immediately queried.

"He will recover." Juan breathed a sigh of relief as he sat down. "His wound is deep, and he lost much blood, but the knife did not sever any major arteries or blood vessels. However, some muscle damage was sustained. The captain is a very fortunate man. He will be seeing no action for months until he is fully healed.

"Thanks be to God."

"I'm sure the hand of God was upon him."

"May I see him, now?" The doctor told the Indian who waited outside in the hallway to show the lieutenant the way to the patient. He was guided through the hospital entrance where numerous cots were sectioned off by white linen curtains. Some of the cots were occupied by sick soldiers, but most of them were empty. Parting the curtains, the Indian let Juan in and returned to the surgeon's office. Jorge was half asleep and looked as white as a sheet. He was unsure as to whether to awaken him when suddenly Jorge opened his eyes.

"Juan, my friend, I'm glad that you have come." The lieutenant sat down next to the cot.

"How are you feeling?"

"It's painful, but the doctor assures me that I will recover in time."

"I thank God that I got to you in time before that savage could do you more harm."

"You saved my life."

"I did nothing more than anyone else would have done."

"You came to my rescue even after the way I have been treating you."

"I am your friend. I've never forgotten that."

"When General de Bivona returns, I am recommending that you be appointed a captain."

"Jorge that is not..."

131

"Do not argue with a sick man," he smiled. "My mind is made up!"

"I will leave you now so that you can get some sleep. I'll come back to see you later."

"Thank you again, Juan."

Lieutenant de Leon's footsteps seemed quicker and lighter, and his mood was much brighter than it had been just minutes before.

CHAPTER 20

Four days later, the army under General Emilio de Bivona marched back into San Cristobal and straight to the fort where the barracks were located. The ranks were somewhat thinned out as they transported the wounded with them.

With the other soldiers and officers, Juan waited at the gate to see if his friend was still alive. His eyes scanned the mounted officers, but he could not detect Sebastian anywhere. As the last captain rode through the portal, the lieutenant snapped to attention, saluted and inquired, "Is Lieutenant Sebastian de Mancera alive, sir?"

"You'll find him among the wounded," the officer related as he rode off. *Thank the Blessed Mother that he is still alive!* Running off to the hospital, Juan came upon the wounded who were being given a cursory look by the doctor. "Bring him in to the surgery room," he heard the doctor announce to the Indian orderlies. Juan looked at the face as they carried him in. It wasn't Sebastian.

From his left, a voice could be heard, "Juan!" The young man turned to see Sebastian, who had been laid in the shade of the building until the doctor could see him. Rushing over, Juan could see the remnants of a broken arrow still embedded in de Mancera's left thigh. "Are you alright?" he inquired as he gripped the patient's hand with a firm handshake.

"I'll live," the wounded man said sarcastically.

"What happened?"

"We were betrayed, Juan!"

"Betrayed! How?"

"The bearers who were scouting for the Cholti for us instead gave them our position and we sustained another sneak attack!"

"Is that how you obtained your wound?"

"No, we were able to drive them back once more but we sustained many losses."

"Were you able to run the enemy down?"

"The general ordered an attack and before too long we came upon the Cholti village." Sebastian took a moment to grit his teeth in pain before he continued his story.

"What occurred then?"

"They fought like devils once we had them in their own village. They did not flee so they could protect their families. That's when one of them shot me in the thigh, but that did not stop me!"

"What did you do?"

"We used their fire pits to light up reeds and throw them on the thatched roofs of their houses. They burned as bright as roman candles."

"And the people?"

"We put every man, woman, and child to the sword. No one was left alive and the village was burned to the ground. They'll never attack and deprive a Spaniard of his home anymore!" The doctor appeared and bent over Sebastian to examine his wound.

"Bring him inside for surgery." The porters did what they were told.

"I'll come to see you soon," called Juan as his friend was carried away. As he returned to the barracks, he thought, *Although the bearers had been Christianized they still turned on us when they had the chance.* He watched the Indian residents as they moved about the town. *How many of them would turn on us before too long?* The possibility of an Indian revolt within San Cristobal made him uncomfortably upset.

The morning was blessed with less heat since cloudy skies held off the intensity of the sun. The humidity clung like a leech, draining the life out of everything it adhered to. By early afternoon, the officers and cadets of the academy stood erect and in perfect formation on the parade field.

The sky grew increasingly grayer as the predictable afternoon rainfall creeped closer. As the horns resounded in unison, General Emilio Bivona marched out with his military aides and entourage until he stood in front of the gathered men.

Juan tried to keep his eyes locked straight ahead, but finally he shifted his eyes around trying to discover whether his godfather was among the other amassed townspeople anticipating the coming event, but he could not see him. Another trilling of the horns and five officers stepped out in front of their fellow compatriots. These five officers had been recommended and approved to receive medals and a promotion in rank because of their actions in battling the Cholti.

The first two officers were called up by name, received a red sash and medal and were given their new commission. "Lieutenant Juan Cesar de Leon!" the officer reading names from the scroll announced. Juan snapped his heels together and with a steady cadence made his way to a point where he faced the general. De Bivona took a red sash from his camp-de-aide and slipped it over the lieutenant's head and arm. Another officer handed the general a silver and gold medal shaped like a starburst and pinned it on the jacket. "Lieutenant Juan Cesar de Leon, for bravery in the field by saving your captain from certain death, you are now commissioned as Captain! Congratulations!" Shaking his hand and kissing both Juan's cheeks, Captain Juan Cesar de Leon saluted and returned to the ranks of assembled men. As he marched back, he saw Jorge, his arm in a sling and Sebastian standing with the help of a cane.

Two other officers followed Juan after which the ceremony was concluded and the men dismissed. Jorge and Sebastian came to congratulate their friend, but Juan was distracted by looking to find Mariano Sandoval. Suddenly, his godfather's grinning face emerged from the crowd. His godson had never noticed the gray hairs that were now crowning his cranium and the wrinkles that crinkled his face. "Juan my boy, felicitations on your new commission!" He shook his hand heartily.

"Gracias, Padrino."

"Your father and mother would be very proud of you today."

"My wife has prepared a sumptuous feast for this happy occasion. Come home with me."

"We better hurry because the skies are ready to open up!" Halfway to the house, the clouds burst and the rain poured down in sheets. Thunder grumbled and crashed while lightning darted in crooked lines like scars across the sky.

When they reached the hacienda, they were both soaked and laughing. Sancha, Mariano's wife, scolded them for getting wet. "Dry yourselves off and come to the table." Sancha kissed Juan in greeting as they all sat around eating and chatting. Their 17-year old son Cesar was hoping to be recommended to the academy next year and his two younger brothers, Julio and Bartolome, sat next to their father. Glasses of wine toasted the newly appointed captain as they all ate hungrily.

While the rest of the family went off into their bedrooms for a siesta, Mariano and Juan stayed to talk. "It goes without saying that I am very proud of you. In fact, in many ways I consider you to be my son."

"And I see you like a father, *Padrino*."

"You have a brilliant career ahead of you, Juanito," he said affectionately. "But..." Mariano hesitated.

"Is something wrong?"

"No, nothing's wrong, but I need to breach a topic with you."

"What is that?"

"You are 22 and not married." Juan had never thought about taking a woman to be his wife. "It is time you settled down and have a family as I do."

"I am still young and have plenty of time."

"An officer with a wife and family moves up the ranks much quicker and easier, Juan. This is a fact."

"I have much more to accomplish before I find a girl to marry."

"And what must you do before marriage?" Juan moved closer to his godfather.

"I want to find the lost city of Nakanjo as my father did." Getting out of his chair, Juan walked over to the loose brick and took out the wrapped object, bringing it to the table. He uncovered the bracelet and stared at its luster and radiance. "I will become rich and build a large hacienda and plantation first before I think of marrying!" Mariano watched as his godson talked.

"I have seen this before," he warned.

"Seen what?"

"I've seen that look before." Puzzled, the young man responded, "What are you talking about?"

"The lust for gold and treasures."

"I don't have any look," the captain answered defensively.

"I have seen it too many times and in too many eyes to be mistaken about it."

"You are wrong!"

"I saw it in the eyes of Cortez and his soldiers who tried to escape from Tenochtitlan and all of our men who stuffed as much booty in their clothing and saddlebags and when they were thrown in the water were weighed down and sank to the bottom of the lake."

"I am not like them!"

"I saw the same look in your father's eyes when he learned about Nakanjo."

"Unlike my father, I will succeed in finding the city and bringing back its wealth."

"His greed led him to an early grave. I'm afraid for you, Juanito. I don't want you winding up in the same cemetery in ignominy like your father."

"It will be different for me. I'll succeed where he failed, you'll see," he answered passionately. "I'm tired now. I think I'll get some sleep." Replacing the bracelet behind the brick, Juan went to his bedroom leaving his godfather alone at the table. *Somehow, I must dissuade Juan from following the same course as his father. It will only end in disaster.*

Five years had passed and even though he hadn't initially agreed with his godfather, Juan Cesar de Leon had been promoted to a Major and now turned his eyes toward settling down. At the age of 27, Juan had distinguished himself once more in the Indian Wars, driving back an English expeditionary force looking to oust the Spanish from San Cristobal. The city had grown and spread out tremendously and grew rich from the trade of coffee and sugar exported to the Mother Country.

With some of his savings, the Major purchased an abandoned coffee plantation, miles from the city. Purchasing Indian slaves, Juan had been able to earn enough to transform the once decrepit hacienda into a vibrant home once again.

It was his godfather who kept insisting that he must take a bride and have a family that would secure and continue his bloodline into the next generation. With great enthusiasm, Mariano suggested one young Mestizo woman after another from prominent town members. Juan declined them over and over for some reason or another. This time Mariano Sandoval arrived at Juan's home with a name he was not going to let his godson refuse.

"Come inside, Padrino and refresh yourself," he greeted Mariano who alit from his horse. The two men walked in as his godfather brushed off the dust of the road from his clothing.

"It is hot today," Sandoval commented.

"Yes, but I have a bottle of Rioja waiting for us inside." Both men settled in the drawing room as an Indian servant poured the wine. "You have done a beautiful job restoring this house and plantation," mentioned his godfather looking around.

"It took a few years, but now the plantation is finally turning a profit."

"I can see that through your fine furnishings." Juan smiled with satisfaction. "Yet…"

"What is wrong?"

"Yet there is something missing that would turn this house into a home."

"You are not going to bring up my marriage again are you?"

"This time I bring with me a name you cannot possibly find any fault with."

"And who would that be?" he answered with some skepticism.

"She is the second daughter of Severino Espinal. Her name is Pilar."

"Espinal, who owns one of the largest sugar plantations of the town?"

"The very same."

"And his daughter, is she less than fair of face?"

"On the contrary, she is rumored to be a great beauty."

"Rumored? Hasn't anyone seen her before this?"

"Her father has been very protective about keeping Pilar at home."

"What makes you so sure her father would want me as a son-in-law?"

"I have brought your name up to him as a possible suitor. Severino was very interested." Juan sat back in his chair to ponder the suggestion.

"I don't know."

"Don't be a fool! He is one of the wealthiest men in the colony. Severino told me that he has been following your military exploits for some time and admires your speedy rise in the ranks. A joining of the two families would be very desirable for both of you."

"I cannot say that it's not one of the more intriguing offers you have brought me. And you have seen this Pilar for yourself?"

"In passing."

"What does that mean?"

"It means that I went over to Severino to try and broker this arrangement, and while I was there, he introduced me to his daughter. You are expected to be there tomorrow afternoon for an introduction."

"You arranged for the two of us to meet without asking me?"

"There is no use in going on and on. The meeting has been set, and you will be there!"

"But..."

"Do not argue with me. It is done and you will go!"

The afternoon was hot, but Juan was sweating not only because of the heat. He had debated sending a message to the Espinal Plantation begging off from the arranged appointment, but his godfather had been so adamant about the meeting, he knew he would have to face Mariano's anger. *It's just not worth it!* Juan was attired in his dress uniform with the medals pinned to the jacket.

His horse galloped off at an easy pace. *There's no use pushing this animal hard in this heat.* The ride was dusty, but the Major did not notice it. All his thoughts were of Pilar Espinal and how he could find an excuse for him to leave early.

After about an hour, he approached the plantation. Over to the distant right, he glanced at black slaves cutting down sugar cane with machetes. As he approached the hacienda's white-washed stucco walls and orange-tiled roof, an Indian waited outside to take his horse. A female Indian waited on the porch saying, "Please follow me. Senor Espinal is expecting you."

He followed her through the lavishly decorated rooms into Espinal's den. The older gentleman with a mane of white hair stood erect as he extended his hand to Juan. "It is a pleasure to meet you, Senor Espinal."

"It is an honor to meet one of the men who distinguished himself in the great victory of the Battle of the Gulf of Honduras against the English. Please, have a seat."

"Thank you, Senor."

"May I offer you some wine?"

"No thank you." Severino poured himself a glass and sat down opposite the major.

"I must say that I was very pleased when your godfather approached me with the idea of a possible connection between our two families."

"Yes, my *Padrino* was very happy too."

"My daughter Pilar is a rare flower, Major de Leon."

"I'm sure that she is."

"She has been educated by the Sisters of the Franciscan Order in *El convento Trinidad Santisima* where she learned to speak Latin and French. Pilar has a beautiful singing voice and can weave wonderful tapestries. I have been approached by many men who asked for her hand in marriage, but until now, I have never given my consent."

"I am honored that you have agreed to see me." *My God, how will I ever get out of this!*

"Please Major de Leon, let me escort you out into the garden where my wife and daughter are waiting for you."

Severino accompanied him up to the iron garden gate, opened it and closed the portal once Juan was inside. He turned to the owner of the plantation asking, "Where will I find your wife and daughter?"

"Follow the path and the sound of the fountain. Once you reach it you will see them anticipating your arrival. Good day."

"The same to you, Senor Espinal."

Juan did as he was instructed passing red hibiscus flowers on trees and a variety of fragrant colored roses. As he turned the corner, the sound of the water splashing into the fountain grew louder. There, on a bench, sat two women. One had white hair and was dressed in a matronly black gown and black-laced mantilla that covered her hair. She whiffed herself furiously with her fan. The other shocked him with her beauty. She was dressed modestly in a pink gown. When she looked up at Juan, he felt as if he had exploded into a million stars. Her mother stood up as he approached. "Good day, Senora Espinal." Juan took the older woman's hand and kissed it.

"Good day, Major de Leon," she answered indifferently. "I will be chaperoning my daughter during your visit," she explained.

"Of course, Senora. I understand completely." Her mother sat across from them on another bench. Juan took his place next to the demure Pilar.

"Not so close," her mother warned him. "Propriety, one must show propriety!"

"Perdoname!" He shifted away from the young woman. Pilar held her fan covering her mouth so that Juan could not see her smile.

"Buen dia se pierda."

"Buen dia," she replied in return.

"You are so lovely," he announced staring at her ebony hair and getting lost in her deep brown eyes.

"Nada de eso," the chaperone cautioned. "Do not get too personal in your remarks toward my daughter."

"Si, Senora."

"Are you alright," Pilar questioned. "You appear to be a little warm."

"It is warm today, isn't it?"

"Yes, but it is pleasant here in the garden, is it not?"

"Very pleasant."

"The splash of the water is cooling and the sweet fragrance of roses permeates the air." Juan was sure it wasn't the scent of roses that was making him lightheaded, but Pilar's scent that caused his feeling of vertigo.

"Your father tells me that you speak fluent Latin and French."

"Quod est verum," she replied in perfect Latin.

"I'm very impressed."

"Merci monsieur," she responded, fluttering her fan by her face. Suddenly, her mother stood up.

"It was very nice that you came for a visit, Major de Leon, but now it's time for my daughter's siesta." As if on cue, Pilar stood as Juan followed suit.

"It has been a great pleasure to meet you, Senorita Espinal."

"I enjoyed our talk."

"Come now," her mother stated sternly. "We must go in!" As he watched the enchanting girl leaving, he told himself, *That is the woman I will marry.*

CHAPTER 21

Major Juan Cesar De Leon peered at himself in the mirror in his bedroom. He brushed off some lint on his military uniform then strapped his grandfather's sword on his hip. *There, I believe that I'm ready now.* He walked into the parlor where two men sat with glasses of wine.

"Come," said Major Jorge de la Campo. "I've poured you a drink."

"Yes," added Captain Sebastian de Macera. "It will help to calm your nerves."

"Strange as it may seem, I already feel calm, but I'll drink anyway."

"To your upcoming marriage," Sebastian toasted, his glass held aloft.

"And to all the sons you will be having," Jorge chortled. Juan clicked his glass to the other two and all three downed the libation.

"We better get going," Jorge reminded them. "You don't want to be late."

The three men walked outside where a carriage was waiting. As the driver opened the door for Juan to enter, his two friends mounted their horses. Climbing into his seat, the driver flicked the reins and the two horses trotted forward.

Juan watched from the window as they passed the jungle foliage. His thoughts drifted to the time when he was a boy, living with his mother in an impoverished life. *How life has changed for me.* He thought about the man who helped him achieve what he had at this point. *Mariano Sandavol took me in when I had nobody else when my mother died. It was he who brought me to the academy and to the one who is now going to be my wife. I owe him so much for all that he's done for me.*

As the carriage and two mounted officers moved through the countryside, the closer they got to the city of San Cristobal, the more they saw signs of civilization. Plantations were more frequently spotted where the black slaves were bending and moving as they labored. As they drew near to the town, a cacophony of sounds assaulted his ears.

The carriage drew up to *La Iglesia del Anuncio* which had completed construction the year before. At the bottom of the cathedral, dressed for the occasion, stood his proud godfather. When Juan got out of the carriage, Mariano approached the young man. "This is indeed a special day my son!" he said beaming from ear to ear.

"I owe it all to you, *Padrino!*" They hugged each other warmly. They turned and entered the house of worship with Sebastian and Jorge trailing them.

The interior of the cathedral was bedecked with fragrant local flowers which intermingled with the smell of sweet incense. The sun streaming through the windows lit up the stained-glass transoms that reflected the stories of the miracles performed by Jesus.

After greeting Sancha and her three sons, who were sitting in one of the pews, Mariano joined his family as the groom and his groomsmen went through a door by the altar to a small room where they could wait until the ceremony began. Juan couldn't sit, he was getting jittery. "Are you alright?" asked Jorge.

"I'm fine, but a little nervous!"

"This is the easy part," Sebastian suggested. "Tonight will be the real test!" The three men laughed at the comment.

"Not to worry, my friend. I'm no longer the innocent who got drunk, wound up fighting in a bar and spending the night in a jail cell." As the talked, the cathedral began to fill with guests.

A door opened and in walked an elderly Brother Tomas who would be performing the ceremony. All three men stood in his presence. For Juan, there came flooding back the stories of his father and his doomed quest to locate the lost city. "Are you prepared my son to receive the sacrament of marriage?"

"I am, Brother." Two Mestizo altar boys came back to hand Brother Tomas his vestments for the marriage ceremony. Once he had finished, he told the three to take their places before the altar. Juan gazed out at the worshipers. He saw a sea of familiar faces. With his two friends by his side, the organ, which had been brought over from Spain, began to play. The sound of the sacred music reverberated within the religious edifice.

Juan noticed a flurry of activity from the back of the church. "She's coming," he whispered to him compadres. From afar, he caught sight of the lace and organza white wedding gown and Pilar's face hidden by a veil. By her side stood her grinning father Severino.

As the wedding march began, his daughter placed her hand in the crook of her father's arm as they walked slowly down the aisle. Father and daughter passed the invited guests who whispered to each other what a lovely bride Pilar made. Kissing his daughter, Severino joined his wife in the pew. Juan walked over to his future wife's side. And, the Mass began.

After the exchanging of vows and slipping on wedding bands, Brother Tomas finished the ceremony, saying, *"Puede besar a la novia."* Lifting her veil, Juan saw her face for the first time that day. *She has the features of an angel!* Leaning in, he kissed her enthusiastically. The congregation clapped their hands vigorously.

The couple moved down the aisle receiving the congratulations of all who were attending. At last, they walked into the sunlight. The guests were invited back to the Espinal hacienda where food, drink, and entertainment were provided. The merriment went on into the night. Finally, Juan suggested that he take Pilar back to her new home. She nodded her assent.

Saying goodbye to the guests, Pilar's mother bawled as her daughter departed. On the way home in the carriage, the newly married couple talked. "I know what I am offering you is not as great as what you have been used to in your father's home, but…"

"I love you, not what you have," Pilar whispered to him and kissed him fully on the lips. Juan's body responded.

"I promise to you that this is just the beginning of our life as wealthy plantation owners."

"I know that you will keep that promise." She laid her head on his shoulder. Juan looked out the window and dreamed. *I have a fine house, a profitable plantation, a commission as a Major and my beautiful Pilar. I have everything that I could want…almost.*

In the decade that passed, Juan's promise to his wife was nearly fulfilled. Their hacienda was expanded to accommodate the four children Pilar had given her husband over the years.

Three daughters and a son were the light of the parents' eyes. Carlotta, the oldest who was nine, was most like her mother in beauty and temperament. Fair of face and sweet, who doted on her father. Leticia, the second born was eight and full of life. She was flirty and high spirited and would do anything on a dare. Her coloring was more like her father's, olive skinned. Tito, their only son who was seven, was a reserved and reverent boy who liked to spend his time praying in the family chapel, and who possessed an even disposition. He had a mass of curly black hair that reminded Juan of Pilar's father, Severino. The last child, Paloma, three years old, was a loving child who followed her mother everywhere. Her father nicknamed her, *La Sombra,* because like a shadow, she was never far away from Pilar.

With the expansion of the *Hacienda de Leon,* so too were the coffee fields enlarged as well as the number of slaves that worked in the fields. Juan had managed to weave his way into the fabric of San Cristobal's upper echelon of society. His export of coffee back to Spain also brought with it luxurious goods that ornamented his home and expensive jewelry that adorned his wife's neck and wrist. His godfather had given him the golden bracelet years before.

The year before, his godfather Mariano Sandoval had died after being thrown from his horse. His godson was devastated by the news. Sancha was in a desperate way for the money that Juan supplemented. Her oldest son Cesar, was now a lieutenant in the army while Bartolome was studying for the priesthood.

Three years earlier, while Pilar was in her last month of pregnancy with Paloma, Severino Espinal suffered a severe stroke that took away his ability to speak and walk. Pilar's grief was so deep that she gave birth to their last daughter a month before she was due. Severino was now being cared for in the hospital by the *Hermanas de la Misericordia* or Sisters of Mercy. Her mother, who watched her husband continually decline, died of a broken heart after realizing he would never recover. Pilar thought it best not to mention this to her father. Once a week, she went to visit her father who was well cared for, but over time, he lost another piece of his memory until he no longer recognized his daughter.

As time passed, San Cristobal grew from a rural town to a city metropolis. The fort was enlarged as the city expanded and the walls that once encircled the town had been demolished as the city grew in population and buildings. Juan wondered what his father would think if he saw the city he had founded. *I'm sure he'd be amazed.*

Juan was decommissioned from the military as a general and had served some time on the city council. As a result, he won many influential and wealthy friends. For each of his children, he had thrown lavish celebrations after their christenings. The names of guests were of the powerbrokers in government, the military, and the church. For any other man, life would seem satisfying. But not for Juan.

Even though his family name was highly regarded, he could not dismiss the blot of shame he thought counteracted everything he had accomplished. Unlike the names, *Cortez and Pizarro* which lived on because of the successful campaigns against the Aztec and Inca, the name de Leon held no such regard. His father's exploits of finding the lost city of Nakanjo had ended in disaster. All that was left of that expedition was the dusty tombstone with his father's name inscribed. After years of not thinking about it, his leisure time was inflamed with the yearning to succeed where his father had failed. "Pilar," he said one day. "I need to talk to you."

"What is it my husband?" she replied with curiosity.

"The plantation is running very smoothly and we are making quite a profit." Pilar thought it strange that he was discussing business with her, something he had never done before.

"I am glad to hear it."

"And the household performs like a well-run timepiece, thanks to you my dear."

"Thank you, Juan."

"And yet something disturbs me."

"Tell me what bothers you, my husband."

"Even with all the accolades I have received in my lifetime, still something is missing."

"And what is that?"

"My father's name has the blemish of disappointment on it for many years."

"In what way, Juan?"

"His expedition to the lost city of Nakanjo ended in disaster with a loss of men and money, as well as my father's reputation."

"What are you saying?"

"I wish to begin another search for the city."

"But Juan, we don't even know if this city ever actually existed." Walking over to his desk, Juan unlocked the middle draw and withdrew a cloth. Unwrapping it in front of his wife, Juan put the bracelet in her hand. "Where did you get this?" she inquired as her eyes were fixed upon the piece of jewelry.

"My godfather removed it from inside my father's clothing when he reappeared in town badly wounded."

"But what does this prove?"

"It proves that he reached Nakanjo! Here is the definite proof that it once existed!" Pilar asked nervously,

"What do you plan on doing?"

"I'm thinking of finding the city myself and restoring my father's reputation."

"My husband, you would leave your wife and children behind in the hope of this city's discovery?"

"It is the one thing I still have to accomplish." Pilar did not answer but prayed that she could dissuade him from following his aspiration.

As the decades passed, the bond of friendship between Juan, Sebastian, and Jorge grew stronger.

Jorge de la Campo eventually was decommissioned as Major General and married a rich merchant's daughter. His father-in-law owned a fleet of ships that plied the waters of the Atlantic Ocean from San Cristobal, Guatemala to Cadiz, Spain. With the wealth he had been able to accumulate, Jorge had a large and luxurious hacienda built for his family that was not far from the city. He had three children, all sons, who had followed their father into the military. The years of inactivity after serving in the army had left Jorge paunchy but there was still the twinkle in his eye when all three friends talked about the good old days.

Sebastian de Mancera had broken ties with his uncle the Marquis de Mancera and was now his own man. Sebastian had decided to make military service his life. As a Senior General in the Spanish army, he owned a beautiful hacienda outside of the city. His pension was large enough to live the good life. For the sake of propriety, he took a wife, a local doctor's daughter, who was thrilled to be married to a great military officer, but they never had any children. Sebastian had not changed very much physically. He was still very much enamored with his public appearance which included the numerous medals he wore proudly on his military jacket. All three had something in common - thin and graying hair.

Now in their late 40's, they got together a few times a week, meeting at each other's homes to catch up with what was going on in their lives, share a bottle of wine, and to look back at their lives together. "It doesn't seem so long ago we were all young bucks starting off at the academy, does it?" reminisced Jorge.

Sebastian sipped at his wine, replying, "No, not so long ago. May I tell you that I miss those days."

"Why is that?" queried Juan.

"It was the thrill of not knowing what you were going to face every day, the adventure of living," answered Sebastian.

"My life has become rather mundane," complained Jorge. "It's the same thing day after day. The repetitiveness is driving me slowly insane."

For years, Pilar had continuously talked him out of his dream of finding the lost city, and for her sake and those of his children, he put his dream up on a shelf until it lay there in his head, dusty and almost forgotten. Now it suddenly sprang back to life. "What if I were to tell you that adventure for us is just within our reach?"

Jorge took a gulp of the red wine before he replied, "What are you talking about? What adventure?"

Before he answered, Juan rose from his chair, walked over to his desk and took out a key from his vest pocket. Unlocking a drawer, he brought over a covered object. He uncovered it and held it out to the others.

"*Dios mio!* Where did you get this?" The bracelet still reflected the bright sunlight while the emeralds and semi-precious stones shone brilliantly as if it had just been crafted. Jorge took it into his hand and examined it.

"I can tell that this is not something that has been handcrafted by any European artisan. How did you obtain this piece of jewelry?"

"What if I were to tell you that it belonged to my father." Sebastian insisted on knowing,

"Where did he get it?"

"My godfather found it in my father's clothing when he stumbled back from an exploration to find the Mayan city of Nakanjo."

Sitting back in his chair, Sebastian laughed and said, "Nakanjo is just a legend, a story people repeat around a campfire when they're making up tall tales."

"Sebastian is right! It is a child's story of a lost city that contains great wealth. It's a figment of somebody's active imagination." Juan voice became serious.

"Then how do you explain this?" he pointed toward the bracelet.

"There's no doubt that it's beautiful but there's no way to tell if this comes from Nakanjo," reasoned Jorge.

"My father led an expedition years ago, to find the city. He was the only one to come back alive. A little while later, he died of his wounds. I believe that he and the members of his party were attacked because they came too close to the lost city."

"I'm sorry about your father," sympathized Sebastian, "but it is said that he was delirious once he reached San Cristobal. Perhaps he was just raving due to the blow to the back of his head." Juan stiffened with indignity toward the remark. Covering the object, he returned it to his desk drawer and locked it once more, his anger rising, "I show my two friends proof that the city of Nakanjo exists and you scoff at the idea!"

"Listen, my friend," Jorge began. "We're not saying that your father was lying, but that perhaps he was out of his mind."

"What further proof do you need to be convinced?" His two friends looked at each other before Sebastian spoke up.

"Someone will need to find the city and show us its wealth before we can believe your father's story."

"I'm sorry Juan, but I feel the same way," concluded Jorge.

"What if I were to tell you that I'm considering putting together my own expedition to Nakanjo?" De Mancera answered without missing a heartbeat. "Then I would tell you that you are going on a fool's mission."

"Juan," counseled Jorge. "Why would you go and waste your time and money?"

"To reclaim my family's honor!"

"You have brought great integrity to your family's name. There is no need for you to go on this foolhardy exploration to prove anything," advised Jorge.

"The two of you are my friends, but the way you have spoken about my father is the way he has been defamed since he returned to this city. I will not rest until his reputation is restored."

CHAPTER 22

No matter how many times Pilar begged him or showed him how imprudent his plan was, Juan could not be persuaded against his plan. "What of your wife and children?" she confronted him.

"My business will take care of you, and as for my children, they are grown and living their own lives."

"But a man of your age cannot just go into the rainforest and hope to come back alive, not at this point of your life!"

"I am only 51 and still as vital a man as when I was younger. Nothing will happen to me except that I will return to you with my family's honor intact."

"Even Sebastian and Jorge are convinced that this is something you should forget about for your own good."

"They mean well, but they can't understand what is in my heart."

"Most of our children have tried to change your mind."

"They have their lives to live and so do I."

"Has the governor given you his blessing for this exploration?"

"I have talked to him and he has agreed that I can go if I muster enough men who want the thrill of an adventure and discovery." Pilar for the first time saw some hope that this expedition would never get started. *Who would agree to go on such an exploration?*

"I doubt that you'll be able to find a full contingent of men to follow you."

"On the contrary, I've had to turn some volunteers away because there are just too many who are eager to go with me."

Pilar was emotionally crushed by this statement. "Then you are going ahead with your plan?"

"As soon as I am able to." Pilar walked away not willing to let her husband see her tears of anxiety and frustration. *I will no longer try to change his mind.* She walked into the family chapel to pray.

It was Juan's only son Tito who had agreed with his father's decision to locate Nakanjo. As a second-year cadet at the academy, Tito had approached his father as soon as he heard his plan.

One afternoon while Tito was visiting home, he sat down with his father. Juan looked at his son and saw himself in his progeny. *I was about his age when I got drunk and was thrown into jail with Sebastian.* A fleeting smile crossed his lips. "Have I told you how pleased I am with you, son?"

"Thank you, father. All I want is to make you proud of me."

"Then you have fulfilled your wish."

"I came to talk to you about your expedition, father."

"Please Tito! If you've come to tell me that I'm too old or that I'm wasting my time and fortune, I've already heard it from more people then I care to think about. I have listened enough to the naysayers. I have no wish to hear more, especially from my son."

"I am not here to try and divert you from your dream."

"Then why are we having this conversation?"

"I want to go with you." Juan looked tenderly into his young son's eyes.

"You are not seasoned enough, my son. You lack the experience of a soldier to go on this expedition."

"Father, you will need me."

"And how is that?"

"These other men you have chosen have volunteered for only one reason, to get their hands on the gold and riches of Nakanjo. They are untrustworthy!"

"Why do you say that?"

"Greed turns men into dogs who are willing to attack each other for a bone. They are no better than rabid mongrels. You will see. First, they will turn on each other, and then they'll turn on you."

"I know these men. Each of them has been highly decorated."

"Father, take me along! I can protect your back. I too want to see our family name reestablished with honor as it should be."

"Your mother is already in a state of apprehension at my leaving. She would be in the throes of depression if she were to hear that you wanted to go too."

"Your dream is my dream. Together we will have the name de Leon honorable once again." Juan could not argue with his son about what he declared. Although he wanted to turn his son away, he could not find a reason to deny his request.

"If your reasons are truly what you have averred, then I welcome you."

"Thank you, father. You won't regret it, but how are we going to convince mother?"

"Leave that to me. I'll find a way.

"No!" she screamed at her husband. "You can't!" Juan tried to take her into his arms to comfort her, but Pilar would have none of it and pushed him away.

"He asked to go and I told him that he was too young and inexperienced."

"Yes, all of that is correct!"

"But then he told me something that really changed the way I was thinking about it."

"What was that?" she demanded of him.

"Tito also wants our family name esteemed and brought back to its rightful place in our community."

"All he is doing is parroting what you have told him all of his life. They are not his words but yours."

"I believe," Juan declared in a calm voice, "that these words come straight from his heart."

"You have lost your mind! I will never accept the fact that he will leave the academy to join you in this irrationality."

"He will not be out of the academy forever. Once we discover Nakanjo, he will continue his military training."

"Now I know you're crazy. You will lead him to an early grave."

"You are losing control of your emotions!" Juan warned his wife. "Have a little decorum for God's sake!"

"Our son's blood will be on your hands. May God forgive you because I never will!"

"You're hysterical Pilar! I can't talk to you when you're like this!"

"I will go to Tito and tell him that I refuse to give my permission for him to go with you on this reckless mission, this dangerous fantasy that you've concocted in your head!"

"You can go to him, but he will not back down. He is determined to come and will not hear a word against it."

"We'll see about that!" she yelled as Pilar walked away from him and out the door of their hacienda.

"Where are you going?"

"I'm going to talk to Tito right now!"

"He's at his classes and should not be disturbed." Pilar ignored her husband's advice and sent for the carriage to be brought around to the front door. As she was helped up, he yelled, "I forbid you to go!"

"To the academy," she instructed her driver and the carriage moved down the road.

She arrived at the academy and the driver helped her down. She walked into the building as the students were being instructed in swordsmanship. The instructor called a halt to the lesson as soon as he noticed her in the doorway. "Senora," he addressed her. "Women are not allowed inside the academy."

"This is an emergency! I must speak to my son Tito de Leon!" Immediately, all the other cadets looked toward the young man.

"Go!" the instructor bellowed at him, "But make it quick, Senora. I do not like my classes interrupted!"

"Mother," he scolded her once they were both outside. "You shouldn't be here!"

"I'm here to reprimand you!" she remarked turning the table on him. Tito suddenly knew exactly why she was there."

"If you've come here thinking that you could change my mind about going with my father, you've wasted your time."

"I forbid you from going!" Pilar said with an irate expression.

"I'm sorry, mother but if father says I can go then I'm doing just that!" She slapped him hard across the face. The shock of her action was expressed in her son's face.

"Go then, and break your mother's heart!"

"Goodbye, mother. I must get back to class." Pilar entered the carriage and sobbed all the way home.

Reports swirled around the city about the impending expedition that was being put together to search for the fabled city of Nakanjo. Many young men, eager to make their fortunes, went to Juan to plead their cases as to why they should be included, but Juan politely and forcefully turned them away.

One morning, Tito visited his father's hacienda to talk about strategies. Pilar refused to talk to either one of them once they insisted that they were bound and determined to go. Tito had questioned about some of his fellow cadets at the military academy. "They are too young and would be too difficult to control," he stated to his son.

"Then what types are you looking for, father?"

"Experienced soldiers are a priority Tito, but also they must be men who will follow orders and not challenge me. A limit of 20 men will be enough to be able to feed them reasonably, otherwise the group size would be too unruly."

"But how will you know what direction to take once we're in the rainforest?"

"From the stories my godfather told me, I think I have a pretty good idea."

"But father, we could be wandering around the jungle aimlessly for who knows how long and still not be able to find it." Juan shrugged not knowing how to answer him.

"I may have an answer to our dilemma," Tito suggested.

"What do you mean?" his father inquired. Tito rose from the chair and stepped outside. He began to wave someone over. Next to his son appeared an old Indian in a straw sombrero. Taking him by the arm, Tito led him inside. Politely, the Indian took off his hat. Looking at him, Juan thought he had seen him before somewhere.

"Father, this is *"El Viejo"*, the old one as he is known around the academy." Although the Indian appeared to be aged, no one knew exactly the number of years he had spent on this earth.

"Yes. Yes," his father reacted. "I knew I had seen you somewhere, but now that I recall it, you worked at the academy cleaning up when I was there."

"*Si, Senor de Leon.* I remember you at the academy too," he responded in a quiet, respectful voice.

"Why have you brought him here?" Juan queried.

"Tell my father what you told me, *El Viejo.*"

"I have heard about your plan to discover the location of Nakanjo, in fact, everyone in San Cristobal has heard about it."

"Yes, I'm sure they have, but tell me now why you have come here."

"I know the way." Juan looked at the old man suspiciously.

"You know the way to what?" the general challenged, throwing down the gauntlet to see what this Indian really knew.

"The way to Nakanjo." Juan didn't say a word as he looked back and forth between his son and the old man. Finally, he replied,

"This old man has either lost his mind or is lying to us!"

"No Master, it is true. I know the way to the lost city."

"And how is it that you know the way?"

"Before I was taken by your people, I lived among my people, the Caltech. The old man suddenly stood erect with pride when he said, "We are the true descendants of the people of Nakanjo." Juan judged him with a suspicious eye. "All of my people knew the way, but many, like me, have been taken or driven deeper into the rainforest." The words were not said with condemnation but just in passing. The general did not know what to think about this new development.

"Is that so! Then why is it that your people never took the gold and treasure from the city?"

"It is cursed. My people believe that the city is protected by evil spirits."

"But you are not afraid of these spirits?"

"Oh no, Lord," he answered humbly as he made the sign of the cross. "I am a good Christian now and I don't believe in them anymore."

"If you know where Nakanjo is, why haven't you taken the treasure for yourself?"

"I am an old man, Lord and there is too much to carry. I would need help.

"What do you expect to get for all this information?"

"All I am asking for is a fair share of the riches that are there."

Tito added, "And what would you do with your share of the treasure?"

"I would buy my freedom, my Lord." Father and son looked at each other as if to ascertain what the other was thinking about this offer.

At last Juan spoke up. "You'll lead us!"

"Thank you, Master!"

"Go now. My son will inform you about when we will leave. And tell no one else what you have told us!"

"No, my, Lord." *El Viejo* left the hacienda.

"Tito," Juan whispered. "Watch him. See if he contacts anyone and report it to me. I do not fully trust him." With a nod, his son left to return to the academy.

CHAPTER 23

The masses of food and equipment that were stored at Juan's hacienda did not go unnoticed by the citizens of the city of San Cristobal. Rumor mills were busy grinding any new story about the expedition and when it would be leaving. Many of the men Juan had rejected from joining his company looked at him with hatred and jealousy. *Not only must I worry about Indian assaults, but now I must watch my back against my own kind!*

At last, the morning came when they planned on leaving. The men assembled outside his home. Each came with his own horse and weapon. *"Buenos dias en General"* They each greeted as he shook their hands. The last to arrive was *El Viejo* and Tito.

"Come into the chapel so we can receive God's blessing for our venture," he told them. Everyone followed him in. The Mass was said, Communion received and the blessing given. When they all turned to leave, Juan noticed Pilar kneeling in the back, her cheeks stained with tears. Father and son walked to her as she stood up.

She opened her mouth to speak the first words they had heard from her in weeks. "I have tried to talk you out of what you're going to do for so long, but at last the morning I've dreaded has arrived."

"Mother..." Tito began.

"Do not say another word, my son. Just know that you go with my blessing and my wish that you remain safe."

"I promise, mother." She kissed him on the lips and sent him outside so that she could speak to her husband in private.

"Give me your word, Juan that you will look after our son."

"I promise you."

"And my love, please come back to me safely."

"I will, my love." Juan took her into his arms and they kissed passionately. Juan pulled away and walked outside. *Please Blessed Mother,* Pilar prayed silently, *let them both come back safely to me.*

Juan walked out into the bright morning light to see that his men were already mounted and waiting for him. Most of these former soldiers were from the regiments that he had led many times into battle and was victorious. His men anticipated that in this expedition, he would be triumphant once more.

Juan got into the saddle on his steed, his son next to him. *El Viejo* sat on a mul, for no Indian was permitted to ride a horse. Leading the group were Indian workers who would cut a path into the jungle. Trailing were the Indian laborers who were in charge of the mules carrying food and equipment. Raising his hand in the air, Juan called out, *"Adelante!"* and the group moved forward.

However, unbeknownst to them, a group of about 27 discontented men followed at a safe distance. Their intent was plain to see.

Moving through the lush plant life, Juan turned to the old Indian asking, "How long will it be before we get to Nakanjo?"

"It will be many weeks, my Lord but in the end, it will be worth all the trouble."

As they moved deeper into the interior, the sounds of wildlife seemed to come from all directions. The screaming of Howler Monkeys mixed with the roars of jaguars as the heat and humidity of midday continued.

Juan Cesar de Leon's thoughts could not help but go back in time and imagine his father's incursion into the jungle. *Did he hear the same sounds? Did he begin his venture with the same high anticipation that I have?* He could not believe that it was any different.

The Indians with their machetes glimmering in the sun chopped off and threw to the side any branch, plant, or leaf that would have obstructed the party's way, the sweat dripping down their naked backs. Water had been rationed until they came to the first place where fresh water could be obtained, therefore no one touched their canteens unless it was absolutely necessary. The soldiers in the contingent of men were hardened warriors who were well disciplined. They knew the importance of following orders if they were to survive this ordeal and come back as rich men.

The day continued as the party moved ahead. Behind them, a man named Hector Davila had assumed authority over the trackers that followed the de Leon contingent because of his size and brutish ways. The others fell into line behind him. Davila had been one of General de Leon's men; an officer who proved through battle that he had acquired tremendous military skills, but there came the day when he was accused of raping another officer's wife. Juan had stripped him of his officer status and he was reassigned as a regular soldier. His resentment about how he was treated led to many nights of drunkenness and brawling in the local bars. Juan had tried to turn a deaf ear to Hector's behavior but his insolence and refusal to follow orders happened one time too often. In a ceremony in front of the rest of the troops, Davila was called out to face his general.

The charges were read to him before his fellow compatriots by one of the general's aides-de-camp. When the charges were finished, Juan had stripped away the medals and badges of honor from his military jacket. Holding out his hand, Juan accepted the sword that had been strapped to Davila's hip. He snapped it in two over his raised knee and threw the halves into the dusty dirt.

Hector's hatred and resentment toward Juan like a poison building up in his body, corrupted whatever was still good in him until he was thoroughly tainted. *I will have my revenge against de Leon. I will not be satisfied until his dead body lies at my feet and his riches and fame become mine!*

The day grew hotter and steamier, but for Davila it did not matter. Nothing was going to turn him back to San Cristobal until he satisfied his blood lust.

It was said that when Hector Javier Davila touched gold it became garbage. It wasn't simply his own fault because it started the moment his mother gave birth to him. Manuela Gomez, a 15- year old scullery maid in the estate of Lord of Rubiano, was taken unwillingly to be bedded by the lord's 24-year old son. Their coupling produced a son nine months later. Outraged, the Lord of Rubiasno confronted the new mother and denounced her as a liar when she identified his son as the father and was ready to throw mother and child off the estate. However, one look at the child's cleft chin, a characteristic physical trait handed down to family members for centuries, had him singing a different tune. To avoid public scandal, he gave them a small stipend and had Manuela and her son shipped as far away from Spain as possible on the next ship leaving for Guatemala.

Mother and child wound up on the streets of San Cristobal begging for food until the Sisters of Charity took her into their convent. And for room, board, and three simple meals a day, Manuela cleaned the convent along with other homeless women who had been taken in. In this loving, religious environment, Hector grew strong as a child. He was afforded an education by the Sisters who taught him to read and learn mathematics. With all this knowledge, he also learned from his mother that he was the son of the future Lord of Rubiano. A flood of pride and resentment of his life coursed through his body.

But there came a time when young Davila was reaching puberty and Mother Superior approached Manuela. "Hector must leave the convent before he becomes a man," the Sister informed her.

"But Mother, where will he go? What shall I do?"

"I can recommend his entrance into the Dominican monastery where he would be able to join the other Brothers one day." Although it was a solution, the former scullery maid did not want this for her son born of noble birth, even if he was considered a bastard. But with little recourse, the woman agreed to the proposal. Ten-year old Hector was taken by a Brother, kicking and screaming from his mother's arms, and brought to the Abbot Brother Luciano's office. When the boy refused to stop screaming the Abbot slapped him hard across the face. Stunned, Hector became silent. "There are rules to follow here if you expect to stay." For the first time in his young life the seeds of hate were planted deep into his soul.

And for a time, Hector studied and worked for his place with the other Brothers, or so they believed. But the first chance he had, at 15, he ran as fast as he could from the monastery. He grew up in the rough streets of San Cristobal learning the art of pickpocketing from the other urchins and ruffians and so his hatred grew for aristocrats.

Like the gangs of boys, he would have grown up as a thief, but for the pity of a wealthy plantation owner who saw the boy as one of the gleaners on his fruit and vegetable plantation. The owner, who was mounted on a horse and riding through the fields, noticed that the boy had the features of a Spaniard and not a Mestizo or Indian. Riding up to him, the owner called out, "Boy."

Looking up, Hector stood by the horse. "You called me?"

"Who are you?" The young man stood up proudly and answered,

"I am Hector Javier Davila, the son of the future Lord of Rubiano!" Being so close to him, the rider could detect the white skin under the redness of the sun and his aquiline nose, distinctive of the Iberian Peninsula and most importantly, the cleft in his chin which was a characteristic of the Lord of Rubiano. *A bastard child!*

"You do not belong here," the rider explicated. "Come with me." Taking pity on the boy, he led Hector back to his hacienda and dressed him in proper clothing of his son who had died two years before.

Seeing Hector in his son's clothing brought the man to tears. He decided to give the lad a chance at a better life and sponsored him as a cadet candidate, paying for his entrance, room and board, and his tuition. However, the good in Hector was withering away and the bad was getting stronger.

As a cadet, his studies came easily and the lessons in swordsmanship fulfilled his desire for violence. The other cadets soon learned that by crossing him, they were asking for a beating. The first time it happened was when another cadet confronted him about his lineage. Along with two other friends, they challenged his right to be in the academy with them. "I hear you're from the gutter," his main antagonist piped up.

"That's no business of yours," he replied casually.

"There's a rumor going around that you claim to be the bastard son of the Lord of Rubiano, but that can't be correct."

"It would be better for you if you turned and walked away from me right now," he replied clearly upset.

"And if I don't, what are you going to do about it?" he mocked. Without saying another word, Hector pounced on the other cadet bringing him to the ground, his fists flailing across the young man's face. "Help me!" Hector's victim screamed at his comrades, but they stood there in fear of his uncontrolled fury. Once Hector got it out, he rose so that the other cadet could stand. "I'm going to tell the headmaster about what you did to me," he whined pathetically. "Go ahead," he challenged and you'll get a worse beating than you got today!" Needless to say, the cadet never mentioned the incident.

Davila had trouble taking orders from men he saw as his inferiors and would often challenge their directions. Because of his disrespect to his captain, he had received 10 lashes each time for his infractions. Each lash left a red welt that crisscrossed his back. Each lash left another seed of hatred in his heart and soul. Despite this, Hector finished his courses and at the graduating ceremony was commissioned as a lieutenant. He immediately was assigned to a battalion.

Within his first year as an officer, he had a penchant for drinking. As a drunk, he could be violent and insulting to his fellow officers. Almost eight months into his commission, the charge of rape was leveled against him. At an officer's ball, he was struck by the beauty of the wife of Lieutenant Calderon. He asked her to dance and she obliged him. Hector danced her out the door, away from the other guests and began to sexually assault her. It was her screams that alerted her husband to her distress. The lieutenant grabbed Hector by the shoulder and tore him away from his sobbing wife and punched him in the jaw. Davila wound up being knocked to the ground but before he could fight back, General Juan Cesar de Luna interfered. "What is going on here?" Calderon explained the situation.

Getting to his feet, Davila brushed himself off saying, "She wanted it!" Calderon lunged for him, but other officers restrained him.

"You are under house arrest," the general barked. "Take him back to the Academy!" Two officers escorted him back where he spent the night.

In the morning, Juan ordered him to his office. He was brought by two cadets who waited outside in the hallway. Hector snapped to attention. "Your record at the Academy has been a series of positives and negatives since you began here. Your schooling and training have been exemplary.

"Thank you, sir!"

"But your self-discipline in following orders has been sorely lacking. What's your explanation for this?"

"Sir, some of the officers under your command are incompetent. Their orders should not be obeyed."

"So, you're saying that I don't have the ability to choose competent officers?"

"In some cases, yes that's the case."

"I find your insolence intolerable."

"I'm sorry, sir but that's the truth as I see it."

"In the past, I have been willing to overlook certain incidents you have been involved in because of your circumstances, but last night was the last straw!"

"But, sir..."

"You will remain silent! The troops will be mustered this morning and will witness you being drummed out of the battalion!"

"She asked for it!" he tried to defend himself.

"Take him back to his barracks!" de Leon shouted out to the cadets in the hallway. "And make sure you keep him under guard there!" Hector was marched out to await his fate and before the afternoon began on that day, Hector Javier Davila found himself out of the army. All the hatred that had built up through his lifetime was now directed toward General de Leon.

The march into the interior of the rainforest for Juan was exactly like his father's, except for one important change. Unlike 36 years before, the jungle to the immediate west of San Cristobal no longer found Indian tribes settled there. The indigenous people had either been killed, taken as slaves, or driven deeper into the tropical forest.

After the first day's march, they had covered just over five miles when Juan decided to make camp for the night. Campfires were lit and bedrolls laid out as food was cooked for the expeditionary force. Sentries were posted around the camp a few yards away from each other as the rest of the men bedded down for the evening.

Although the temperature had dropped a few degrees when the sun went down, it remained unbearably hot, and those trying to get a good night's rest awoke time and time again because of the heat. When dawn broke, a meager meal was distributed, camp was abandoned, and the men continued onward.

Day followed day in the same manner. The routine never changed and soon became monotonous. Yet there was no grumbling by the men, no calls from them to turn back. The thought of the riches of the lost city kept their determination to see this venture through to the end.

While they moved slowly through the underbrush, *El Viejo* told the legends of Nakanjo that had been told by the Jacalteco Indians over the centuries. "The wealth there is fabled for its gold and jewels," the old man related. Juan pondered this information. *If the bracelet my father brought back is any indication of what else can be found there, we are in for quite a haul.*

"And you've seen the treasure?" de Leon's second in command, Major Fulgencio Dominguez inquired with interest.

"Oh, yes! There is too much for one person to carry out. Much of it was commissioned by a king who was called Jaguar Claw. It is said that in his tomb, he is dressed with some of the most valuable items that decorate the body. *I wonder if the bracelet was taken from this king's sepulcher?*

"Tell us more about this King Jaguar Claw?" Tito begged the old man.

"It is said that he was a great warrior king!"

Dominguez inquired enthusiastically, "What did he do?"

"As the legend reveals, he turned back and defeated a king from another city who was trying to invade Nakanjo."

"You were in the tomb and saw the treasures?" Juan wanted to know.

"As a young man, many times," responded *El Viejo*.

"What was there?" Cadet de Leon queried.

"Many things," the old man answered. "Arm bracelets and necklaces made from gold and studded with emeralds. There are jade earrings with brilliant turquoise, and rings with opals as red as blood in the funeral chamber. As well there are amber necklaces and quartz crystals of many color varieties also there.

"It must be quite a sight," stated Juan.

"It is, my Lord. Even with the men you have it would be impossible to completely empty the treasure that is found there." This news made them even more excited to arrive at their goal.

This story was also heard by a scout who Davila had sent to carefully watch what was happening and being said by the group headed by General Juan de Leon. When the man returned to Davila's band of stalkers and related what he had heard, Hector thought, *Soon, it will be all mine and de Leon's men will be killed. I will take care of de Leon by myself!*

Forty-eight days into the mission to discover Nakanjo, Davila's group of discontents was starting to create waves of dissatisfaction. Unlike the general's group of soldiers who had come with supplies to get them through each day of the march, Davila's cutthroats and murders had not planned that far ahead.

A few were sent into the jungle each day to shoot any animals they came upon for sustenance. Fresh water was hard to come by so the men were reduced to suck the moisture that accumulated on leaves. It was less than adequate in the tremendous heat and humidity, but they moved forward, fueled by the stories that had been heard from *El Viejo* and the greed to possess the fantastic treasure they had heard about.

And so, this band of desperados went on until the morning of the 49th day. A man named Carmelo Bega, a ruthless lout who had served time in jail in San Cristobal for blackmail and robbery caught the attention of Hector who began to see discontent in the ranks. "We should turn around," Carmelo told the others. "This is a fool's mission and we will all die in this jungle if we continue to follow Davila!"

One evening while Bega was again encouraging others to abandon their enterprise, Hector confronted him. "What are you waiting for?" Carmelo Bega questioned the others after they had stopped for the night. "Who of you will follow me back to San Cristobal tomorrow?" The men, who were grumbling between them, suddenly stopped talking and looked up. Bega got a funny feeling that someone was standing right behind him. Carmelo stood up and turned around. A furious Davila was positioned face to face with the rabble-rouser.

"So, Bega, I've heard that you are unhappy with my leadership. Is that true?" fumed Hector.

"Yes, that's true," his antagonist fired back. "You're leading us all into an early grave. We'll never get back to San Cristobal again!"

"Do you think you could do a better job if you were leader?"

"I certainly wouldn't keep chasing after some myth of a lost city when there is no proof that it ever existed!"

"So now you're trying to turn these men against me?"

"Put it to a vote! Ask these men if they want to continue on this flight of fantasy you're leading us on!"

"Go ahead, ask!"

"Who's with me to leave here and make our way back to San Cristobal?" Before any of the men could answer, Hector took a knife from his belt and plunged into Bega's side. He screamed in pain and shock as their leader kept plunging his knife into the body. At last, he crumpled to the ground and drew his last breath.

"Anybody else want to take over this group and return to San Cristobal?" No one uttered a sound. "Think!" Hector reminded them. "Think of the riches that you will possess. We can all go back to San Cristobal as poor or rich men! What will it be?"

"Rich men," was the unanimous response.

"Then let there be no other talk about giving up the mission."

Months of painfully sluggish marching were finally paying off. The group led by General Juan Cesar de Luna came upon a rushing, white-capped river, the sound of which could be heard before they came upon it. They had finally broken out of the rainforest and now could see for miles. It was decided to make camp where fresh water was plentiful. Immediately, soldiers, Indians, horses and mules drank their fill. "This is the first sign that that we will be coming upon the city," *El Viejo* informed the general and his son. "We are just weeks from our destination."

"Where do we go after this?" queried Tito.

"We must follow the river until it empties into a lake. That is where the lost city of Nakanjo can be found." Juan added,

"You are sure of this?"

"I am very sure, my Lord."

As camp was constructed, Tito approached his father. "Should we call the group together and tell them how close we are?"

"There is no reason to get the men prematurely excited. There will be time enough to celebrate after we come upon the city." Juan began to feel a certain exhilaration building in his chest. *Father, I am almost at the point of redeeming your reputation. Give me the strength to see this mission through to the end.*

The men he was leading had been good about this arduous trek. There were aches and pains in backs, shoulders, and legs, yet there were no complaints or calls from them to turn back for San Cristobal.

A hunting party was sent out to bring back fresh meat that would supplement the group's meager amount of food that was left. The men came back carrying on their shoulders a mature, white- tailed buck. The group ate well that night. Stomachs full and thirsts quenched, the soldiers slept well. Only the sentries posted around the encampment stayed alert during the night.

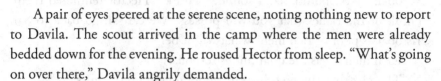

A pair of eyes peered at the serene scene, noting nothing new to report to Davila. The scout arrived in the camp where the men were already bedded down for the evening. He roused Hector from sleep. "What's going on over there," Davila angrily demanded.

"They've eaten and gone to sleep. There is nothing else to report."

"Go get some sleep!" he barked as he lay back down. *Damn de Leon! When the hell will they come upon Nakanjo? I don't know how much longer I can keep my men under control. If we don't come upon the lost city soon, they'll all turn on me!*

The morning came and so did the rain. It soaked through everything on the ground. The soil became muddy and mired Davila's band of murderous thieves as they tried to move forward. Because the horses were having such a rough time moving, Hector ordered the men off the animals so that they could help lead them onward. Soaked to the skin, the hair from their heads and beards dripping, the progress remained slow. The only good news their leader received was that Juan's party was having the same difficulty, but it did little to lift his men's bad mood.

It was at that point that Davila's party reached the river. There was a collective sigh of relief as they finally could gulp as much cold water that they needed. Their somber mood seemed lifted.

When the sun finally broke through the gray clouds, the moisture slowly began to dry and the men, as soon as the soil was once again firm, mounted their animals. Fights between the men broke out constantly as they took out their frustrations on each other. More than once, Davila had to break up the brawls by inserting himself into the fights. It usually ended with the combatants both on their asses. Each conflict ended with the same infuriated demand. "How much longer before we come to the city?"

"How should I know?" he answered them. "I'm as much in the dark as you are!" After witnessing Bega's death at the hands of Davila, nobody said another word. They just cast their eyes down and moved on.

A tapir had been shot and the fresh meat and full bellies lightened the group's mood. Hector felt a sense of reprieve as the men ate their fill. The dregs of society slept for the first time in a while without their stomachs grumbling. The next morning, they followed the beaten down grass where de Leon's troupe had marched out.

The sun was beginning to dip below the horizon and the sky turned a pinkish orange that lit up the white clouds. Juan de Leon and his men came upon a large lake that covered an extensive area in the valley. *El Viejo* suddenly halted, looking in all directions. "Is this the place?" Juan asked in great anticipation. The old man nodded saying,

"We are at last here!" There was great jubilation among the men as they realized they had at last reached their destination. Some of them wanted the old man to show them the city immediately but their leader calmed them down telling them, "When the sun comes up tomorrow, we will have plenty of time to make our discovery." The men knew he was right and settled down for the evening, but sleep did not come easily. The men thought about the riches they would soon accumulate and their triumphant return to the city of San Cristobal. When they did fall asleep, dreams of their new lives pervaded their thoughts.

The scout rode hurriedly into Davila's camp, his men already waking up. The speedy pace of the horse had Hector believing that there might at last be good news. Dismounting, the man came straight to Davila. "They've arrived!"

"Are you sure?"

"I heard the old Indian tell them so."

He personally awakened the rest of his men. Some of them grumbled about being shaken awake while it was still early. "Quiet!" he shouted out. "After a very long wait, I at last have some good news." The men looked eagerly at their leader. "Juan de Leon and his men have reached the area where the lost city can be found." They all shouted in relief and elation.

"What do we do now?" one of them questioned.

"We attack!"

"Now?" the scout inquired.

"There is no better time for it. They won't be expecting us because they don't know we've been following them."

"What about their sentries?"

Davila looked around and called out, "You men are all skilled in using the garrote to quietly strangle an opponent without them calling out for help. You will sneak up behind the sentries and dispatch them. When your jobs are done, the rest of us will charge into their encampment, swords drawn and kill them all. We will spare the old Indian's life until he has revealed the site of the city of Nakanjo" A great shout arose from the group. "All of them will die except de Leon," he specified.

"Why not de Leon?" one of them shouted back at him.

"Because... he is mine!"

Mounting their horses and by the light of what was the rapidly fading moon, the scout led the rest of them to the place where de Leon's men were encamped. Dismounting, the four murderers crawled through the high grass in search of their victims. One by one, the guards were asphyxiated without making a sound. The four men crawled back after their murderous deed was completed. They joined the others who had been waiting for their return. "Are they all dead?" whispered Davila. A man named Duarte nodded.

"They're all taken care of." Digging their spurs into the flanks of his horse and with a whoop, they charged the slumbering camp.

Those who were first to be awakened, including de Leon, reached for their guns and dropped some of the killers entering their sanctuary, but they were soon overwhelmed as slashing swords brought down one after another of Juan's party. Resistance was futile and those who were left dropped their weapons and were rounded up with their leader.

Looking at them, Juan did not see Tito among those being herded to the center of the camp. "Tito!" he screamed out in panic. "Tito! Where are you?"

"I have a gift for you de Leon!" Hector spoke up. With a wave of his hand, a body was dragged to Juan's feet. There was no mistaking the deep wound that had taken his son's life. Juan cried out in anguish as he looked at his son's bloody face.

"Kill me too!" cried out Juan.

"Tie all of them up!" Hector ordered that the old man be brought to him. The survivors' hands were tied behind their backs. *El Viejo* was brought to Hector. "Tomorrow, old man, you will lead me to Nakanjo!"

"What do we do with the others?" one of his men asked him.

"Kill them!" was his cold-hearted response. One by one, each of de Leon's men were killed.

"Why have you let me live? Kill me as you killed my son, for without him, I'm already dead."

"You don't remember me, do you?" queried Davila. Juan's dead eyes looked up at his tormentor. Suddenly, the light of recognition shone in them.

"Davila, isn't it?"

"Yes, that's right."

"So, all of this killing is due to being drummed out of the army?"

"That and more."

"You are a man without honor," spat Juan. "I knew it then as I know it now!" Davila simply laughed. "What do you plan on doing with me?"

"Take him to the lake!" Two men grabbed him by the arms and dragged him to the edge of the water. Juan immediately understood what his fate would be. *I am to die as many of my comrades in arms had that night of the Aztec assault. I'm to lie at the bottom of a lake.*

"Do what you came to do with me," de Leon challenged him.

"Goodbye old man!" With a mighty shove, Hector pushed the general into the water and watched with glee as Juan struggled to keep his head above water. After a few minutes, Juan Cesar de Leon's head sank below the water and never came up again. All that Davila could think was, *Tomorrow, I will be a wealthy man!*

Morning broke in brilliant sunshine and as Davila arose from his bedroll, he exclaimed, "God is blessing our endeavor today. Quickly, the entire camp saddled up and got ready to leave. Davila's second-in-command, another man dishonored and drummed out, former Lieutenant Vicente Touro brought the trussed up *El Viejo* to him. "Untie him!" Hector commanded. "Now tie the rope around his neck, tightly!" Once this was done, Touro guffawed, "He looks like your dog".

"Si, mi perro!" Davila joined in the laughter. Then he grew serious. "Old man, if at any time, I feel as if you are leading me astray, I'll hang you by the neck from the nearest tree! Now take me to the city of Nakanjo!" *El Viejo* never uttered a sound but began to lead them all through the valley.

Like waves parting before the bow of a great ship, the tall grasses parted before the Spaniards' horses.

Fresh water was abundant as they circumnavigated their way around the blue lake. Hours passed and Davila and his men were losing their patience. Suddenly, Hector pulled viciously on the rope that tightened around the old man's neck and dropped him to the ground. "Where is it?" he screamed at the Indian. Getting up on his feet, he pointed to the land that lay before them. Shading his eyes with his hand Davila looked in that general direction. "Where!" he yelled once more.

"Over there," the old Indian replied finally finding his voice.

"There's nothing there except some grassy knolls! If you're trying to mislead me, I'll have Tuoro cut out your lying tongue!"

"No, my Lord. The city is there covered by vegetation."

"If you're lying…"

"No, my Lord. It is true!"

"Move!" The Spaniards followed the man until he stopped at the base of the first hill. Dismounting, his men drew near. "Rip out the plant life!" he barked. "We'll see if this dog has been telling us the truth."

All of them began to rip the rooted vegetation away until one of them called out," I've found something!" The others gathered around to see what had been revealed. It was a partial limestone step. A smile crossed Davila's lips. "Start climbing and ripping the plants away until we get to the top!"

They hacked away for almost an hour before they reached the summit. Hector took a moment to look at the spectacular view around him before he turned back to the Indian. "And the treasure will be found inside?"

"Yes, my Lord."

"Show me!" Before *El Viejo* took a foot inside, he let out a loud, shrill piercing whistle.

"What are you doing?" Touro confronted him. What he was doing soon became dreadfully apparent. At the sound that carried over the valley, the rainforest vegetation parted and out swarmed what looked like hundreds of Jacalteco warriors armed with war clubs, spears, and bow and arrows as their screams reverberating throughout the valley. Arrows, like guided missiles, whistled through the air, some finding their marks in stunned Spaniards.

"Get inside!" he ordered his men and those who were still alive gathered inside the top of the pyramid. Davila did not drag the old Indian in, but simply slit the man's throat. Raising his sword in the air, Davila thrust it violently in a downward movement and screamed, "Fire!" The gun shots went off killing the warriors that were the first to scale the pyramid, but others took their places and ran to the top. The Spaniards didn't have time to reload their weapons before the Indians were upon them. Hand to hand fighting began but before too long, the Spanish were overwhelmed by the attackers who outnumbered them.

Only Davila and Touro were left alive. The others had been murdered. Their hands were bound behind their backs as warriors cleared away the plant life revealing a round flat stone which seemed to be stained with human blood. Grabbing Touro by the hair, they dragged him to the stone as they ripped off his armor and clothing. As he was stripped, two other Indians lit a brazier that was nearby. The Indians pulled the naked Spaniard until he was flat on his back on the stone. Pushing his legs and arms down, his chest rose. One Indian walked toward him incanting words the Spanish did not understand. Vicente Touro screamed in panic as he saw the Indian reciting Mayan words, raise a knife up in the air. "No," he screamed out loud. "Oh God, please spare me!" he cried as the knife was suspended in the air.

"Vicente, die like a man and not as a coward!" Davila cried out just before the blade dropped down and pierced his flesh. This time Touro screamed out in excruciating pain as the knife separated his heart from his body. He stopped struggling. The heart, still beating, was tossed into the brazier where it crackled and sizzled in the flames. The dead body was tossed down the stairs.

Now it was Davila's turn and they quickly stripped him as he was walked to the altar. Without their help, Hector got up on the stone and lied down. *Is this how my life is to end?* He watched as the blade struck down and he blacked out.

THE SEARCH

CHAPTER 24

In April of 1958, in Shelburne, Massachusetts, a son was born to Margaret and Edwin Cummings. The birth had been a difficult one, so much so that a day later, Margaret died of a heart attack due to an aneurism. The baby, who was named Martin by his mother before she died, was left in the incapable hands of his father. Edwin had no interest in the responsibility of raising a child, especially since he blamed his son for his wife's premature death. He packed up his belongings, left his house in a real estate agent's hands, and with the infant, traveled about three and a half hours back to Harvard University where he was a Professor of English Literature.

When he arrived, he hired a middle-aged woman named Louisa to take care of his child, and found a house to rent. He was again able to concentrate on his profession, eventually being promoted to Department Chairman. As he grew up, Martin only got to see his father a few days a week. His son longed for a relationship. His father did not.

At three years of age, Martin developed an eye infection that left them red and painful. It went unchecked for over a week when Louisa called Martin's father, but received no calls back. By the time he was taken to an ophthalmologist and learned that the condition was called orbital cellulitis, it was too late. Because it went untreated, Martin's eyes became weak which forced him to wear eye glasses for the rest of his life.

As Martin Cummings grew, he learned to depend on his nanny rather than his father whom he saw infrequently. At the age of ten, Louisa was let go and replaced by Meredith who was fired three years later to make way for Christine. It was only after time had passed that Martin realized that each of his nannies had a sexual relationship with his father. Unlike other boys his age who were playing baseball or football or any other sport, Martin did not find the need for friendships, and instead read books in the house or the front porch. He was fascinated by ancient civilizations, especially those in Mesoamerica.

The boy was of superior intelligence with an I.Q. of 141. He was a dedicated and high-achieving student. Dating was out of the question; first because Martin showed no interest in giggling girls, and second, because the girls laughed at him. Edwin continued to take little note of his offspring, burying himself in his work. It was not surprising that after he graduated high school, Martin was accepted into Harvard, but he had enough of his family. Instead, he escaped to the other side of the continent and attended a little-heard of college named Trinity University in Oxnard, California. He majored in archeology and minored in history.

He earned a Bachelor's Degree in Science, and began his studies as a graduate student. It was while he was in his "Archeology of Central America" class that his professor Dean Adamson took notice of his questions during his lectures. "You have a quick and intuitive mind, Martin."

"Thank you, Professor."

"I'd like you to work for me as my student assistant. Would that interest you?"

"Definitely, sir. I'd be honored."

And so, Martin's career began to form. Adamson became a substitute father; someone he could talk to with little effort. When he was to graduate with a Master's Degree, Adamson was going to retire and he recommended Cummings to take his place in the classroom. "He's young," he informed the executive board, "but he's got the makings of a top-notch teacher." The board overwhelmingly approved the recommendation and Martin was approached by the president of the university.

Martin was shocked but delighted by the invitation to join Trinity University's faculty. He thanked Adamson for his recommendation. "I know you'll make me proud," his professor said.

"I'll try, sir."

The following September, Martin joined his colleagues and began his teaching career. He saw no need to inform his father about his decision.

Esmie Hastings had come from a humble beginning. Born in San Francisco on July, 1989 to an English-American father and a Japanese mother, she was determined at a young age to leave her old life behind. She watched as her mother, Kimiko, was subservient to her husband who was a military graduate of Annapolis and a newspaper editor, her dictatorial father Everett. She swore that she would never be dominated by a man once she left her father's house. Even the name he had given her, Esmeralda, she had abhorred all her life and had changed it to Esmie as soon as she entered her freshman year at college.

She was a stunning combination of both her parent's physical and mental attributes. From her mother, she took long black hair that dropped to her shoulders, delicate facial features and almond shaped eyes, and her tendency toward a soft heart. Her blue eyes that reflected dogged determination and stubbornness, she inherited from her father. "You are a combination of the best of both worlds," she often heard her mother tell her. It made no difference to the young woman. She had been teased unmercifully about how she looked by the children of the Albright School, a private institute whose students came from white, financially privileged backgrounds and who were not used to being with students of mixed ethnic origins. Her persistent attitude eventually came in handy once she grew past her early life and attended Trinity University in Oxnard, California in 1984. It was there that she met the noted academic and archeologist, Martin Cummings.

Esmie never thought she could be interested in a college course in archeology, but the more she heard Dr. Cummings relate his experiences in the jungles of Central America, the more it sparked her imagination and inquisitiveness.

Dr. Martin Cummings could not be described as handsome. His hair was thinning and his receding hair line left him with a high forehead and the tonsure of a monk at the top of his head. His skin was spotted and wrinkled and his failing eyes were deep set, which was not surprising since he was 59, 31 years her senior and at that point an avowed bachelor. But there was something about his stories that made him absolutely fascinating to Esmie. He was typically dressed casually in a light blue button-down shirt and a brown tweed sports jacket. His horn-rimmed glasses were perched on the edge of an elongated nose. After the lecture room emptied, she would engage him in conversation before he could gather up his notes and leave the lectern.

Following many of these dialogues, he concluded that Miss Hastings possessed a brilliant and inquiring mind. Cummings began to grow fond of his pretty student and suggested, "Would you be interested in becoming my student assistant?" Esmie jumped at the opportunity. It was in his faculty office that she had access to the works of many men as well as those of Dr. Cummings. *Publish or Perish*, was the adage that she heard from her instructor as he bored it into her head. "If you are thinking of a career in this subject, you must publish!"

She remained his student assistant for the next two years, reading him his pupil's theses, and organizing his papers while she made sure she attended all his classes. When she was about to graduate with a Bachelor's Degree in Social Sciences and told him she was going to enter her graduate studies, he offered her a permanent position. Esmie accepted enthusiastically.

In time the teacher began to tell her about the next archeological dig he was planning in Guatemala. "I am after a lost city in pre-Colombian Mesoamerica called Nakanjo located in what is now Guatemala," he whispered to her cautiously. "It will make anyone who finds it a celebrity as huge as Howard Carter, the archeologist in Egypt who uncovered Tutankhamen's tomb in The Valley of the Kings." Esmie's eyes opened wide at the bold statement.

"If the city is lost, how can you be sure that it even existed?"

Martin winked and replied to his young protégé, "I just know."

CHAPTER 25

GUATEMALA CITY, GUATEMALA

Salvador Hermoza had been born to a middle-class Guatemalan couple in Guatemala City in 1986. His father was a mid-level bureaucrat in the government, a pencil-pusher who was only too happy to follow the orders of his superiors. His parents were proud because their son Salvador was an outstanding student in school and he also played soccer on his school's team. He had been provided with everything he needed by his parents and sometimes even more. This might have spoiled most children, but Salvador was different. He was possessed of a kind, generous, and sensitive heart. His friends totally admired him for these qualities.

Graduating high school with honors, Salvador entered the Universidad Mariano Galvez de Guatemala to study accounting. The tall, good-looking, curly-haired student with an affable smile met a female student a year older than he, who was about to change his whole life.

She was a spit-fire named Miss Lola Espinosa (which in Spanish means thorny). Lola was a 5' 8" red-headed bombshell with light green eyes that drew Salvador in the first time he saw her. She could prove to be extremely prickly when someone dared to confront her over her political views. Lola Espinosa had even taken a swing at a cop during a student demonstration against the current government. Anyone who was attracted and loved her would be in for quite a rollercoaster ride of emotions. Theirs became a tumultuous love affair flaring into arguments from time to time and then into their smoldering fiery lovemaking. Hermoza fell swiftly and hard for Lola and after a few months, they became engaged.

His parents violently protested but to no avail. "You barely know her!" his father pointed out.

"I know enough to be convinced that I love her and want to be with her for the rest of my life."

His mother added, "Who are her people?"

"What you're really asking is if she is of our class, isn't that right?"

"Well, after all," she responded haughtily, "There are such things as social conventions that should not be broken." His father took him by the arm.

"You are going to introduce us before you're married, aren't you?"

"I believe that would be a disaster based on our present conversation."

"But Salvador..." his mother began, but she was quickly interrupted.

"Goodbye mother and father. This will be the last time we see each other!" He slammed the door of the house in which he had grown and spent a happy childhood, but he would never visit again. His parents were not going to change his mind.

Once he was hers, she introduced him to her radical friends who often took to the streets to rally against the oppressive government of Guatemala. Posters of Fidel Castro and Che Guevara hung in a room of a dilapidated building they were using as their headquarters. They gladly showed him the reason for their protests and demonstrations.

Salvador had spent all his life looking the other way at the squalor of the poor of the city, gazing at the people, but never really seeing them before. To him, they were like the trees on the avenues. He knew they were around but didn't notice them. The poor people's revolution or *Revolucion de los pobres* was a movement to force the rich and powerful of the country to share their wealth with the disadvantaged, voluntarily at first but forcibly if they resisted. The more Hermoza listened to their arguments and saw the great poverty of the people, the more he began to see their point.

Besides their own wealthy, the student movement blamed the imperialistic American government for skewing the greedy of their country into heartless wolves who ravenously fed on the disadvantaged. The students called themselves, the *La Neuva Luz,* the New Order. Salvador Hermoza dropped out of the university and wholeheartedly joined them.

RIO DE JANEIRO, BRAZIL

Armand Thierry, French by birth but a citizen of the world, had chiseled features and cold blue eyes. His hair was a white mane that crowned his head. Never married, he dated model types whom he treated like tissues; used once then throw them to the side. He sat quietly in his tufted office chair in his posh decorated study. Behind him was the view of Sugarloaf Mountain, atop which stood the Statue of Christ, his arms wide open. If he looked down from his richly adorned mansion in Rio de Janeiro, he could see the city spread out before him, or if he gazed out he caught sight of the blue color of Guanabara Bay.

Armand had kept his eye on Dr. Martin Cummings for a very long time. The first son of a man who massed-produced munitions, Armand had inherited the firm on his father's death. The business he now controlled grew to became a multibillion-dollar operation. That is because, unlike his father, he lacked ethics. Armand sold his product to the highest bidders on the black market and had clients which included Al Qaeda in Iraq, Boko Haram in Nigeria, Taliban in Afghanistan, Hezbollah in Lebanon, Isis terrorists in Syria and Al-Shabaab in Somalia. As a wealthy man, he owned residences in Paris, New York, Rio de Janeiro, the Isle of Malta, and Istanbul.

Educated in some of the finest universities in the world such as Oxford, the Sorbonne, and Harvard, the lifelong womanizer became thoroughly engrossed in the field of archeology. The thought of discovering ancient civilizations and finding their treasures sparked his imagination. He learned about the lost city in Guatemala named Nakanjo and its supposed fabulous treasure. *It is already mine,* he told himself.

In his research, he read all he could find about the famed and fabled Mayan city. He also learned about his main competitor, Dr. Martin Cummings of Trinity University. He knew that he possessed unlimited funds and did not have to go begging to some college board of directors for money, which sent Armand Thierry into the throes of exhilaration. *He is no competition for me,* Thierry snarled inwardly. *I will just "borrow" from him the work that he has already accomplished.* Moving to the computer, he Goggled Cumming's name. Thierry found out as much as he could about his adversary to use against him. He smiled smugly to himself.

"Ramon!" he yelled out. Standing just outside the door stood his henchman, dressed in black, big and burly with a jagged scar on his left cheek. He had buzzed black hair and looked like an escaped convict. He opened the door to his boss's office.

CHAPTER 26

TRINITY UNIVERSITY, OXNARD, CALIFORNIA

More and more, Esmie had to take over the professor's work, as Martin's eye condition deteriorated. It was Miss Hastings who finally accompanied him to the eye doctor. After going to the specialist, it was determined that he had glaucoma. The distressing news did not break the man. He had been preparing an expedition to find the lost city of Nakanjo and nothing was going to stop him.

Approaching Esmie, he inquired, "Would you be interested in joining me on this exploratory endeavor to Guatemala? Without you there, I doubt that I could have a successful outcome." His assistant's heart nearly beat out of her chest with euphoria.

"Of course I will. I'll be right by your side." Cummings breathed a sigh of relief.

"But what evidence do you have of the city's location?" she queried.

"This is for your ears only," he whispered. "The last time I was in Guatemala an old Indian told me a tale he said had been passed down through generations. But I had run out of money and could not follow up on it to discover if he was telling me the truth."

"What did he say?"

"I cannot tell you that…" Esmie looked at him with a strange expression on her face that reflected her frustration with him. "Why not, don't you trust me?"

"I could reveal it, but only to my wife." Hastings was now more confused than before.

"Are you married?"

"No, that's not what I mean." Esmie stared at him once more with incomprehension. Suddenly a light went off in her head.

"Are...are you asking me to marry you?" Martin reached into his jacket pocket and pulled out a box. He opened it revealing a diamond ring.

"I've kept this ring for years after my mother died but I never found a woman who was as remarkable as you, a woman who was my intellectual equal. Will you marry me?" Esmie had never heard such an unromantic proposal. She hesitated and then said, "Yes." Hastings was certainly not in love with him, but by marrying Cummings she deduced that his name had a certain cache that would open doors for her that probably would have remained as obstacles to her success in her own archeological career.

Taking her in his arms he kissed her. Esmie kissed him back unenthusiastically. As far as she was concerned, this was a business deal and not a love match made in heaven. After all, he had not said he loved her and she was sure he was doing this because of her value as his eyesight kept dimming. *I can live with that!*

"What did the old man say?"

"That will be my wedding gift to you."

"Then we'll have a civil ceremony as soon as possible. No guests, just the two of us."

"I agree." She did not bother to inform her parents of the upcoming event.

Two days later, they marched out of city hall and onto the steps outside. Esmie was wearing the diamond ring. She was dressed in a cream shift dress and carried a bouquet of yellow daisies. Martin was dressed in the best clothes he had, a slightly worn blue suit and tie. It had the scent of mothballs that clung to the fibers.

As they reached the sidewalk, they called a cab and went to a local restaurant to have brunch and celebrate their nuptials. After the waiter took their order, Esmie spoke up. "Well..." Martin looked at her.

"Well what?"

"Are you going to tell me what the old man said as you promised? We are married now." Leaning over across the table he uttered, "He told me that just south of the lake named Lago de Ayarza lies the river Rio Los Esclaves which flows into the Pacific Ocean. He told me that somewhere in the river's delta, in a thick jungle, I would find what I was looking for, the lost city of Nakanjo. I have been looking for it for over 27 years. I drew a rough map on the information he related to me."

"What is it about this city that drives you to uncover it for such a long time?"

"It is supposed to be the mythical city-state of King Jade Ocelot and it has been untouched for centuries. Besides the recognition I would receive for such a discovery, it is said that he was buried with a fabulous treasure of gold and jewels." His eyes lit up as he relayed his story to his new wife.

"When do we leave?"

"The budget has to be approved by the university board before I can set out, but these things take time."

"How long has the board had your proposal?"

"Almost three months, but you have to remember that I've been on one other expedition to Guatemala that did not result in finding Nakanjo. They're probably reluctant to fund another lost cause."

"But you must explain to them the old man's story!"

"I have, but I was told by the president, without going into too much detail, that the story was not much to go on."

Esmie Cumming looked crestfallen. "Is that it?"

"I haven't officially received word of their decision, but I have great hope that I will soon return to Guatemala and make the greatest find in almost a century."

"I hope so."

"The Executioner", as he was sometimes called, but never to his face, had a rugged physique and strong chiseled features giving him an outdoorsman appearance. His eyes were a soft brown, which beguiled females, and his skin had olive tones enhanced by a constant suntan. He appeared nothing like the killer that he really was.

Bonifacio Millian had been born as a twin boy in Mexico City to a father who ran a family banking business in the city, and a mother who lived for her husband and family. The affluent family sent their sons to be educated in private schools and they all got very used to cossetting in the best that life could offer.

For years, things went well for his family, living in a mansion outside the city limits, until he turned 14 when his brother Carlos was killed in a water skiing accident. His mother never recovered from the tragedy although she put on a brave front for other people. But in her private moments, she was reduced to tears that would not end.

However, the family business continued until his aunt and uncle, his father's younger siblings, cheated his father out of the business which left them destitute. They were forced to leave their home and move into one of the city's many slum neighborhoods.

The young man watched his family crumble before his eyes. First his mother died and his father turned to drink which eventually killed him. Bonifacio swore that he would pull himself out of his current situation. He started running drugs for one of the Mexican cartels, and educated himself, even learning to speak English. He practiced to become a marksman for a reason. One day he walked into his family's bank and shot his uncle, execution style; one bullet to the back of his head. He broke into his aunt's home and shot her in the chest. Because of this, he earned his nickname, "The Executioner."

His intelligence and his penchant for not being squeamish about killing saw his quick rise in the cartel. It wasn't long before he had done away with the top man and took over for himself. He gathered around him young men who hoped they could coattail their way up the cartel ladder. Millian made sure that anyone who pitted themselves against him wound up in an unmarked grave.

Millian purposely did not live ostentatiously and did not believe in conspicuous consumption. Unlike other drug lords who wore multiple diamond rings and gold chains around their necks, Millian lived a low-key existence with two exceptions; the private jet he used for drug drop offs, and a small villa that he owned in Puerto Vallarta.

The drug lord had swarms of young beautiful women in his life but never considered getting married. Women for him were simply blood sucking leeches who drained his "machismo", his power that might jeopardize his place at the top. *I'll never let myself fall to the bottom like my father did!*

Climbing into the cockpit of his private jet, Millian checked his instrument panel. Turning on the engine, the pilot released the brake and started to taxi. Slowly, the plane picked up speed and lifted off the ground, and he retracted the landing gear. Millian loved the freedom and pleasure he felt when he was in the air. It was as if he left all his concerns on the ground. He could have hired someone else to fly and make the drug drop but for two reasons; he didn't trust anybody else. And he loved the adrenaline rush he received with the sensation that he was skirting his life on the sharpened edge of danger.

Flying below the radar surveillance, the jet seemed to skim over the different shades of green that made up the jungle canopy, and then the aquamarine expanse of the Caribbean dotted with islands that looked like a string of emerald stones.

After almost 90 minutes, Millian got on his radio and signaled a message using the code name "Fire Fox." A static sounding voice returned saying, "You are cleared to land."

Bonifacio made this trip four or five times a week and never had a bit of trouble with the authorities. The dispersing of bribes made sure that the wheels were thoroughly greased and that there would be no problems with the business.

The pilot turned inland until a landing strip came into view. He descended until the wheels touched ground. Breaking gently, the plane came to a halt. "Welcome back!" an unshaven short man in grubby clothes and a cap greeted Millian.

Climbing down from the plane, Millian shook the man's hand. "Hello Ignacio! How are your wife and five children?"

"Carmelita is pregnant again!"

"Aha!" he laughed in response. "Good for you!"

As they conversed, some peons unloaded the cocaine and packed and tied them on mules that would be lead to the coast and then into shipping containers that were loaded onto what looked like innocent fishing boats. These ships were destined for a small port town just south of the Mexican border with Texas. From there they were smuggled under the cover of darkness across the border.

When the count of the packages of cocaine was done and approved, Ignacio led the pilot back to a cabin. In the corner of a closet, a safe was located. "I'm sorry my friend," began Ignacio, "But I must ask you to stand by the front door while I work the combination."

"Of course." Millian stood by the closed door while Ignacio worked the tumbler. He counted out several packets of one hundred dollar bills. Closing and locking the safe door, Ignacio laid the bundles on the table. Bonifacio walked over and thumbed through the bundles. Ignacio took a few plastic bags and placed the bundles inside. "As always, it is a pleasure to do business with you," said Millian as they shook hands.

"Have a safe trip back, my friend!"

Bonifacio strolled out to his jet to make the journey back.

"Los American cuatro ojos esta de vuelta," Ruben Tobon told his boss. The drug kingpin laughed hysterically.

"Four-eyes is such a gringo term. You saw him yourself?"

"I was paying off the local official when I saw his boat dock and his people disembark." Drug lord Bonifacio Millian shrugged indifferently.

"As long as he explores away from our cocaine trafficking and airstrip, as he has before, this should not be a problem.

"But this time something was different."

"And what is that?"

"He has brought a woman, a beautiful oriental woman, and they both wear wedding rings." Bonifacio winked and poked his elbow into his henchman's rib. "Everybody needs a little recreation, my friend." They both laughed knowingly. "Now back to business," Millian declared. "Is my plane loaded up and ready to go?"

"That's what I came to tell you. You can take off any time you want to."

Bonifacio walked out of the makeshift cabin and glanced up to the sky. *A clear day with not a single cloud in the sky, a great day for a plane ride!*

The 6'2" slightly balding man with a well-groomed moustache, who always carried a Glock in a shoulder holster, walked toward the airstrip hewn out of the jungle where his Cessna Citation jet waited for the short hop of 1 hour and 49 minutes to Mexico.

PUERTO VALLARTA, MEXICO

Bonifacio lounged in a deck chair overlooking the blue Pacific that expanded just beyond the white stucco deck inlaid every few feet with colorful Mexican tile. A slight breeze rustled the fronds of the surrounding palm trees and a big blue sun umbrella shaded the area that Millian occupied. A half-finished cold glass of Tequila Sunrise lay on a low tiled table an outstretched arm's distance away. He had flown in the day before just to get a little rest.

His villa, set away from the tourists and the hotels they frequented, was off the beaten track. A private beach of fine white sand sprawled out like a carpet in front of him.

Sunday morning in Puerto Vallarta was Bonifacio's favorite time of the week. The seaside village was quiet, due to the heavy drinking and partying that went on every Saturday evening. The recovering tourists in their hotel suites called for room service for their breakfasts. Millian could walk undisturbed along the cobblestone streets of the village and stop in his favorite shop for coffee and to read the morning edition of *"El Norte"* in peace. The few people he might bump into at that time of the morning knew who he was and treated him with respect and caution. Millian left as soon as the first tourists started milling about in the streets and he retreated to his hideaway.

As soon as he returned, his middle-aged butler approached him. "Sir, a Mr. Thierry called and asked that you call back as soon as you returned."

"Thank you, Carlos." Bonifacio walked into his den and closed the doors. All the plantation blinds on his windows were open to the ocean, the sound of the waves pounding on the beach. An overhead fan spun around as the heat of the day began to settle in. Bonifacio dialed the number and waited for it to be picked up on the other end. A big voice came from the other side, "Hello Bonifacio!"

"Hello, Armand! How the hell are you?"

"I'm well my old friend. I got your message."

"Good! I've been hearing about a new assault rifle called the Fama. What can you tell me about it?"

"It's an excellent rifle that is equipped with night and day video sights. It's a bullpup-styled assault rifle, and it uses a lever-delayed blowback action and all the latest technology."

"I like what I'm hearing. How soon can you ship 200 to me?"

"Right away, but don't you want to talk about price."

"Screw the money. I'll pay whatever the asking price is!"

"Now that our business has been concluded how are things going in your venture?"

"As long as Americans keep shoving spoons up their noses, I'll continue to do a booming business. And you, Armand?"

"I can't get arms and munitions off the shelves fast enough."

"Well, take care and stay well my friend."

"To you as well, Bonifacio." He hung up and turned toward the open window to let the sound of the sea and the cool breeze washed over him. It was very therapeutic.

He walked to his bedroom, closed the door and undressed so he could put on his swimming trunks. The maid had already cleaned his suite and put together his bed. Slipping on his flip-flops and gathering up a pool towel from the closet, he made his way outside. He rang for the butler who appeared promptly. "Yes, sir?"

"Get me a fresh drink."

"Right away, sir!"

Dropping the towel over a chair, and letting his gun holster hang from its spindle, he walked to the edge of the tiled pool and stared into the water. A moment later, he dove in with one graceful motion. He began swimming underwater.

Like his time in his jet, his weekend escapes to his villa were chances to recharge his battery. He felt entirely insulated from the rest of the world. *Someday I'll leave this business and retire permanently here, but until then, I'll take full advantage of my weekends.*

Bonifacio's head broke above the water on the opposite side of the pool and he clung to the edge. Brushing his wet hair from his eyes, he observed the beauty and serenity that surrounded him. He climbed out of the pool and made his way to the towel, leaving behind puddles from the drops of water that fell from his body.

Toweling himself off vigorously, Millian grabbed his drink and dragged his lounge chair into the sun. Taking a few gulps from his icy glass, he lay down. He closed his eyes, and allowed himself to bask under the warm rays. He felt like an adobe brick left drying in the sun. The rays of the sun felt so healing on his body and mind. Above his head, a yellow and black Altamira Oriole whistled its melody as it perched on a high palm frond.

Falling asleep to the bird's sweet melody, he luxuriated in the warmth. He lay there until the coolness of a cloud that covered the sun overhead woke him. He saw the fast-moving thunderhead clouds covering the sky. *The usual afternoon storm is moving in.*

He moved inside. *Well, the weekend is most likely over.* He would fly back to the Guatemalan airstrip early the next morning.

TRINITY UNIVERSITY

"A letter has arrived," Dr. Martin Cummings noted.

"From whom?" his wife inquired. Ripping the envelope open with his letter opener, he slipped the folded piece of paper out.

"Here," he said passing it to Esmie. She began to read silently. "Who is it from?"

"It's from President Lewis." Martin gave her a bewildered look for a moment.

"That's strange," he at last answered. "He usually just calls me directly when he wants to get in touch. What does the letter say?" His wife hesitated to read him the contents of the letter. "Well, what does it say, Esmie?" Once more, she did not answer his inquiry. "Is something wrong? You must tell me!"

"Montgomery has set up an appointment for you to answer questions of the board members." Martin became suddenly subdued by this information.

"When is the board meeting?"

"Tomorrow morning at nine."

"This does not bode well for me," he gravely announced.

"Why do you say that? It's probably some minor issue." Even as the words came out of her mouth, they rang hollow to her.

"This is a formal invitation to a board meeting. There's something serious going on."

"I'm sure it's nothing," replied Esmie trying to remain as cheery as possible.

"No, something's up." His wife could think of nothing to say to him that would be reassuring.

"Will you go with me tomorrow?"

"Of course, we'll attend as a united front! There's no reason to be concerned." He simply shook his head and returned to his work.

Esmie Cummings did not want to admit it to her husband but she was also worried about this meeting. *This is the first time Martin has ever been ordered by the board to answer questions. I have a sneaking suspicion that this is about his waning eyesight. No, it does not bode well at all.*

The rest of the day was spent on their research into the lost city of the Maya in Guatemala. With a magnifying glass, Martin poured over volumes of work while Esmie worked at typing his notes. She noticed little indications that the professor was continually losing concentration and he often cursed himself and his eye condition for his losing track of his research.

Finally, by eight at night, Esmie called a halt to their work. "What you need is a good dinner to help you get things off your mind."

"I don't think I could stomach any food right now."

Taking him by the arm she replied, "Let's go to Santorelli's and share a bottle of chianti and have the spaghetti and clams in a spicy tomato sauce and dunk the Italian bread in it. You know how much you love that."

"I don't know..."

"You don't have to know. Leave everything to me." She guided him a few blocks until they reached the restaurant with the burgundy canopy with the establishment's name inscribed in gold letters. The hostess led them to their favorite table. "How are the two of you?" the waitress questioned.

"Mimi, how are you?" Esmie inquired.

"The same as usual since my feet are still killing me! What'll you have tonight?"

"Our usual," Martin indicated.

"Coming right up!" The hefty woman took their order back to the kitchen. In a few minutes, she returned with a bottle and two glasses. She poured the ruby liquid into the glasses. "Your food will be out as soon as possible."

"Thanks, Mimi," Mrs. Cummings replied. She waited for their food server to wander away before she raised her glass, "Here's to us!" Martin raised his glass and Esmie clicked her glass against his. He did not answer her toast but took a long drink of his wine. "Talk to me," his wife begged of him.

"The weather's been warm lately."

"Don't try to be cute because it's just not working."

"What do you want me to talk about?"

"Let's talk about the letter you got today."

"What about it?"

"I know you were upset about it. What are you thinking?"

"I'm most likely going to be fired."

"You can't be sure of that." He put his wine glass down and stared directly into her eyes.

"Poor eyesight, nothing published in three years and the lost city still not discovered, it's a no brainer!"

"I'm not so sure about that," she replied half-heartedly.

"We'll see tomorrow."

After finishing their dinner, Esmie drove them home and Martin went straight to bed. He remained asleep until 1:30 a.m. when he abruptly woke and could not get back to his slumber. By 2 A.M., he gave up in exasperation. He carefully made his way to the den, sat down on his easy chair and turned on CNN. He could not clearly see the picture on the set but listened discouragingly to the home and overseas disasters. *This planet is a disaster!*

No matter how he tried, he could not get the meeting out of his head. He felt like a prisoner waiting for the guillotine blade to drop on his neck.

After a few hours, he fell asleep. Esmie found him in the chair at 7 A.M. and woke him. "Had a rough night?"

"You could say that," he yawned.

"Do you want breakfast?"

"No, I'm just going to take a hot shower."

They avoided each other until it was time to drive to work. The trip ensued in silence. They went to their offices and tried to do some work. Five minutes before the meeting, Martin got up from behind the desk. He found his wife waiting in the hallway for him. "I'm perfectly able to find my way to the president's office by myself, but I'm glad you're going with me."

They walked into the outer office where Lewis' secretary was sitting. "Go right in Professor Cummings. The board is waiting for you."

Dr. and Mrs. Cummings entered the board room with its oak-paneled walls and stained glass windows with the university symbol in each one. Five people - one woman and four men - sat at the oak table, including the president, Dr. Montgomery Lewis. It was as silent as a tomb until Lewis spoke. "Martin, Esmie; it is good to see you again. Please have a seat." Esmie guided her husband to an empty chair and sat down beside him.

"I received your letter about this meeting," Martin droned, his voice cold and distant. "Why have I been summoned here today?"

"We would never demand anything from a distinguished professor and archeologist as significant as yourself. It was more like an invitation than a summons," Ann Vickers, the female board member replied sweetly.

Esmie responded, "Let's do away with all these banalities and cut to the chase. Why are my husband and I here?" Silence again blanketed the room as each member of the board turned their head toward Lewis. Clearing his throat, Lewis began. "First, I want to thank you for all your hard work at this university. We are truly appreciative of all your efforts."

Martin interrupted saying, "Thanks, now why am I here?"

"This is very difficult to say." Esmie recognized a stall when she heard one. "As you know, your last expedition in Guatemala to find the lost city Nakanjo was fruitless." One of the other male board members joined the discussion.

"At an expenditure of over 10 million dollars, I might add."

"And your point?" his wife queried.

"We can no longer fund your archeological travels to Guatemala," stated Lewis.

"In other words," Ann Vickers stated, "We refuse to throw good money after bad!"

"But we are very close," Martin protested. "This cannot be repeated to anyone outside this room. Do you understand?" Everyone on the board nodded in agreement. Martin appended, "We are closer to finding this Mayan city than we have ever been before!"

"There is another problem," interjected Montgomery without making comment on the bit of information that he had just learned. Esmie knew what he was about to bring up. "There's the issue of your diminishing eyesight."

"How dare you!" his wife raised her voice.

"Now, now, Mrs. Cummings. There is no need for you to take on a hostile tone of voice."

"So now we come to it! Martin raised his voice. "I'm to be given a pink slip. That's what this is all about, isn't it?"

"On the contrary, the board wants you to stay on and continue teaching," another board member retorted.

Martin was furious at the proposal. "Is this done out of pity? Because under those circumstances, I refuse your offer!"

"It's out of the question," his wife barked. "There are plenty of other higher learning institutions that would be pleased to have my husband on their staff." *With his eye condition, they too would probably not be interested in hiring Martin.* "Maybe we should start contacting them," she told her husband.

"You have misunderstood," spoke up Lewis.

"How is that?" questioned Martin.

"Not only do we want you to continue teaching here but you are to continue your work in Guatemala."

"I'm confused. I thought that you said that this university could no longer grant funds for this endeavor."

"I did, but now something has changed." Husband and wife looked at each other with bewilderment.

"Not too long ago we received a huge donation of money."

"How large?" Martin wanted to know.

"10 million dollars."

"The donor had only two conditions; that all the money be put toward the next expeditions to find the lost city; and that you would continue as the leader of the expedition." Both Martin and Esmie's jaws dropped to the floor.

"Is this a joke?" inquired the professor.

"Not at all."

"What is the name of the donor?"

"He wishes to remain anonymous. In fact, if he finds that his wish is broken, he threatens to stop payment on the check." The Cummings could not believe their good luck.

CHAPTER 27

GUATEMALA

Chocko Renteria was in and out of consciousness. The heat in the corrugated tin hut where he was being held was intensified with the break of each new day. Streams of sweat formed on his neck and face and his clothes were saturated with perspiration. When he was left alone, he struggled against the ropes that bound him hand and foot to the chair, but he was not successful. Frustration added to his anxiety. The last thing he could remember before he was thrown into his present situation was that he had been home sleeping when he was roughly rousted from his bed, his hands tied behind him, and a black hood forcefully put over his head. There had been a rough truck ride until the vehicle came to a jarring stop. The prisoner thought that it had been at least three days since he had been taken, but he couldn't be sure. He hadn't seen anyone and his throat had become sore from the screaming for help that had gotten him nowhere. Suddenly, he could detect two male voices talking outside, but he could not make out what they were saying.

"Ayudame! Por Dios, me ayude!" The door unexpectedly flew open. Four men entered. Three of them had AB-3 assault rifles slung over their shoulders while the third carried a Glock 43 in his hand. All four were dressed in camouflage uniforms. The four with the rifles seemed like young men. Someone suddenly yanked the hood off his head. Their leader had a moustache and goatee that looked like it was overgrown from lack of trimming. The man held a cup of water. He lifted it to his lips and he drank deeply. The captive watched helplessly as the liquid was swallowed. *"Agua, por favor,"* the cracked lipped man croaked. The leader held the cup to his lips and allowed him two gulps. *"Mas agua, por favor!"*

"You will get more water after you answer my questions, Senor Renteria." Chocko pleaded with his captors. "I am a poor person with very little money! You have taken the wrong man!"

"There has not been a mistake made. We wanted you!" Chocko looked at his abductors with a wary eye.

"Why am I here?"

"For information."

"Who are you people?"

"We form the group Nueva Luz, the New Order!"

"For what purpose?"

"We and our compatriots have formed a guerilla group set on freeing our people from the ruthless dictator who calls himself the President of Guatemala."

"What does all of this have to do with me?"

"Along with the president, we intend to drive out all foreign influence from our land."

"I still don't understand why I was taken." With a flick of their leader's head, one of the soldiers moved up and drove the butt of his rifle into Renteria's midsection and he doubled up. The wind was knocked out of him for a few minutes. Once his breathing became regular, he sat up erectly.

"Do not play us for fools, senor! We know about your dealings in our country with the foreign pig!"

"I don't know who you mean!" This time their leader delivered a vicious blow across Chocko's face. The wallop cracked the prisoner's lip as his head was violently turned left. Immediately, his bloody bottom lip began to drip unto his sweaty shirt.

"I can get the truth out of you the easy way or the hard way. It's your choice to make."

"Yes, that's true," he sputtered as blood flew from his mouth.

"Good! Now we are getting somewhere. And who are these people you work for?" Renteria balanced the information he had with his strong desire to stay alive.

"They are an American couple called the Cummings." He hoped that he would buy it and not be forced to give up Thierry's name.

"Why are they here in our country?" *They bought it. My biggest benefactor is safe but when I get out, it will cost Thierry a pretty penny for what I am going through. If he refuses, I will give up his name to the New Order.*

"They are archeologists from the United States looking for a lost city."

"What is the name of the city?"

"That I don't know."

"Have they discovered it yet?"

"No." Chocko watched as the man raised his hand once more. "That's all I know! I swear it!" The leader stood for a moment his hand poised to strike like a lethal cobra, but after he thought about it, he let his arm drop down to his side.

"I believe you, Chocko." He took the cup of water and once more held it to his prisoner's lips until it was drained.

"Now that I've told you everything, will you let me go?"

"Yes, I will release you but under one condition."

"What is that?"

"If these people make contact, you will send me word."

"How do I contact you?"

"There is no need to worry about that. One of my men will have you under constant surveillance. Do you understand?"

"Yes, I understand."

"If I feel that you are holding back information from me, you will be taken back here and you will not remain alive. I hope that is clear to you."

"Yes, very clear." The man with the facial hair snapped his fingers and one of the guards untied him from the chair, retied his hands, put the black hood over his head and marched him out to the truck.

Once the truck pulled away, the leader, Salvador Hermoza related to the man standing next to him, "The stupid American couple are looking for this lost city because they believe it holds treasure. We will not stop them from finding it and when they do, we will kill them and the others and use the treasure to buy more armaments to free our country. The other man nodded enthusiastically in agreement.

CHAPTER 28

RAINFOREST OF GUATEMALA, JULY 2004

The Cummings and their expeditionary party boarded the ship, *The Panama Queen*, that set sail from Miami. Husband and wife could have taken a plane to Guatemala City but it involved layovers and a long difficult trip to the coast to meet the ship. By traveling with the others, they could make daily checks of their equipment. For Esmie there was an air of excited anticipation since this was her first chance to leave the familiar campus and explore the unknown.

The ship plodded along for eight days until the port of Flora was in sight as the daylight pushed away the inkiness of the night sky. The heat of the day was oppressive as the ship was docked. Coming down the gang plank with his wife guiding him, her hand on his elbow, Martin and Esmie presented their passports to the local official whose name was Esteban Morales. The outside of the building was dilapidated and the interior was even worse. Plastered walls were slowly falling apart and the electric fan above turned so slowly that it could not possibly beat back the overwhelming heat and humidity. Morales reflected his surroundings. He was a plump man who had a ragged moustache and wore a dirty khaki uniform that had sweat stains under the arms. The official sat behind a row of desks in which he was the only government employee to be seen. Esmie thought, *It's no wonder this place doesn't see too much tourism!* The man took their passports and looked carefully at the pictures of the man and woman who stood before him.

"And what are you doing in my country, Dr. Cummings? Is it for business or for pleasure? Mrs. Cummings thought with incredulity,

Pleasure? He must be joking! Esmie hadn't moved but already her forehead dripped with perspiration.

"We are an expeditionary group on an archeological exploration." The official rubbed his scruffy chin with his hand and looked at them with a skeptical eye.

"Tomb robbers?" he smirked.

Martin indignantly answered, "We are most certainly not! My wife and I are respected archeologists from Trinity University in the United States!" He handed over the official permission from the Guatemalan government allowing them entrance to the country. Esteban scrutinized it carefully. In time, he looked up and shrugged saying, "You may enter." He stamped both passports. The Cummings waited while each of their group also had their passports stamped. Then they began to unload the equipment.

Exiting the building, Martin told the others to wait for him as his wife accompanied him down the dusty street. The people stared at them with blank expressions. Car horns went off as they maneuvered around slow-moving horses and carts that were everywhere kicking up clouds of dust that choked the air. Esmie Cummings wondered if the town looked any different than the one founded by the Spanish in the 16th century. She doubted it.

"Where are we heading?" requested Esmie.

"I have to hire some porters. We're going over to the next plaza where laborers wait to be hired." Esmie noticed that there was not one single flower that she could see from the street. *This place's name sure is a misnomer!* They walked until they saw a congregation of mestizo men, smoking and talking as they waited for someone to hire them. As they approached, Martin called out, "Chocko Renteria, I'm looking for Chocko Renteria!" From out of the mass of males scurried a man who more closely resembled a native rodent called the capybara because of his elongated nose and his general unkempt appearance. A smile flashed that revealed yellowed teeth and gaps where teeth once had been. Taking off his straw hat and wiping his forehead with his arm, he stretched out his hand. "It is good to see you again Senor Cummings."

"It is good to see you too. This is my wife," he announced.

"Senora Cummings, a pleasure," he declared as he kept bobbing his head like a bobble head doll. Esmie only smiled. "Are you on another expedition, senor?"

"I am. I'll need 20 good bearers."

"Si, and how many quetzal will you pay a day, senor?"

"Five dollars a day."

"American dollars?"

"Yes."

"But Senor, the question is what will you pay me for my managing them?" Martin smiled expecting this mercenary inquiry. "Double what I pay the others. Now go and pick out the best men." As soon as Chocko told the men what the American was willing to pay, they eagerly called out to him.

"Chocko is an unusual name," observed Esmie to her husband

"It is slang for the Spanish word chocolate something that Renteria has a penchant for eating."

"I don't like him," she started, "and there's something about him that tells me he shouldn't be trusted."

"Ridiculous, he has been my guide every time I've come down here and there's been no trouble."

"Will you explore the area the old man told you along the Rio Los…"

"Quiet!" he warned her. "And make sure you leave all the talking with Chocko to me! Understand?" Esmie nodded like a dutiful wife. She was suddenly reminded of her own father's browbeating toward her mother. *I hate myself right now!*

The expedition began on rented trucks along dusty, bumpy paths that lead to the tropical jungle. On the outskirts of the green rain forest, the trucks were unloaded and then turned toward the port of Flora.

Dividing up what was to be carried, Chocko yelled, "Okay, move out!" With a machete in hand, Renteria slashed at the vegetation, creating an entrance that had not been there before. The exertion in the hot, stifling, and humid air slowed the pace and required frequent breaks. Their sweat quickly drew swarms of mosquitoes which they had to constantly swat away. The jungle was alive with the sounds of chirping birds. Esmie was forever beside Martin, brushing away leaves that would have hit him in the face, and giving him water to make sure he was hydrated. With great difficulty, they tramped on until they finally put up tents and made camp for the evening.

A bonfire was lit to cook as well as to keep jaguars at a distance. Once she had Martin on his cot with netting draped over him, Esmie retired to her own cot, but sleep did not come right away. Even without moving, Esmie was aware that she was continually drenched in her own perspiration. She could tell by her husband's snoring that he was exhausted. She wondered how long Martin could keep up this grueling pace.

When the sun broke through the tree canopy, Esmie got up, feeling as exhausted as when she went to bed. She found Martin lying down but wide awake. "Did you get enough rest?"

"I've been awake for a little while." She helped him to his feet. "I feel it," he announced unreservedly.

"You feel what?"

"I can sense that this time we will find Nakanjo!"

"How can you be certain?"

"Something deep inside me says that this will be the time!"

"I hope you're right."

"You must believe," he added in a voice that sounded like that of a preacher.

Esmie walked her husband outside where breakfast was being prepared by Chocko. "Sit, sit," he told them and poured them both a cup of coffee. Esmie wished she could have something cold but in this wilderness, modern conveniences were nowhere to be found. Tortillas filled with cut up plantains were devoured by the group. While the couple ate, Chocko made sure that everything was packed before they left and then once more they followed him closer to the Rio Los Esclaves.

For six days, this scenario continued as Martin Cumming's fatigue kept slowing the party down. All at once Chocko stopped slashing. "Why have you stopped?" inquired Mrs. Cummings.

"Listen!" instructed their guide. Esmie listened carefully to a soft rumbling.

"What is that?" she asked with some confusion.

"It is the rush of water from the Rio Los Esclaves. We are within reach of it!"

"Thank God! Let's move forward." The whole party was excited by the news. Even Martin perked up when he heard they were close to their destination. As they drew closer, the sound of the river grew louder. Finally, the last of the fronds was cut away, revealing the cascade of foamy water that rushed from the mountains and drained into the Pacific Ocean. "We'll make camp here!" Dr. Cummings declared. Chocko looked up to the sky.

"But Senor, I don't understand. It is just past midday. We can go on because there are many more hours before sunset."

"We'll stop here. I'm too tired to go any further today." Shrugging at the gringo's words, Chocko ordered the men to set up camp. Although he was tired, Martin wanted the time to speak to his wife privately. Once their tent was up and the flap closed for confidentiality, Martin opened a waist pack that he never took off. He pulled out a rolled parchment. "What is that?" his curious wife asked.

"Keep your voice down," warned the professor. "Come sit by me." They sat on his cot before he unrolled a map.

"Is this a map to Nakanjo?"

"It is."

"How were you able to get your hands on it?"

"Remember when I told you that I drew a rudimentary sketch based on the old Indian's story?"

"I recall."

"I lied. This was his map. I took it when the old man died."

"Who drew it?"

"It is believed it was Brother Gallego who accompanied Cesar de Leon's army on his conquest in 1524. He drew it from the time they left this river until they reached the city."

"My God, if this is correct we are assured success!"

"But there is something off about it. I have tried to pinpoint it and failed."

"It has to be close by," exclaimed Esmie optimistically.

"Still, look at this carefully and memorize the route and where the city is located."

"But why, we can just use the map."

"If something should happen to it, the city would be lost again."

"Are you saying that Chocko might steal it?"

"Just memorize the right side of the fold of the map. I have already learned and committed to memory the left side."

"Why do we have to do that?"

"Because if we are questioned, neither one of us knows the complete directions. Besides we will need each other to get where we're going. Using her index finger, Esmie followed the route on the aged map. Her finger followed the route of the river to the southwest until she came to Lago de Ayarza. To the north were three hills and then northeast from there, the map said Nakanjo.

"Have you memorized your part?"

"I have." Without warning, Martin grabbed the map from her hand and pulled out a cigarette lighter. He lit the map at its corner.

"Are you crazy? What are you doing?" She tried to grab it from him but in what seemed like a second, the paper was completely consumed by flickering flames.

"Don't worry," he tried to calm his exasperated wife. "As long as we both stay alive, we will find it." Martin was sure that the plan would not blow up in their faces.

Sunlight had barely broken over the horizon as the raging waters of the Rio Los Esclavos roared in the background.

"Martin! Where are you?" Esmie screamed with a terror that rose every second she could not locate her husband. Her cries awoke the other members of the expedition.

"Senora!" Chocko Renteria shouted and grabbed the hysterical woman by the arm. "What is wrong?" The other members of the party gathered around in distress.

"Martin is gone!" she cried wrenching her arm from Guatemalan's hand.

"Are you sure?" Esmie gave him a look that could kill. She restrained herself from slapping him across his cheek.

"He was not in the tent when I woke up! I looked for him outside our tent but I could not find him anywhere. I've called his name to no avail."

Chocko turned to the others instructing them in a loud voice, "Fan out and cover the area. If you find him call out." The bearers quickly broke up and went into the jungle calling out his name. "Do not worry, Senora! We will find him." The American aides who had traveled with the couple joined the others in the search for their beloved employer.

"Oh no," she gasped. "What if he fell into the river?" Renteria hesitated to tell her that if anyone had fallen into the torrent of water, they were most likely drowned.

"Join us in the search, Senora," he suggested.

"No, I'll stay here on the chance that he comes back into camp!" With that said, he too disappeared into the green foliage of the tropical rain forest.

Esmie Cummings watched Chocko disappear and heard her husband's name being called in the distance. She watched the turbulent water thunder pass her. She paced along the bank looking for any sign that her husband had been there. She found nothing. *My God, even a sighted man would have a hard time surviving in these tempestuous waters. Martin would never survive if he fell in. Still, even though his eyesight is poor, there was nothing wrong with his hearing. He would never have wandered so close to the river.* She ran along the bank screaming his name until she was almost hoarse.

Hours dragged by as the sun rose to its apex and the heat became intolerable. Esmie was inconsolable as her tears flowed down her cheeks. Suddenly, the skies darkened with black clouds shutting out the sun. Within a few minutes, the cracks of lightning and the thumping of rain drops plopped on the green leaves surrounding the camp before the pelting rain and furious thunder drowned out the sound of the river. Reluctantly, Esmie retreated to her tent. Before she was undercover, Martin's wife and collaborator was drenched to the bone. Drying herself as best she could, she collapsed on her husband's cot. *Where did you go on your own? Why didn't you wake me as you usually do to help you? Where could you be?* She hoped to hear the answers to these questions from his own mouth. *If he is even still alive! Stop it!* She told herself. *I can't think like that. Renteria and his men will find you, I know they will! Then you will be safely back in my arms again.*

For the first time since they had met, Mrs. Cummings came to the startling realization that she had actually fallen in love with her husband. This feeling made her even more desperate to find him alive. *Will he ever hear it from my lips?* Dr. Esmie Cummings had a sinking feeling in her stomach that it would never happen.

The rain slackened slowly until it finally came to an end. She opened the flap of the tent and stepped out to discover that the clouds had moved on and the sun had broken through. There was even a rainbow that stretched across the sky. The Rio Los Esclavos seemed even more swollen with water after the storm's soaking rain.

From behind Esmie, there came the sound of something approaching. She hoped that one of Renteria's men was leading her lost husband back to her. Her spirits rose as the wet plant life was parted by a hand but it was not her husband's face, although she so desperately wanted to see him again. Two of the bearers returned soaking wet. Mrs. Cummings approached them saying, "Dr. Cummings?"

"No, Senora. We looked all over but could not find him anywhere." In time, as the others returned, she received the same reply to her inquiry. Nobody had found him. It was as if he disappeared off the face of the earth. Esmie's last hope had eroded as each succeeding party came back to camp with the same news. Retreating into her tent, the missing professor's wife dissolved into tears.

"Mrs. Cummings," Esmie heard Chocko's voice come from outside her tent. "May I talk with you?"

"Come in," she answered desperately trying to control her emotions. Renteria entered the tent.

"I'm sorry to say that with all our searching we could not find your husband. We tried very hard but it was no use."

"I know Chocko and I want to thank you for your efforts. Please express that to your men for me."

"I will."

"We will start back to San Cristobal immediately. After that, I will fly to Guatemala City to see the American ambassador. Hopefully, he will be able to order a more extensive search. Go and tell your men to pack everything up."

She had been so preoccupied with finding her husband that she had not thought about the expedition. Without Martin's remembrance of his part of the map, the quest for the lost city was over. The two parts of the map had been burned until there were only ashes left behind. As she packed, disturbing thoughts crossed her mind. *Why did he feel the need to burn the map? Was he being intimidated by someone? Had someone threatened his life to obtain it?*

CHAPTER 29

THE ISLE OF MALTA

Armand Thierry stood outside on the balcony of the villa he owned on the island of Malta. Located on the mesa of Ta' Dmejrek Mountain, 830 feet above the blue Mediterranean Sea, the view was usually magnificent. But today a storm was sweeping up from North Africa and forcibly pushing forward. Far below, the number of whitecaps increased as the wind whipped up the water. The rumbling of thunder began to boom in the distance as the sun was overcome with the vastness of gray clouds that gradually became black. A huge storm was about to break over him.

His white hair, usually in place, now began to blow in the wind and he decided to go in before he was caught in the downpour. Ramon sat inside, thumbing through a magazine. *Why haven't I heard from him yet?* He wasn't used to being kept waiting and he detested it. "Can I get you anything, boss?"

"No, nothing!" Armand was expecting a very important phone call that hadn't come through yet, and he was beginning to develop a stress headache. The customarily cool and calculating person was now anxious with anticipation.

"What's the matter boss? I've never seen you like this before."

"Nothing's wrong with me!" Armand snapped. *He's right of course. I need to hold it together!* Ramon went back to his magazine

Sitting down in his plush leather chair in his study, he decided to gaze at some of the artwork he owned. *That never fails to quiet my jangled nerves.* Thierry leaned back in his chair and focused his eyes on the wall on the opposite side of the room. Hanging there was a frieze of two dancing girls which was taken illegally from Angkor Wat in Cambodia and smuggled to him. *It cost me millions but it was well worth it!* On the wall behind his desk hung a landscape painting created during the Tang Dynasty in China by the painter Li Sixun, called *Misty Mountains* which was worth millions. A glass case protected it. Both pieces of art were bathed in low lighting from the ceiling. It was like this in every one of his houses. They were the repositories of illicitly-gained works of art from around the world.

He walked over to the bar and grabbed the brandy decanter and a glass and poured himself a "liquid Prozac". His attention was diverted to the first drops of rain that hit against the window. *Damn him! Why hasn't he called? It's been days since I last heard from him.*

In an instant, the patter of rain became an angry downpour that beat against the glass windows. His cell phone finally rang and he was startled as it shattered the silence. Thierry removed it from his inside jacket pocket and watched as Ramon left the room. Whenever his boss was talking to a person in the room or receiving a phone call, his henchman knew not to hang around. Armand waited for him to leave the room before he pushed the green phone button and put the device to his ear. "Yes?"

"Senor Thierry, it's Chocko Renteria."

"Do you have good news for me?"

"Si. Senor Cummings is dead!"

"Excellent!"

"A military detachment was sent over to find him. They recovered his body miles away and said that it was, mostly likely, an unintentional drowning. They're assuming he woke up and was disoriented, went outside and fell into the river. It has been listed officially by the police as an accident, senor."

"And the map, do you have it in your possession?" The phone went suddenly hushed. "Hello, Renteria? Have we been disconnected?"

"No senor, I am still here."

"What about the map? You do have it, don't you?"

"No, Senor Thierry. I don't have it." Armand lost his patience.

"Why the hell not?"

"I searched his pockets, the inside of his hat, took off his shoes…I searched him completely but he didn't have the map on him." Thierry's voice grew low.

"I'm disappointed, very disappointed, Renteria." At that moment, a tremendous clap of thunder rang out and a crooked flash of lightning cut a jagged path across the sky. The downpour of precipitation became even more violent than before.

"Senor, I did my best. I believe Mrs. Cummings must have the map in her possession. I could not search for it because she was always inside or not far away from the tent!"

"I suppose so."

"Senor Thierry, you will send the rest of the money as you promised?"

"You only accomplished half the job. You'll get no more of my money."

"But Senor, I risked my life and besides…" Armand hung up. *I see that I'll have to take control of this situation myself if I want things to get done right!* He pushed a button under his desk.

"You called me, sir?" inquired Ramon.

"Call the airport and tell my pilot to be ready to take off when the weather decides to cooperate, understand?"

"What will be your destination, boss?"

"Someplace in the United States called Oxnard, California, wherever that is."

"Yes, sir." Armand sat back in his easy chair and thought about all the pleasant conversations he would have convincing Mrs. Cummings to turn over her husband's work to him. *If the professor willingly gives me the information I want, there will be no problem. But if she resists me, she will know how unpleasant I can be!* Oh, how he hoped Esmie would resist.

CHAPTER 30

GUATEMALA

Search parties were sent out by United States Ambassador Colin Speeks once Esmie explained the dire situation of her husband. She took a room at a small hotel and waited for some word of the fate of her husband. Every day she called Speek's office to find out if he had been found, and every day she received the same answer. "There is no information yet."

Esmie contacted Trinity University and spoke directly to Montgomery Lewis. "He's missing, she explained to the president.

After the first shock of the news faded away, he inquired, "How could that have happened?"

"It seems he wandered away from the tent at night or just before dawn."

"And you didn't hear him?" A flash of rage coursed through her veins at this question.

"Don't you think I would have stopped him if I'd heard anything?"

"Of course you would," Lewis said regretting his inquiry. Trying to placate her, he added, "Please keep in touch. We all will be praying for the two of you."

Hanging up, Esmie pondered, *Should I pray for him even though neither one of us ever talked about our lack of religious beliefs?* She felt awkward talking to someone she couldn't see but she didn't know how else she could help her husband.

Eleven days after she had registered in the hotel, a black limousine with two miniature American flags fluttering in the breeze pulled up and someone knocked on the door. "Ambassador Speeks would like to see you."

"Has he been found?"

"I don't know but the Ambassador has asked you to come to the embassy."

On the ride, her mind bounced back and forth as to whether she would hear good news or bad news. Esmie wished the chauffer would speed up so that she could finally hear something.

Two armed American Marines opened the gate and the limousine drove up to the embassy door. At the top of the marble stars, she arrived at the ambassador's office. His secretary ushered her inside. "Mrs. Cummings, please have a seat." Esmie could tell from his grave expression that the news would not be good.

"Is he alive?" she demanded upon sitting down. Speeks took his seat behind his desk before he spoke up.

"I'm afraid the news is not good." Esmie visibly shrank in depression after hearing this.

"Where was he found?"

"Apparently, he fell into the river and because of the strong current, drowned and was washed miles downstream." Esmie's hand flew to her mouth.

"My God."

"His body has been brought here for you to identify. Do you feel up to it?" Esmie nodded her head and replied, "I am."

The ambassador walked around his desk and took her hand. Esmie stood up. "I'm truly sorry for your loss. I had hoped the outcome of the search would have turned out better than this."

"Thank you for your assistance." The ambassador's assistant accompanied her down an elevator to the basement. He took her to a room where a covered body was laying on a table. For a moment, Mrs. Cummings felt as if her feet were cemented to the floor. With great force of will she walked to the body. The assistant pulled off the sheet. What Esmie witnessed forced the acrid taste of bile into her throat. The clothes were her husbands but his body was bloated from the length of time it had been submerged in the water. "It's him." The sheet was once more drawn over the body. "The ambassador wants you to take his private plane back to Oxnard with your husband's body. Please advise us as to when you want to leave."

"Please, thank him."

Dr. Cummings could not remember the ride back to her hotel, but somehow found herself sitting on the bed. She just wanted to lie down and close her eyes, but arrangements had to be made. She called a local funeral home so that Martin could travel in a coffin, and afterwards called Montgomery Lewis. "He's dead," she sobbed over the phone.

"Esmie, I'm so sorry. His death is a great loss not only for you but for his students and this university."

"I have a favor to ask of you."

"Anything you need."

"Since Martin and I have no religious affiliation, and since he dedicated most of his adult life to his students and Trinity University, I was hoping you would be agreeable to burying him somewhere on the campus."

"Think of it as already done. We will hold a memorial in the university chapel for him once you return."

"I should be back in a couple of days."

When she hung up, Esmie phoned the embassy to let them know that she wanted to leave with her husband's body as soon as possible. Once more she broke down into tears. *This is so unlike me. I feel so vulnerable right now*

Dr. Cummings had one more phone call to make. Looking at her husband's phone directory, she located Chocko Renteria's phone number. She dialed and listened to it ring. *It's only right that he should know about Martin's death. After all, he has acted as a guide for him for many years.* "Hello?"

"Chocko? It's Mrs. Cummings."

"Has there been any word about the professor?"

"I'm sorry to tell you that he was found dead in the river today."

"This is a sad day, Senora. He was truly a great man."

"Yes, he was. I am flying his body back to California and I wanted you to know because of your long affiliation with my husband."

"Thank you, Senora. If one day you decide to continue his search for the lost city, I hope you will call upon me for my help as your husband did." With this, the phone call ended. *With all that has happened, I've forgotten the reason we both had come down here in the first place. But after Martin had burned both pieces of the map, there's no way it will be found any.*

CHAPTER 31

OXNARD, CALIFORNIA, OCTOBER, 2005

Esmie received an offer from Trinity University to replace her husbands. The budget it offered wasn't as large as some from the bigger colleges, but she was promised free reign over how it was to be spent. Being Mrs. Cummings had finally paid off big time.

She became a permanent resident of California and within a few months, she was shown her cutting-edge modern lab by the president of the university. With the decision to hire Dr. Cummings, Trinity University was now on the map.

It took months to interview and hire competent assistants before Dr. Cummings could begin working on the next journey through the thick jungle of Guatemala. As she prepared for the trip, she could not help but think back to the last time she was there when her husband had disappeared.

Just because Trinity University had given her department a generous budget, Esmie didn't feel the compunction to squander it away. She bought equipment sparingly and only if it would help her research. Besides, she was not eager to return to Guatemala since her husband had died there. She was much more comfortable in the lab than she ever was in the field. But she knew she would have to eventually go back.

In the first year in Oxnard after her husband's death, she had ventured out to the Mississippi to explore the American Indian mound cultures. In the county of Chickasaw, a previously undisturbed area outside the city of La Croix, Mississippi there was a region consisting of six conical mounds covered in grass where the dig had begun. Along with her assistants, she brought with her some promising archeological students who would do the grunt work of digging. A suitable place was chosen for their campsite.

Within a few weeks, the first artifact was uncovered and after a few months, Esmie returned with her prized discoveries. She was extremely pleased with what had been accomplished.

The group arrived on their flight back to Los Angeles and then to Oxnard, and Esmie waited impatiently for the artifacts to be delivered. When they did, the chairperson of the department invited the board to a viewing. As the professor unwrapped each in front of the board, the members smiled politely but were strangely silent. After all was laid out, Esmie turned toward the board members. The expressions she saw on their faces reflected disappointment instead of elation. "What's the matter?"

President Montgomery Lewis with a strained smile that was plastered on his face, paused before he said, "I really don't know how to put this to you."

"Just tell me."

"Your time in Mississippi although productive, is not what the board expected when we hired you to replace your husband."

"In what way?"

"Well, we expected that you would continue your husband's work in search of the lost city of Nakanjo. When you requested the field trip to Mississippi, well, we were hoping for more dramatic finds." The members of the board spoke up in agreement with Lewis. Esmie was determined not to let this gaggle of bureaucratic pomposity get the upper hand.

"I am not one of those department heads who spends university money without thinking things through. My husband made two trips to Guatemala and came up empty handed. The last time he sadly disappeared and died."

"Such a horrible tragedy," Lewis attempted to console her.

"Yes, it was. After that, I didn't have the heart to continue his search. All Martin had to go on were bits of information and an old Indian's story about the city's location. If I continue in his footsteps I will not only be wasting your money but wasting my time. I will not attempt another trip there until I have more concrete information to work with."

"We were hoping that you would continue his work by doing research in Madrid. I'm sure Dr. Cummings did, but perhaps he missed a piece of vital information that could solve this puzzle. What do you say to that proposal?"

"Is the board willing to pay for this excursion?"

"Of course, within reason."

"Then I'm going to formally ask for a year's sabbatical in which to do my research for the upcoming school year.

"This is such short notice. I don't even know who I would put in your place."

"As chairman of the department?"

"Never," he answered reassuringly. "Just as a teacher."

"I believe Kevin March, an adjunct professor here, would be an excellent choice. I'm sure he would accept the offer. I don't know him very well, but I am confident that he would."

"Good! I will get the formal paper work done immediately." Lewis swallowed hard and looked at the other board members before he turned to face her. "I believe that all of what you asked for can be arranged."

"Then I'll start making arrangements right away." She was elated by the decision. *I just kicked their asses!*

CHAPTER 32

MADRID, SPAIN

When Iberia Airlines Flight 457 landed at Madrid's airport, the sun had been up for hours. An exhausted Esmie Cummings disembarked and after collecting her luggage, hailed a cab and instructed him to drive to a small but satisfactory hotel named Puerta del Sol, conveniently located near El Escorial. She checked with the accommodating desk clerk, and when a young man showed her to her room and she tipped him, Esmie immediately crawled into bed and slept for the next three and a half hours.

It was late afternoon when she finally was awakened by the bells of a nearby church. Yawning and stretching, she realized that it was already too late to start her research. After taking a hot shower, Dr. Cummings dressed and took the elevator down to the lobby. Just across the street from her hotel was a quaint restaurant where she went to have some dinner. Enjoying a dish of paella and a half bottle of claret, the researcher decided to walk it off by touring Madrid at night.

As daylight faded into a starlit night, she strolled among the natives and listened to their lilting language as she passed them on the street. After an hour, Esmie made her way back to the hotel sufficiently tired so that she could get a good night's sleep.

With the rays of the sun shining on her face, and the traffic noise outside her window, she woke up refreshed. After a breakfast of a roll with butter, curd flavored with honey, and a cup of coffee, Esmie got into a taxi carrying a brown leather portfolio. She was driven through heavily trafficked streets to a palace, now a museum known as the El Escorial. She showed her documents to the guards and one of them escorted her to the office of the director. The door was opened by a young woman who allowed her into Senor Rebolledo's office. Standing immediately when she appeared, he came from behind his desk to lift her hand to his lips. He was a diminutive man of 5'6", dressed impeccably with a neatly trimmed moustache. "Senora Cummings, it is a pleasure to meet you at last. Please have a seat."

"Thank you."

"May I offer you some coffee or tea?"

"No thank you, I've already had my morning coffee." Dr. Cummings reached for her portfolio and began to remove her identification as well as letters of introduction and permits issued to her by the Spanish government. Rebolledo waved them away with his hand.

"Please, Senora that will be unnecessary. Your husband's stellar reputation has preceded you. Let me just say how saddened I was on learning of Dr. Cumming's death. He was truly a great man."

"Thank you for your kind words."

"He spoke of you often." *That's interesting since the last time Martin was here it was before we were even married.* Esmie suddenly stood up indicating that she was through with small talk.

"I must get started with my research." Kissing her hand once more, he said,

"If there's anything I can do to help expedite your work, please feel free to contact me any time, night or day."

"Adios, Senor Rebolledo."

"Adios, Senora Cummings."

The young woman who had opened the door for her escorted the professor to the Ancient Manuscripts Department where a sentry stood guard. He unlocked the door and turned on the lights in the room. In the middle of the room stood a wooden table and chairs surrounded by stacks of books.

Before her escort left, she indicated that a pair of surgical gloves was required to eliminate any body sweat that would deteriorate the centuries-old books. The guard stayed inside the room and closed the door. *So much for trust!*

She glanced around the room taking it all in. *I have my work cut out for me in the next weeks.*

CHAPTER 33

RAINFOREST IN GUATEMALA

While the cocaine was bundled into easily-handled packages by some workers, others weighed each so that they were an exact weight. Local peasants with low-paying or no jobs at all were recruited with higher wages then they had ever seen. Farmers were enticed by cash incentives to pull out the crops they were growing and root coca plants in the soil instead. Anyone who balked at the idea was shot down.

Bonifacio Millian had the whole business running like a well-oiled machine. He personally oversaw every part of the process, trusting no one else to do it for him. He had his hand in every part of his enterprise, even to the bribing of local and national government officials.

Twice a year he flew his jet to Guatemala City, the capitol of the country, to visit with its president, Miguel Soza. One day he had called Soza to say that he was flying in and that he should clear his calendar. There was no argument from the president. With him, Millian carried a plain brown leather attaché case. It was a short flight that took less than an hour to arrive at the private airport. Renting a medium-priced car, he drove from the outskirts of the city to the presidential palace, parking in a "No Parking Zone" in the front of the building. The guards all knew who he was and Millian was permitted to pass freely in and out of the magnificent edifice.

Bonifacio walked up the staircase to the presidential office, bypassed the receptionist, opened the door and brazenly walked in. The two soldiers standing guard on either side of the door made no attempt to stop him. Miguel looked up from behind his impressive cherry wood desk. "Bonifacio, my friend, how have you been?" The president, a short dumpy fellow with a smattering of hair on his head, got up, walked around the desk and gave his visitor a hug. Miguel could feel the holster and Glock positioned under Millian's jacket. "The Executioner" patted the president's back as a sign to release his hold of the drug king.

"I'm well, and yourself?"

"Even if I am having a bad day, seeing you always makes me feel better." *I'm sure that the money I bring has something to do with his pleasant attitude,* thought Millian.

"That is good to hear," responded Bonifacio.

"Come and sit with me for a while." Millian sat in a brown leather club chair next to a small table. He put the money case on it. The president could not take his eyes off the case. *It's like watching a wolf just before it springs on its prey.* Miguel walked over to a hidden bar behind two glass doors and queried, "You will join me in having a little drink of cognac, no?"

"With pleasure." As Bonifacio watched the man pour the Remy Martin Black Pearl Cognac, one of the most expensive cognacs in the world, he knew that one of the reasons he could afford such a luxury was because of him. The other reason was that the United States government was paying huge amounts of currency to Guatemala to destroy any drugs being produced in the country. This money was going directly into Soza's pocket. *Americanos estupidos!*

Miguel took a seat next to his guest. Holding a glass out to Millian, he said, "To our mutual interests! May we continue our prosperity!"

"Most assuredly." They clicked their glasses and let the smooth liquor flow down their throats. Soza's eyes returned to the case lying on the table.

"May I?" the president inquired in a foxy manner.

"Be my guest." He snapped open the locks and opened it. His eyes immediately glazed over with greed.

"Two million American dollars as we agreed upon?"

"It is all there." Soza put his hand on the paper money and fondled it as if he were touching a woman's breast. Bonifacio found it unsettling to watch.

"Why don't you put it in your safe?" the drug king suggested. His words seemed to snap Miguel out of his reverie and back to reality.

"Yes, of course." Taking the case to his desk, he sat down and worked the tumbler of the safe under his desk. He quickly piled the bundles into the safe and closed the door. He brought the case back to its owner and sat down. "It is good to see you again!" Bonifacio simply smiled at the statement. *You mean it is good to see my money again, you pig!*

"Well, I must be going."

"I'm sure you are a very busy man."

"The Executioner" got up out of his chair. "Very true. Until we meet again, take care of yourself".

The president got up to hug him again. Bonifacio stuck out his hand to indicate that a handshake was more than enough as a farewell.

"You do the same," the president said shaking hands.

Bonifacio left the office, walked down the marble staircase to the lobby and left by the front door. He got in the car and drove back to the private airport. Returning the car, he dropped by the office for his clearance to fly out.

"We are recommending," the woman behind the desk announced, "that all flights be cancelled for the next few hours."

"Why?" Bonifacio demanded angrily.

"A storm is traveling west and is almost upon us!" The pilot looked up at the sky.

"The sky is clear! Besides I have less than an hour in the air."

"Still, this is a strong recommendation. I cannot stop you if you will not take my advice."

"Good, because I don't intend to hang around here for the next few hours."

Walking over to his jet, he got in and started the engine. He contacted the tower and was given the same advice. "Clear me for takeoff," he warned them "or I'll go without it!" The voice in the tower hesitated and then said, "You are clear for takeoff."

Taxing down the runway, the jet accelerated and lifted off the ground. As soon as he steadied the plane, he noticed the increasing buildup of gray and black clouds at his back. *Maybe I can outdistance this storm before it hits!* Almost immediately, the jet shook with air turbulence. The first drops of rain fell on the windshield. Rumbling thunder was accompanied by a streak of white lightning that lit up the sky. The crackle of electricity was conducted through the air.

The jet went from mild turbulence to increasingly volatile shuddering of the whole plane. Keeping a cool demeanor, Bonifacio turned on the windshield wipers as the rain pounded on the jet making a horrible noise. The steering wheel became ever more difficult to control but the pilot was not going to let the weather dominate him. Another cacophonous sound of thunder almost deafened him, as swift and deadly lightning strikes crisscrossed the progressively darkening sky.

Boniface felt the sweat on his hands, and the droplets of perspiration on his forehead and upper lip. *Maybe I should have waited on the ground until the storm passed, but there's no turning back now!*

The plane bounced violently as if it were a wild stallion refusing to be tamed. The muscles in Bonifacio's hands, arms, and neck began to ache from the pressure and stress. He tried to radio the man on his private airstrip but the cracking of forked lightning prevented clear communication. Still, he did not give up. "This is Fire Fox, Fire Fox! Come in Land Control, come in!" After repeated attempts, all he received in return to his urgent message was the sound of constant static. "Damn it!" he screamed trying to drown out the thunder. He was unsuccessful.

What seemed like an hour in the air was in fact only about 27 minutes in real time. Boniface wondered how far he had traveled because he could not get his bearings from the islands below. His navigation was still working, but he felt as if he were flying by the seat of his pants. It wasn't a very comforting sensation. He hoped the strong tail wind would get him to his destination much quicker and that he wouldn't have to spend much more time in this dire situation.

It was with a sense of relief that he sensed the turbulence abating. *Am I dreaming or are the clouds growing less threatening?* His answer came in a few minutes as the clouds began to break up and streams of sunlight shone through. Suddenly a call came in from his landing strip. "Land Control calling Fire Fox! Land Control calling Fire Fox! Come in Fire Fox!"

"Fire Fox here! Go ahead!"

"We received your messages but I guess mine never got back to you."

"I never received them."

"I didn't think you would be arriving until after the storm passed."

"I decided to ride it out. Am I cleared for landing?"

"You are cleared." As soon as the message had been delivered, the clouds broke and the sun dominated the sky. Dropping his landing gear, he bounced down, his wheels touching ground. *Neither God nor nature has any dominion over me!*

CHAPTER 34

SALAMANCA, SPAIN

Like the El Escorial, Salamanca University was an imposing edifice to Esmie. The elaborate decorations on both buildings directly reflected the wealth and power that Spain possessed in its "Golden Age."

After Dr. Cummings rented a room in a hotel and dropped off her luggage, she walked a short distance to the university. Inside she presented her papers, including letters of introduction. The sentry on guard duty carefully read the letters and looked her up and down. Picking up the telephone in his booth, the young man dialed a number and had a quiet conversation with the person on the other line. Hanging up, he turned to her, mumbled something in Spanish and pointed up the marble staircase saying, "Director Acevedo." The stairs and hallway were teeming with young men and women jabbering as they made their way to their classes.

Nodding her head to indicate that she understood, she walked the hallowed halls that Christopher Columbus once traversed. Finding the right office, she was prepared to meet a slightly balding, overweight older male official. To her surprise, she was guided into the private office to find an attractive middle-aged woman with jet black hair pulled back into a bun. She smiled and held out her hand to Esmie Cummings.

After the introductions were made, Amalia Acevedo announced, "You have very impressive letters of introduction." She indicated that Esmie should have a seat.

"Thank you."

"Would you like a cup of coffee or tea?"

"No thanks, I would really like to get started on my research."

"Yes, and what will you be researching?" *If she had read the letters, she wouldn't have found the need to ask me that question.*

"I'll be looking at Brother Manolo Gallego's years of teaching at this university." *Is she purposely trying to put up barriers to waste my time?"*

"To what end?"

"To study some of his early treatises while he was teaching at this university." The director had her chin in the palm of her hand and tapped her index finger against her cheek. Finally, she spoke. "You understand that the Inquisition found his writings to be heretical and he recanted his earlier books."

"I know that and I understand that the Catholic Church reversed its opinion centuries ago."

"That is true but I am sure that his books were destroyed long before the Holy See changed its mind." *Why is she trying to discourage me?*

"Still, I'd like your permission to see what I can find of his works."

Acevedo shrugged her shoulders and stood up. "I suppose if you are so eager to waste your time in this endeavor, I should give you my acquiescence." *She has no other choice. The letters from higher Spanish officials indicated that they have already given me their approved!*

"Then, may I get started?"

With a sniff from her nose, she retorted, "Be my guest. A guard is waiting outside in the hallway to show the way."

In the weeks that followed, Esmie found that Acevedo was right. Very few works still existed and although she poured over what little there was, nothing of his years in Guatemala could be found. Each day she arrived with hope, like the flame on a small candle, and each evening it was snuffed out. *If I can't find what I'm looking for here, the search for the lost city will be over. Am I missing something that will reveal to me the object of my searching?*

She sat back in her chair, her hand pressing upon her forehead. *Think! Think!* She paced back and forth in the room disturbing the centuries of dust that covered everything. *Think! Think!*

That night as she tried to sleep, she suddenly sat up with a smile on her face. *That's it! If he was a Brother, he must have been from a particular order of monks!* The next morning, she was up early, showered, and on her way, denying herself breakfast to find the answer to her question.

Searching the books she had already looked through, she noticed several quotes attributed to Saint Dominic. *Could he have been a Dominican? There is only one way to find out. I will need to make inquiries.*

She left the university early and strolled to the information desk at her hotel. "Tell me," she asked the young woman who greeted her with a smile. "Is there a Dominican monastery near here?"

"Just a moment," she replied. Suddenly she displayed a pamphlet and pointed to something in it. "Here, the Convento de Juan el Bautista." Esmie looked down on the picture.

"Where is it located?" The girl took a yellow magic marker and highlighted the address.

"Plaza del Concilio de Trento. Here, you can keep it."

She walked immediately to the address. The building was massive with towers and spires that housed many storks that had nested there for centuries. She found the shadowy interior of the church was several degrees cooler. It was illuminated by countless candles, their scent wafting in the stifling air around the church. A few people scattered around, prayed with the rosary entwining their fingers. Nearby a few parishioners waited quietly for their turn in the confessional.

She exited at the front of the church by a side door and found herself in a rose garden. The heavily scented flowers, in the extreme heat of the day, made her feel a little nauseated. She followed a stone path, and came to a wooden door that had a small barred window. The door had no handle and she wondered how she could gain entrance. It was then that she noticed a rope dangling nearby. Esmie pulled it and heard a small brass bell ring. When no one appeared, she pulled the cord again. This time a monk, dressed in a black robe and hood, made his way to her. "How can I help you?"

"I'd like to come in and speak to your Abbot."

"Do you have an appointment with Brother Rafael?"

"No, but I will need to see him only for a little while."

"It is impossible. Brother Rafael sees nobody without an appointment." The monk turned away and Esmie saw her opportunity begin to vanish in the air.

226

"Brother!" she called after him. He turned to face her. "I have letters of introduction. Please bring them to Brother Rafael and let him decide!" Reluctantly he walked toward her as Esmie passed them through the bars. He glanced through them and then looked up.

"Wait here!" he commanded and disappeared inside. Esmie waited by leaning back on the stone wall. It was miserably hot and humid. Waves of steam rose from the street and rippled into the air. There was not even a wisp of a cloud above to offer a small temporary respite from the unmerciful sun. *I'm so thirsty! My mouth feels like the sand in the desert.*

"Dr. Cummings," a voice startled her. It was the monk once more.

"Y...yes?"

"Brother Rafael has agreed to see you."

"Thank you." He unlocked the door to let her pass through and locked it after she entered.

"Follow me."

CHAPTER 35

FOREST IN MEXICO

As soon as he landed in the secretive airstrip in Mexico, Bonifacio could detect the scowl on Ignacio's face. "We need to speak," he stated walking away from the others.

"What's got you so upset?" inquired "The Executioner".

"Your deliveries have been coming in lighter in weight."

"Impossible! It must be somebody on your side of the process." Bonifacio waited and then queried, "Are you sure?"

"Come with me." The two walked over to where his jet was being unloaded and the packages of cocaine being weighed. "Is there the same problem with the weight with this shipment?" he asked his worker.

"Five to six ounces lighter per package." Boniface looked at the scale reading. Successive packages reflected the same problem.

"It is obviously a problem on your end that needs your immediate attention." The drug king fumed at the idea that someone was cheating him. "Don't worry! I will handle it!"

His sudden outburst of rage made Ignacio hesitate before he spoke again but he spoke up anyway.

"You understand that the money I give you will reflect the missing product." Bonifacio wanted to reach into his holster, pull out his Glock and shoot this bastard between the eyes because of this bad news. Two reasons stopped him from making this rash decision. First, it was a problem among his own workers, and second, Ignacio's guards carried sub-machine guns. Ignacio passed the duffle bag full of money. "So sorry to give you the bad news."

"Save the 'sorry' for someone who will appreciate it! I don't!" Marching back to his jet and sitting in the cockpit, Boniface turned the ignition key. The engine roared alive. *One or more of these bastards is not going to live to see the sunset today!*

The usual length of the flight seemed to take even longer that day. His index finger itched to pull the trigger and empty a shot into somebody's head. But as he flew, he cooled down and tried to be more calculating in his actions. *I need to come in with a pleasant mood as if nothing has happened and catch the thief off guard. I'll give whomever it is enough rope to hang himself!*

At last, the jungle airstrip became visible and the pilot banked his plane to turn for the approach. As the jet descended, the landing gear was engaged. Touching the ground, the brakes were applied. As he alit to the ground, his second in command, Jorge, a man who had been his associate in Mexico and who had been handpicked by Bonifacio to join him in the enterprise in Guatemala, greeted his mentor. "How was everything, boss?" Boniface didn't want to think that his second had stolen from him, but everyone was suspect.

"It went as smooth as silk. Why would it be any different?" "The Executioner" watched for his reaction to his statement.

"No reason," shrugged Jorge.

"I'm going to put this money in the safe," Bonifacio never mentioned the incident or the fact that he carried back less money than he had before.

The drug lord put the money into his safe and locked it. He made his way outside to the corrugated roofed building where the cocaine that was grown in the fields was delivered, packed, and weighed. Boniface's entrance caught everyone by surprise since the workers rarely saw him. Jorge approached him. "Hey, boss. What are you doing here? Anything wrong?"

"What could be wrong? I'm here because this is my business and I like to check in on it every once and a while."

"Sure, boss...sure." Work had come to a halt as soon as Bonifacio showed his face.

"Get them back to work!"

"*Volver a trabajar, todo el mundo!*" shouted Jorge clapping his hands. Instantly, they all had their heads down and their hands moving.

"Walk with me," he demanded of his second in command. Jorge fell in line as Bonifacio walked down the lines past each table where two workers were busy weighing and packaging. He turned to his associate and instructed, "Tell them to line up against the wall!"

"What for, boss?"

"Just do it!" he snarled.

"Atencion!" he yelled. *"Todos se alinean contra la pared!"* Men and women looked at each other and then did as they were told. The armed guards in the building were on high alert.

"Check them!" Boniface addressed the guards. Jorge seemed panicked.

"Check them for what, boss?"

"See who is hiding any filched cocaine! If you find anyone, pull them out of line!" The guards immediately did what they were told over the boisterous protestations of the workers.

"Empty your pockets, Jorge!"

"You suspect me?" he remonstrated with shock.

"I suspect everyone!" Jorge turned out his pockets. Except for the usual items, there were no hidden drugs on him.

A woman screamed as her husband was dragged out of line. Others followed - three more men and a woman - until five in all were found with cocaine on them. Bonifacio barked, "Take them into the jungle and do away with them." The thieves screamed and begged for mercy, but "The Executioner" turned a deaf ear to their cries.

"I can't believe they stole from you. They were paid very generously!" Jorge exclaimed as he put the objects back in his pocket.

"They are dead because they dared to steal from me!" Boniface told him. "You will die because you are incompetent!" Jerking the Glock from his holster, he fired one bullet between the stunned man's eyes. His body dropped like a stone to the ground, a stream of blood trailing down the bridge of his nose. "Everyone get back to work!" *I'll have to appoint a new manager and find a few more workers,* he thought as he walked away.

CHAPTER 36

SALAMANCA, SPAIN

The Dominican Brother led Esmie to the monastic library. Along the way, several Brothers of the Order plodded down the stone hallway, their leather sandals keeping a rhythmic beat. Their cowls covered most of their faces as they kept their eyes down, but the distinct sound of high heels caused them to look up. The expression of shock that crossed their faces was momentary and then quickly replaced with disgust. It was clear to Esmie that they resented this intrusion of a female into their male-dominated world.

Turning a few corners, the Brother stopped at an ornate iron door. Taking the keys hanging on his waist, he chose one, inserted it and turned the lock. With squeaking resistance, the door was opened. Esmie stepped in and immediately heard the door close and key turn. "You're locking me in here?"

"I can't babysit you all day! Besides, noon Mass is about to start."

"But how will I get out when I'm finished?" The Brother pointed to a brass bell and rope that hung from the rafters alongside the door.

"Ring it when you are done and I will come back to unlock the door. I must go now." He turned and the sound of his sandals faded down the hallway. Esmie never wore a watch so she wasn't sure of the time until the Abbey's bell struck 12 times. Immediately, from a distance, she heard male voices celebrating Mass in a Gregorian Chant. The sound of it raised goosebumps on her flesh. She certainly didn't like the idea of being left alone in a locked room, but she was here to do some research. Esmie had to keep her mind focused on that.

Dr. Cummings turned to look at the library room, the only chamber in the complex that had air-conditioning so that mold and rot could be kept at abeyance, a respite to the hot and humid day outside. It was a vast room with book cases that almost touched the 10-foot ceiling. There were tables and chairs aligned in the center and book cases on either side on which were hung sliding ladders. There were numerous windows that let the rays of the light in with colorful streams. Each of the windows was decorated with stained glass images of saints who had died as martyrs for their belief. Hanging from the rafters in the back of the room, was a large crucifix with the image of Christ wearing a crown of thorns, His hands and feet bleeding, and an image of an open wound in His side. *Get a hold of yourself! You're not a scared child anymore!*

I guess it would be too much to expect to find a computer with all the listings of the libraries content! She found the card catalog and pulled out the draw with the letters Ga to Ge. She fingered through the cards until she came to Gallego, Manolo. *Stack 23.*

Esmie looked up at the top of each book case where the number was printed to get her bearings. She followed the bookcases to the left until she got to the correct number. She stopped to see the books at the bottom and worked her way up to those at the level of her eyes. Esmie couldn't find any of his writings. Breathing a deep sigh, she realized she would have to climb a ladder. She made her way to the ladder at the next bookcase and rolled it over. Stepping on the first few bottom rungs, she realized that her high heels would make it difficult to climb, so she kicked them off and let them drop on the floor.

Cautiously, she started to climb, stopping at each new shelf, hoping she would find what she wanted without climbing to the top. But nothing that she needed was found. The arches on her bare feet were beginning to ache, but she tried to put the pain out of her mind. Esmie was beginning to conclude that she was uncomfortable with heights, but still she pushed herself up to the next rung. She scaled to the uppermost shelf and scanned the books from left to right. Then, the name Gallego seemed to jump out at her. *At last!* From the amount of dust that had accumulated on the top of the books, she realized that these volumes had probably not been touched in centuries.

Gathering the dusty books to her chest, she gingerly made her way back down until her foot touched the cold stone floor. She strode over to the table and laid the dusty tomes down.

The professor sat down to examine each book carefully after she had slipped on a pair of white linen gloves to protect the pages from corrosive human sweat. Esmie withdrew a legal size yellow pad and her ballpoint pen from her briefcase. Blowing off as much dust as she could, she poured over each page of the three books of the expedition of Cesar de Leon; the first one written by de Leon himself, the next written by the second in command, Juan Martinez and the third from a Brother Francisco Urbano, Abbot at the time.

Although she copied a few pertinent facts, the information about where the lost city could be found was not amongst them. The chapel bell rang three times indicating that it was midafternoon. *Three hours of research and I have nothing substantial to show for it.* She slammed her palm down hard on the table. "Ouch!" Her voice echoed in the cavernous space as the voices of the Brothers were once again raised in song.

She wished she was a believer so she could ask for God's help in this matter. *Still,* she thought to herself, *I'm more of an agnostic than an atheist. I guess there is some superior being determining each of our lives.* Sheepishly, she made her way over to the carved wooden crucifix and looked into His eyes. *I know you've never heard from me before and because of that I really shouldn't expect your help, but could you possibly see to it that I find the information that I'm looking for, if you don't mind.*

As soon as she had finished, she regretted her weakness. *I'm more than capable of finding what I'm looking for!* Shrugging her shoulders, Esmie picked up the volumes and marched over to the shelves. As she climbed one foot at a time, hanging precariously with one hand on the ladder as the other held the books tightly, the familiar pain in her arches started up again. *"How much more of this do I have to endure?"*

Finally, she reached the top shelf and balanced her footing so that she could return the books to their proper place. As she returned them, she felt her foot slipping and instinctively grasped onto the shelf to rebalance herself before she fell to the stone floor. It was then that she felt something lying flat towards the back of the shelf that she hadn't noticed and withdrew it. It too was covered with dust and she wiped it clean with her hand. The title nearly caused her to lose her balance again as she read, *The Diary of Brother Manolo Gallego.* At last, she found what she had been looking for. Before she climbed down, her eyes wandered over to the crucified Jesus. *Thanks!*

She climbed down the ladder and sat at the table and opened the book. As she read, she concluded that the old Indian's tale told to her husband had been correct except for one important difference. According to Brother Gallego, the city of Nakanjo was located not on the banks of the Rio Los Esclavos but along the shores of Lago de Ayarza. Still the old Indian might have purposely led Martin astray. *Amazing! All this time and money was spent looking for the city in the wrong place!*

Then she thought to herself, *If these volumes are so dusty, I'm sure the Brothers have never taken them down from the bookcase. Therefore, if I took the diary of Gallego, I'm sure they'd never miss it!* She smiled to herself until she gazed up once more on Christ's image and had second thoughts. *I guess I can stay here and copy the pertinent information.* She resigned herself to do the right thing and began to read and copy what she needed.

It took weeks of careful research and note taking as she poured through dusty volumes that Esmie located in the library of the El Escorial until she realized that what she had found was information she already possessed from Martin's investigations. It was all so exasperating!

Turning her attention to Brother Gallego's private life instead of his years in Guatemala, she discovered that before he started his missionary work, he had a career teaching theology at the University of Salamanca. *That will be my next stop I guess.*

As she rode in the back seat of the taxi taking her to her hotel, she came to an awareness that it had been almost three years since her husband had died, and in all that time, she had poured herself into her work at the university. *It's time for me to kick back a little and get some relaxation.* She had even skipped her paid vacations because if she was working, her thoughts could not go back to that day in Guatemala. *I think I will get some rest, shower, and dress and go out to the best restaurant in Madrid.* And that's exactly what she did.

Exiting the elevator, she walked to the reception desk. She wore a black frock that flirted at her knees and just above her shapely calves. A gold chain necklace that Martin had given to her on their last anniversary lay at the top of her bosom. She inquired, "Can you give me the name of a good restaurant near this hotel?"

"I enjoy a meal at *Indice Restaurant Ay Ac Palacio Del Retiro*. It is famous for its traditional Mediterranean dishes and the views of the beautiful gardens of Retiro Park."

"That sounds wonderful. Thank you." The young man behind the desk smiled at her. She was driven by taxi to her destination. The doorman moved to the taxi and opened the door. Esmie entered a classically furnished restaurant. The maître d', a man in his 40's, dressed in a brilliant white shirt and a black tuxedo approached her and asked, "Table for two?"

"No," Mrs. Cummings responded politely. "I'll be eating alone." She thought she saw a flash of an expression from him that she interpreted as, *Poor dear; she has no man in her life.*

"This way, please." He led her to a corner table that was by an open window overlooking the gardens. *So picturesque.*

"Your waiter will be here in a minute."

Almost at once, a young man appeared at her table. "Senora, I will be your waiter this evening. My name is Ricardo. Would you like a cocktail?"

"No thank you, but may I have the menu?" Without any hesitation, he placed one before her. "Do you have anything you would recommend?"

"Everything is delicious here but we are famous for our fish stew." He pointed it out on the menu.

"Then that's what I'll have."

"And some wine?"

"I'll trust your judgement."

"Very well, Senora!"

He returned carrying a bottle of Albarino named for a white grape grown in Galicia region of Spain. He poured a little in her glass to taste. "Delicious!" she exclaimed as he smiled and poured her a full glass. She took another sip and luxuriated in the flavor. Holding on to the glass, she rested her elbow on the table.

As she looked out the window, the maître d' passed, leading a male patron to his table. Unexpectedly, the patron seemed to stumble and bump into Esmie's arm. Startled, her glass fell from her hands to the tiled floor and shattered into sharp shards while the wine splashed all over. "I'm so sorry," the man said apologetically. The maître d' snapped his fingers calling Ricardo over. In a state of shock, Esmie looked up to see a handsome man about 30 years her senior staring down at her.

As Ricardo and two other employees cleared up the mess and changed the table cloth, the professor checked her dress and with her napkin began to mop up the few drops of wine that had landed on it. "Please send me the bill from the dry cleaner. I will gladly pay."

"That won't be necessary," she feebly beamed. "Most of the wine landed on the table."

"Then allow me to pay for your dinner. It's the least I can do!" Esmie wanted to decline his offer, but there was something about this attractive man that prevented her from doing so.

"Okay, if you insist."

"Good. Are you dining alone?"

"Yes."

"So am I. Might I join you this evening? I just hate dining by myself." Esmie was very familiar with that feeling. Trying not to sound too enthusiastic, she replied,

"I suppose so." Ricardo laid out another place setting as the gentleman took his seat.

"I believe introductions are in order."

"Hello, my name is Esmie Cummings." He took her hand and shook it as the waiter brought over two glasses that he filled with wine.

"I'm Armand Thierry." Armand looked up at the waiter. "I'll have the Grouper a la Mallorquina."

"Very well, Senor." Esmie looked up with surprise.

"You didn't even look at the menu."

"I eat here quite often." Picking up his glass, he toasted saying, "Here's to our chance meeting although I wished it weren't because of my clumsiness."

"No harm, no foul." They clicked their glasses and took a sip.

"So where are you from, Esmie. I know you're an American from your accent."

"Very astute. I'm originally from San Francisco but now I live in Oxnard."

"Oxnard, that's a funny name. And what do you do for a living in this Oxnard?"

"I'm a professor at Trinity University."

"Very impressive. What is your background?"

"My father was English and my mother Japanese."

"Are you in Madrid for business or pleasure?" She began to take note that he was asking all the questions and decided that it was time to turn the tables.

"I'm on vacation," she lied. "And what about you? Your accent is French I would guess."

"I was born and raised in Alsace-Lorraine just outside of Strasbourg. My father was French and my mother was German."

"Where do you live now?" Before he could answer, their meals arrived. They both began to eat.

"I've forgotten your question."

"Where do you reside at this point?"

"I have a few residences around the world." *This guy must be loaded.*

"And what do you do for a living?"

"I'm more interested in my hobbies which are collecting art and antiques." Mrs. Cummings raised her eyebrows.

"My goodness, these are expensive hobbies."

"They are but luckily I don't have to worry about money."

As dinner was finished and coffee was done, Armand paid for the bill and afterwards they strolled out onto the street. "Is your hotel near here?" inquired Thierry.

"A little way down the boulevard." Armand hailed a cab which immediately pulled over.

"Let me escort you there."

"That won't be necessary," and before he could object, she quickly added. "It was nice getting to know you. He smiled and lifted her hand to his lips and kissed it.

"Enchante." His blue eyes sparkled, reflecting the beams from the street lights. Once she was in, he closed the taxi door and the vehicle took off. Thierry stood on the sidewalk and watched until the cab turned the corner. His eyes had now turned cold and calculating.

Days later, Armand Thierry sat in an armchair overlooking the front entrance of a four-star hotel named *El Palacio Jardin*. This was not the type of hotel Armand frequented, but sacrifices had to be made if he was going to gain the prize that in his mind loomed before him. He had ordered one of his agents to follow Professor Cummings to determine the hotel in which she was staying in Salamanca. He had already asked the desk clerk, "Is Professor Cummings in?" The young man turned to the key rack and discovered that the hotel guest's room key was hanging there and replied,

"She is out for the moment. May I take a message?"

"No thank you."

Thierry had found himself a place to sit next to a fake palm tree in the marbled lobby and pretended to read a newspaper, keeping one eye on the door. Beside his chair, a piece of his luggage rested next to him. He waited for some time, while he checked his wrist watch. Forty-three minutes after talking to the desk clerk, Esmie walked through the hotel door. He held the paper just under his eyes and took in her image. *She really is very attractive, this combination of occidental and oriental beauty. If she would just wear some light makeup and dress in clothing that flattered her curves, she would be a knockout. Also, that ponytail has to go.* Esmie had a faint smile that crossed her face. *She is definitely a natural beauty.*

Folding the paper as he stood up, he dropped it on his chair and bent to pick up the luggage before he walked back to the desk. A new desk clerk was getting her key. *Perfect, he wouldn't remember me.* "I'd like a room please," he announced. Esmie turned to look at him as she received her room key and was surprised by who it was. Recognizing him from the other night's shared dinner, she said,

"Well, hello!"

Armand casually turned and feigned a surprise reaction. "Look who it is!" he answered as if he were caught by surprise. "What are you doing here?"

"I have a room here. Are you just checking in?"

"I am. Well isn't this a pleasant surprise? When I saw you the other evening, I never thought I would see you again!"

"The same here!"

"I hope you don't think that I've been following you," he laughed as he signed the guest book while the clerk processed his credit card. When she laughed at his statement, he breathed a sigh of relief.

"That would be a stretch of the imagination, wouldn't it?" Armand looked at his watch.

"It's almost dinner time. May I ask if you have an engagement for dinner this evening?" Mrs. Cummings blushed at the question. *He's very good looking. What harm would it be to have such an engaging gentleman have dinner with me once again?*

"No, I'll be alone again tonight."

"Would you like to share a dinner table with me?"

"I'd love to." The clerk handed the key and credit card to Thierry. Looking at the room key, she declared, "Well isn't this a coincidence. We're both on the seventh floor."

"The gods must be pushing us together," she giggled as they made their way to a bank of elevators. They entered the elevator along with another woman who pushed the button for the fifth floor. They remained quiet until she got off. The doors reopened on the seventh floor. As they made their way down the hall, Thierry asked, "Do you think you can be ready in an hour?" Esmie raised her eyebrows. "An hour? Mr. Thierry, it's obvious that you have never been married."

"What makes you say that?"

"A woman needs time to make herself perfect."

"I see. Well then, what about an hour and a half?"

"Where shall we meet?"

"I'll knock on your door."

"It's a date," she rejoined as she unlocked her door and entered the room. Armand walked two doors down on the other side of the hallway. Unlocking the door, he entered. After a few minutes, Ramon knocked on the door and his boss let him in. "Have you brought everything?" Ramon pointed to the clean shirt, tie, and underwear and laid them on top of the bed. His highly-polished shoes he placed near a chair.

"Go and wait in the car. I'll call you if I need you. After dinner, you can drive me back to my room in The Ritz Carlton."

"Yes, sir."

After a shower and some grooming, Armand waited impatiently for the time to pass. The hands on his watch seemed to move in slow motion. He turned on the television as a source of distraction. At last the watch read 8:30 and with a sense of relief he got ready. Slipping on his suit jacket, he closed the room door and walked down the hall knocking gently on her door. "I'll be there in a minute," he heard her voice say from the room interior. When she at last opened the door, he was taken aback. She had transformed herself for the evening. Her hair was done up and held by an amber comb. Her dress was black organza, cut just low enough to catch a glimpse of her breasts. "I'm ready if you are," she remarked as she locked her door and walked down the hallway to the elevator with him.

"May I be permitted to say that you are looking ravishing this evening?" She smiled up at him. *My God, I could almost fall for her right now.* Mentally, he shook himself. *Don't forget what you're here for,* the voice inside his head reminded him.

In the elevator Esmie turned to ask, "Where are we going to dine tonight?"

"I made a reservation for us at Casa Las Conchas. I've eaten there before and I think you'll enjoy it."

"I'm sure I will." They climbed into a taxi hailed by the doorman, and the cab took off down the avenue. The traffic was heavy as they continued to their destination.

"You look pleased with yourself this evening," Thierry offhandedly mentioned. "Did something happen to cause that expression?"

"No, not really," she lied.

"I guess I was hoping that it had to do with our chance meeting."

"Well, I guess it might have something to do with it." Light conversation continued between them until the cab pulled over to the curb." Paying the driver, Armand escorted her into the establishment.

The room was crowded with patrons talking and eating with gusto. The maître d' walked over and greeted them.

"Bienvenido de nuevo, Senor Thierry. Es Bueno verte otra vez."

"It's good to be back, Bernardo."

"Let me show you to your table." They followed Bernardo to a table in the furthest corner of the restaurant. The brick and stucco wall softly reflected the candlelight at each table. Given the menus, they looked over the selections.

A waiter approached and asked, *"Te puedo recibir una bebida?"*

"He wants to know what you'd like to drink."

"I just don't know. Can you order for me?" *He's not wearing a wedding ring but that means nothing in today's world.*

"Of course, a bottle of Monastrell." The waiter went off to fill the order.

"The last time we met I told you about myself. Now it's time for your big reveal."

"I am not that interesting," he laughed purposely.

"Come on now, don't make me have to coax you."

"Very well, I'm a private gem buyer." The lie sounded genuine.

"Sounds fascinating. What does that entail?"

"I seek out gems for private clients." *This will easily explain my wealth.*

"You must travel a lot."

"All over the world."

The waiter returned with the bottle of wine, uncorked it and poured a taste into a crystal goblet and handed it to Armand. He sipped it and swirled it in his mouth before he swallowed. *"Perfecto!"* The wine was poured in the two glasses. Raising his glass, Armand toasted the occasion by saying, "To chance meetings." Esmie clicked her glass with his.

"May I order for you?"

"Since you are familiar with the cuisine here, please do." Armand ordered rare steaks, rice pilaf and grilled vegetables.

"Do you like your steak rare?"

"Yes, I do."

"As I recall, you told me that you were an archeology professor. That hasn't changed, has it?"

"No," she laughed. "That hasn't changed."

"Are you here to do some field work?"

"Just here on vacation."

A lie.

"I'm more likely to be grading papers than getting dirty digging in some excavation."

Lies and more lies, he told himself.

"Are you married?"

"Not presently."

"Divorced?"

"No, he died." Esmie didn't bother to get into the details of Martin's demise. As the conversation continued, it was interrupted by Thierry's cell phone ringing in his inside jacket pocket. He retrieved it and glanced at the number.

"Excuse me, but I must take this call."

Robert C. Novarro

"Go right ahead. Armand left the table and walked outside.

"Why are you calling me? I said I'd get in touch with you." he demanded of Ramon.

"I got a frantic call from Renteria."

"Forget him."

"He says he has important information to tell you and that you need to call him back right away."

"I'll do that later but now that you've called, go up and search the woman's room. Search it thoroughly but don't make it seem as if someone's been rummaging through her things, got it?"

"Yeah, I got it."

"I'll try to keep her out as late as I can. Find that map whatever you do! Call me when you're done." Armand hung up and walked back inside, painting a smile on his face.

The search proved to be futile; the map was not found.

CHAPTER 37

FLORA, GUATEMALA

The door to the Chocko Renteria home was suddenly kicked in. Insurgents of the New Order stormed past the toppled door and stormed into the interior of the home led by the mustachioed, burly-built younger man. Rosita Renteria screamed holding her apron over her mouth. Chocko came in to see what the turmoil was about. *"Oh, Dios mio!"*

Salvador Hermoza snapped, *"Cierra boca de su esposa gorda antes de la tiren!"*

"Rosita," her frightened husband hissed. "Shut your mouth before he kills you!" Turning toward one of his men, Hermoza instructed,

"Take her into the kitchen and keep her mouth shut!" Grabbing her by the arm, the soldier led the terrified woman to the back of the house.

"Why are you here?" the traumatized Chocko queried.

"Keep your mouth shut! I told you the last time I saw you that you were going to be watched!"

"I've done nothing wrong!" Gruffly, Salvador laid his hands roughly on the quaking man.

"You lied to me."

"I swear…" Hermoza did not wait to listen to another lie but thrust him across the room making Renteria crash into a table and chairs. The victim was sprawled over the tile floor. Holding up his arm, he pled for leniency. "Please, no more!"

"You told me that the only people you were in touch with regarding the lost city were the Cummings." Renteria blanched. *Has he somehow found out about Armand Thierry?*

"That is true!" Hermoza took his boot and kicked the prone man in the ribs again. Chocko screamed out in pain. Stepping back, he glowered at his simpering victim.

"And still you lie to my face!"

"I don't know what you want me to tell you!"

"I want you to tell me about the other man involved in finding the Mayan city, a man named Armand Thierry." *It's too late, Hermoza knows everything. There's no use in my trying to hide it any longer.*

"Y…yes! Mr. Thierry is involved." *I'm not going to risk my life to hide Thierry's participation. Besides, the bastard has never even bothered to return any of my phone calls.*

"Now we are getting somewhere. Your phone calls to this man have been monitored. Now what does he have to do with the lost city?"

"He is a silent partner and financer of Mrs. Cummings expedition although she doesn't know anything about his involvement."

"And what does this Thierry do to afford financing such an expensive project?"

"He is a munitions manufacturer." Salvador's eyes suddenly lit up.

"Munitions you say. That sounds very interesting."

"He is a man with a vast fortune, a man who can help you get all the guns and ammunition you will need to overthrow this government!"

"Yes, you are right. Therefore, you have outlived your importance. You are just a small fish trying not to get swallowed by the sharks." Hermoza raised his gun in Renteria's direction.

"No…no! I can still help you!"

"How is that?"

"He will not speak directly to you. Of the two of us, it is me that he will call back. Without me, you will get nowhere with him." The rebel leader seemed to ponder what he had just been told.

"Call him, now!" *What if Thierry refuses to talk to me again? I am as good as dead!* But the pudgy man knew he had no other choice but to make that call. Getting up from the floor, he walked into his bedroom where his cell phone rested in its charger. Chocko lifted the phone and dialed. He heard the phone ring but Thierry did not answer. *Pick up, pick up damn it!* Finally, a recording went on. "Please leave a message after the tone."

Renteria found his voice and addressed his boss. "It's me. I've got a proposal that I think will interest you…" Before he could finish, the phone was picked up on the other side.

"Renteria, you better not be wasting my time. What is the proposal?"

"I have a man here…" Hermoza ripped the phone from his hand.

"Am I speaking to Mr. Thierry?"

"Who the hell is this and where is Renteria?"

"Sir, my name is Salvador Hermoza. I am the leader of the revolutionary army named "New Order." We are dedicated to overthrowing the corrupt government of Guatemala."

"What does any of this have to do with me?"

"I've been told you manufacture guns and munition, is that true?"

"I suppose Renteria mentioned this to you."

"Answer my question." On the other side of the line, there was complete silence. "Mr. Thierry, are you still there?"

"I am. Let's for argument sake say that I do manufacture those items. Why would you care?"

"I'm interested in getting a supply of them for my rebels."

"Can you pay for them?"

"Not in money."

"This conversation is over!"

"Do not hang up, Senor! It will cost Chocko his life!"

"What do I care? Shoot the stupid bastard!"

"Senor Thierry, I can give you something valuable in exchange for your goods."

"And what is that?" he asked with mild curiosity."

"Free passage to wherever you need to travel in my country." Armand laughed out loud.

"I already have that!"

"Not once we take over the government - and believe me senor, it will happen." Thierry contemplated the proposal.

"Alright," he responded. "Put Renteria back on the phone." Salvador handed it back to Chocko.

"I am here, Senor Thierry."

"Listen to me very carefully, you ass." Chocked bristled at the comparison. "I want you to make sure that whatever I send them gets into their hands, understood?"

"Si, Senor Thierry."

"Make sure they cause me no interference when I'm down there."

"Si, Senor."

"Don't screw this up or you'll find yourself hanging from your balls."

"Si, Senor. I understand," he answered with resentment.

CHAPTER 38

OXNARD, CALIFORNIA

It all crystalized for Esmie as she settled back for the long flight from Madrid to Los Angeles. She hated to leave Spain behind. Madrid and Salamanca were culturally enriching, its people so cosmopolitan, while Oxnard was dull and so provincial in comparison. The professor detested the idea that after a year abroad, she was forced to return to the culturally unartistic void that was Oxnard. The only thing pulling her back was information she had copied from the diary of Brother Manolo Gallego and how it might help her pinpoint the Mayan city of Nakanjo. Mrs. Cummings had decided to keep the discovery of the diary close to the vest. *The more people who know about my discovery, the more chance there is for someone to beat me to the prize Martin and I have worked so hard to discover.*

Esmie arrived in her office at Trinity University the next morning, and like a plow horse in a yoke, went about her daily routine as if she never left for Spain. She fell into her brown leather office chair that over time now fit her like a glove. It was then that she went through her mail and found an envelope that had been handwritten with her name on the outside. Ripping it open and unfolding the note she read,

Dear Professor Cummings, I hope you enjoyed your time off. Please come to my office at your earliest convenience.

President Montgomery Lewis

No point in putting off the inevitable, I suppose. She made her way to the executive board floor. On the way, she shook hands and made small talk with employees who were glad to see her back. Esmie arrived at Lewis' office and his secretary opened the door for her. Not only was the president there but he was accompanied by a young man. "Good to have you back,

Dr. Cummings," Montgomery greeted her. He reached out his hand and Esmie grasped it to shake.

"Good to be back," she fabricated.

"You remember Kevin March, the young man who took over your classes while you were gone."

"It's so good to see you again," Kevin gushed with enthusiasm.

"Have a seat everyone." *Why is this kid at the meeting?*

"Esmie, I first want you to know how well Kevin handled your classes."

"That's nice."

"Yes, so much so that he has been hired as your assistant." *Oh hell no! I'm not having this snot-nosed kid looking over my shoulder as I research Nakanjo's precise location.*

"I'm sure he would be very helpful but I'm in no need of an assistant." Turning toward the young man, Lewis said,

"Would you excuse us, Kevin?"

"Of course." March got up and left the office. Montgomery's voice became more somber.

"It's not a question of needing him. He's already been hired for the position."

"Kevin is which board member's nephew or maybe he's yours?" she retorted sarcastically. Montgomery chose to overlook her ridicule. He sat closer to the edge of his seat.

"We didn't get much information from you while you were gone. Have you brought us back any good news?"

"I'm sorry to say that every time I thought I might have a lead, it turned into a dead end." Lewis seemed crushed by what had been revealed.

"You've come back with nothing at all after a year?"

"Sadly, I've come back empty handed."

Lewis slid back in his chair. "This is a bitter pill to swallow. I'm not looking forward to relating this to the rest of the executive board."

"I'm sure they'll be disappointed but I'm not giving up on locating the city. In time, it will be found and bring prestige to this university."

"That's the problem; time may have already run out on any more expeditions."

"What is that supposed to mean?"

"It means that our anonymous donor will be reluctant to financially support this project since you came back with nothing new!"

Esmie was disconsolate upon hearing this statement. "Maybe I could talk with him and help to change his mind."

Now it was Montgomery's turn to use mockery. "What part of 'he doesn't want to be identified' don't you understand?"

"Still..."

"It's out of the question and that topic is now closed." He stood up indicating that the meeting was over. "You'll find that Kevin will be a great asset to you," he informed her aloofly. *It's* quite *a change of attitude since I first walked into his office.*

"I'm sure he will be." She left the office and walked back to her room. *There's got to be a way that I can get rid of this Kevin character.*

CHAPTER 39

PUERTO VALLARTA

It wasn't his usual habit upon returning for the weekend in Puerto Vallarta to drop in on a club, but Bonifacio Millian had just finished a particularly stressful week. A new manager had been hired and new workers were brought in. Six graves were dug in the jungle on his order with six bodies dropped in.

Millian didn't know what possessed him to walk into a tourist trap like *"El Gatos Azul"* but he just felt like getting away from his usual routine. The music was throbbing and the young people dancing to Gloria Gaynor singing "I Will Survive".

All the young and beautiful people were there, rich young American women dancing with beautiful men to the intoxicating rhythm of the music, as well as ladies from the town looking for a good time and a free ride that only people with lots of money could provide. Millian made his way to the crowded bar and elbowed people aside. Some of the people tried to confront him but once they recognized his face, quickly backed down. Banging on the bar counter, he got the bartender's attention and he moved quickly to serve this customer. Bonafacio said, "Jack Daniels." He held up three fingers across his chest indicating to the man behind the bar how much he wanted him to pour.

The drink was brought to him and Millian laid some cash on the bar. Taking a sip, he turned to watch pulsating bodies on the dance floor under colored lights. They were all the same, these Americans, so beautiful, searching for the next new experiences and sniffing coke that he had probably supplied. He laughed to himself as he took another sip.

Turning back, Bonifacio noticed a new person standing next to him. Unlike most of the other girls, this raven-haired beauty was in full blossom of her womanhood. *No doe-eyed damsel is she, but a woman with some experience.* She was trying to get the barkeep's attention but the bar was crowded with people trying to get a drink. Millian banged his hand on the bar. The bartender returned and Boniface pointed to the woman standing next to him. "What can I get for you?" he asked.

"Bourbon and Branch," she ordered. *I'm impressed. She didn't order some fruity cocktail.* Turning toward Bonifacio, she said, "Thank you."

"My pleasure." The bartender brought it over. Millian spoke up. "Put it on my bill."

"Oh, no!" She objected. "I pay my own way." The bartender did not wait around.

"I'm sure you do, but indulge me this one time."

"Once again I'm indebted to you." They clicked their glasses together.

"I must ask you for a favor now."

The woman eyed him suspiciously. "And what is that?" she asked.

"May I know your name?"

She hesitated for a moment before she replied. "Cheryl Donnelly, but my friends call me Cher."

"I hope you'll see me as a friend."

"Only time will tell."

"From New York, aren't you?"

"I guess I don't hide my accent very well, do I?"

Bonifacio laughed.

"And what's your name?"

"Bonifacio Millian."

"What do you do for a living, Mr. Millian?" "The Executioner" had a pat answer every time he had to reply to the same question.

"Import-export. And you?"

"I'm an algebra teacher."

Millian gave her curvaceous body a quick glance. *She doesn't look like any math teacher I ever had.*

"I usually don't frequent places like this." He felt almost apologetic.

"Neither do I. The two women I'm traveling with asked me to join them but now they've met guys and I'm by myself."

"Not anymore," he pointed out. "When did you arrive in Puerto Vallarta?"

"Yesterday morning."

"And how long are you staying?"

"We're here for a week."

"How would you like me to show you around this weekend?"

"I couldn't put you out like that - besides I don't know you."

"Well, what better way to get to know each other."

"I don't know…"

"Think about this. I can show you a far better time than you'll have hanging around with your girlfriends."

"I guess it will be okay."

"Wonderful! I'll send a car for you at nine in the morning. We'll have breakfast at my villa. How does that sound to you?"

"I'd like that very much."

"Where will the car pick you up?"

"At the *'El Oasis de Palmeras'*. That is where we're staying."

"Stay in the lobby. My driver will have you paged. Until tomorrow." Boniface lifted her hand and kissed it.

"Until tomorrow then."

Millian walked away but suddenly turned back. "Bring your bathing suit if you like." He turned around once more and walked out the door. *It's no sin to indulge in a little weekend distraction.*

CHAPTER 40

RIO DE JANERO

There was no turning back for Armand Thierry. The thought of possibly getting his hands on one of the world's greatest fabled funerary treasures had the arms dealer salivating, but he had been bogged down for months without any progress. There was only one thing to do. He would have to identify himself to Esmie as the anonymous donor and make a play for her. Slowly at first but never diverting himself from his real goal, the cache that lay hidden just out of his reach. "Ramon," he spoke up. "Get my pilot on the phone and tell him to prepare for a flight from to Oxnard."

"Oxnard?"

"Yeah, it's in California."

It was 13 hours in the air during which Thierry contacted Montgomery Lewis to tell him that he would be arriving the next day for a meeting. "I want Esmie Cummings to be there."

"You do? Are you saying that you want to reveal yourself as the anonymous donor to her?"

"That's it exactly, but I want to be the one to tell her. Do you understand?"

"I understand completely. I'll have the rest of the board assembled for our meeting."

"Don't bother. I want just the three of us there."

"I see. When will your plane arrive?"

"My private jet will land in Los Angeles approximately 2 P.M."

"I'll have Dr. Cummings join me at 2:30 P.M. There'll be a limousine waiting for you to take you to Trinity University."

"That won't be necessary. I'll have my own car waiting for me once I have landed."

When his private jet had come to a stop, his driver located Armand and they proceeded out of the airport and onto the highway for the trip that took about 75 minutes. As he entered the administration building of the university, he was greeted by a cute blonde senior intern. "Mr. Thierry?" she inquired, walking up to him.

"Yes, I'm Mr. Thierry."

"Follow me, sir." She led him to an elevator bank and pushed the "Up" button. The elevator cage arrived, and they both stepped in. They were the only two occupying this elevator. "So," he said breaking the silence, "Are you a teacher here in the university?" His obvious blunder resulted in the response he had anticipated.

"Oh no," she tittered coquettishly. "I'm just an intern."

"And what a beautiful intern you are."

"Thank you," she answered blushing involuntarily.

"And your name?"

"It's Peggy, Peggy Somerset."

"Well, Peggy Somerset, I hope we bump into each other again."

In a meek voice, she retorted, "I hope we do too."

The elevator stopped at the 5th floor and the door opened. "This way Mr. Thierry."

"Please, call me Armand. Why should we be stifled with formality while we're chatting, and may I call you Peggy?" There was a slight hesitation before her answer was forthcoming.

"Of course, Armand." She led him to a wooden door that had a gold sign that read "President. M. Lewis".

"We're here," Peggy announced. Armand took her hand and kissed it. *A tasty little morsel!* She looked down at the top of her hand in amazement.

"I'll be sure to tell President Montgomery what a huge help you were to me."

Peggy looked at him as if she were looking at a star filled sky. "Thank you so much…Armand."

Armand Thierry entered the outer office and was greeted by the receptionist. After introducing himself, she rang the phone in the president's office. "Your 2:30 appointment is here." Once she received her answer she said, "You may go right in." He opened the door as Lewis rose to his feet to greet him. Esmie turned around and felt like her jaw had fallen to the floor. Cummings got to her feet although later she could not recall anything at all about their meeting.

"Mr. Thierry, welcome back."

"Good to see you again, President Lewis." Thierry made no attempt to make eye contact with the doctor. Finally, Esmie found her voice.

"What a surprise!"

"The two of you know each other?" Lewis queried in astonishment.

"I've had the pleasure of bumping into Dr. Cummings a few times." He gently took her hand and pressed it to his lips.

"You have been the anonymous benefactor who's funding my search for Nakanjo?"

"Me and no other," he replied as he let her hand go.

"Please, have a seat." Armand sat opposite the shocked Esmie.

"I had no idea," she muttered still stunned at his sudden presence.

"And that's the way I wanted it until I had the good fortune of meeting you at dinner."

"How did you make the connection that I was the one looking for funding in finding the lost city?"

"President Lewis told me your name the first time we had spoken about donating my gift to Trinity University."

"You mean you knew who I was when we accidently met or was it an accident at all?"

"It was a most fortunate accident, Professor Cummings, a fortunate accident for me."

"But why didn't you tell when we were sharing a meal?"

"I wasn't sure I wanted to give up my anonymity. But after we met the second time, I knew I could no longer keep it a secret from you."

"You could have knocked me over with a feather when I first saw you walk in!"

"I hope it wasn't too much of a shock."

Esmie smiled. "Not at all." President Lewis felt uncomfortable interrupting what seemed like a private conversation, but he felt that he needed to get down to the purpose of this impromptu meeting.

"Mr. Thierry, I hope you're not here to tell us you've decided to drop your funding for Dr. Cumming's expeditions to find Nakanjo."

"That's not why you're here is it Armand?" her voice was filled with the trepidation of a person preparing herself for the bad news.

"On the contrary, I'm here to donate another ten million dollars and to offer my services as an amateur archeologist."

"We would be working together?"

"I hope that pleases you." Cummings glowed like a woman in love.

"Nothing would please me more."

CHAPTER 41

RAINFOREST OF GUATEMALA

For Salvador Hermoza, his increasing power acted like a formidable aphrodisiac. The more he garnered, the more he desired to acquire until he spiraled out of control.

It started when he decided to make demands for money from Thierry. With the money he had already spent, the forces of New Order were now equipped with the most modern weaponry. Now Hermoza decided to push the envelope.

Sneaking into town with his girlfriend Lola and a few men, he made his way back to the house of Chocko Renteria. Banging on the door with his fist, he yelled, "Open the door, Renteria!" A terrified Chocko opened the door to give them entrance.

Chocko inquired, "What do you want from me now?" Renteria asked in a frightened tone. "You already got your armaments."

"Now I want more!"

"More? That wasn't the deal you had with Mr. Thierry."

"Get him on the phone. I want to speak with him and make a new deal."

"He will not accept a phone call from you." Salvador moved threateningly toward Thierry's flunky and grabbed him by the shoulder. Holding his gun to Chocko's head, he sneered, "He will if he knows that I'm ready to kill you!"

A moment of clarity crystallized in Renteria's head. "Do you think he cares if someone like me is killed? He will just find another to take my place. Thierry doesn't care about anybody but himself!" Hermoza realized that the fat man was probably right and that he and the munitions manufacturer were probably two of a kind. The New Order leader let him go realizing that he wasn't going to get anywhere with this kind of tactic.

"When he does get in touch with you, tell him I now want more money to ensure his safety when he arrives in Guatemala. Do you understand?"

"Yes, I get it."

"That's good because if you don't, you're a dead man

Thierry better come through with the money!

Chapter 42

Trinity College

For Esmie Cummings, this was the first time she'd experienced anything like this. With Martin, it was respect and a certain level of caring. But love had never entered the picture for her until he had disappeared. Once she had discovered that Armand Thierry was the university's secret donor to her project, she felt totally devoted to him. *Cut it out, Esmie! You're not a school girl anymore!* But although this became her mantra, she could not help falling head over heels for this handsome, debonair man. He seemed to have the same feelings for her, but like any man, he kept them to

himself. Still, it was the little things he did that kept her thinking that he felt the same way about her. It had started after their meeting with Montgomery Lewis. She had showed him around her lab. "This is woefully inadequate," Thierry declared

"I suppose so, but I've spent most of your last donation preparing for my next trip to Guatemala."

"Well, with the next donation I want you to purchase some cutting-edge modern technology for this lab."

"I certainly intend to do just that!"

"Hello," a voice from behind interrupted them. The lanky frame of Kevin March stood in the doorway.

"Oh, yes," Dr. Cummings said, not bothering to hide her disparagement of the man. "This is my intern assistant, Kevin March."

"How do you do," Thierry greeted him extending his hand.

"It's a pleasure to meet you. There's a rumor going around the university that you are the school's anonymous donor. Is that true?"

"Guilty as charged," laughed Armand.

"I'm sure Mr. Thierry doesn't have the time to answer your silly questions, Kevin. Besides, don't you have some papers to grade? I think you had better get to it!"

"Of course, Doctor." Kevin turned around and left.

"What a nuisance he is. The board forced him on me. I really don't trust that little worm!"

"Let's not talk about him," he suggested. "Instead, start making a list of equipment you will need." While the list was created, Armand promised to call her and left the room. As he walked down the hallway, he bumped into Kevin March. "It was an honor to meet you, sir" Kevin explained in a surreptitious tone of voice.

"Tell me something, Kevin. What does an intern assistant like you get paid?"

"Well, let's just say that it's not enough to pay all my bills."

"Would you be interested in making some money on the side?"

"I'd be very interested, sir."

"Good!"

"But what would I have to do to earn this money?"

"I would want you to keep me abreast of any discoveries found by Dr. Cummings about a lost city named Nakanjo. Of course, all this must be kept from her."

"Do you mean spying on Dr. Cummings? I don't really think I could do that."

"That's alright. I wouldn't want you to do something against your conscious." Armand began to walk away.

"Wait a minute, Mr. Thierry," the intern called out to him. A smile spread across Armand's face. Putting on a serious expression, Thierry turned around.

"Yes?"

"How much would a job like that pay?"

"Let's just say that I'm a multi-billionaire and that I pay very well for the things I want, understand?" Kevin put out his hand.

"It's a deal sir."

"Good man!" They both shook hands on it. Armand gave him his card.

"Don't you want the lab number to reach me?"

"I already have it," he smiled walking away.

He called Esmie that afternoon to ask her to join him for dinner to celebrate. He picked her up that night in a limousine and drove to a five-star restaurant. There they drank and ate and continued their conversation.

Back in the limousine, Armand instructed his driver to drive around for a while. Thierry sat back and moved himself closer to Esmie. "Maybe this is too soon in our relationship to say but I think I'm beginning to have feelings for you."

"Oh, Armand, I feel the same way. Thierry moved in for a kiss but she turned her head.

"Is something wrong?"

"The driver," she whispered. "He'll see everything!"

"Don't worry," he responded calmly. He pressed a button and a smoked window went up, separating driver from passengers. "Now let's get back to it." Armand moved in and pressed his lips to hers. While his tongue flicked the roof of her mouth, his right hand explored her body.

"Oh, Armand!" Esmie wanted to give her mind and body to him... except for the discovery of Brother Gallego's diary. That she kept locked up in her head.

CHAPTER 43

You couldn't label it a whirlwind romance because it had happened much faster than that. Esmie was head over heels in love, a sense she had not felt before this. After all, what was there not to love? Armand was handsome, sophisticated, and wealthy and lived his life with a certain, *joie de vivre*. This eligible bachelor had chosen her to join him in this first-class journey through life.

Their first trip was planned to his home in Rio. "But what about my work?"

"You can take a break from that, after all I'm the one paying the bills," he responded.

"But I don't have the right clothing!"

"Don't worry. We can buy anything you need while we're there." And he was right. When they landed his private jet and took his limousine to his villa, he made a few calls and before the hour was up, he had salespeople from the best designer clothing stores stop by with everything from apparel to cosmetics. He purchased all that she needed for her.

Armand introduced her to the staff and Ramon. "Ramon is like my man Friday. He does the jobs I cannot find anyone else to do."

"Hello, Ramon. It's a pleasure to meet you."

"The pleasure is all mine, Madam."

Thierry took her on a tour of his villa, showing her the guest bedroom first. "It's gorgeous!" the professor exclaimed as she looked over the room. He led Esmie to some French doors which he opened to reveal a balcony.

"You see," he said stepping out and pointing down. "You have your own personal view of Rio just below."

"My God, it takes my breath away."

"Come with me, this is only the beginning."

They walked around for what seemed like an hour before they reached his study. The door was opened to a massive room with white-washed walls and French provincial furniture. The windows were opened and the white sheer curtains fluttered in the breeze, which brought with it the fragrance of the salty sea. "Each room is more impressive than the one before it."

"Is it all too much for you?"

"No, not at all." She moved around the room admiring the art work. She stopped in front of a large oil painting behind protective glass. "Is this "The Virgin and Child" by Jan van Eyck?" Thinking for a moment, she continued, "No, but it couldn't be the actual painting, could it?"

"You are very knowledgeable about the arts. It cost me a lot of money to have the painting reproduced." She moved over to a wall niche which housed a statue of Mary and the child Jesus.

"And is this also a copy of the statue sculpted by Michelangelo in Bruges, Belgium?"

"As a matter of fact, it is."

"Fantastic, simply fantastic! They're almost like the real works of art. Only experts would be able to tell the difference between them!"

"That's what I paid a fortune for," he perjured himself with a smile on his face. "All the art in each of my homes is an almost exact replication of the original." His smile nearly melted her heart. The butler knocked on the door and entered the room.

"Sir, lunch is served."

"Thank you. You must be starved," he said to Esmie. "I know I am."

He led Esmie to the dining room where luncheon was laid out on the table. Crab legs chilled in individual ice bowls were spread before them. Wedges of lemon and cocktail sauce were placed within reach. Glasses were filled with German Riesling wine. He raised his glass saying, "Here's to us!" Esmie raised her glass and touched it to his, making a gentle sound.

"To us!" They both drank. After taking a bite of the crab, she said, "These are delicious!"

"I'm glad you're enjoying it. I had them flown down from Boston this morning to make sure they were fresh." *Is there anything this man can't do?*

After one more course of grilled mixed seafood, Esmie put down her napkin. "I couldn't eat another bite!"

"Let's change and go out to the pool to cool off." Esmie went to her room and closed the door. She found that all the clothing that Armand had bought for her that morning had already been put away by the maid. Opening the bureau, she located several swimsuits. She chose a black bikini and a white lace cover-up and sandals. Esmie put on her sunglasses and went out to the pool area. On top of posts that surrounded the area were white flower pots filled with bright red geraniums.

Esmie walked over to a cabana where bright yellow umbrellas shaded two lounge chairs. She strolled over and slipped off her cover-up. It was at that moment that Armand arrived outside. He made his way to her and exclaimed, "God, you're beautiful."

"Why thank you, sir." The butler arrived with a pitcher of margaritas which he poured into two glasses with salted rims. After taking a sip, Armand removed his shirt and made his way onto the diving board. His body was toned and tanned. *My God, he has the physique of a young athlete.*

After a few springs, he dove into the water and started to swim laps. As he swam, Thierry thought, *Now, that I've got her out of town, my people can search her home and lab without interruption. That map must be somewhere.* Leaning back in her lounge chair with a chilled drink in her hand, she thought, *I could easily get used to a life like this!*

CHAPTER 44

PUERTO VALLARTA, MEXICO

The morning was sparkling from the reflection of rain drops that had fallen during the storm the night before. Everything seemed fresh and new.

After the driver had been sent to pick up his guest, Bonifacio rang for the cook and ordered everything he could think that she might like to eat. *"Huevos Rancheros,"* he began, "Some Sweet Breads, cut up some fresh fruit and serve some yogurt."

"Si, Senor Millian."

"And don't forget the coffee."

"I will remember." Hurriedly, he went out to the patio where the breakfast table was just being set under a big red umbrella.

"Cut some of the red hibiscus and put them in a vase in the middle of the table".

Millian had chosen his clothing carefully that morning. He was wearing a collared, powder-blue shirt over white linen pants. A fawn-colored belt and pair of slip-on shoes finished the look. He had splashed on some Christian Dior cologne. Bonifacio wanted everything to be perfect. He sat on a chair in the patio wearing sunglasses and waited patiently for his guest to arrive. The sound of the water lapping on the sand relaxed him.

The sudden ringing of the phone woke him from his daydream. "Sir," the guard at the front gate said. "Your car is now coming up the driveway."

"Thank you." He made his way to the front door just in time to see the car pull up. His chauffer got out and went around and opened the back passenger door. Cher stepped out into the shade of a huge Banyan tree. Walking out from underneath the tree, he caught his first sight of her in the sunshine. Cher looked dazzling. She was dressed in lime green pants, tapered at the ankle, and a lacy blouse. She wore silver sandals and her hair was done up in a ponytail with a green scarf. With barely any makeup, he could not help but think back to the painting of "Venus Rising from the Sea" by Sandro Botticelli. Cher was simply stunning.

"Welcome to my home," he greeted her as she walked inside.

"Thank you again for your invitation. My God, your home is magnificent!"

"I'm glad you like it." The chauffer walked into the entrance with a small piece of luggage." Turning to his butler, Bonifacio stated, "Take Miss Donnelly's bag to the second guest bedroom." He added, "I think you'll like the room. It has a beautiful view of the ocean."

"I can't wait to see it."

"That will need to wait. Breakfast is ready on the patio." Millian led her outside. Cher's eyes opened widely. "This view is gorgeous!"

"Please have a seat." The cook uncovered platters of the food.

"This all looks so delicious but there is so much!"

"Eat whatever you'd like."

"I think I'll have some yogurt and fresh fruit." The butler spooned it out into a dish and passed it over.

"I'll take the *"Huevos Rancheros"*.

"Yes, sir." Bonifacio was given his plate. As they ate, the coffee was poured. The butler was dismissed.

"So, what did your girlfriends say when you told them where you were going?"

"One said that it might not be safe staying with a stranger, but the other one told me to go and have a good time."

"I'm glad to see that you took the second friend's advice.

"I'm going to love sharing this with you today."

"And I'm glad to hear you say that."

CHAPTER 45

FLORA, GUATEMALA, SEPTEMBER

Night time brings no rest for the wicked they say, and it was the truth. For Salvador Hermoza, his patience waiting for more money was exhausted and he was going to do something about it. With two henchmen, he silently drove just outside the city and then furtively went on foot to the house of Chocko Renteria. The only thing that made Salvador hesitant was the full moon that shone incessantly on the town.

The three came upon the door, but it was locked. Going to the side of the building, Salvador saw the bedroom window open so that a cool breeze could enter. Sleeping in bed were Chocko and his wife Rosita. With deadly silence, they climbed in through the window.

Hermoza motioned with his hand and one of the thugs walked over to the wife's side of the bed and put his hand tightly over her mouth. The woman woke up and started to scream but the hand muted it. Still, there was enough of a racket to awaken her husband. "What's the matter, Rosita? Are you having a nightmare?" he yawned rubbing his tired eyes.

"No nightmare," Salvador rejoined. "It is the real thing because I'm your worst nightmare!" Chocko looked up to see two armed men, then turned to see another man's hand on his wife's mouth. Rosita's eyes rolled in dread.

"What do you want Hermoza?" To Salvador, the man's answer seemed almost submissive. Definitely, it was a change of attitude.

"Where's my money?"

"What money?"

"Don't play games with me fool, or someone will get hurt! Where is my money from Thierry?"

"There will be no more money, now or ever again."

"What are you saying?"

"Any fool could understand why Mr. Thierry refuses to pay you."

"And why is that?"

"He says he doesn't like paying bribe money."

"Did you tell him that I will protect him and his party the next time they come here?"

"I told him, but he's not impressed." Hermoza whipped his gun to the fat man's head, saying, "Maybe, you should call him right now and explain the dire situation you and your wife will be in if he doesn't send the money right now!"

"Mr. Thierry doesn't like being threatened. He's the one who does the intimidating." Hermoza nodded his head and the brute who was over Rosita withdrew a knife from his jacket pocket. He held it against the woman's throat.

"What if I told my man to slit the throat of your pig of a wife?"

"Go ahead and do it!"

Rosita's terrified sobs came out in muted sounds.

"You think I won't?" he answered, voice raised in rage.

"No, I don't think so!"

"And why not?"

"You may be many things, but you're not stupid! You cannot reach Mr. Thierry yourself. You will need to be in my good graces if I am to speak to him and get him to change his decision. Let one drop of blood fall from my wife, and you'll never see another centavo. Is that plain enough for you?"

"How long must I wait!"

"As long as it takes! That's the best answer I can give you!" Salvador stared at the man who had found his backbone. With another nod, his henchman backed away from the woman.

"What if you don't change his mind?"

"Then you don't get the money, not from Mr. Thierry anyway."

"I need that money!"

"It wasn't a wise decision to give him an ultimatum. He wasn't happy when I told him what you said."

"Let's go!" Hermoza told his men. The two left the room. "When will you call him?"

"I don't know. He always calls me," he responded with a shrug. Hermoza sneered, wanting to get the last word.

"Well, he better call very soon!" *And if he doesn't, what am I going to do. That fat pig Renteria is right. Without him, I would not have access to Thierry.* He walked away in a rage but could do nothing to change his situation.

Rosita sobbed uncontrollably and then punched Chocko in the arm.

"Ouch!" he yelled at her. "Why did you do that?"

"You told that dog that he could slit my throat!" Once again, she struck him on his arm.

"No more punching!" he warned her. "Besides, I knew he wouldn't do it."

"How could you be so sure?" she asked as she began to calm down.

"Once I realized that I was his only connection to Mr. Thierry, I knew I had him under my thumb. Go back to sleep, Rosita. He doesn't have the balls to try that again!"

CHAPTER 46

RIO DE JANEIRO, BRAZIL

It was not unusual in Rio, that in June it turned out to be a chilly, misty midmorning, the kind of morning when you want to bundle your coat close to the neck. It started off that way when they set off for Galeao International Airport. The limousine stopped on the tarmac and the chauffer opened the door. A tram was waiting to pick up Thierry and guest and drive them to Armand's private jet, a Dassault Falcon 900. For Esmie, she was getting another taste of the good life, and it was delicious! She thought, *No crowded terminals, no crying babies, no security check, and no lost luggage! This is all so incredible!*

The tram glided on until the plane was in sight. A flight attendant came down the steps. "Good morning, Mr. Thierry!" the young man with a broad smile said. "It's good to see you again!"

"See to it that my luggage and Dr. Cumming's bags are safely stowed away."

"Yes, sir."

As the bags were unloaded, Armand escorted his guest aboard the plane. The pilot welcomed them aboard. Tipping his cap, he returned to the cockpit and closed the door. They both took their seats in faun-colored plush leather chairs and buckled up. The flight attendant came back on board and closed the jet door behind him. A phone rang next to Armand. He picked it up and listened. "I understand," he said and then hung up.

"Is there a problem?" quizzed Esmie.

"The pilot informed me that we have ten minutes before we receive the okay to take off." Esmie reached for *Time Magazine* and started to thumb through the pages. She realized that this dream she was living had to come to an end, and that she needed to get back to Oxnard and to her work. She could imagine Montgomery Lewis already blowing his stack about how much time she had taken off. When she told this to her host, he had replied, "Then I'll go to Guatemala with you." Esmie had been stunned by his declaration.

"You will?"

"I want to be with you. I want to help you with your life's ambition."

"Are you sure you know what you're letting yourself get in for? It's a lot of hard and dirty work that 90% of the time results in nothing and leads to a dead end."

"You can't frighten me away! I've had some experience with archeological digs in Cambodia and Mesoamerica." Stopping for a moment, he said, "Don't you want me working side by side?"

"Of course, I do." The phone rang again and this time the steward picked up.

"We are ready to take off," he announced as he sat down and buckled up.

The engines revved and the sound grew louder. They began to taxi down the runway. Suddenly a tremendous thrust lifted them off the ground. Objects that had appeared in normal size outside the window soon became dots on the ground. Breaking through the gray cloudbank, an azure sky appeared with small puffy clouds. The flight attendant approached. "You may unbuckle your seat belts." Both passengers complied with the directive. "May I have your drink order?" he inquired of the doctor.

"Just some club soda on ice."

"And for you sir?"

"A scotch, neat." The flight attendant retreated to prepare their drinks. "You are happy that I'll be working with you, aren't you Esmie?"

"Of course I am," she declared reaching over to take his hand."

"You do agree that there should be no secrets between us if this collaboration is to work well, don't you?"

"I totally agree." The flight attendant came back to serve the drinks and then retreated to the back of the jet.

"I can't help but think that you've been holding something back from me concerning the lost city." He watched to see what effect this statement would make on her. She remained as cool as a cucumber.

"What do you mean?"

"Is there something you haven't told me yet? Isn't there something pertaining to Nakanjo that you have in your possession?"

"Can you give me a clue as to what you are talking about?" *Is he referring to Brother Gallego's diary?* She sipped her drink.

"Isn't there an old map leading to the Mayan city?" *Thank God, he didn't mention the journal. I'm not ready to reveal that to anyone yet.*

"Oh that," she tried to answer as insouciantly as she could. "It was in my possession once but it proved to be incorrect." With that, Armand downed his drink with one gulp.

"You used to have it? Where is it now? I'd like to look at it."

"Oh, Martin and I burned it a couple of years ago, in Guatemala once we learned how useless it was." Armand called for another drink and the attendant got busy.

"You've got to be kidding me!" he answered in shock. *I've wasted all this time looking for a map that no longer exists.* The steward handed him his drink and he took another gulp.

"It's not a joke. It's gone!"

"But why?"

"Martin was afraid somebody else might try to get their hands on it." *And he was right.*

"Then you have no way to find Nakanjo?"

"Well, I wouldn't say that."

"What are you holding back from me?"

"The map was right about one thing." Thierry's curiosity was peaked but he didn't want to give any emotions away.

"And what would that be?"

"I believe that the map did show the general area in which the lost city can be found."

"Then why haven't you found it?"

"The area contains mountainous terrain and thick dense jungle growth. It would be harder than finding a needle in a haystack."

"So, you're saying it's hopeless? If you had told me this fact, I never would have invested as much money as I have!"

"I'm not saying it's hopeless, but only that it's going to take time and a lot of work. Do you like getting your hands dirty?"

A causal smile spread across the billionaire's face. "The dirtier, the better!"

"Then this is the beginning of a beautiful working collaboration!" *And so much more I hope!*

"Have you ever experienced Carnival in Rio before?" Thierry inquired after dinner had been served.

"I haven't experienced Carnival anywhere," answered Esmie. Armand smiled broadly.

"Then you're in for a real treat tonight." Taking the limousine into the city, they were dropped off on the sidewalk at a favela held in one of the poor shanty towns of the city. The crowd was already electrically anticipating the world-famous event. "It's so exciting!" Esmie enthusiastically announced getting caught up in the crowd's anticipation.

"You haven't seen anything yet!" Armand was right. When the hypnotic music started, the people began to sway and dance. The first of the sumptuous allegorical floats came rolling down the avenue. It was decorated with towers adorned with bright red hibiscus blooms scattered among plaster figures painted in gold that seemed to gyrate. In the middle of it was a young woman dressed in a gold bikini and fiery red feather plumes. She danced as if she were possessed. On every side of the float, rhythmic young women dressed in elaborate and extravagant colorful yellow plumes danced the samba in flesh-revealing clothing. Young men beat out a mesmerizing pulsation on their drums that was accompanied by ringing bells and whistle blowing. Colorful confetti dropped from the heavens as revelers stood on balconies above and tossed the colorful paper squares coating everything and everyone below. People danced provocatively with their partners as well as strangers on the street. Hips swayed, arms gesticulated wildly as they let go of all their self control and became uninhibited. Voices were raised in total abandonment. Individuals were passing around bottles of liquor.

Esmie could not help getting caught up in all the jubilant mayhem. Her cheeks were flushed and her eyes lit up and burned bright like roman candles. She had never felt anything like this before and loved every moment of the festivities.

Armand raised his voice. "Let's move down the street to get a better look at the second float!"

"I'm right behind you!" He grabbed her hand and guided her past bodies, but immediately the partying throng pressed closer to the curb to get a better view. Then without warning, her hand slipped out of his manly grasp and they were pulled apart by the celebrating crowd. "Armand!" she screamed as she soon lost sight of him. "Armand, where are you?" The people around her pushed and jostled her out of their way. "Armand, I'm lost!"

Suddenly, two inebriated young men caught hold of her. They laughed as she struggled to get out of their grasps. The taller of the two shouted, *"Beber e celebrar conosco!"* in Portuguese. Esmie could not understand what he was saying, but when he forced the bottle to her lips, it all became clear. As the liquid was forced down her throat, she coughed and sputtered,

"Leave... me alone!" She shrieked in terror as they started to feel her flesh through her clothing. But although she continued to shriek, no one in the crowd came to her assistance - they were all too busy reveling, her screams getting lost in the cacophony of street pleasure seekers. With sudden brutality, the other man pulled up her blouse and started to kiss her along her neck. Esmie wanted to slap him, but his partner held her wrists with a firm grip behind her back.

All at once she felt the man behind her being pulled away. Reacting to this sudden interruption of their pleasure, his friend pushed her aside and came in swinging his fist at a person behind her. When she turned, she saw that Armand had already knocked the man behind her to the ground and with one swing of his fist in the drunken man's solar plexus, the other gasped for air before he crumpled at her feet.

Taking her by the arm, Armand pulled her close to him. Getting his cell phone out, he dialed. "Come around and pick us up at Arcos de Lapa right now!" he raised his voice to be heard by the chauffer. He pushed their way to the corner with Esmie in tow, to where the black limousine was waiting. The chauffer got out and opened the passenger doors of the vehicle. Esmie and Armand clamored inside. Armand commanded, "Take us home right away!" The vehicle made a U-turn and took off down the street. "Are you alright?" he turned his attention to the woman putting up a façade of normalcy as she was trying to straighten her chemise in the back seat as best as she could.

"I was scared for a moment but no real damage was done except for a few popped buttons on my blouse. It was just a bit of a shock." she fibbed.

"I'm so sorry this happened to you."

"Where were you? I kept calling and calling your name but you never came to me!"

"I'm sorry, but once we were separated, I tried to get back to you. The crowd was too dense. I heard you call my name and I shouted back. I guess it was just too noisy for you to hear me."

"Nobody around me helped or even seemed to care about what was happening to me."

"I apologize."

"It's alright. You got to me just before anything too serious happened, thank God!" Armand smiled and sidled toward her, cradling her head between his arm and broad chest.

"It's okay now, you can relax. You're safe with me." Esmie closed her eyes and let herself breathe easier in his paternal doting.

Suddenly, it started to rain, the sound of it lulling Esmie into a state of semi-consciousness. She must have drifted off to sleep because before she knew it, the vehicle slowed to a stop in front of the villa. They both ran from the vehicle to get into the dry shelter. Once they were inside, Thierry soothingly said, "Come with me." She followed him to his study and he had her sit down. A low fire had been conveniently started in the fireplace. He walked over to the bar behind mirrored doors and poured two glasses of brandy. He handed her one. "Drink this," he instructed. "You'll feel much better."

"Okay, I'll do what the doctor orders." She sipped at it and felt the warm liquid as it traveled down her throat and into her stomach.

They sat in silence for a while, neither one wanting to bring up the earlier incident until Esmie at last spoke up. "I'm feeling a little tired."

"That's very understandable."

"I think I'll go up to my bedroom."

"I believe that's a good idea. May I escort you there?"

I was hoping you would ask me that question.

"Thanks so much." Taking the stairs and getting to the landing, they turned into the left hallway. They stopped at his bedroom door as Armand began to say, "Have a good night's sleep. The rest will do you good."

"I'm sure I'll feel a whole lot better in the morning." *Ask me to come in.* She tried to influence his actions but he turned to walk away. Esmie was not about to let him get away.

"Sleep is good but I know something that would help me even more." Armand turned to face her.

"And what would that be?" She meandered over to him and took him by the hand.

"You know! By having your company for this evening. Besides, I haven't really properly thanked you for saving me tonight." She tugged gently on his hand and Thierry followed her through the door. Once the door was closed, Esmie looked up into his deep blue eyes and seemed to be drawn into them.

She kissed him on the cheek. "Thank you," Esmie said. Then she pressed her lips against his and slipped her tongue into his mouth. He immediately responded by taking her by the waist and unrelentingly pressing her body to his. She could feel his sex organ as it became aroused. "I want you," she whispered. "I've wanted you practically from the first moment I met you."

"I've longed for you too, right from the start." Before the two of them realized it, they were undressed and joined each other under the sheets. Esmie had never felt this way with Martin throughout their marriage. With Armand as her lover, it was the sweetest sensation. As they both climaxed, she kissed him passionately. He responded with just as much hunger. Armand finally slipped to her side as he looked at her and smiled.

"I love you," she told him.

"And I love you too."

Esmie turned on her side, her back to her lover. Armand moved over and spooned her. Esmie thought, *My God, I've never been so much in love!* Thierry at the same time thought, *Damn, that map still alludes me. I'll just have to be more direct, but my God, the plan for tonight worked to perfection! I've got her hook, line, and sinker.* They both drifted off to sleep.

CHAPTER 47

PUERTO VALLARTA, MEXICO

Swimming and lounging in the sun with a cold tropical drink was pleasant and Saturday was almost gone, but Bonifacio suggested they go to one of his favorite restaurants in town. "I really didn't bring much in the way of clothing with me. I never expected to be here all day."

"It's a casual place, not fancy and whatever you decide to wear will be fine. While you shower and change, I'll call and tell them we're coming."

Cher luxuriated under a warm flow of water in the marble shower. The sun hovered over the horizon, creating a shimmering gold and pink sky that any painter would have wanted to reproduce on a canvas. As the glowing orb sank, it uncovered the flickering light of a myriad of stars. As she dressed, Cher stared out her window. "This is truly paradise on earth!"

She came downstairs in rose-colored capris, a flowing pink flowered blouse and gold sandals. At the bottom of the stairs, Millian watched as she descended. *She is so lovely!* The car was waiting for them outside the front door. "Are you ready to leave?"

"If you are." The chauffer assisted them inside, climbed into the driver's seat, and they took off down the driveway. At the front gate, a guard opened it to allow the car to pass.

"I hope you're not a vegetarian or one of those vegans," Bonifacio stated.

"No," she remarked, "I eat almost everything."

"Good, because this restaurant we're going to, *"El Toro Carga"* is famous for its thick, juicy steaks."

"I love a good steak." For the rest of the journey into town, the conversation turned to their upbringing. Bonifacio told his story leaving out the part his relatives played in bringing his family down and his bloody revenge. "I don't have much to tell," Cher began. "My father abandoned my mother and me before I was 5 years of age. My mother struggled to raise me. By the age of seven my mother was diagnosed with advanced breast cancer. A year later she was dead."

"I'm sorry."

"That's all right because my grandmother raised me. I had a wonderful childhood with her. I graduated high school and went to college for my teaching degree. My grandmother died five years ago and I really do miss her. I owe her so much."

"I'm sure she's happy now. So, you don't have any other relatives?"

"No, I'm pretty sure that I'm it."

"It must be very difficult for you," Millian answered sympathetically.

"I have lots of friends. It's not that bad."

The car pulled up to the restaurant and the couple stepped out. Cher took one look at the crowded seating and remarked, "We'll never get a table here!"

"Don't worry about that," he replied taking her hand and walking in.

As soon as the maître d' recognized him, he came over. *"Buenas noches, Senor Millian. Eres mesa estalista."* They followed him upstairs into a private dining room. Only one table was set for dinner with a single candle burning. They sat down and the maître d' handed them menus.

"Would you mind if I ordered for both of us?"

"No, not at all.

"Two Steak Tampiquena," he ordered as soon as the waiter came over. "How do you like your beef cooked?"

"Medium-well."

"Both medium-well."

"And to drink?"

"Bring a bottle of your best cabernet sauvignon." The waiter made a note of the wine then rushed to the kitchen to place the orders.

In seemingly very little time, the wine and meals were served. As the waiter poured the wine, Cher remarked, "It's good that you called ahead."

Millian smiled and answered. "I have a standing reservation here even if I don't come every night." Bonifacio gazed into his guests' eyes. The lambent light of the flame was reflected in her glistening eyes.

As they ate and drank, Cher looked back on the wonderful day they had spent together. "I guess your driver should take me back to the hotel tomorrow morning." Bonifacio wiped his mouth with a linen napkin and said, "Why not stay here tomorrow, that is if you had a good time today."

"Oh, I've had a fantastic time but you know what they say about guests who stay too long, don't you?"

"Do you mean the one about fish?"

"I do."

"Believe me, the last thing I think about you is a comparison with malodorous fish."

"That's sweet of you but I don't think I can. My roommates are expecting me back."

"Call them, and while you're on the phone, tell them you're spending the rest of the week in my villa."

"You're kidding, aren't you?"

"I'm serious. Stay on."

"Well, if you don't think I will be in the way."

"You don't have to worry about that. I will be working away from my home during the week but I'll join you for dinner every night."

"Alright, you have a deal." They clicked their wine glasses together to seal their agreement.

As they drove back, Cher mentioned, "All the rest of my clothes and cosmetics are back at the hotel."

"I'll simply call the hotel and have your things packed. My driver will pick them up. Anything else you need, you can find in town."

Once they arrived back, she said, "I'm really feeling exhausted tonight. I think I'll go to bed." Before she could climb the stairs, he took her hand and drew her body towards his.

"I've had a truly wonderful day and it's all because of you." He pressed his lips onto hers and they stood there kissing for the next few seconds.

"Good night. I'll see you tomorrow morning."

"I look forward to it, Cher." She climbed the stairs and closed her bedroom door. She looked into her luggage and unzipped a small compartment inside. She withdrew her cell phone and took it into the bathroom. She closed and locked the door. First thing she did was turn on the shower, after that she opened the sink faucet and lastly, she flushed the toilet. Quickly, she dialed a number on her phone. It rang only once before it was picked up. A male voice on the other side asked, "Do you have anything to report Agent Kowalski?" Cher replied,

"I'm in!"

Kimberly Kowalski, posing as Cheryl Donnelly waited until the house was asleep before she slipped out of the bedroom at 2:17 in the morning in her nightgown and robe. Bonifacio's snoring convinced her that she could make her reconnaissance around the house without being surprised by anyone. She crept barefoot into Millian's study and stopped before she entered. The villa remained silent. She closed the door and made her way to his desk. A full moon allowed her to see without turning on a light. *I heard the phone ring a few times in the day and passed the study door once to see the butler answer the phone and jot some information on a notepad.* Kim hoped that one of these notes might lead her to make an arrest of the drug lord. So far, Millian had been clever enough to avoid being charged and there was no extradition treaty between the United States and Guatemala to transfer a Mexican citizen.

Kim walked over to the desk and looked for the notepaper. It wasn't there. She checked under the blotter. There was no sign of it there either. She pulled out the chair and sat down. The wastepaper basket had been emptied by the butler before he went to bed. *Shit!* Pulling out the middle draw revealed nothing but writing utensils. The draw on the left side revealed the writing pads. She took out the one laying on top and brought it to the window. The paper with the message was gone but the pad retained the impression of the message on it.

Kowalski opened the drawer of the writing utensils and took out a lead pencil. Placing the pad on the desk, she began to rub the pad with the side of the pencil until the words became discernible. It read,

Mr. Armand Thierry called. Wants you to call back as soon as you get in.

"Holy crap! Millan's in contact with Thierry the munitions manufacturer and dealer. This couldn't get any better!" she whispered. "What a feather it would be in my cap if I could apprehend them both!"

Ripping the note from the pad, Kim replaced the pad and pencil in the drawers. She pushed the chair back to where she found it. Kowalski lifted her cell phone from her robe pocket and quickly punched in the numbers and waited. A familiar voice answered. It was her direct supervisor, Abraham Prentiss. "Kowalski, what's going on?"

Abe was a pudgy, middle-aged man whose bushy white eyebrows made him look older than he was. He had worked for the C.I.A. for a little over 32 years, and over time had been an intricate part of the takedown of crackpots from Christian militias to Islamic extremists. He had recently been promoted to his present position, e had handpicked and he had handpicked Kim for this mission.

"Abe, I've got information that will blow you out of the water."

"What did you find out?"

"Millian is doing business with Thierry."

"You're joking!"

"No, they know each other. Do you know what that means?"

"Kim, I'm starting to really worry about you!"

She selectively ignored his comment. "I have to cast a bigger net if I'm going to catch these two sharks."

"I'm going to pull you out of this situation."

"Don't you dare! I started this and I'm sticking around to finish it!"

"Then I'm putting more agents in the area to follow you. I'm afraid for your life!"

"I was thoroughly trained for this kind of job. Besides I can take care of myself. Don't place any more agents here. My life would really be in danger if Millian detected their presence."

"I don't know, Kim!"

"Listen, we're never going to get another chance like this. You chose me because I have the look in women that he likes. Trust me to know what I've been trained to do, okay?"

"I'm still not sure. I should have chosen a more experienced female agent."

"That ship has sailed! I have almost five years of experience. I'm here now. Millian is not stupid. If I were to suddenly pull out, he would suspect something was wrong. Do you think you would ever get the chance to do this again with another female agent?"

"Probably not."

"Ok. Then stop with all the negativity and let me do my job!"

"Are agents Kravitz and Monihan still hold up in the hotel?"

"Nate and Dan are there, but every day, one of them takes a hidden position near the gate and follows me whenever I go into town."

"Alright, I suppose, for now I'll keep the operatives the way they are."

"Don't screw this up for me, Abe!"

"Try and find out what Thierry and Millan talk about and get back to me when you know something concrete."

"I will!"

"Remember, you only have a small window of opportunity to catch them breaking the law."

"I might convince him to let me stay longer but we'll see."

"Just watch your step. I don't want you returning to Ronald Reagan Airport in a body bag."

"Relax, you worry too much."

"I get paid to worry."

Bonifacio walked through the front door at 4:37 in the afternoon. His butler was notified that his boss was driving up to the villa by the guard at the front gate, and he was waiting for him in the foyer. "Where is she?" the owner of the villa inquired in a whisper, then he walked through the entrance.

"She's resting by the pool."

"That's good", he replied as he walked into his study. The butler followed him there. "Has she used the house phone today?"

"Not once, sir."

"Did she leave the villa at any time?"

"She said she was going out for some sundry items."

"And?"

"The chauffer reported that she went in, shopped, paid for the items and then came out and got back in the car."

"Did you check her luggage?"

"There was nothing unusual."

"What about the chest of drawers and the closet in her bedroom."

"Again, there was nothing, sir."

"Did she walk around the house looking into rooms?"

"The maid kept her eye open and said except for going into the guest room a few times, she's been out by the pool all day."

"Alright. Did you check downstairs to monitor the videotape of the guest room?"

"Nothing unusual, sir."

"Thank you. You're dismissed." Millian checked his phone messages and wrote down the numbers of the people he needed to call back. He walked through the French doors to join Cher.

She was lying on a lounge chair in the sun, her skin glistening with sun protection lotion. Cher was wearing a light pink bikini with a print of hot pink flowers. She wore a big brimmed straw hat with a pink sash running around the bottom of the crown. Her flip flops lay at the side of the chair and a pink and white striped beach bag lay on the low glass table next to her. "Pretty in pink," Bonifacio remarked as he drew near and kissed her on the cheek.

"Do you really like it?"

"I really do!" Millian sat down on a chair next to her.

"Have you ever seen that movie?"

"Yes, that's why I said that." Cher checked the watch on her wrist.

"Are you done with work for today?"

"Yes, and I came running home to you."

"You must have left very early this morning. I didn't hear you leave."

"I left about six. I did not want to wake you to say goodbye. The woman flashed a cozy little smile.

"How have you been entertaining yourself all day?" *Let's see if there are any inconsistencies in her story.*

"Mostly I stayed by the pool but I did ask to go into town for some things. I hope you don't mind that your chauffer drove me."

"Not at all. That's what he's there to do."

"This bikini was one of my purchases. I could not wait for you to see me in it."

"Did you hear from your girlfriends today?"

"I spoke to them last night about my plan to stay for the week. They said that they were happy for me but I believe they really were jealous." Bonifacio laughed.

"If you'd like to invite them for a day, please feel free to do so."

"Oh, no," she countered. "I want you all to myself." "The Executioner" suddenly changed the subject.

"Do you mind if we eat dinner here tonight?"

"Not at all. You must be exhausted."

"Thank you. I'm going to go upstairs and change into my bathing trunks and rejoin you out here. I want to cool off in the water before we eat."

"I'll wait here for you."

Bonifacio climbed the stairs to his bedroom and closed the door. He changed, grabbed a towel and went back to the pool. Cher was already in the pool waiting for him, her wet hair pushed back with her hands. "Come in," she shouted at him. "The water feels terrific!" Millian ran to the pool and cannon balled next to his guest, splashing water on her. When he reemerged above the water, she said, "You're such a little boy!" He swam next to her and held Cher in his arms.

"If you like, I can show you the real man I am after the lights go out tonight."

"I'll be looking forward to it." They kissed passionately.

Chapter 48

Thousand Oaks, California

There was no longer any pretense of sleeping in separate bedrooms. Armand had contacted a real estate agent in Thousand Oaks, California, not far from Oxnard. When they exited the jet, Esmie and Armand were whisked away in a limousine and taken to the house that Thierry had bought for them on Hidden Valley Road.

It was a stately but modest mansion consisting of four bedrooms, three and a half baths, 3,200 square feet located on 5 acres. When the vehicle pulled up in front, Esmie gasped at what she saw. "You bought this for us?"

"I know it's smaller than my other residences but I hope you like it."

"Like it? I love it! It's certainly better than the present place I'm living in."

Strolling up the brick walkway, Thierry took out the house key and unlocked the front door. In the foyer, waiting for them, stood, Ramon.

"Is everything in order, Ramon?"

"Yes, sir." Esmie looked into the rooms decorated in a grand style.

"You had time to refurnish all these rooms?" she inquired.

"When I bought the house, I demanded that all the furnishings be included in the price. At first the old owners bristled at my demand but with a little persuasion, they eventually came around." *Thanks to Ramon.*

"How much did you pay for all this?"

"Let's not talk money, for you the sky's the limit." She gave him a peck on his cheek.

The next morning, the limousine picked them up and drove them to Trinity University to face President Montgomery Lewis. "He's going to be peeved with me for taking so much time off from my teaching."

"I wouldn't worry about it darling. I have the feeling that he will be very compliant." Esmie was met by Montgomery in his office welcoming her back with a broad smile. It was as if Armand had a crystal ball, but Esmie hadn't realized that her boyfriend had called Lewis directly threatening to cut off his monetary gifts to the university if Esmie were to be fired.

"I have some wonderful news!" she told Montgomery. "Mr. Thierry will be joining me on my next expedition into Guatemala!"

"Wonderful! Just wonderful!" the president exclaimed in his most enthusiastic tone of voice.

"Now, I'd like to get back to my lab and classes."

"Very well," he grinned. Esmie couldn't remember another time when Lewis smiled so much.

Armand followed her down to her office where Kevin March sat behind her desk marking test papers. "Welcome back," he said sarcastically.

"Everything running smoothly, Kevin?"

"With me at the helm, of course." From the door, Armand used his index finger to call Kevin out in the hallway. "Excuse me," he said to Dr. Cummings as he left. Armand pulled him over to the side of the hallway where only a couple of students were walking between classes. "Kevin," he began. "I no longer need your services."

"Mr. Thierry, I know Dr. Cummings has not been back in months but that wasn't my fault. Now that she's back, I'm sure I can be of service to you again." Mr. March was hoping that the nice check he got would not stop coming.

"You see my plans have changed, Kevin. I have relocated here and I plan to be at the university much more."

"But what about my money?"

"I'm afraid that's coming to an end." Kevin could not help but show a bitter frustrating expression on his face.

"I'm sure you could find another way to utilize my talents."

"I'm afraid not. Now, if you'll excuse me, I have to go." Turning, he walked away and entered Esmie's office. Kevin lingered in the hallway steaming. *That's it? I'm just cut off?* With some strain, he strived to put a less angry expression on his face before he walked into the office. When he turned the corner, he caught the two of them in a lip lock. "I just came for my test papers," he announced, elated that he was interrupting them. The two lovers separated. "You have a class in ten minutes," he stated checking the clock on the wall.

"Yes, I know."

"Do you want me to cover it for you?"

"Thank you, but no. Now that I've returned, I might as well get back into the swing of things."

The grin on Montgomery Lewis' face was almost wide enough to expose all 32 pearly whites. Dr. Esmie Cummings announced that the following summer, she would lead the next expeditionary foray into the Guatemalan jungle to find the lost city of Nakanjo.

To join the expedition was a plum appointment and so she weighed the positives and negatives of each candidate. Many of the men that had been on the last trip with Martin and Esmie were either dead or had left Trinity University for other placements.

Months before the trip, Esmie began to receive applications and resumes applying for the positions. One thing Dr. Cummings knew for sure is that Armand Thierry would be right by her side. It was while she was looking through the applications and making phone calls that Kevin March approached Esmie in her office. "Excuse me, Dr. Cummings."

"I really can't talk right now, Kevin. I have to finish going over these applications for the mission to find the lost city."

"That's what I wanted to talk to you about." Esmie laid down her papers and responded,

"Well, make it quick!"

"I was hoping that you would take me on your archeological trip to Guatemala."

"Kevin," she began in a somewhat patronizing way, "Everyone who is going to be chosen comes with a needed skill. What can you bring to the table?"

"I figured that since I was already your assistant, I could join you in the same capacity." Esmie smiled as if she just caught him with his hand in the cookie jar.

"Really, Kevin, I don't think I'll be needing someone to grade papers or run errands for me while I'm down there." March's expression turned ugly and in a raised voice inquired,

"I suppose Mr. Thierry is going with you?"

"Yes, he is."

"And what may I ask does he bring to the table?"

"He brings a check, a big fat check of two million dollars. Can you do the same?" This answer left Kevin with no comeback.

"You know," he replied after a moment. "I just don't think my talents are appreciated here." He hoped to shake Esmie up to change her mind.

"You're probably right." Esmie lifted an application from her desk and adjusted her reading glasses. March was incensed by her lack of a reaction.

"I think it's best that I start looking for a position at another university."

"You have to do what you think is best for your career." March wanted to blow his top, but restrained himself. Instead, he walked out. Watching him leave, she smiled thinking, *He's never leaving Trinity!*

After a day of teaching classes and doing paperwork, Esmie was looking forward to getting home and seeing Armand. Traffic was brutal this time of day. After almost two hours, Esmie moved onto the off ramp where local traffic was much more bearable. Fifteen minutes later she was pulling up to her home in Thousand Oaks. She walked past the beautifully manicured lawn and blooming flower beds. She unlocked the door, went inside, and got out of the heat. The air conditioning felt wonderful, but the sight of Armand holding out a vodka and tonic for her was even better.

Giving him a kiss, she took the glass and downed half of it. "Traffic was worse today?"

"As bad as usual, I suppose."

"Come back to the patio, kick off your shoes and relax in the lounge chair for a while. Cook says dinner will be ready in a little while." They went outside hand in hand.

"I'm so glad I'm home!"

"Rough day at the office?"

"I had even more paperwork because of applications to join us on our trip."

"I'm sorry you had a hard day." Dr. Cummings took another swallow of her cocktail."

"It wasn't all difficult today. There was one moment of hilarity."

"What happened?"

"Kevin had the nerve to come and ask me to take him with us."

"You're joking!"

"No, it took all my self control to keep from laughing in his face, but that was not the end of it."

"You said no, of course."

"Of course."

"What did he do next?"

"He asked if you were going with me, and when I said you were, he wanted to know why you and not him."

"What did you tell him?"

"I said you were donating two million dollars and I asked if he could match that. He wasn't very pleased after that."

"That is hilarious!"

"Wait, there's more. He threatened leave Trinity."

"How did you react to that?"

"I told him to do what he needed to do. He's such a strange duck!"

Kevin hadn't heard the remark Dr. Cummings had made about him, but it wouldn't have surprised him at all. Mr. March dreamed of making his mark as an archeologist, but at each turn, Esmie thwarted his attempts. *What does that bitch have against me anyway?* It was the same question he had asked himself about anyone throughout his life.

"Mr. March," a cute, cheerleader coed called out to Kevin as he came out of Esmie's office.

"What?" he asked impatiently.

"I'd like to talk to you about the grade you gave me on my last paper."

"Not now! I'm busy!"

"But..." Kevin did not bother to look back. *I'm going to find out who this Armand Thierry character is!* he swore to himself as he roughly elbowed his way through students in the hallway.

CHAPTER 49

PUERTO VALLARTA, MEXICO

The sunlight seeped through the plantation shutters creating patterns of light on the bed. Kim awoke with one thing on her mind. *I need to get Millian to ask me to stay on so I can get more damning evidence on him.*

The last night in Puerto Villarta had been spent going out to dinner, dancing at a disco, and walking hand in hand on the powdery sand.

She recalled their conversation as they walked. "I hate having to go back home. I've had a wonderful time here with you." Bonifacio had smiled at her but said nothing. "It's going to be very hard for me to go back to my classroom and leave all this beauty behind."

"I'm sure it will be."

"I'm going to really miss you."

"I feel the same way." There was nothing in his voice that smacked of encouragement. Kim became desperate as she thought about her two fish slipping from her net.

"I'm sure you've been with many women," Kim baited him hoping he would say that there was no one like her. He simply smiled. Kim stopped talking at that point and she continued to walk with him in reticence.

When they finally reached the villa, the hour was late. Bonifacio kissed her on the cheek and said, "Goodnight." Walking up the stairs, he disappeared around the corner. Kim was crushed, but she knew she would have one more opportunity during breakfast to get Bonifacio to ask her to stay with him.

The next morning, she packed her bags anticipating her departure, took a quick shower and got dressed in the outfit she had first arrived in a week ago. She entered the breakfast room where the credenza was already set up with chaffing dishes of food. The butler pulled out her chair. "Juice and coffee, miss?"

"Yes, please!" She uncovered the dish and served herself some scrambled eggs and a croissant. "Will Mr. Millian be down for breakfast soon?"

"Mr. Millian has already had his breakfast." Kim's fork paused between her mouth and plate.

"Where is he?"

"I don't know miss, but he left early this morning before you were awake."

"Will he be back soon?"

"He didn't say." She glanced at her wristwatch and remarked,

"I was hoping to thank him for his hospitality."

"Mr. Millian asked me to tell you that he had a wonderful week and that you should have a safe flight back home." Kim was devastated. She would not be having one last conversation with him.

Finishing her meal, she turned to the butler and said, "Please call for a taxi to the airport. I'll be leaving immediately."

"The limousine will be waiting outside whenever you are ready to leave."

"Thank you. Will you see to getting my luggage in the car?"

"Yes, Miss." Kim went up to check her makeup and then turned around to leave, not looking back. *My leaving without having the two men taken into custody is a bitter pill to swallow!* She got into the limo and they took off for the airport. She wanted to call Abe and tell him that the whole plan was a bust but she couldn't talk in front of the chauffeur. The drive seemed never ending but in time they arrived. "Would you see if you can get the porter to take my luggage?"

"Yes, Miss Donnelly." She tried to tip him but he graciously refused. She took her luggage and got on the ticket line. There were a few people ahead of her. Checking to see if there was anybody who would overhear her, she removed her cell phone from her purse and scrolled until she got the number she was looking for. "What's going on?" Abe asked.

"It's a bust! I threw him all kinds of hints but he never asked me to stay on."

"You knew that might happen."

"Yeah, but I thought I had him really interested in me. To make matters worse, he wasn't home this morning so I couldn't try to convince him one more time."

"Well, I guess you're no Mata Hari!" Kim was about to answer when she felt a hand on her shoulder. Turning around, she met Bonifacio Millian's eyes. She was stunned by his sudden appearance at the airport. She left her cellphone on so that Abe could hear the conversation.

"What are you doing here?" Her voice reflected pleasantness and astonishment.

"Cher, I tried not to feel anything for you. I told myself that it was better for me to let you walk away, but I was lying to myself. I can't face another day without you."

"But what about my job? I have to be back at work on Monday." *Don't resist him too hard or you'll really screw this up.*

"I want you with me. I want you to share my life with me. I tried to deny it but I couldn't get past the fact that I'm in love with you." The phony persona, Cher Donnelly, nodded.

"I love you too. You've made me so happy." She threw her arms around his neck and kissed him.

"Next!" the ticket agent called out. Kim turned to the man behind her and said, "I've changed my mind about leaving, you're next." Cher followed the porter and Bonifacio to the door and quickly got back on her phone. "Did you hear?"

"I heard," Abe Prentiss responded.

"I'm in again!"

"Be careful, Millian is a dangerous man to have as an enemy."

"Don't worry! I'll be fine!" she said loud enough for Bonifacio to hear before she hung up. As the porter loaded his car, Boniface asked with inquisitiveness, "Who were you talking with?"

"It was my mother. I told her I was staying on in Puerto Vallarta for an extended period of time."

"I guess you should call your girlfriends and tell them to go home without you." Millian to tip the porter.

"I'll do that right now." She dialed the hotel room of agents Kravitz and Monihan and asked, "Have you checked out yet?"

"Not yet," Kravitz answered.

"Well don't! It's back on!" Hanging up she walked to the convertible where Millian was behind the wheel waiting for her. "Have you told them?"

"Yes, it's done". Millian put his car into drive and hit the gas pedal.

CHAPTER 50

Esmie sat back in her plane seat while Armand unsnapped his seat belt to speak to the pilot. She watched as the white billowy clouds passed by her. She couldn't help but think how the clouds were like her life. More than three years had passed since her last trip to Guatemala with Martin, three years since his body had been recovered from the river. A lump suddenly grew in her throat as the emotional grief revisited her heart and mind.

At that time, funds were limited and their traveling accommodations were substantially less luxurious than how she now was travelling. She loved the life that she and Armand were creating for themselves, but she thought back to how much simpler her life had been with her husband. *Have I lost myself in this lifestyle? It's been three years since I tried to find Nakanjo. Have I lost my edge as an archeologist?*

Dr. Cummings realized that if it hadn't been for Thierry's money to Trinity University, she would have been fired from her job long ago and Kevin March would probably have taken her place. *It's no wonder that he hates me so much.*

"Esmie," a voice called to her.

"Yes?" she asked gazing up.

"What were you thinking about? Your mind seemed to be a million miles away."

"I was just thinking about my last trip to Guatemala."

Armand retook his seat beside her. "Would you mind if we took a couple of days' detour?"

"Why is that?"

"A businessman I have some dealings with needs to see me. He asks that we stay overnight until our transaction is completed. Is that alright with you?"

"Well, the men I've hired and the equipment for the expedition won't arrive right away. It will take a couple of days for them to arrive in San Cristobal, so I don't think that will be a problem."

"Thank you, my love," he responded kissing her hand.

"Where are we headed?"

"It's a beautiful resort in Puerto Vallarta, Mexico. He has a lovely villa down there."

"Who is this person?"

"His name is Bonifacio Millian. He is an importer-exporter." Armand sat back in his chair and reclined the seat until he was stretched out comfortably. In a few minutes his eyes began to blink as he started to fall asleep. Esmie watched him in serene slumber. He was a man of limitless money and contacts with powerful people around the world. *He could have any woman in the world, any number of models and socialites and yet he has chosen to be with me.* She wasn't questioning his motives but only thinking she was a very fortunate woman.

A few hours later, the jet began its decent into Puerto Vallarta. After landing, the two passengers disembarked and walked over to a waiting limousine. The chauffer sat behind the steering wheel and sped away.

After about 25 minutes, the limousine turned into a long driveway. The view of the villa was breathtaking. As they drew near to the front entrance, Esmie noticed two beautiful people waiting for their arrival and thought, *this is the everyday life of the idle rich, I suppose.*

The vehicle pulled to a stop and the chauffer came out to open their doors. Armand got out and greeted the man with a bear hug and a kiss on each cheek. "Bonifacio, my old friend, how have you been?"

"Well, my dear friend." Thierry turned and gave his hand to Esmie to help her out. "Let me introduce you to my associate Esmie Cummings. Millian kissed her hand.

"A pleasure. This is my guest, Cheryl Donnelly." Armand kissed her hand, and Esmie said, "It's nice to meet you Cheryl."

"Please don't be so formal. My friends call me Cher."

"Come in out of the heat," invited Millian. I've had luncheon prepared for us." All four walked in with Bonifacio leading them to the canopied terrace in the back.

"You have such a lovely home," stated the professor as they all sat down at the table. Four goblets of cracked crab over ice waited to be consumed accompanied by glasses of ice tea.

"I love crab," cooed Cher.

"It's a special occasion," Millian announced. "It's not every day that my old friend comes to visit me."

"We are both businessmen with demanding schedules," remarked Armand. "I'm glad that we could arrange this, thanks to Esmie."

"Thank you, Esmie for allowing this get together," Bonifacio remarked.

"You're very welcome." The four began to dig into the crab meat.

"This is so fresh and delicious," remarked Esmie.

"I had it flown down especially for our luncheon from Boston," smiled Bonifacio. Esmie was surprised by this statement. *It sounds as if Millian expected our visit way before Armand brought it up to me on the plane.*

They ate and drank, whiling away the time listening to the surf break on the beach and having a congenial conversation. After a time, Bonifacio remarked to his friend, "Let's go into my study for a good cigar and to work out a deal between us."

"Good idea."

"Esmie," Millian remarked. "Why don't you and Cher enjoy the sun while we discuss boring business."

"I would love to," responded Esmie. *I may have even less access to roam around the place with Armand and Esmie here, but I can still pump her for information*

Esmie commented, "This is such a lovely house."

"I know. I just adore being here. So, Esmie what do you do for a living?"

"I'm a professor of archeology at Trinity University in Oxnard, California."

"That's interesting because I'm a teacher also."

"Really," Esmie answered unimpressed.

"I teach math in a middle school in Hawthorne, New Jersey." Esmie thought, *Our jobs are not quite the same.*

"What does Armand do for a living?"

"He's a jewel broker." *The poor sap doesn't even know what she's gotten herself into.*

"His career must be fascinating and very financially rewarding." *This woman is either playing dumb or is totally clueless,* thought Cher.

"It must be." Esmie sat back and closed her eyes hoping that it would indicate she was no longer in the mood to talk. That didn't stop Cher at all.

"So how long have you known your boyfriend?"

"Not quite three years, but he's not my boyfriend."

"Really! Then how would you describe your relationship with him?"

"We're just friends who share a lot of common interests." *Boy, she's very nosy. I'll just turn the tables on her.* "And how long have you been with your boyfriend?"

"Like you, he is not my boyfriend. I'm just a houseguest on an extended stay here." *God, I wish that I could be a fly on the wall of the study and listen to what the two of them are talking about. I hope Nate and Dan are listening to them with the bug I planted in that room.* "After you leave here, where are you heading?"

"We're on our way to Guatemala."

"Going to a resort?"

"Not really," Esmie said with an air of disdain. "Armand and I are searching for the long-lost Mayan city of Nakanjo."

"Sounds exciting!" *She's such a bitch!*

"And when do you plan to go back to New Jersey?" Esmie inquired.

"Whenever the mood strikes me!"

"It must be great to have so much time on your hands." *I wish a large van would hit her right now.* "It's such a beautiful day, isn't it?"

"Just perfect."

CHAPTER 51

TRINITY UNIVERSITY, OXNARD, CALIFORNIA

"Thank God for the Internet," Kevin March expressed as he sat at his home computer. "I can find anything I need in a matter of seconds. March had typed in the name "Armand Thierry" and waited for the screen to light up with information. The listings for the "man of mystery" appeared like magic. Clicking on the first site, he began to scan the data. There was the usual place of birth, birth date, and his multiple residences around the world, but Kevin found this all very generic and not what he was looking for. *I need something by which I can nail this bastard to the wall!*

Site after site, it was all the same, there was nothing he could exploit to his advantage. He ran his fingers through his brown hair and adjusted his reading glasses. *There must be something, anything!* As he scrolled down and clicked on each different site, it was all the same, and he had spent hours in fruitless research. March was about to give up when he came upon a site labeled, "*The Dirt*" and clicked on it. The site opened to a screen on which the flames of hell seemed to be burning. Kevin began to read. At first, the site was filled with the same old information that he had scanned before, until he came to a part that made him yell, "Eureka!" He clicked on "print" and the computer spit out 50 copies. For the rest of the day, he spent his time highlighting pertinent and damning statistics. When that was completed, he put one copy in a brown manila envelope and locked the other 49 in his desk drawer. Kevin imagined the scene that would unfold tomorrow after the information was received. Smiling, he went into the kitchen to microwave a frozen dinner.

Because Dr. Cummings was away, Kevin March took over her first period class. Since he had no classes the next two periods, he marched himself over to President Lewis' office, the manila envelope under his arm. He announced loudly, "I'd like to see President Lewis."

"He's on a phone call right now, but have a seat and when he hangs up I'll tell him you're waiting to see him."

"Don't bother," he answered in a dismissive tone as he opened the president's office door.

"You can't do that!" his secretary admonished, but March was not going to be stopped. Surprised abruptly by this intrusion, Montgomery barked,

"What are you doing here?"

"I suggest you hang up."

"I'm sorry, but he just wouldn't listen to me!" his secretary announced stridently.

"I strongly suggest that you hang up immediately!" March loudly mandated.

"I'll have to call you back," the president said to the caller. "I need to deal with a crisis."

Kevin remarked, "That's more like it."

"You may go back to your desk," Lewis told his secretary and waited for her to close the door.

March stood in front of him grinning with supreme self-confidence. "We need to have a conversation."

"How dare you barge into my office and tell me to break off a phone conversation that I was having with an alumnus!"

"I bring you news of rather great importance."

"I'm not going to invite you to sit down because you won't be remaining in my office very much longer!" Kevin undid the envelope, pulled out some stapled papers and slammed them on Lewis' desk.

"Read!" he ordered pointing to the papers.

"Have you lost your mind? Who do you think you are ordering around, one of the students?"

"Shut up and read the parts of the paper that I have highlighted!" Jumping up at this insult, he retorted, "You have your nerve..."

"I suggest you read it carefully. It has everything to do with your future here at Trinity University!" Montgomery Lewis stared at the upstart for a moment before he turned his eyes toward the papers. There was complete stillness in the room. Finally, the president looked up and sat back down.

"Interesting, but what does this have to do with me?"

"It has plenty to do with you! You've allowed a murderer like Armand Thierry, an international illegal munitions dealer, to establish a toehold at this university!"

"First, I had no idea what he was involved in; and secondly, his donations have put this small university on the map!"

"Yes, it's on the map. But I wonder what the Board of Administrators would say if they had this information in their hands. And even if you didn't know about Thierry's background, your lack of knowledge about who you have admitted into our midst smacks of incompetence, don't you agree?" Quickly darting his arm like an attacking serpent, Lewis snatched the papers from the top of his desk and locked it in a drawer.

"Where's your proof now?"

"Oh, that's alright you can keep that copy. I have 49 others. In fact, besides giving a copy to each of the board members, I'm toying with the idea of hanging the rest around the campus for the student body to read." Kevin watched with satisfaction as Montgomery blanched at what he heard.

The president's voice took on a quiet timbre as he queried, "What do you want from me, my resignation?"

"Not at all, there's no need for such a drastic measure."

"Then tell me what you have in mind."

"I want to take Esmie Cummings place at this university."

"Are you joking? You don't have her credentials!"

Sharply snapping back, March declared, "I'm not done with my demands!"

"What else?"

"I want to receive a contract from this university that reflects her salary with a big sign-on bonus."

"You are out of your mind! The board would never agree to any of your demands!"

"It will be your job to convince them. That's why you get the big bucks!"

"What reason could I use to say that I intend to fire Dr. Cummings and replace her with you?"

"Are you kidding me? Look at all the absences she has taken over the years. It's disgraceful!"

"You've put me in an awful position."

"You've put yourself in that position, not me!"

Lewis dropped his head into his hands. "What if I refuse to fulfill your demands? What If I were to tell the board that you were blackmailing me?"

"Go ahead, but my dismissal will not make any headlines. Your firing will be big news especially when they discover that you have been taking money from an arms dealer."

"Oh, God!" Lewis moaned.

"Just imagine all the television and newspaper reporters who will camp out on your front lawn, snapping pictures of your wife and daughters and asking them embarrassing questions. I can almost picture it now."

"You son of a bitch!"

"I give you 48 hours to dismiss Cummings and offer me the job. If not, your worst nightmare will come true for you and your family." Kevin walked to the door and opened it. Before he stepped out, he turned around and said, "Have a nice day, Montgomery, I know I will!" The door closed behind him as he departed.

CHAPTER 52

PUERTO VALLARTA, MEXICO

Cigars were lit and snifters were filled with cognac. The two men clicked their glasses together and downed their drinks. "It's always a pleasure doing business with you, my friend," Thierry announced. "When my shipment arrives, the money will immediately be delivered."

"It is the only way to do business, Armand," Millian responded, "Otherwise, it just gets too messy." Each of them took a puff on their cigars and blew the smoke in the air.

"There's nothing like a good Cuban cigar and a glass of cognac to seal a deal, is there?"

"You always know how to treat a guest, Bonifacio. Speaking of guests, who is that delicious dish you have staying with you?"

Millian grinned from ear to ear. "She's a school teacher from New Jersey."

"My teachers never looked anything like that." Both men laughed at the joke.

"What about your woman, you dog? Where did you find her?"

"It's a coincidence that they're both educators. Esmie teaches archeology at Trinity University." He did not bother to mention how they were both on the track to find the lost city." *No use having a rival trying to find it. I've spent too much time and money to lose its discovery to somebody else.*

Armand's cellphone began to ring. He saw that it was Ramon on the line. "I'm sorry my friend, but I must take this call."

"Go right ahead." Armand got up from his chair and walked out of the office and through the front door to stand in the brick courtyard. Dialing the number, Armand waited until Ramon answered. "Boss?"

"Yes, it's me. I couldn't talk before. What's going on?"

"Chocko Renteria called and said he had to talk to you right away. He claims that it is an emergency."

"He's always claiming it's an emergency."

"Something's different, boss. He just didn't sound the same as he usually does."

"Alright, I'll give him a call. So help me if this isn't an emergency, I'll drown him in a vat of chocolate!"

"Okay, boss." Armand pushed the buttons of Renteria's phone number. It rang three times until it was picked up.

"Hola," Chocko's voice answered.

"It's Thierry. I only spoke to you last week to remind you that when I get there with Esmie you are to pretend as if you don't know me."

"I remember boss, but I don't think you'll be allowed into Guatemala."

"What are you blabbering about? I've already paid Soza his money."

"That's the problem. Soza is dead! He was assassinated!"

"You've got to be kidding!"

"No, he's dead alright, but you'll never guess who killed him."

"I'm not in the mood for games."

"You remember perhaps, the name Salvador Hermoza." Armand didn't even bother to try and remember.

"No, I don't know him!"

"He was the leader of a revolutionary group called New Order, you remember him. You paid him off for a while."

"I do recall him." Suddenly it dawned on Armand. "Are you saying that Hermoza killed him?"

"That's right."

"Well, it doesn't matter. I'll pay off whomever follows him as president."

"That's the other problem. A military coup has taken over the government. A junta headed by General Inocencio Castillo has taken charge."

"It doesn't matter. Whomever takes over has their price! He's no different from any other person! They're all greedy."

"He is different. Already he has given a speech condemning foreign interests in our country. He has ordered all foreigners out of Guatemala and the borders are already closed. What are we to do, Senor Thierry?"

"I have to think about this. Once I've decided, Ramon will call you."

"Okay."

Armand called the pilot to get ready for a return home. He walked back into the house and straight to the back where the two women were sunbathing. "Esmie," he whispered shaking her from her slumber.

"Yes," she replied as she awoke. Thierry put his index finger on his lips and led her away while Cher slept. "Thank God you got me away from Cher! She's so nosy!" Esmie looked at the concerned feature on Armand's face. "Is there anything wrong?"

"I'm afraid there is. We're not going to be able to go to Guatemala. I just got a call from one of my agents that Guatemalan President Soza was assassinated."

"I'm very sorry about that, but it shouldn't stop us on our expedition to Nakanjo."

"There is more. The country is now ruled by a military junta led by a General Castillo. He has ordered all foreigners out of his country and closed the borders to anyone trying to get in."

"This can't be happening!"

"I'm sorry to tell you that it is and the expedition must be called off. Contact the other people who are coming down and tell them to turn around."

"Damn it!" Esmie whispered. "Of all the damn luck!" Taking out her cellphone, she made her call.

When she was done, Armand said, "We must say goodbye to our hosts so that I can get back and start making a few phone calls to turn this all around."

Waking Cher to say goodbye, they entered the house and approached Bonifacio. After explaining their situation, their host said, "I'm sorry to see you go so soon. The two of you must visit again. Please take my limousine to the airport."

Gathering their things from the bedrooms, and with kisses and hugs of farewell, they sat back in silence in the vehicle as they drove away.

The private jet received clearance to land from the tower. The landing was smooth, much smoother than the current situation in Guatemala. Thierry got off his cell phone. "I just spoke to the chauffer and I'm going to send you home in the limousine," Armand announced as they taxied to a stop near the terminal.

"You're not coming home with me?" a disappointed Esmie inquired.

"No, I'm going to Guatemala."

"Not without me!"

"The country is in turmoil. It is no place for a female to be."

"But you're going! It's just as dangerous for you!"

"I still have some contacts which I'm going to use to try to get entry into the country." The jet door was opened and the steps brought down by the flight attendant.

"I'm not comfortable with you going there! I don't like it at all!"

"Calm yourself," he advised her. "If we ever hope to go back and find Nakanjo, I have to make some inroads with General Castillo. It's the only way."

"I'm going to miss you. Promise me that you'll phone every day."

"I promise." They kissed goodbye.

The flight attendant announced, "The limousine is here and your bags are already in the trunk."

"She's coming," Thierry said. "Now go on. The sooner I get there, the sooner I'll arrive home."

Esmie scrambled off the jet and entered the limousine. The chauffer got in and started the vehicle. As they entered the highway, Esmie announced, "Take me to Trinity University."

"But I was told to take you to Thousand Oaks."

"Well, I'm changing my mind. It's off to Oxnard."

"Yes, madam." The chauffer took the next exit, turned around and drove the highway in the opposite direction. Gray clouds were building up and by the time they arrived at the campus, the rain began to patter on the ground.

Running up the stairs, she entered the office. She was surprised to see the gold letters spelling "Montgomery Lewis" being scrapped from his office door. She approached his secretary.

"You sure came back in a hurry!"

"There's a political revolution going on in Guatemala."

"Oh."

"What's been going on here?"

"We've had our own revolution here while you were gone."

"Why is Lewis' name being scrapped off?"

"He suddenly handed in his resignation without giving a reason. Not even to me and I've worked for him the last 16 years!"

"My God," Esmie exclaimed, her jaw slackened.

"And that's not all," she whispered.

"What do you mean?"

"Your assistant, Kevin March was fired this morning by the board. He's in your office right now gathering up his things."

"You're kidding. I don't understand any of this!"

"I don't know much either but word is that blackmail was part of the equation."

"Who was being blackmailed?"

"That's all I know. Everything is very hush hush."

"Who's taking Lewis' place as president?"

"The rumor is that someone on the board will step in for the time being until another person is hired."

"This whole place has gone topsy-turvy since I left." Suddenly the office phone started ringing.

"These phone calls have been going on all morning! Sorry, I've got to answer this."

Esmie went to her office to see if she could catch up with Kevin before he left the university. She bumped into him as he was coming out with a cardboard box. "Kevin, what's going on?"

A scowl appeared on his face when he saw her. "As far as I'm concerned, you are as guilty as your boyfriend!" he barked out, causing everyone in the hallway to stop and look at him. "But I take comfort in the thought that you'll get yours soon enough!"

"What are you talking about?"

"Drop dead, bitch!" were his parting words before he scurried down the hall and out the door.

CHAPTER 53

Millian received an imperative phone call which needed his immediate attention. He excused himself from Cher and entered his study, closing the door. Kim could tell it was important because she could hear him screaming through the open window. "The Executioner" was really upset. "Hello?" he said after he picked up the receiver.

"Bonifacio, it's Armand."

"You just left an hour ago. What's the matter?"

"I couldn't talk to you in front of the women but this General Castillo is about to ruin both of our lives!

"What has he done?"

"The belief is that he has already started sending soldiers into the countryside to uncover drug mills."

"What?" he screamed at the top of his voice.

"That's not all. If these drug manufacturers are found, they will be shot and the place set ablaze!"

"No, he can't do that!" yelled Bonifacio into the telephone receiver. "He has to be stopped!"

"When my jet lands, I'm taking off for Guatemala City. I'm going to speak to this bastard one way or another. I suggest you join me there as soon as you possibly can. I believe he's trying to pressure men in the drug business to squeeze more money out of them. If that's not the case and he can't be bought, he has to be taken out!"

"I'm on my way!" He called the pilot of his private jet and told him he wanted to leave for Guatemala City as soon as he got to the airport. He told the butler to call the chauffer and tell him to pull the limousine outside the door. "Then tell one of the maids to pack my bag for a few days, and get it done now! I'm leaving immediately."

Millian walked out to the patio where Kim pretended that she was asleep.

"Cher," he said tapping her on the shoulder.

"Mmm," she said pretending that she was just waking up. "Come swimming in the pool with me."

"I wish I could but I'm leaving for a few days on business."

"But this is the weekend. You're always here with me on the weekends," she answered her lips becoming pouty.

"I'm sorry my dear, but this is an emergency. I'll come back as soon as I can." He bent over, lifted her chin up and kissed her lips.

"I guess that will need to do for a while."

"I'm afraid so, but I'll be back before you know it."

The butler came out onto the patio. "Excuse me, sir. Your bag is in the trunk and everything is ready."

"Thank you. I've got to go."

"Please, come back soon."

"I will," he replied as he left the patio.

Finally, I can have free reign in the house. Kim realized that she still had to be careful around the maids and butler, but now she could take her time searching the villa. Kim heard the limousine pull away but stayed in the lounge chair just to make sure that the employees didn't get suspicious.

At last she got up and stretched so she could determine that she was still alone. She was. Kim wandered to the study and looked inside. It was empty. She entered and quietly shut the door. She walked over to the phone, lifted it and unscrewed the receiver. The bug she had installed was still in place. Screwing it back, she replaced it in the cradle and left the study. Kim climbed the stairs to her bedroom and opened the door. She found one of the maids making up her bed. "I'm sorry, Miss Cher. Should I come back later?"

"Yes, thank you, Florencia." The young women left the room closing the door. Kim went into the bathroom and closed the door. She searched through her beach bag and removed her cell phone. She turned on every tap and flushed the toilet. She dialed a number on the phone.

"Dan," did you hear Millian's call?"

"Loud and clear!"

"I could tell he wasn't happy. What's going on?"

"He got a call from Thierry about General Castillo. It seems that the new leader of Guatemala is rumored to be ordering all drug manufacturing in the country to be burned down, employees shot, and the border closed to all foreigners."

"Has that been confirmed?"

"Yeah, but I think it's a ploy to extract more money out of them."

"Anything else?"

"They're both headed for Guatemala City. We are sending agents to take them both down, but stay put in case anything goes wrong."

"I'm going to go through the house and see if I can find any incriminating evidence."

"Just be careful," advised Dan.

"Yes, mother."

Changing out of her swimsuit and into a sundress, Kim carefully wandered and searched the house, making sure she stayed out of the way of the employees. She found very little until she came to the only locked door in the villa. *Interesting! What does he have behind the locked door that he doesn't want anyone else to see?*

Pulling out a credit card, she inserted it between the door and the door frame. It stubbornly resisted but finally clicked open. She faced a flight of stairs that descended into darkness except for a strange glow at the bottom. Kim searched for a light switch and turned on the light. Closing the door behind her, she moved cautiously down. When she reached the ground floor, the source of the glow became very clear. To the right side of the basement room, the wall was filled with computer monitors. *Maybe they are just for outside security.* No one was there monitoring the computers. She approached tentatively and looked at the monitors. Not only were there cameras outside the residence, but every room in the villa were also covered. Kim gasped in surprise. *He's been watching everything I do?*

CHAPTER 54

TRINITY UNIVERSITY, OXNARD, CALIFORNIA

First period class was concluded when Esmie returned to her office and picked up the telephone. She dialed Armand's cellphone number and waited for him to pick up. It rang a few times without being answered and she wondered if leaving a message would be a good idea. She didn't have to conjecture about this because Thierry answered, "Hello?"

"Armand, it's Esmie. How are negotiations going?"

"Not very well."

"Why not?"

"Right now, I'm cooling my heels in Castillo's outer office. I've been sitting here waiting for an audience for almost three hours."

"This doesn't sound very promising for the renewal of our expedition."

"Don't give up just yet. If I've learned anything about dealing with these people over the years, it is that they all have their price to do business."

"The house seems so empty without you and I miss you."

"I feel the same...I've got to hang up. I'm being called into his office."

"Call me back when you know..." Esmie realized that the call had already been cut off and that she was speaking into dead air.

Disappointingly, she hung up. Dr. Cummings opened a folder of undergraduate papers that she was going to read and grade. Suddenly, the phone rang and Esmie excitedly picked up. "Armand?"

"Dr. Cummings, this is the president's office calling."

"Yes," Esmie replied annoyed that it wasn't the call she wanted or expected.

"The acting president would like to see you in the office, immediately!" It was the way the secretary said "immediately" that set off an alarm in Esmie's mind.

"I'll be right there." Locking the office door, she walked down the hallway to the president's office. The removal of Montgomery Lewis' name was now complete.

"Go right in," the secretary told her. "You're expected." Esmie opened the door to find Board Member Anne Vickers sitting in the president's chair.

"Come in Dr. Cummings and have a seat." The fact that Anne used Esmie professional name instead of her given name, which was her usual custom, gave the professor an uneasy feeling. Esmie walked over to the desk.

"Let me congratulate you on your appointment, Anne."

"Thank you, but I'm only acting as an interim president until they hire someone permanently. I guess you're wondering why I called you in this morning."

"Yes, I am."

"I am sorry to tell you that the board has decided to terminate your contract with Trinity University." Dr. Cummings bristled at the statement.

"Is this some kind of joke?"

"I must say that I am somewhat surprised at your reaction."

"You just fired me. How am I supposed to react to that news?"

"This has been a long time coming, and it was only because of the objection of Dr. Lewis that you were kept on here in your position."

"Am I hearing you correctly?"

"Come on, you must have seen this coming, Dr. Cummings. You can't be in that much of a shock to hear about your termination."

"I certainly am! What is the reason for my sudden departure?"

"Really, do I have to go into all of this with you?"

"I demand that you do!"

"As you wish. First, there is the issue of all the time away from the classroom."

"Any time that I've taken has been for the research to find the lost city of Nakanjo."

"And that's the other thing. You still remain unpublished."

"I am about to begin my book entitled, "The Lost City of Nakanjo"."

"Let's be honest with each other, Doctor. All of your time was not spent in research. I know for a fact that you went to Puerto Vallarta recently. What investigation was that attached to?"

"You had no right in looking into my private affairs!"

"Speaking of affairs, how is yours going with Mr. Thierry?"

"Are you objecting to me cohabitating with an eligible bachelor? I feel like I've been in a time machine and I arrived back to the 1950's."

"That is not the board's objection to your relationship with him."

"Then what is?" Anne opened the top drawer of the desk and pulled out a set of papers that she shoved in front of Esmie. Her eyes were drawn to the top where Armand's name was centered, and then to the yellow highlighted sentences and words. As Esmie read, she became more alarmed. After scanning the papers, she set them down, her face red with rage. "This is definitely a case of libel and defamation of character. I'll be contacting Mr. Thierry and I am sure he will get in touch with his lawyer!"

"Be that as it may, you are still terminated."

"This is so unfair! My husband Martin put this school on the map with his archeological discoveries and now, when I'm on the verge of finding Nakanjo, you are tossing me out?"

"On the verge, on the verge; do you know how many times you intimated that you were on the verge of discovering the lost city? Too many times! You're like the boy who cried wolf."

"If you fire me, the grants that Mr. Thierry generously gave to this university because of my research will all dry up!"

"Mr. Thierry's dirty money is made by questionable dealings with nefarious organizations. His grants have led to the denigration of our once fine university."

"Your accusations are baseless and uncalled for! They disparage your reputation!"

"My reputation? Dr. Cummings, don't be so ingenuous. Why do you think Dr. Lewis was forced to resign?"

"I wouldn't know."

"He saw the writing on the wall when he faced the reality of accepting money from a known munitions manufacturer and illegal arms dealer."

"You have this all wrong! Who gave you this slanderous article anyway?"

"It was your assistant Kevin March."

"He has a personal grudge against me and I'm sure he used this to try to bring me down professionally, and now he's succeeded with the board's assistance!"

"All this discussion is leading us nowhere. The board's decision is final!" Dr. Cummings glanced at her wristwatch.

"I've got to get to my next class. I'm already five minutes late."

"That won't be necessary. Your termination is immediate."

"But what about my classes?"

"We have a visiting professor covering your teaching assignments until a new department head is selected."

"I have to go back to my office to gather up my personal items."

"No need to worry about that. While we were talking, your things were packed in a box that is waiting for you in the outer office. *God, they work fast.* Anne got up indicating that the discussion was over. Esmie rose from her chair. "I hope you find another teaching position soon."

"Whatever!"

"Just one piece of advice, Esmie." *She used my given name.* "You need to drop your association with Mr. Thierry before you wind up as dirty as he is."

"Thanks for nothing!"

Walking out to the outer office, Esmie found her possessions packed in a box and a security guard waiting for her. The bearish man dressed in a blue uniform and cap had a reddish complexion and a moustache and goatee. A pistol rested gently in a holster on his hip and he carried a baton in his belt.

"Why are you here?" she asked.

"I'm to escort you out of the building."

"No need for that. I've been finding my way out of here for about seven years."

"That was my order and I intend to follow through on it."

"Then let's go." The secretary never looked up to say goodbye to Esmie as she left the office. The two of them made their way down the hallway to the faculty parking lot. A few of her students watched her leaving and one of them asked,

"Dr. Cummings, where are you going?"

"I've been fired!" Her students stood in shock. The security guard opened the door, passed the box to her and after she passed through the portal, slammed it shut behind her.

Chapter 55

Guatemala City, Guatemala, The Presidential Palace

The Presidential Palace was abuzz with men in military uniforms coming and going up the great marble staircase. Upstairs in an anteroom outside the president's office sat an assortment of politically connected Guatemalans and foreigners. In their midst sat Bonifacio Millian and Armand Thierry. The cacophony of voices speaking in different foreign languages reverberated in the marble room as impatient men waited irascibly to speak to the new head of government, General Inocencio Castillo.

Occasionally, a woman who sat at a desk received a phone call and as the current petitioner left, a new petitioner was sent in. They passed the door where two soldiers, armed with sub-machine guns stood on guard. Armand recognized the weapons he had supplied to the Guatemalan army. *Now they are being used to keep me out!*

"This is ridiculous," Millian stated to his friend. "We've been waiting for more than three hours to see the president."

"There's not much we can do about it, is there?" Thierry stated with resignation in his voice. Armand looked at the others who sat around the room. Some were influential men seeking favors from the new president, but others were dressed poorly and they seemed to be the ones Castillo wanted to see first.

Suddenly, Thierry's cellphone rang. After a few minutes of conversation, he hung up. "Who was it? Someone from the new government?"

"No, it was Esmie."

"What did she want?"

"She called to find out what was going on and to tell me how much she missed me."

"Are you serious about this woman?"

"I'm as serious about mine as you are serious about yours," laughed Thierry. Bonifacio thought, *I can't believe that I'm falling so hard for Cher.*

"Yeah," Millian replied.

Armand could not stop glancing at his gold Rolex watch, but the hands on the expensive timepiece moved so slowly. Gradually, the number of petitioners in the anteroom began to dwindle down. At last their names were called out. The two men made their way into the office. Behind the gold ornamental desk sat the new president. The 48-year-old man was very imposing. He was dressed in a military uniform, numerous medals hanging from his broad chest. His hair was completely gray for such a young man, and he had a robust figure. Inocencio's deep brown eyes sparkled with intelligence and charm, and his dimpled chin set the whole look off.

A soldier stood by the desk and extending his hand announced, "Passports, please!" The two men handed them to the soldier who placed them in front of the president. Inocencio gestured to two chairs opposite his desk. His guests sat down. One by one, he lifted the passports opened them to look at the pictures and then scrutinize their owners. Time passed without a single word between them. At last, the generalissimo inquired in a baritone voice, "How can I help you, gentlemen?"

Armand responded. "May we speak privately to you President Castillo?" Inocencio looked them in the eyes before he told the soldier, *"Me dejan por ahora."* The soldier left the office for the antechamber outside. "You may speak freely now."

Armand began. "Mr. President, I represent Trinity University in America. A professor named Dr. Cummings has for the past number of years been searching for the lost Mayan city of Nakanjo."

"I have heard of Dr. Cummings."

"As well you should since she is a noted archeologist in the field."

"This I already know. Why have you come to me?"

"I am here to petition you to allow her into Guatemala so she can search for this ancient city."

"And what is her nationality?"

"She's an American, of course."

"I see and your passport says you are from France, is that right?"

"It is."

"I believe I made it very clear that foreigners were to clear out of Guatemala."

"But President Castillo, if Dr. Cummings finds the city, it will bring great fame to you and your country as well as a cut of the riches that are found."

"I understand." Castillo turned and addressed Bonifacio. "Are you here to petition me to allow you back into my country too?"

"I am, Mr. President."

"And why do you wish to return here?"

"I run a business in your country."

"I see, and what kind of business is that?"

"I am an importer-exporter."

"And you are a Mexican citizen?"

"That is correct." Castillo grinned at both men.

"Gentlemen, you have wasted both my time and yours. I will not be changing my mind especially for such disreputable men as the two of you."

"There is no point in calling us names, sir," commented Bonifacio.

"I call you who you are. You sir…" he gazed at Millian, "are a drug manufacturer and dealer. You sir are an arms manufacturer and dealer. Sadly, it is men like you who did elicit business with my predecessor. The two of you are a cancer in my country and must be cut out if I am to save my patient."

"Okay," Bonifacio spat out. "How much do you want?"

"Yes," Thierry concurred. "Give us a number." Inocencio Castillo smiled once again.

"I am not greedy, gentleman."

"Yes, we understand that," answered Armand. *He's going to ask for an outrageous number.* Bonifacio added,

"Tell us your bottom line."

"I want double what Soza was getting."

"Double?" shouted both petitioners.

"You understand that it is now the price for doing business in my country." Millian thought, *He is a wolf in sheep's clothing. He pretends to be the representative of all the people, but only intends to line his own pockets as every other corrupt president has done before him.*

"Do you agree to my terms?"

Millian and Thierry looked at each other with a knowing look. "We agree," Bonifacio reluctantly responded.

"I will expect your contributions to be sent to me in the next 48 hours. If not, you will be hunted down and executed if you ever step foot in my country again." The two men nodded their heads. "You may leave now," the president uttered dismissively. Bonifacio and Armand had their passports returned to them. They walked out of the office, through the antechamber, down the marble staircase and out the door. "Avaricious asshole!" Bonifacio spat out the words as if there were poison on his tongue.

"Yes, he is, but at least we will have access to the country."

"At double the price!"

"Yes, that's true."

CHAPTER 56

PUERTO VALLARTA, MEXICO

In that moment, Kim Kowalski C.I.A. agent, came to the realization that if her goose wasn't cooked already, it soon would be over for her. Taking her cellphone, she rang her supervisor. "Abe? It's Kim."

"What's the status of the operation?"

"I have some very disturbing news."

"What's that?"

"Millian has the whole villa monitored with cameras, inside and out."

"Is there anything condemning on them that would reveal what you've been doing?"

"There is an image of me rummaging through his study which will give me away if he's seen it."

"He hasn't confronted you about it?"

"He hasn't approached me about it if he's been down here in the basement."

"Bonifacio is still in Guatemala, isn't he?"

"Yes, but I don't know when he'll be coming back."

"Clear out of there now! Don't wait! Make sure you keep the help in the dark as to where you are going. Call up Nate and Dan as if they were a taxi company and order a cab. I'll get in touch with them and give them their instructions. Hang up from me and call them. Then get busy packing."

"I'll call them right now."

Kim called her fellow agents. Nate answered. "What's going on, Kim?"

"Abe's pulling the plug on this operation."

"What went wrong?"

"Millian has been taping me. Some of them are incriminating. I can't be here when he gets back."

"We'll be right over."

"Give me ten minutes to pack. Abe wants you to pick me up in a taxi."

"Not a problem. Get busy, we'll be there to pick you up soon." Cutting off the conversation, Kim came up from the basement and peered out the door. *Damn it!* She caught sight of the butler sorting through the mail that had just arrived. Florencia came down to join him. "Have you made up the bedrooms?" the butler inquired of her.

"Yes, I have. Now I'm going to tackle the bathrooms. I just came down for the mop and pail."

"Okay." Florencia walked toward Kim who was hiding behind the basement door. Her heart and breathing seemed to stop as Kim heard the maid's footsteps approaching. In the next 30 seconds, she heard the door open but it wasn't the one she was so desperately using as a shield. Gathering up the mop and pail, the maid carried them up the stairs.

At last, the butler concluded his task and left the foyer. Making sure the coast was clear, Kim left her hiding place. Unfortunately, she did not close the door all the way and it was left slightly ajar.

Kowalski walked up as casually as she could, hoping not to bring any uncalled-for attention. On the second floor, she came face to face with Florencia. "Such a beautiful day," the maid said.

"Yes, it's just lovely." Quickly, Kim entered the bedroom and closed the door. Getting her bag from the closet, the agent got busy throwing in her clothes. *There's no time for folding or being neat!* She had just snapped her luggage shut when she heard the doorbell ring. Picking up her bag, she opened the door and went down stairs. The butler had answered the door. Kim heard him say, "No one here called for a taxi." Kowalski saw Nate dressed as a cabbie standing by the front door.

"I'm telling you that someone in this house called to be picked up."

"I'm afraid you have the wrong address."

"I called for the taxi," Kim stated as she walked through the foyer.

"You did?" the butler asked in shock.

"Yes, thank you for a very pleasant stay." Kim did not wait for an answer as Nate took her bag. From the corner of her eye she watched Dan rush from a red Alfa Romeo Spider parked just outside the door and climb

318

into the open trunk of the cab. Nate placed the luggage next to him and slammed the trunk shut. Kim got in the back seat and Nate got in and drove through the gate. The butler stood watching the taxi drive off, still wondering what had happened.

When the cab was out of sight of the villa, Nate stopped and popped the trunk. Dan emerged, slammed it shut, and got in the back with Kim. "What have you been up to?" asked Kowalski.

"Let's just say that the next time Millian gets into the Spider for a ride, he'll get a big bang out of it." Nate hit the gas as the cab continued down the road.

Bonifacio Millian sat back in his private jet flying back to Puerto Vallarta. It had cost him double the American dollars he had given Miguel Soza to satisfy Inocencio Castillo. He had been kept waiting for days just to have an audience with the new president of Guatemala. *It was all worth it so that I could continue my multibillion businesses in drug trafficking without government interference.*

Taking his cellphone out of his jacket pocket he dialed his home. Millian hadn't spoken to Cher in days and he was dying to be with her again. As he waited, his cellphone gave off a distress signal and a voice came over saying, "Your call cannot be put through at this time. Please try again later." Bonifacio stared at the instrument in his hand as if it were demented. Still, he tried again. The same message was repeated. Picking up the phone by his chair, Millian called the pilot. "Do you know of any reason why I can't make any phone calls?"

"It's reported that there have been a number of solar flare activities which are interfering with all communications."

"Damn it!" he replied hanging up. *I guess I'll just have to wait until I get home to talk to her.*

A car was waiting at the airport for him and he was whisked home. As he climbed the stairs to his front door, he told his butler, "Bring my bags in and put them in my room." Millian went immediately to the back of the house expecting to see Cher laid out on a lounge chair under the sun. She wasn't there. He looked out on the beach. It was vacant. Turning around, he went back into the house. He ran into Florencia in the foyer. "Do you know where Miss Donnelly is?"

"I don't know exactly, Senor Millian. She is gone."

"Is she shopping in town?"

"Oh no, Senor Millian. She packed her bags and left."

"Left? Left to go where?"

"She didn't tell me, but I suppose she left to go home."

"Does anyone know?"

"No, she told us all goodbye and got into a taxi she had called and drove off." *I don't understand what's going on. Was she a scam artist? Had she robbed him blind since I've been away from the villa?*

Dismissing Florencia, he decided to check the bedroom. He checked his bureau draw. Everything was in place. He went into his closet and pressed a button. A panel drew back revealing a wall safe. Nothing was gone. Even his stacks of bundled money lay just as he had left them. Bonifacio relocked and hid the safe once more. *None of this makes any sense.*

Millian wandered about the villa looking to see if anything had been stolen by Cher. *If that's even her real name!* Everything seems in place. His search had only fostered a feeling of exasperation in him. He just couldn't comprehend what had driven her from his house. He had fallen for her like a ton of bricks hitting the pavement. Bonifacio was inconsolable.

He turned to the basement door and thought something was wrong. As he got closer, he fully grasped his uneasiness. The door was slightly ajar and was no longer locked. He felt for the door key that he wore on a chain and never took off his neck. Grasping the door knob, he pulled it open. Only the butler, two maids and Cher were in the house. One of them had violated his privacy. Bonifacio decided to go down and check the tape to discover who that person was.

"The Executioner" had been remiss about going over the tape each day to follow what was going on in the villa, but he had been utterly remiss after meeting Cher. He had mistakenly let his routine slide. Now he was afraid to see what had been going on in his absence.

He saw that all the computer monitors were still working. He sat and grabbed the mouse. He clicked on each monitor and reviewed each tape. Time after time, he saw his servants going about their chores with diligence. Then Cher made an appearance. At first, she made her way back and forth from the patio to the bedroom, to the dining room and to the bathroom. *There's nothing suspicious about any of that.*

Then the tape showed something curious. Cher passed the basement door with caution a few times. She kneeled in front of the door and withdrew what looked like a credit card. She slipped it between the door and its frame jiggling it back and forth until the lock gave way. "That bitch! She saw my monitoring equipment! It's no wonder that she left in such a hurry!" *Cher thinks that she has escaped my reach. She's about to learn just how long my reach is! I'll just stop by her hotel and find her address in Hawthorne, New Jersey. Boy, will she be surprised when she opens the door and finds me standing there. I'll get the truth out of her one way or another and then I'll kill her.*

He took the key from around his neck and locked the door. He slipped the chain over his head and grabbed his car keys from the foyer credenza. He ran to the door but the butler's voice stopped him. "Will you be back for dinner, Senor Millian?"

"Yes, I'll only be gone for a little while. Keep my meal warm."

"Yes, Senor." Bonifacio couldn't be bothered calling for his chauffer and jumped into his red Alfa Romeo Spider parked on the side of the house. Millian inserted the key in the ignition and turned it. A bright flash of light and a deafening explosion followed. It blew out the glass from the windows facing the front of the house. The hood of the car was jettisoned 30 feet in the air before it crashed back to the ground as the automobile was consumed by flames. The "Executioner" was now executed.

CHAPTER 57

THOUSAND OAKS, CALIFORNIA, APRIL, 2016

There was a bitter taste left in the mouth of Dr. Esmeralda Cummings after her unceremonious dismissal from Trinity University. Days later she still bristled at how she was just shown the door without warning, but there was something else that disturbed her even more. It was the article that Ann Vickers had shown her during her firing. If she were to believe it, Armand Thierry was nothing more than a warmonger selling arms to the dregs of society, and not a jewel broker as he claimed. *But he's always been kind and loving towards me.*

It had been almost a week since he left and even though she had talked to him on the phone, she felt this conversation should be postponed until they were face to face. She sat around their Thousand Oaks home feeling desperate and gulping down cups of coffee. *I've got to get my mind focused on something else for the time being.* Then it came to her. *I'll start writing my book!*

Sitting in front of her computer, she typed the title. After that, her ideas dried up. Esmie sat staring at the monitor and watching the clock as its minute hand, torturously slow, made its way around the clock. Dr. Cummings grew disgusted by her lack of progress and turned on the television to CNN. "The top story of the hour," the reporter announced, "Is the assassination of "The Executioner" Bonifacio Millian." Esmie almost fell off the chair because of what she heard. "We now have some video of the blast that took place at his home." Esmie recognized what was left of the red Spider that she had seen parked outside his residence. *What the hell! We were just there!* "It has been theorized," the reporter continued "that this may have occurred as a revenge to many of "The Executioner's" assassinations, or due to a rival drug lord's attempt to do away with a competitor."

"Oh my God," Esmie cried out. "He was a drug lord?" She began to remember how, on their way to Guatemala, Armand had suddenly decided to make a detour to Millian's villa in Puerto Vallarta. *If Millian is a drug lord, how does Armand know him unless he too is a shady international criminal?* Esmie turned off the television and walked away from the computer. If she could not concentrate on writing her book before, she certainly could not now after the news report she had just watched. She spent the rest of the day and all night unable to erase the facts that she was facing. *How is Armand really involved with Bonifacio?* Cummings was to get her answer the next day.

Armand Thierry arrived in California the next day wanting to surprise Esmie. While he flew back, he had read the paper on the flight and was caught off balance by Millian's death. He wondered if Bonifacio had been caught unaware by that girl he was housing in his villa. *Love and business are a deadly combination!* He was not going to get caught in that web of problems.

The limousine was waiting for him at the airport and Thierry decided to go home and dress in clean clothing before he caught Esmie off guard in her office in Trinity University. Getting out of the vehicle, he instructed the driver to leave his bag inside the entrance hall. He unlocked the door and began to climb the stairs to the master bedroom. Armand was shocked to see Esmie at the top of the landing, slovenly attired. "My God, you're home. Why aren't you at the university?"

"I was fired!" she exclaimed fervently.

"Fired? That seems grossly prejudicial. What reason did Lewis give you?"

"First, I was confronted by Ann Vickers."

"Not Montgomery Lewis? Where was he?"

"He was forced to resign."

"What the hell?"

"Yeah, he was unceremoniously ousted from his job just as I was."

"But what was the reason she gave you?"

"We both lost our jobs because of our association with you."

"This makes no sense after the millions of dollars in grant money I have given to that university!"

"Vickers confronted me with an article."

"What article?" Thierry suddenly was filled with concern.

"It was an article that accused you of selling armaments to revolutionary splinter groups that were causing worldwide destruction."

"And you believed it?" he questioned with indignation. *I need to think fast!*

"I didn't know what to believe and then there was the news report about how Millian was killed because he was a drug lord. What am I supposed to believe?"

"You could have believed in me. These unfounded reports about me have been put out by jealous competitors."

"But there is your association with Millian!"

"He misrepresented himself to me," lied Armand. "When I was introduced to him, he told me that he was an importer-exporter and that we could do some business together. That is why I wanted to stop in Puerto Vallarta. He pulled the wool over my eyes too!"

"My God, if we were still there we would have been caught up in this whole mess," she replied relieved that Armand didn't know "The Executioner" very well.

"Perhaps he was trying to use me as his cover, but that is no longer something I have to worry about. Now, what are you going to do about your situation?" Thierry inquired.

"I'm at my wit's end about that. I tried to start a book based on my research of Nakanjo but all of this turmoil has clouded my thoughts."

"You can still do your work on finding the lost city."

"How can I? All of the equipment your grant money paid for is owned by the university and I no longer have access to it!"

"Have you forgotten that I am your benefactor? I will build you a cutting-edge laboratory right here in our home."

"Oh Armand, really?" she asked throwing her arms around his neck.

"I'll build you the finest lab with the newest technology money can buy. We'll make the lab at Trinity University look amateurish, I can promise you that!"

"What would I do without you?" she queried kissing him. *Just find Nakanjo so I can finally cash in on all the attention and money I've given you.*

In a matter of months, the basement of the Thousand Oaks home was equipped as a first-class lab. Machines at the estate were newer and more powerful than those she had worked with at Trinity University. Added to those was an Infrared Vision Technology machine which could scan dense jungle to locate objects previously hidden. Their neighbors looked askance at the delivery of this technology, but never said a word about it.

Once it was installed and running, Esmie entered the coordinates found in Brother Gallego's diary. Immediately the screen became cloudy as the latitude and longitude were entered in the computer. As the machine ran its course, Esmie thought, *I've got to tell him about the diary.*

Because of Armand's extreme generosity in creating her lab, Esmie felt that she could no longer keep the secret of Brother Manolo Gallego's information from him. "Armand, I have something that I need to get off my chest."

"What is it, my dear?"

"Do you remember the time we bumped into each other in Salamanca?"

"How could I forget?"

"I was there not just for a vacation."

"Really? Then what were you there for?"

"I was looking for some evidence that would give me the coordinates to Nakanjo."

"And did you succeed?"

"I did. In a Dominican monastery, I came across a discarded diary in which the approximate longitude and latitude were revealed."

"Then what's the problem?"

"I've been keeping this fact to myself, not even telling you!"

"You didn't know if the coordinates were correct. Now we will finally find out."

Throwing her arms around him, she cooed, "You're so understanding, and I love you so much."

At that very moment an image began to take shape on the computer monitor. They both moved toward it, gazing at the image on the screen.

"What are we looking at?" inquired Armand as three green hills came into view within the dense green jungle foliage.

"Those mounds are not natural," Dr. Cummings excitedly replied. "They are man-made!"

"How can you be sure?"

"They are too symmetrical to be natural."

"Then..."

"Then we could be looking at the lost city of Nakanjo!"

"What are we looking at?" inquired Armand as three green hills came into view within the dense green jungle foliage.

"Those mounds are not natural," Dr. Cummings excitedly replied. "They are man-made!"

"How can you be sure?"

"They are too symmetrical to be natural."

"Then..."

"Then we could be looking at the lost city of Nakanjo!"

"This is a cause for celebration!" Walking to the refrigerator, he withdrew a bottle of champagne. Esmie brought two plastic cups over to the counter while Armand unwrapped the silver paper around the bottle neck and the cork. He rocked the cork with his thumbs until it was dislodged with a loud pop. He poured them each a cup and exclaimed, "To you, Esmie for finally succeeding in your endeavor."

"To both of us, Armand! Because without your funding, I would still be in the dark!" They sipped the fermented wine.

"So delicious," commented Armand.

'You know", Esmie began, "we still will not know if it's correct until we leave on our next expedition to Guatemala."

"Don't be such a wet blanket," Thierry scolded her. "Stay positive that you will finally find what you were looking for all these years."

"You're right. This is the first positive hit that I've ever had."

"That's more like it!"

"Are you sure we will have access to Guatemala?"

"I certainly gave that crook Castillo enough money to smooth our way!"

"Great! I'll get in touch with the people we hired last time to see if they are available."

"So, we are leaving immediately?"

"The sooner the better!" While Esmie made her phone calls, Thierry dialed a number on his cellphone. It was picked up. "Hola"

"Renteria? It's Thierry."

"Yes, Senor. What can I do for you?"

"Expect us in a couple of weeks."

"Si, Senor."

"Tell your men that they should clear their schedules."

"I will, Senor."

"And like last time you will forget that you know me."

"I understand."

"Then I'll see you when I get there." Thierry didn't bother to wait for an answer, but simply hung up. Putting the cellphone in his pocket, he thought, *I'm so close to it now that I can almost taste it!*

CHAPTER 58

FLORES, GUATEMALA

Our private jet is cruising above the clouds while the world below seems so insignificant, thought Dr. Cummings as she looked out of the window. The plane was carrying eleven passengers; a pilot and co-pilot, a flight attendant, five technicians, Esmie and Armand and Thierry's shadow Ramon always close by his side. The equipment was being shipped in a cargo plane that would arrive hours after they had landed in Guatemala. Three of the technicians sat at a round table playing poker and keeping the attendant busy refilling their glasses. Another technician sat reading a book while the last was sound asleep. "Did you get in touch with your man in Guatemala? What's his name again?" Thierry inquired knowing full well his name.

"Chocko Renteria," stated Esmie. "Yes, he knows when we are supposed to arrive. He told me he would be waiting with his men at the private airstrip."

"That's right, Chocko Renteria. What about transportation?"

"It's all been taken care of by Renteria. Everything and everyone will be waiting for our equipment to arrive."

"Very good. Now we can sit back and relax until we land." Getting the flight attendant's attention, he ordered. "I'll have a scotch and water. What would you like, my dear?"

"Just some club soda with lemon, please."

"And cut off the liquor to those guys in the back. We don't want them inebriated when we finally land."

"Yes, sir."

Armand pushed his chair into a lounging position and laid his head back while he daydreamed of the new wealth and the objects d' art he was going to get his hands on. *I'll propose an even split with Esmie, but if she balks, well, who is ever going to find her body in the rain forest.*

After 4 hours and 40 minutes, the pilot located the airstrip and set the jet gently on the ground. As promised, Renteria, the bearers, the mules, and the trucks were all waiting for them. As they descended the stairway, Renteria ran up to meet them, sombrero in hand.

"Senora Cummings, it has been a while since we last saw each other. Unfortunately, it was the time when your husband died."

"Yes, I remember," she replied solemnly.

"But I'm so glad to see you again." Esmie looked at Renteria and saw the difference in him that time had changed. The first wisps of silver hair were scattered amongst those that were still black. Renteria looked thicker around the middle than he used to, and he had lost a front tooth. Chuckling to herself, she thought, *He looks like a Guatemalan hillbilly!*"

Snapping out of her reverie, she said, "This is Senor Thierry."

"A real pleasure to meet you, Senor Thierry!" Renteria pumped his hand in a vigorous handshake as if he were lifting his car with a jack to change a flat tire.

This idiot is hamming it up! Pulling his hand from Renteria's grip, he answered, "A pleasure I'm sure."

"I see everything is here as we agreed."

"Yes, Senora, just as you requested." The whole party went to a shed located on the side of the strip and sat in the shade to cool off while they waited for Esmie and Armand to present their papers to the customs official. "I'm not sure about this," the customs agent sputtered. Armand could feel the bile rise in his throat.

"What do you mean you're not sure? Our permits have been signed by the president!" he pointed to the paper, using his index finger like a spear.

"Yes, I see it but I'll have to call the Presidential Palace." He went to the back room to make the phone call.

"This is ridiculous!" Thierry shouted so that the official could hear his enraged voice.

"What's happening?" a concerned Esmie inquired.

"I paid Castillo directly for these permits. He'd better not be thinking of double-crossing me!"

The two sat on some rickety chairs against the wall. A small fan mounted on the wall ineffectively spun around. The perspiration poured off them and onto their khaki clothing. Pasted on the front of the counter was a worn travel posted that read

Welcome to Guatemala! The Garden Spot of Central America!

While the custom official dragged his feet, they sat in silence. Conversations were limited due to the excessive heat and humidity. Almost an hour later the official returned and the two foreigners joined him at the counter. "Well?" Armand questioned.

"I am sorry, Senor but I can't get connected to "El Presidente".

"What is this?" shouted Esmie, "some kind of scam?"

"Scam?" the man said as if he didn't understand the word. Armand pulled out of his wallet, and a $50 bill was placed it on the counter. Snatching it up and slipping it into his pocket the official simply stamped both permits.

"I hope you enjoy your stay in my beautiful country." As they both walked out the door, Armand grumbled, "Drop dead!"

Two hours later, the cargo plane came into view and landed. The technicians brought over the bearers and supervised the unloading of the equipment and the loading of the trucks. One of the techs whistled that they were finished and Armand and Esmie joined them. "Well, here we go!" exclaimed Esmie.

"I've got my fingers crossed," responded Armand.

Once they were all boarded, the trucks took off, kicking up clouds of dust from the unpaved road. They traveled a few miles until the road came to an end at thick green foliage at the edge of the tropical rainforest. The men unloaded the mules first and then the equipment was loaded on their backs. Two burros loudly brayed in protest to the weight.

When everything was loaded, two of the bearers took out machetes and cut a swath into the thick vegetation as Esmie, using a compass, pointed the way. "You're sure you know where you're going?" Armand quizzed hating the idea of being lost in this environment.

"You're such a worrywart, Armand," she chuckled. "Don't forget, I have been here before."

"Yes, of course," he answered still thinking of the fabulous wealth that he would soon possess.

The going was slow and by the time the sun was setting, they had gone just a few miles. Stopping for the evening, they set up camp. A fire was started and camp tents put up, cans of meat and vegetables were opened for the starving expeditioners. The bearers had their own food packed and the mules chewed on the foliage around them.

After supper, everyone went into their tents, leaving Esmie and Armand to discuss the plan for the next day by themselves. "We'll keep traveling in a southeastern direction."

"How long will this little jaunt take?" inquired Armand.

"Just a couple of weeks."

"A couple of weeks? We should have stayed on the trucks!"

"It wouldn't have helped. Sooner or later, axles would have broken and oil pans punctured and leaked. No, this is slower but much more reliable."

"I guess you're right." Thierry moved closer to where his woman was sitting and put his arm over her shoulders.

"I don't think so," she laughed lifting his arm and placing it in his lap. "During this expedition, we must not be side tracked by anything. The discovery of Nakanjo is our absolute goal. Nothing, not even making love to you, will distract me."

"Okay."

"Let's go to bed. We start again early in the morning."

The days were a misery. The slow pace through the tangled undergrowth of the rain forest soon got on everyone's nerves, and occasionally tempers flared up hotter than the afternoon sun.

"Stop bumping into me!"

"Shut up! You talk too much!"

331

"Be quiet or I'll kill you both!" A few times a third party had to step in between the two verbal combatants before they came to blows with each other.

The chopping of vines and leaves soon brought out swarms of mosquitoes that nearly drove the bitten crazy. The jungle came alive with the screeching of birds and the chatter of monkeys as their habitat was disturbed by the invaders.

If the days were miserable, the nights were unbearable. The heat and humidity did not abate once the sun went down. A fire had to be built every night to deter jaguars and other wild cats from entering their campsite.

Every morning, they went through the motions of packing up camp and returning to the monotonously slow movement through the tropical rain forest. Each night, they stopped and made camp for the evening and ate food out of cans even though their appetites were suppressed. They climbed onto their cots, adjusted the mosquito netting, and tried to fall asleep. If it weren't for exhaustion, they probably wouldn't have gotten any sleep at all.

Hours turned into days that finally became weeks, but no one even suggested that they turn back to the coast. The lure of the lost city kept Esmie and her team focused, but for Thierry it was the thought of the acquisition of fabulous wealth that drove him forward. The flame of covetousness burned brightly in him so that he could think of nothing else but the procurement of the Mayan treasures.

Seventeen days after they first set foot on their expedition, a constant roar could be heard in the distance. As they made their way further into the interior, the reverberation intensified. "What the hell is that?" grumbled Armand.

"It's the sound of the rapids of the Rio Los Esclaves," Esme answered as she brushed the hanging vines out of her path. Before the end of the day, they came upon it. "We'll set up camp here," she announced to the group, who were only too happy to stop for the night and fill their canteens with fresh water. Some of the men stripped off the shirts and splashed water on their exposed flesh.

As the tents were erected, Dr. Cummings stood quietly at the edge of the shore. Armand approached her saying, "You seem to be far away. What are you thinking about?"

"I'm remembering my late husband, Martin. The last time I was here, he was swept away by the river." Thierry stood silently next to her never flinching at her statement.

"That's awful. I'm truly sorry." Thierry did not show an ounce of remorse for the archeologist he had ordered Renteria to kill years before.

"That is why this expedition is so important to me," she answered turning around to face him. "If I find Nakanjo, it will be the culmination of my dead husband's dream." *She's going to give me a hard time taking what I want from the graves and if that's the case, I'll just have Chocko kill her as he did her husband.*

"How many days do you think it will take until we're in the location of Nakanjo?" queried Armand.

"Just a few, but the going will be much easier since we'll follow the river to Lago de Ayarza."

"And that's where the Mayan city can be found?"

"According to my calculations and the information I gleaned from the equipment you bought me for the lab, the city should be found somewhere in the vicinity."

That night, after fishing in the river and roasting their catch on a spit over an open fire, the members of the expedition were in much more of a contented mood. Their bellies were full and they had almost reached their destination. For the first time in weeks, conversation and laughter emanated from the campsite. They slept well until the fire was spent and the first rays of dawn encroached into their encampment. There was a spring in their steps as the camp was dismantled and they started out for the day.

For three days, they made their way along the river created by the melting mountain snow. Each day the roar of the river decreased as the water leveled out, approaching an unseen valley. On the third day, they walked onto a rise that revealed the basin just below them where the water gently flowed into Lago de Ayarza. The gleam of the sun on the water gave it a golden glitter. A flock of Roseate Spoonbills that had been feeding in the shallows rose like a fluttering pink cloud into the azure sky and flew off once they had been disturbed by the entrance of humans into their environment. "Is this it?" Thierry demanded in excited anticipation.

"We've arrived." Armand scanned all the area around the lake. His expression immediately became disgruntled.

"You must be mistaken!" he whined like an indulgent child denied a piece of candy. "There's nothing around here but more jungle!"

"Somewhere in this jungle the city is hiding." Esmie's eyes flashed in a rush of ecstasy. "It's our job to uncover it." Turning to the others who were also caught up in the rapture of the moment, she proclaimed. "It's getting too late to start our search. Let's set up camp here and tomorrow we'll go down, set up camp in the valley, and then get started on our quest." The group went about their chores.

That night there was very little sleeping going on. All of them anticipated the adventure of the next day. Armand wandered out to the rise and carefully sat on the edge. In the moonlight, the lake waters took on a silvery hue, but Thierry never noticed that. His mind was on something else. He tried to curb his exhilaration but it was like an unbridled wild mustang, its spirit unbroken and unwilling to be tamed. *So many years I have waited for this and now I can't believe it's laying somewhere down there before my eyes. Perhaps tomorrow I will get my hands on Nakanjoan treasure!* Just the thought of it made his heartbeat rapidly. *I need to get to sleep to be prepared for tomorrow.* He walked back to the camp and stepped into his tent.

CHAPTER 59

Dr. Esmie Cummings awoke that morning to the sound of rain drops drumming against her canvas tent. She stuck her head outside her tent flap. It was misty and drizzling but that didn't dampen the archeologist's spirits. *It always rains for a little while before the sun comes out and dries the rain.* Instead, she felt fired up by the aspect of the culmination of a dream. *Martin, I believe that before we leave this valley your theory will come to fruition. Stand by my side and guide me today, dear.*

The camp was starting to stir as the others got up to have a quick bite before they packed up. In less than an hour, everyone in the group was ready to travel to the valley below. Gingerly, they slipped and slid down until their feet were on level ground.

Once camp was again set up, Esmie gathered the group around her. "This is it," she said with a smile. "I have a feeling that by the time we leave here, Nakanjo will no longer be considered a lost city." The nodding of heads indicated that the rest of the group was in total agreement.

"How should we start?" one of the techs asked. "The lake looks extremely large."

"We have to do this analytically and meticulously, searching one part of the land at a time. Today we are going to scan the land north of the lake. Find a long stick to push away dead debris to make the search easier, and a shovel. Do not use the shovel, however!" she emphasized. You could easily disturb or break the thing you find. Instead," Esmie directed, "I'm giving each of you a whistle to wear around your neck." Handing one to each member, she watched as they slipped it over their heads. "If you find something blow on the whistle and I'll come to you. The rest of the group will keep on searching for anything they can find. We'll fan out about 30 feet apart and then move inland. Keep your eye on the sun and when it reaches late afternoon, come back to the lake." As if on cue, the sun broke through the grayness and scattered the rain clouds away. "Are there any questions?"

"Not a question but a statement," announced Thierry.

"Go ahead, you've got the floor." indicated Esmie.

"I'll kill anyone caught stealing from the site," announced Thierry as he took out a pistol from his shoulder holster.

"Armand!" Dr. Cummings voice sounded reproaching.

"I am sorry my dear, but that is something I just will not tolerate!" Ignoring his outburst, Esmie guided them to the north side of the lake. With a short blow on her whistle, each member of the expedition moved forward. Moving the dead foliage off the ground, they marched ahead.

Hours passed with not one whistle being blown. As the sun came down, they all met on the shore of the lake. "Nothing?" she asked of them.

"Not a thing!"

"I didn't see anything!" Their answers were all the same. Somewhat crestfallen, they marched back to camp to wash, eat, and go to bed to be ready for the next day.

At daybreak, Esmie specified that they would be looking on the western side of the lake. Reminding them of the method they would use, they started out. Near the end of the day, the results were disappointingly the same.

A seed of doubt was being planted in Esmie's mind. *Did I read the infrared machine in the lab correctly? Did I mistakenly copy the information down incorrectly from Brother Gallego's diary? No, I looked at both many times. I could not have been wrong.*

Discussion was limited during dinner mostly due to fatigue, but also because no one had anything positive to say. But Armand Thierry attached himself to her side and kept talking about his disappointment. "This has to the wrong place to be looking! I tell you there must be another lake nearby! We should pick ourselves up and look somewhere else!"

"Armand!" she raised her voice in frustration. "We still have two other sides of the lake to search! I'm not leaving until we have searched every inch of land and turned over every rock! Until then, we'll remain here looking for Nakanjo! Moreover, I can't be around such negativism. It's counterproductive as far as I'm concerned!" Armand stared at her because she dared raise her voice to him.

"Nobody talks to me like that!" he barked stridently.

"Why don't you go back to your tent with Ramon and try to get some sleep," Esmie replied conciliatorily. "Besides, I have a terrible headache." Armand spun around and stormed off. *On the day we find the city, I will cure you of your headaches.*

The next morning broke with bright sunshine and heat. The optimism of the last two mornings had evaporated faster than the dew off the jungle vegetation. When they gathered for breakfast, it was evident that the mood of the group had become suddenly sullen. The silence was deafening!

Without saying a word, Armand sat next to the professor and ate his meal. *I'll be damned if I am going to apologize to her for only speaking my mind.* "Listen everybody," she spoke up as they were finishing their meal. "I know we've been disappointed the last few days and that we've come back to camp dog tired. But there are still other areas around the lake that remain unexplored. We can't give up hope this early, agreed?" They all nodded except Thierry. "Armand, can't you have a little hope that Nakanjo can still be found at this location?"

"I suppose so," he answered with as little enthusiasm as he could muster. Esmie knew she would have to accept his answer as backing down. *That rarely ever happens.*

"Today," she announced, "we'll search the eastern shore of the lake. The same rules will apply as the last two days. Let's get our tools and start walking over." The group traipsed along the lake bank until they reached their destination. With the blow of her whistle, they started back into the shadowy world of the secretive jumble of plants, roots, trees, and vines.

The repetitious and tedious routine of searching through the lifeless and yellow remains of decaying vegetation seemed endless. The heat made it even more insufferable and Esmie was forced to sip from her bottle of water a little more often than she wanted.

The sun traversed the sky in slow motion and Esmie began to sense the first seeds of doubt enter her mind. For the first time since she had heard of the legend of Nakanjo, she began to believe that she may be on a fool's errand. *If today proves to be a failure, how am I going to energize the rest of the group for our last day's exploration?*

Then the hot stifling air was shattered by a shrill whistle blow. *My God, is this it?* Without a thought for her own safety, Esmie ran back to the lake crashing through the greenery. *Blow the whistle again!* The sound again resounded through the jungle. "I'm here," she screamed joyously. "Where are you?"

"Keep coming forward," Renteria's voice called out to her. Running ahead, she brushed large green leaves out of her way. Soon the image of Chocko became clear to her in the dimness of the light.

"What have you found?" she asked almost breathless.

"Look," he said pointing to the ground. "I almost tripped over it!" Peering down, Esmie caught sight of a limestone block about 5 inches thick and 12 inches long that was sticking about 2 inches out of the ground. As Dr. Cummings bent down to scrutinize it more closely, Thierry enthusiastically bounded up to them to get a view of what had been uncovered.

"What have you found?" he demanded of the Guatemalan.

"Stop shouting," Esmie warned him. Thierry closed his mouth. After a few minutes, Armand could not contain his overwrought inquisitiveness.

"Well, what is it?"

"Whatever it is, it looks promising!" Taking a small brush, she began to whisk away the dirt surrounding the object to get a better look. She blew her whistle in short, shrill staccato blasts. The others came running to find out what had been uncovered. The enthusiasm was contagious! "Start digging around the object carefully," she instructed. Keep about an inch width of dirt around it so it's not hit carelessly by anyone's shovel."

Four of them took one of the sides and started throwing shovels full of soil and debris to the side. When the heat got to them, four others took over and they alternated like this until they had dug about 6 feet down. "Stop where you are and get out," she told them. She brought out a small trowel and a brush, then she jumped in the pit, and started removing the dirt from the top of the object. It fell to the bottom of the pit. Brushing off the last layer of dirt, strange square images began to appear.

"What has been discovered?" Thierry said in a commanding voice.

"It seems to be a stele or monument stone." Taking out her camera, she took shots of the object.

"Is it over a tomb?" Armand demanded.

"It's not that kind of monument," Esmie countered. "It was erected as a way of glorifying the deeds of some great person, usually a king."

"Is there a tomb below it?" Thierry belabored the point.

"No." *God, he has a one-track mind!*

Taking out her water bottle, she carefully poured it over the stone making the glyphs even clearer to read. With her fingers, she traced over the symbols. "What does it say?" one of her techies inquired.

"It is dedicated to a king named Jaguar Claw." Her hands continued down the length of the limestone block.

"Does it give directions about where to find the treasure?" feverishly asked Armand.

"It tells about a great victory achieved over another king named Holy Snake Lord."

"Ay, joder!" one of the bearers screamed out. Everyone turned around to see him sprawled out on the ground.

"Que estas hacienda?" yelled Renteria. The man got to his feet and brushed the dirt from his clothing.

"Algo se me ha disparado!"

"What is he saying, Chocko?" Dr. Cummings queried.

"He said that something tripped him." Esmie walked over to the bearer.

"Where?" she uttered staring at Renteria. Chocko translated the answer.

"Right in front of you." Esmie moved ahead, scrapping the jungle floor until the tip of her boot hit an object practically hidden by the dead vegetation and soil that had interred it out of sight.

"It's here!" Esmie announced. "Start pulling off the leaves and vines," she told the others. Ripping and cutting the foliage apart soon revealed the first few stepped blocks of limestone. Examining what had been uncovered, Esmie gasped. Armand inquired with great anticipation,

"What is it?"

"These appear to be limestone blocks that maybe a part of a temple pyramid."

Thierry expressed his eagerness at this sudden discovery. "You mean…"

"We may have just stumbled upon a pyramid complex that could be a part of Nakanjo!"

The clearing of jungle debris and growth around the edifice continued to reveal that Esmie had been correct about her estimation. It was a temple complex. Daylight faded rapidly as Esmie decided that while the others went back to camp she would assign two of her techies to stay on guard over the recently excavated sight. It was not unusual for grave robbers to stalk an expedition to be the first to get their hands on funerary riches left in ancient graves. Although Chocko had been a tremendous help so far, Dr. Cummings did not trust Renteria or any of his hand chosen bearers to do the job. *They'd steal the gold teeth out of each other's mouths if they had a chance!*

Giving the two guards some of the food they had leftover, the others left to go back to their base camp. There was a distinct uplifting of spirits as they walked. The chatter between them was incessant and continued through the meal. As always, Armand took a seat next to Esmie. Ramon stood near, Armand's constant shadow. "So, have your feelings about the site being unproductive and that we should move on changed today?"

"I guess I was a bit too hasty." *A bit?*

"I would say so."

"But tell me, what do you think?"

"Think about what?" She purposely acted clueless to rile him.

"What do you think? Is this the fabled Mayan city of Nakanjo?"

"All indications seem to lead me to believe it is, but there must be more definitive proof before I can say decisively one way or another."

"It has to be Nakanjo! It just has to be!"

"Why does it have to be Nakanjo?" she inquired already knowing what his reply would be.

"After all the millions of dollars I've spent on this project, it can't be anything else." *I definitely want to get my hands on that stele for my New York penthouse. It will make a great conversational piece!*

"Well, I'm sure that we'll see in the next few days."

Stoking the fire with wood that had been stacked and cut, she made her way to her tent. "Are you going to bed already?" he queried wanting her to stay and answer his questions.

She turned toward him and replied, "Today was a big day, but tomorrow will be even bigger. I suggest you try to get to bed early too and get some rest."

Sitting by the fire, Armand responded, "How can you sleep when tomorrow may be the day our names go down in history?

"Goodnight, Armand," answered Esmie as she entered her tent and dropped the flap down.

The next morning, before the sun had risen over the horizon, and after a quick repast, they gathered some food for the two they left behind and made their way back to the site. The members of the expedition were up and anxious to get back to work with renewed energy.

As the two guards ate, the others made their way up the temple steps and began cutting and discarding the vines and leaves that had grown over the man-made building. As they moved up and uncluttered the temple, the details of the steps became evident. The friezes were filled with disembodied skulls which indicated that human sacrifices had taken place at the top. A charge of excitement pulsated through each member of the expedition.

The morning continued, uncovering a small part of the building until a shout rang out. "What is it?" Esmie asked of the worker who had yelled. He simply made the sign of the cross. Armand and Esmie climbed carefully until they reached the worker. Esmie looked to see a human skeletal hand on one of the steps. "Keep uncovering it!" When he did, an entire skeleton was revealed sprawled along the stairs, its body armor and helmet intact. Esmie took a few pictures of the body.

"Is this the body of a Nakanjoan?" Armand asked.

I don't specialize in bone analysis, but from the larger size of the skeletal frame, I would say that this was not the body of a Mayan. It is more likely that of a Spanish conquistador. Also, the steel armor appears to be made in the Spanish city of Toledo typical in the 16th century." Armand was certainly amazed at the wealth of knowledge that she seemed to possess.

As they made their way further up the staircase more skeletons were found. "There must have been some kind of battle here," Esmie told Armand.

"I bet they were after the treasure," added Armand.

"I suppose so."

After three days of backbreaking hard work, a third of the pyramid was exposed to the rays of the sun. It gleamed from the reflection of light from its limestone surface.

Esmie wondered how many more of these buildings there were in the complex. Another few years of work would determine that answer.

After a few more days, a path was cleared to the top of the Mayan pyramid. Climbing up the platform, all the workers stood at the bloodstained altar stone and imagined the ghastly rituals that must have occurred. Esmie shuddered at the thought.

"Do you think the treasure is hidden inside?" Thierry theorized. It had become plain to Dr. Cummings, that Armand was not interested in an archeological discovery if there was no monetary advantage gained for him.

"Well, it has been discovered by other archeologist's finds in Central America that king's tombs were placed inside the temples, such as in the works of Sylvanus Morley and my role model, Tatiana Proskouriakoff."

"Then what are we waiting for?" admonished Armand as he rushed into the interior of the temple. The others followed. Inside, the walls were sculpted with painted frescos dealing with the royal lives of the king and queen. Some of the color was faded, but some parts still reflected the traces of vivid colors. Much of what was painted had peeled off the wall due to the high humidity. "I don't see anything in here!" Armand sounded crushed.

"Guys, search around for a floor tile with hole perforations in the corners," instructed the female archeologist.

Walking around and brushing away dead leaves, one of the bearers finally called out, "I've found it! It's right here!" Everyone moved to that tile and stared at the only obstacle left that would possibly uncover the treasure.

Esmie stated, "The tile must be lifted off the floor. All of you put your backs into it!"

Bending over, they counted, "On the count of three...one, two three..." Grunting, they lifted the thick tile and laid it gingerly on the floor. The interior of the chamber was dark, dank, and dusty as they all stared into the blackness.

"Flashlight," Dr. Cummings asked of one of her techies. The tool was handed to her. She turned it on and the light penetrated the inky murkiness.

"Oh, my God," exclaimed Thierry.

"What do you see?" Renteria asked with heightened curiosity.

"There's no doubt about it! We've finally found what we have been searching for. It's the tomb of a king!" announced Cummings. Esmie began to take flashlight photographs of the interior. Armand wanted to immediately climb down the stairs, but Esmie stopped him.

"It must remain in *"in situ"* until I've taken some pictures, but I need to take more." Armand was annoyed by the rebuke, but waited. *It will soon be all mine anyway. I can afford to wait a little longer.* Esmie's flash went off with each photograph she took. *Ann Vickers and the rest of the university board are going to regret firing me now that I've finally found it. I get the last laugh!*

Armand could restrain himself no longer and climbed down into the tomb. The body was wrapped in a woven cloth that Esmie examined closely. Thierry was tired of waiting and began to unwrap the head. As the others watched from above in excited anticipation, the billionaire tore the cloth off and it shredded in his hands. "What the hell are you doing?" Esmie screamed as she tried to pull his hand away.

"Get off me!" Thierry commanded gruffly as he pushed her to the floor. Finally, he uncovered the head completely, finding a jade funerary mask studded with precious and semiprecious stones. "We've found it!" Armand screamed to the others above. "We've found the treasure of the lost city of Nakanjo!"

Before he could utter another word, rapid gunfire could be heard. Suddenly, above their heads the men screamed as bullets riddled their bodies. Thierry's bodyguard, Ramon was killed and his lifeless body fell into the tomb preventing Armand from making a quick escape with the mask. Esmie was screaming in terror.

All at once, soldiers appeared at the top of the stairs with AK-47's still smoking from the barrels. Esmie stood in silent shock traumatized by Ramon's killing. They leveled their guns at the billionaire's body. "Listen," Armand exclaimed as if he were in charge, "You're making a terrible mistake. He ignored the bullet-ridden body of the dead man who had protected him for years. I've already paid Castillo for the right to be here!" Renteria came up and peered down at Thierry. "Chocko," help me make them understand!"

343

"Oh, they understand, Senor and so does the president. They understand that you are a grave robber who is attempting to steal and take out of our country our cultural heritage."

"What are you talking about?"

"I have been the eyes and ears of the president while you've all been distracted by the expedition. The soldiers have been following us at a distance ready to spring the trap on a rat like you!"

"You've betrayed me?"

"Si, Senor Thierry. Who has the power now? All your money cannot buy you one more moment of your life." Armand, in desperation, began to negotiate with him.

"I have a lot of money, Chocko, lots of money! Name your price to spare my life and it is yours!"

"No thank you, Senor. I do not want to wind up before a firing squad!" Nodding his head, the soldiers blasted Thierry until his dead body hit the floor. Esmie screamed over and over, as she found herself in this nightmare.

"Please," she begged. "Get me out of here!"

"Senora Cummings, there is no need for you to scream. I do not kill women!"

"Then please be good enough to give me a hand up."

"But there is one small problem with that."

"What do you mean?"

"You have seen me give the order to shoot Senor Thierry."

"Chocko, you have nothing to worry about. I won't tell a soul about your involvement!"

"You see, Senor Thierry has rich and powerful friends who might come after me if they were to find out that I was the one who ended his life."

"I can assure you that they'll never find out from me!"

"I can't take that chance, Senora!"

"But you said you wouldn't kill me!"

"I will not break my promise, but I have something to tell you that I have kept a secret from you for years."

"What is that, Chocko?"

"Senor Cummings did not die from an accidental drowning." Esmie stood looking into his eyes afraid of what she was going to hear next.

"Then what really happened?"

"When Senor Cummings came out of your tent that night, I took him to the river and threw him in."

"This can't be true."

"I'm sorry Senora, but he was getting too close to Nakanjo. I had to stop him and I was hoping that your husband's death would end your quest to find the lost city, but it didn't."

"Please, Chocko. I won't reveal any of this to anyone," she chattered, terrified of what would happen next.

"Date prisa, cubrirlo!" he told the soldiers waving them forward. The men lifted the floor tile and began to slip it back into the grooves on the floor. Esmie screamed over and over, as she held her hands on the sides of her head.

"Noooooo!" The blood curdling scream reverberated around the funerary chamber. Stillness was once again restored when the tile was replaced and Esmie had been sealed inside.

"It's too bad!" he told the others. "She was beautiful and smart, but her name appeared on a death list once she hooked up with Thierry. *Asi es la vida,"* he said, shrugging as he turned to leave.

Printed in the United States
By Bookmasters